MAX

Mallika gav... hoped was a s... professional sm...

'I'll tell you if I change my mind,' she managed, as she pulled together her scattered thoughts.

'The salary is negotiable,' Darius added, but she shook her head.

'It's not about the money,' she assured him.

Darius knew when not to push—he also knew he wasn't going to give up so easily.

'I need to go,' she said. 'Thanks for being so nice about everything.'

She put her hand out, and Darius got to his feet as he took it.

'Nice' wasn't the impression he wanted to leave her with. *'Nice'* suggested she'd forget him the minute she stepped out of the hotel. And he wasn't going to let that happen.

Dear Reader

This is my sixth book for Harlequin Mills & Boon®, and it was perhaps the most fun to write. The idea popped into my head when I was talking to a colleague who'd taken a few months off to travel around Europe. What if I had a hero who was wildly successful at what he did and had made more than enough money to fulfil his boyhood dream of spending some years just travelling around and discovering more about the world? And what if, just before he left, he met a woman who made him think that perhaps there was more to life than just living out his dream?

It took a while to get my characters just right, but Darius in the book is now exactly as I imagined him— successful, strong-willed and very, *very* attractive. Mallika is different—she's been through a lot and she's always put family ahead of anything else. As a result, while she's resilient she's also very risk-averse. She's instantly attracted to Darius but she fights the attraction, thinking that it can never work between them. Darius, however, has completely different views on the matter!

Happy reading!

Shoma

AN OFFER
SHE CAN'T REFUSE

BY
SHOMA NARAYANAN

Published in Great Britain 2014
by Mills & Boon, an imprint of Harlequin (UK) Limited,
Eton House, 18-24 Paradise Road, Richmond, Surrey, TW9 1SR

© 2014 Shoma Narayanan

ISBN: 978-0-263-25329-0

Harlequin (UK) Limited's policy is to use papers that are natural, renewable and recyclable products and made from wood grown in sustainable forests. The logging and manufacturing processes conform to the legal environmental regulations of the country of origin.

Printed and bound in Spain
by Blackprint CPI, Barcelona

Shoma Narayanan started reading Mills and Boon® romances at the age of eleven, borrowing them from neighbours and hiding them inside textbooks so that her parents didn't find out. At that time the thought of writing one herself never entered her head—she was convinced she wanted to be a teacher when she grew up. When she was a little older she decided to become an engineer instead, and took a degree in electronics and telecommunications. Then she thought a career in management was probably a better bet, and went off to do an MBA. That was a decision she never regretted, because she met the man of her dreams in the first year of business school—fifteen years later they're married with two adorable kids, whom they're raising with the same careful attention to detail that they gave their second-year project on organisational behaviour.

A couple of years ago Shoma took up writing as a hobby—after successively trying her hand at baking, sewing, knitting, crochet and patchwork—and was amazed at how much she enjoyed it. Now she works grimly at her banking job through the week, and tries to balance writing with household chores during weekends. Her family has been unfailingly supportive of her latest hobby, and are also secretly very, very relieved that they don't have to eat, wear or display the results!

Other Modern Tempted™ titles by Shoma Narayanan:

TWELVE HOURS OF TEMPTATION
THE ONE SHE WAS WARNED ABOUT

**This and other titles by Shoma Narayanan
are available in eBook format from www.millsandboon.co.uk**

To my family

CHAPTER ONE

DARIUS MISTRY WAS NOT used to taking orders from anyone. And especially not orders that came from a woman he was supposed to be interviewing. The fact that the woman had turned out to be surprisingly attractive was neither here nor there—this was strictly work, and her behaviour right now seemed more than a little strange.

'Hold my hand,' she was saying. 'Come on, she's almost here.'

Her current boss had just walked into the coffee shop, and Mallika was reacting as if it was a massive disaster. Granted, being caught by your boss while you were being interviewed for another job wasn't the best start to an interview, but it wasn't the end of the world. Mallika's expression suggested a catastrophe on a life-threatening scale—like the *Titanic* hitting the iceberg or Godzilla stomping into town.

'Please, Darius?' she said, and when he didn't react immediately she reached across the table and took his hand. 'Look into my eyes,' she pleaded.

He complied, trying not to notice how soft her skin was, and how her slim and capable-looking hand fitted perfectly into his.

'At least try to *pretend* you're my date,' she begged despairingly.

He laughed. 'You're not doing a great job either,' he pointed out. 'The whole "deer caught in headlights" look doesn't suggest you're crazy about me.'

She managed to chuckle at that, and her expression was so appealing that he sighed and put on what he hoped was a suitably infatuated look. Actually, after a second he found he was quite enjoying himself. He had a keen sense of humour, and despite his attempts to remain professional when faced with such an attractive interviewee, the situation was so completely ridiculous it was funny.

He was supposed to be evaluating Mallika for an important role in his company, and instead here he was, holding her hand and gazing deeply into her eyes. Rather beautiful eyes, actually—the momentarily helpless Bambi look was gone now, replaced with an apprehensive but intriguingly mischievous little sparkle.

'My goodness, Mallika, what a surprise!'

The woman who'd stopped by their table was middle-aged and plump and terribly overdressed. Purple silk, loads of fussy jewellery, and make-up that would have put a Bollywood item girl to shame.

'Hi, Vaishali,' Mallika looked up with a suitably friendly smile, but she didn't let go of Darius's hand.

'So this was your "urgent personal meeting", was it?' Vaishali leaned closer to Darius. 'Mallika's kept *you* a pretty closely guarded secret, I must say.'

'We…um…met recently,' Darius said, trying not to gag at the cloud of cloying perfume. It was like being smothered to death by lilies—the woman must have poured an entire bottle of perfume over herself.

'Ah, well, you deserve to have some fun,' the woman

was saying to Mallika, patting her hand in a surprisingly motherly way. 'I'll leave you with your young man, shall I? See you at work tomorrow!'

Her husband had been waiting patiently by her side, and Vaishali tucked her hand in his arm and trotted off with a final wave.

Mallika sighed in relief. 'Close shave,' she said as she released Darius's hand.

Clearly it was no longer of any use to her, but Darius felt absurdly bereft. When he'd first seen her he'd thought Mallika strikingly good-looking, in a natural, outdoorsy kind of way—not his type at all. Now, however, he found himself wishing that she'd held on to his hand just a little bit longer, and the feeling surprised him.

He wasn't entirely sure how he had lost control of the situation, and why he had not asserted himself in his usual role. He usually went for graceful, ultra-feminine women—the kind who'd learnt ballet when they were young and who dabbled in poetry in their spare time. While she was conservatively dressed, in a business suit, Mallika looked as if she'd spent her youth playing cricket with boys and beating them in every game.

Writing off his reaction to her as a momentary aberration, Darius tried to make sense of what had just happened.

'Is she that scary?' Darius asked, and when Mallika didn't answer, he prompted, 'Your boss?'

She bit her lip. 'No, she isn't,' she said after a brief pause. 'She's actually rather nice.'

He was about to ask her why she'd been so nervous, then, but he held the words back. This was a business meeting, and the fewer personal questions he asked the better. Only he didn't feel very businesslike right now.

When she'd bitten down on her lower lip his eyes had been automatically attracted to her mouth, and now he couldn't look away. Her lips were full and soft-looking and utterly feminine, and completely in contrast to her direct gaze and the firm lines of her chiselled face…

Okay, this was crazy—sitting and staring at a woman he'd met fifteen minutes ago. One whom he was supposed to be interviewing for a directorship.

'We didn't get very far with our discussion,' he said, trying to sound as if his interest in her was limited to her suitability for the role he'd been telling her about. 'There's a decent restaurant on the twenty-first floor. Would you prefer going there? Less chance your boss might pop up again.'

Mallika hesitated. It had seemed so glamorous when someone from the Nidas Group had headhunted her to discuss a director level role. Nidas was big—it had been set up by a bunch of young dotcom entrepreneurs a decade ago, and they'd struck gold in almost every business they'd tried their hand at.

They'd started off with online share trading and investments, but later branched off into venture capital and real estate and done much better than players who'd been in the market for thrice the time. Being considered for a directorship in the firm at the age of twenty-nine was a huge ego-boost—it wouldn't have been possible in any other firm, but at Nidas the directors were quite young, and they didn't hold her age against her.

Her first few meetings with Nidas had been preliminary ones, screening her for this final interview with Darius Mistry. For a few days she'd actually thought she could do it—be like any of the other women she'd gone to business school with, take charge of her career, interview with other employers, pretend that she had a *normal* life like everyone else. Reality was sinking in only now.

She glanced across at Darius. When she'd heard the name she'd imagined a paunchy, cheerful, white-haired man—she'd had a Parsi drama teacher at school who'd also been called Darius, and he'd looked just like Santa Claus minus the beard. Darius Mistry had come as a bit of a surprise.

True, his Persian ancestry showed in his pale colouring and hawklike features, but he was in his early thirties, tall and broad-shouldered, and as unlike her former drama teacher as an eagle from a turkey. Not good-looking in the traditional sense, more disturbingly attractive, and he emanated a quiet power and control that had Mallika caught in its glow.

He was still waiting for her to answer, she realised. 'No, I'm fine here,' she said. 'Actually, I just made up my mind. I don't think I want to take the interview any further. I'm sorry—I should have thought this through properly.'

Darius frowned. This afternoon really was *not* going to plan. Mallika had been interviewed by his HR team, as well as by one of his colleagues, and everyone who'd met her had been very impressed. Apparently she'd come across as being sharply intelligent and very, very good at what she did. He'd also looked at the performance of the real estate fund she managed. It had done extremely well, even in a volatile and completely unpredictable market, and before he'd met Mallika he'd built up an image of a hard-nosed, practical businesswoman.

The reality was different enough to be intriguing.

For a few seconds he wondered if she was playing hard to get. People used all kinds of techniques to drive up the benefits package they were offered, but very few started so early in the process. And Mallika looked troubled, a little upset—whatever the reason for her sudden decision to stop the interview process, it definitely wasn't a hard-nosed or practical one.

'You've spent almost five years with your current firm,' he said. 'I know the thought of switching jobs can be a bit overwhelming, but there's no harm going through with the interview process, is there? Once you hear what we're offering you can always say no.'

'I guess…' she said slowly. 'I just don't want to waste your time.'

'My whole night is dedicated to you,' he said.

Promptly Mallika thought of all the things they could get up to together. Her cheeks flushed a little and she took a hasty sip of water, hoping he hadn't noticed her confusion.

'So, how much has Venkat told you about the job?' Darius asked.

'He told me about how you and he set up the share trading division,' she said. 'And how you got a real estate fund going, and that you now want to concentrate on the venture capital side and hire someone to manage the fund for you.'

'That's right,' Darius said. 'The fund was an offshoot of our investments business and it's been doing well—we've consistently outperformed the market.'

She seemed interested, Darius noted as he began telling her more about the role. She was frowning in concentration, and the few questions she asked were focussed and showed that she'd done a good deal of research on the firm and on the job. He asked a few questions in turn, and it was clear that Venkat hadn't been wrong. Mallika knew pretty much everything there was to know about running a real estate fund.

'Does it sound like something you'd like to do?' he asked finally.

It was as if he'd shaken her out of a daydream—her vibrantly alive expression dulled, and her shoulders slumped just a little.

'I love the sound of the job,' she said, almost unwillingly. 'But the timing's not right for me. I have a lot going on right now, and I think maybe it's best I stay where I am.'

'Do you want to take a day to think it over?'

Mallika shook her head. 'No, I…I think I'm pretty clear that it won't work out. I'm so sorry—I know you have a busy schedule, and I should have thought this through properly before agreeing to meet you.'

She looked so genuinely contrite that he impulsively leaned across the table to cover her hand with his, making her look up in surprise.

'Don't worry about it,' he said, masking his disappointment. 'I'm meeting other people as well, but if you do change your mind let me know.'

Mallika blinked at him, uncharacteristically at a loss for words. It was like being hit by a train, she thought, confused. She'd been so focussed on what he was saying, on trying to stay professional, that she'd forgotten quite how attractive he was. Then he'd smiled and taken her hand, and the feel of his warm skin against hers had sent her long-dormant hormones into overdrive.

We like this man, they were saying excitedly. *Where did you find him? Can we keep him? Please?*

So much for a dispassionate admiration of his looks, she thought, trying to quell the seriously crazy thoughts racing through her brain. There was good-looking, and there was scorching hot—and Darius definitely fell into the second category. The first time she'd grabbed his hand she'd been too worked up to notice—this time a simple touch had sent her hormones into overdrive.

Gingerly, she slid her hand out from under his and gave him what she hoped was a sufficiently cool and professional smile.

'I'll tell you if I change my mind,' she managed as she pulled together her scattered thoughts.

'The salary is negotiable,' he added.

She shook her head. 'It's not about the money,' she assured him. 'But thanks for letting me know.'

Darius knew when not to push—and he also knew he wasn't going to give up so easily.

Mallika looked as if she was all set to leave, and he glanced at his watch. 'It's almost eight-thirty,' he said. 'I'm starving, and I'm sure you are too. D'you have time for a quick bite?'

Perhaps he could get to the bottom of her sudden withdrawal and convince her otherwise.

He was almost sure she was going to say yes, but then her phone pinged and she gave the display a harassed look.

'I need to go,' she said, her attention clearly torn between him and whoever had just messaged her. Her expression was distracted as she stood up hurriedly, her short curls swinging around her cheeks. 'Thanks for being so nice about everything.'

She put her hand out, and Darius got to his feet as he took it. 'Nice' wasn't the impression he wanted to leave her with. 'Nice' suggested she'd forget him the minute she stepped out of the hotel. And he wasn't going to let *that* happen.

'I'll be in touch,' he said, keeping her hand in his a fraction longer than strictly necessary.

She didn't reply, but she blinked once, and he realised that she wasn't quite as unaffected by him as she was pretending to be. It was a cheering thought, and he smiled as she walked away.

He'd found her intriguing—an unusual mix of the ultra-competent and the overcautious. And the attraction between them had been hot and instantaneous—if it hadn't been a work meeting he would definitely have taken things further. As it was, he was forced to let her walk away with only a tepid assurance of being in touch later.

The smell of freshly baked bread wafted past, reminding Darius of how hungry he was. He glanced around. Eating alone had never appealed to him, and if he stayed Mallika's boss might see him and come across to ask where Mallika was. He felt strangely protective of the intriguing woman he had only known for a couple of hours.

Mentally he ran through his options. Going home and ordering in. Calling up a friend and heading to a restaurant. Turning up at the excruciatingly boring corporate event he'd earlier declined.

The corporate event was the least appealing, but it would give him an opportunity to network with a bunch of people who could be useful to Nidas in the future. It wasn't too far away, either, and if he left now he'd be able to get there, hang around for an hour or so and still get home in time to catch the last bulletin on his favourite news channel.

He was handing the attendant his valet parking ticket when he spotted Mallika getting into an expensive-looking chauffeur-driven car. She was talking on the phone, and he caught a few words before the doorman closed the door for her and the car zoomed off.

'I'll be home in twenty minutes,' she was saying. 'I *told* you I had a meeting, Aryan. No, I haven't decided. I'll talk to you later…'

Whoever Aryan was, he sounded like a possessive control freak. Darius frowned. He hadn't asked Mallika, but he could have sworn she wasn't married. No *mangalsutra* necklace or rings—but lots of married women didn't wear those. And the way she'd looked at him for that one instant…

Darius shook himself. He was rarely wrong about these things, but meeting Mallika seemed to have seriously addled his brains. He was missing the obvious. She'd hardly have asked him to pretend to be her date if her boss knew that she had a husband.

Restored to his normal confidence once he'd figured that out, he tipped the valet parking attendant lavishly as he got into his car. Not married, and probably not in a serious relationship either. Hopefully this Aryan was her interior decorator, or her tax advisor, or someone equally inconsequential.

'What d'you mean, she wasn't interested?'

'She doesn't want to change jobs,' Darius explained patiently.

He and Venkat had joined the Nidas Group on the same day, and had spent the last decade setting up the businesses they now headed. Darius was the stable, intelligent one—the brains behind most of what they'd achieved together. Venkat was a typical sales guy—competitive, pushy, and notoriously impatient. Outside of work he and Darius were close personal friends, but right now Venkat's expression was that of a bulldog being asked to let go of a particularly juicy bone.

'*Why* does she not want to change jobs? Did you tell her how much we're willing to pay?'

'I did,' Darius said. 'She said she doesn't need the money.'

'You need to meet her again,' Venkat said flatly. 'I have absolutely no clue about this fund management stuff, and if you're leaving we'll go under before you know it. This girl's really good, and she seemed keen until she met you. I'd have thought it would be the exact opposite—girls usually fall for you on first sight. What in heaven's name did you do to put her off?'

'Told her that she'd be working with a bunch of total scumbags,' Darius said, deadpan. 'Look, I'm not prepared to let her go, either, but it will be better to give her some time to think things over and change her mind. I'll make it happen. But in the meantime I've got a bunch of other CVs from HR. Some of them with equally impressive track records.'

Venkat grunted. 'I'll go through the CVs, but you need to work your magic with this girl. Otherwise you can jolly well put your exciting plans on hold and stay here until you can find someone to replace you. I'm terrible at all this HR sort of stuff—you're the one who gets everyone eating out of your hand. Make this Mallika an offer she can't refuse.'

Darius bit back a sigh. Once Venkat decided he

wanted something he was like an unstoppable force of nature.

'I'm a businessman, not a Mafia don,' he said drily. 'Let me do it my way. I have an idea on how to win her…'

CHAPTER TWO

THE FLAT WAS DARK when Mallika let herself in, and she
felt a familiar pang of loss as she put the lights on and
surveyed the empty living room. Nothing was the same
without her parents, and having a brother who'd completely retreated into his shell emphasised her loneliness
rather than reduced it.

It had been a gruelling week. Her job involved meeting builders and visiting construction sites and then
spending hours hunched over her computer, calculating
the possible return she'd get from each investment she
made for her fund.

The Mumbai property market had been at its volatile best these last few months, and investors were wary.
Which meant that there was a risk of projects stalling—
which in turn meant that buyers who'd already invested
found themselves with large amounts of capital locked
up and no hope of returns in the short term. And the
fund that Mallika worked for was seriously considering stopping investment in properties that were under
construction.

The kitchen was dark as well. The cook would have
gone home some hours ago, leaving dinner out in mi-
crowaveable dishes for Mallika and Aryan. She wasn't

particularly hungry, but dinner was the only meal she could make sure her brother actually ate.

The lights in his room were on, and she knocked before entering.

'Aryan? Dinner?' she asked, her heart twisting as she watched him hunch over his laptop. It was as if he didn't see the world around him any more, finding reality in the flickering screen of his computer instead.

'In a minute,' he said, not even looking up.

'Did you have lunch?' she asked, and he shrugged.

'Lalita gave me something,' he said. 'You go ahead and eat—you must be tired.'

It was a measure of how little she expected from him that she actually felt pleased he'd realised how exhausted she was. Leaving him to his computer, she went back to the kitchen—she'd make sure he had something to eat later.

For the last couple of days she'd not been able to get Darius out of her head. The way he'd looked at her, his smile, his voice—it felt as if she'd spent hours with him rather than just a few minutes.

He'd said he'd be in touch, but two days had gone by and he hadn't called. Maybe he'd found someone else more suitable for the role. Someone who *didn't* spot their boss and freak out halfway through a discussion, or run out on him without warning.

Idly she opened the contact list in her phone and stated scrolling down it. Darius Mistry. She had his mobile number and his email ID, and the temptation to drop him a text or a short email was huge. She could apologise once again for running out on him. Or tell him that she'd changed her mind about the job.

When it came to professional communications she

was confident and practical, but somehow with Darius she found herself prevaricating. Her shyness prevented her from getting in touch for anything other than strictly business reasons.

She was still mulling things over when her phone rang, and she almost dropped it in surprise.

'I was just thinking about you,' she blurted out, and then blushed furiously. Darius was probably already convinced of her weirdness—she didn't need to make it worse. 'I mean…I was just thinking over what you said about this being the right stage in my career to change jobs…'

'Reconsidering, I hope?' he said smoothly, and went on without waiting for her to answer. 'Look, I know you've said you're not interested, but I've interviewed around a dozen completely unsuitable people and I'd really like a chance to pitch the job to you again. Preferably in a place where your boss isn't likely to land up and ruin my sales pitch.'

One part of her felt disappointed that he hadn't called just to speak to her, but she shook herself crossly. *Of course* his interest in her was purely professional. What had got into her?

'I'm really not interested in changing jobs, Darius,' she said, firmly suppressing the little voice in her head that told her to go and meet him anyway. 'And I've wasted your time once already—I wouldn't want to do it again.'

Darius briefly considered telling Mallika that time spent with her would definitely not be wasted, but he bit the words back. This wasn't a seduction, and he'd already made it clear that when it came to business he was as determined as she to get what he wanted.

'It's part of my job,' he said lightly. 'Even if you don't want to join us now, at least I'll get to tell you about the company—and who knows? Maybe you'll want to join at some later time.'

'All right, then,' Mallika conceded. 'When shall I meet you?'

'Tomorrow,' he said decisively. 'Lunch at one of the restaurants in Lower Parel? That's nearer my office than yours, and hopefully we won't run into anyone you know.'

Darius was beginning to wonder if he'd been stood up when Mallika finally walked into the restaurant. The first thing that struck him was that there was a strained expression in her lovely eyes. The second was that she looked anything but tomboyish now.

Granted, her hair was still styled for convenience rather than glamour, and her make-up was kept to the bare minimum. But she was wearing a sari today—a dark blue silk affair, with a muted print—and her figure was spectacular in it. And her spontaneous smile when she saw him was the best welcome he could ever have hoped for.

He stood as she walked up to him, and Mallika began to feel ridiculously nervous. It was a Friday and he was dressed casually, in a white open-necked cotton shirt over jeans. His thick hair looked slightly damp from the shower, and she had a second's insane urge to reach up and run her fingers through it.

To cover her confusion she held out her hand, and he took it, briefly clasping it between both his hands before he let go.

'Hi,' she said. 'I'm not too late, am I?'

He shook his head. That smile had lit up her face, but now the worried expression was back in her eyes.

'Is everything okay?' he asked quietly once they were both seated and the waiter had put their menu cards in front of them and retired to a safe distance.

Her eyes flew up to his. 'Yes, of course,' she said, sounding just a little defensive.

Aryan was going through a particularly problematic phase, and in the normal course of things she wouldn't have left him alone at home. But she'd promised Darius, and there were meetings in the office that she couldn't avoid. Just this once Aryan would have to manage on his own, with just Lalita the cook to check on him.

'You look tense,' he said. 'Like you're trying to remember whether you locked your front door when you left. Don't worry about it—burglars are usually deeply suspicious of open doors. If it's unlocked, there's absolutely no chance of a break-in.'

She laughed at that. 'What if I did lock it?'

'Ah, then I hope you have a good security system.'

'A simple lock, and a brother who won't notice if someone puts every single thing in the house into packing cases and carries them away under his nose. As long as they don't touch his computer.'

He smiled, his eyes crinkling up at the corners in a maddeningly attractive way. 'Sounds like my kind of guy. Younger brother?'

Mallika nodded. She hardly ever mentioned Aryan in casual conversation, and the ease with which the reference had slipped out surprised her. Darius was beguilingly easy to talk to—she'd need to be on her guard a little.

The waiter was hovering behind her, and she turned her attention to the menu.

'The fish is good,' Darius said.

'It looks delicious,' Mallika said, glancing at the next table, where another waiter had just deposited two plates of grilled fish. 'I'm vegetarian, though.'

'Then the gnocchi?' he said. 'Or the spaghetti in pesto sauce?'

Mallika finally chose the spaghetti, and a glass of wine to go with it—Darius, who'd never paid good money for a vegetarian meal before in his life, found himself ordering grilled vegetables and pasta. A lot of strict vegetarians were put off by someone eating meat at the same table, and he definitely didn't want to risk that. He was on a charm offensive today, and determined to win her over.

'How's your boss?' he asked.

'She's miffed I didn't tell her I was dating someone,' Mallika said with a sigh. Vaishali was a lovely person, but the concept of personal space was completely alien to her. 'She wanted to invite both of us to her house for dinner—I had a devil of a time wriggling out of that one.'

'What did you say to her?' Darius asked, unable to keep a glint out of his eye.

'That I'd been wrong about you and you were actually really self-centred,' Mallika said, delighted she'd managed to keep a poker face. 'And possessive—and controlling.'

She sounded remarkably cheerful about it, and Darius's lips twitched.

'So we aren't dating any longer?'

'We are,' Mallika said. 'You have a few redeeming qualities, but I'm not as sure about you as I was. We're dating, but I'm not introducing you to friends and family just yet.'

'Wouldn't it have been easier to remove me from the scene altogether?'

'If I'd written you off she'd have tried setting me up with a perfectly horrible second cousin of hers. She's spent the last two years trying to palm him off on every unmarried woman she knows.'

'Maybe he's not so bad?' Darius suggested carefully. 'You should meet him—keep your options open.'

Mallika shuddered. 'No, thanks. I've met him once, and that was once too often. He spent forty-five minutes telling me how rich he is, and how he made his money. And he breathes really heavily.'

'Hmm…'

Darius's eyes were dancing wickedly, and Mallika felt a little jolt of awareness go through her. It had been so long since she'd spent any time with an attractive man that she was ridiculously susceptible.

'Can I ask you something?'

She gave him a wary look. 'Yes.'

'Are you atoning for the sins of a past life by working for Vaishali?'

'She's been very good to me,' Mallika said stiltedly, and when he raised an eyebrow she went on in a rush. 'No, really. She can be a bit overpowering at times, but I owe her a lot. I didn't mean to make her sound like a nightmare boss.'

She sounded as if it really mattered, and Darius nodded.

'If you say so.' He was silent for a few seconds as the waiter put their drinks in front of them. 'So, should I tell you a bit more about the job and the company? You can make up your mind then.'

She nodded, and listened carefully as he explained again about the company structure and the role that he was offering. Unlike her current company, which invested solely in real estate, the Nidas Group had evolved into a conglomerate of companies that included a brokering house, a consumer lending company and the fund where Darius was offering her a job. Darius himself was moving on—he didn't give her any details, but she assumed it was to head up a new division—and he didn't have enough capacity to manage the fund as well.

'I have a question,' she said, once he'd finished telling her about the job. 'Why do you think I'm right for the position?'

'You have a superb track record,' Darius said. 'And Venkat was very impressed after he interviewed you.'

'But *you* haven't interviewed me,' she pointed out. 'Or do you trust Venkat that much?'

'I have every intention of interviewing you,' Darius said, his brows quirking. 'The second you tell me that you're actually interested in the job I'll start firing questions at you.'

Mallika stared at him for a few seconds, and then burst out laughing.

'You have a point,' she said. 'So—the job sounds perfect. It's the logical next step in my career and like you said, I've been in my current job for five years and I'm beginning to stagnate.'

'I can see a "but" coming,' he murmured.

'Yes… I mean…'

'It's not convenient from a personal point of view?' Darius supplied when she hesitated.

Mallika nodded. 'That's it. I can't tell you the details, but...'

'I don't need to know the details,' Darius said. 'But if you tell me what exactly it is that your current company is doing to help you maybe I can see if we can work something out.'

Darius could smell victory, and he wasn't about to let this one go.

'I don't have fixed hours,' she said in a rush. 'Some days I reach work at eight, and some days I go in only in the afternoon. And I do site visits on my own when it's convenient to me. Sometimes I work from home, and there are days when I'm not able to work at all.'

She ground to a halt, her eyes wide and a little apprehensive. Clearly whatever was happening on the personal front was very important to her. He wondered what it was. The kind of flexibility she needed was normally required only if an employee had to care for a sick child or an elderly parent. Mallika wasn't married, and from what she'd said her younger brother sounded responsible. A parent, then, he decided.

The unwelcome thought that she might be going through a messy divorce came to mind, but he pushed it away. A divorce might need her to take time off work, but it wouldn't need her to work from home. It was far more likely that one of her parents needed to be cared for.

He thought for a while. 'We might be able to let you do the same,' he said slowly. 'Can I work this out and get back to you?'

'But when I asked Venkat he said you don't have a flexible working policy!' she said.

'It hasn't been formally approved yet,' Darius said. 'We're still working on it. Yours could be a test case.'

Their food had arrived, and Mallika took a bite of her spaghetti before answering. 'You know,' she said conversationally, 'the job market's really bad nowadays.'

'It is,' Darius agreed, frowning a little.

'And bonuses are dropping and people are getting fired every day.'

'Yes.'

'So you could probably hire anyone you wanted, right? With just as much experience and no complicated conditions. Why are you still trying to convince *me* to take the job?'

When it came to work, Mallika was sharp and to the point. She was intelligent—obviously she was, or Venkat wouldn't have considered hiring her. But Darius found himself wondering why exactly he *was* trying so hard to convince her. He'd never tried to recruit an unwilling candidate before—he'd never had to. And while she was definitely his first choice for the job, there were at least two others who could do the job equally well.

Had this just become about winning? Or perhaps he hadn't been thinking clearly since taking her hand in that coffee shop several days ago. What was going on?

'Venkat's interviewed pretty much everyone in the industry,' he said. 'You're the best fit for the role.'

'But the second best might end up doing a better job,' she said. 'He or she'd be more inclined to take the offer to begin with.'

'It's not just about technical skills,' Darius said. 'We think you'd adjust well to the organisation's culture. And we also need to improve the firm's diversity ratio, now that we're likely to get some foreign investment into the company. That's one of the things investors are likely to look at. There are a lot of women at junior levels, but very few at middle or senior management. There weren't too many CVs that fitted the bill *and* belonged to women—and other than you none of them made a decent showing at interview.'

'But I'm sure you have male candidates who're suitable,' she said, her brow wrinkling. 'Surely this diversity thing isn't so important that you've not interviewed men at all?'

'Venkat's interviewed quite a few,' Darius said. 'Apparently you did better than them as well. Diversity's not more important than talent—it's just that now we've found you we don't want to let you go.'

His gaze was direct and unwavering, and Mallika felt herself melting under it. The attraction she'd felt the first time she'd met him was back in full force—if he told her that he wanted her to join a cult that ate nuts and lived in trees she'd probably consider it seriously. Shifting jobs was a no-brainer in comparison—especially when he was guaranteeing a higher salary and no change to her timings.

She was about to tell him that she'd join when a shadow fell across their table.

'Darius!' a delighted male voice said. 'It's been years, my boy—how are you?'

The speaker was a stalwart-looking man in his early forties, who beamed all over his face as he clapped Darius on his shoulder. The blow would have pitched a weaker man face-down into his grilled vegetables, but Darius hardly winced.

'Gautam,' he said, standing up and taking the man's hand in a firm grip. 'Long while… I didn't know you were back in Mumbai.'

'Just here for a visit. And…? You're married and everything now? Is this the new Mrs Mistry?'

He looked as if he was about to clap Mallika on the shoulder as well, and Darius intervened hastily.

'No, Mallika is…a friend.'

'Aha! A Miss Mystery, then, not a Mrs Mistry—is that right?' Clearly delighted at his own wit, Gautam smiled even more broadly. 'I'll leave you to it, then. Catch you online later—I'm in Mumbai for a week more…we should try and meet.'

'Yes, I'll look forward to that.'

Darius waited till the man had moved away before sitting down, shaking his head.

'It's fate,' he said solemnly. 'Last time it was your boss—this time it was Gautam. We can't meet without running into someone we know.'

Mallika chuckled. 'He seemed a cheerful guy. He reminds me of a story I read as a kid—there was a man who smiled so wide that the smile met at the back of his face and the top of his head fell off.'

'That's such an awful story,' Darius said. 'Were you a bloodthirsty kind of kid?'

'I was a bit of a tomboy,' she said, confirming Darius's first opinion of her. 'Not bloodthirsty, though.'

She frowned at her plate as she chased the last strand of spaghetti around it. Finally managing to nab it, she raised her fork to her mouth. The spaghetti promptly slithered off and landed on her lap.

'And *that's* why my good clothes never last,' she said, giving the mark on her sari a resigned look as she picked up the pasta and deposited it back on her plate. 'I'm as clumsy as a hippopotamus.'

Anything less hippopotamus-like would be hard to

find, Darius thought as he watched her dab ineffectually at the stain with a starched table napkin. Her curly hair fell forward to obscure her face, and her *pallu* slipped off her slim shoulder to reveal a low-cut blouse and more than a hint of cleavage.

Darius averted his eyes hastily—looking down a girl's blouse was something he should have outgrown in high school. The one glimpse he'd got, however, was enough to make him shift uncomfortably in his chair. Really, Darius was so off-kilter he could hardly understand the effect she was having on him.

'Here, let me help with that,' he said, after Mallika had dropped the napkin twice and narrowly missed tipping her plate over. He got up and, taking a handkerchief out of his pocket, wet the corner in a glass of water and came to her side of the table to attend to the sari.

Mallika went very still. He wasn't touching her—he was holding the stained section of sari away from her body and efficiently getting rid of the stain with the damp handkerchief. But he was close enough for her to inhale the scent of clean male skin and she had to fold her hands tightly in her lap to stop herself from involuntarily reaching out and touching him.

'Thanks,' she said stiltedly once he was done.

'You're welcome.' Darius inclined his head slightly as he went back to his side of the table. 'Dessert?'

'I should choose something that matches the sari,' she said ruefully as she recovered her poise. 'I love chocolate, but I'm not sure I dare!'

'Blueberry cheesecake?' he asked, his eyes dancing with amusement again. 'Or should we live life dangerously and order the sizzling brownie with ice cream?'

'The brownie, I think…' she started to say, but just

then her phone rang, and her face went tense as she looked at the display. 'I'm sorry—I'll need to take this call,' she said.

'Haan mausiji,' he heard her say, and then, *'Ji. Ji. Nahin,* I had some work so I had to go out. Calm down… don't panic. I can get home in ten minutes—fifteen at the most, depending on the traffic.'

Her face was a picture of guilt and worry as she closed the call, and his heart went out to her.

'I'm sorry,' she said. 'I need to go. It was a lovely lunch, and thank you so much for putting up with me. I'm really sorry about rushing off again…'

'Don't worry about it,' he said gently. 'Do you need a lift anywhere?'

She shook her head. 'I have a car. Is it okay if I go now? I hate leaving you like this, but I really do need to get home as soon as possible.'

'It's not a problem at all,' he said. 'Take care, and we'll talk soon.'

He put enough money on the table to cover the bill plus a hefty tip, and walked her to the door of the restaurant. Her driver took a couple of minutes to bring the car round, and Mallika was clearly on tenterhooks until he arrived.

'Bye,' she said as the car pulled up and she slid into the back seat. 'I'm really, really sorry about this.'

She clasped his hand impulsively before she closed the car door, and Darius was left with the feel of soft, smooth skin on his. The subtle fragrance of her perfume hung in the air for a few seconds after she left.

He gave himself a shake before turning away to walk back to his office. This was not the way he'd planned to end their meal. He'd sensed she was on the point of accepting the role when they'd been interrupted and he could not be more frustrated with his lack of success so far. But it wasn't over—not when he was this close to getting what he wanted.

CHAPTER THREE

'Welcome to Nidas,' Venkat said, giving Mallika a broad smile. 'I'm so happy you finally decided to join.'

'Same here,' Mallika said cautiously as she shook his outstretched hand.

All the old doubts about changing jobs had come flooding back now that she'd actually done the deed. She'd told Vaishali about the job the day after she'd met Darius, feeling like a complete traitor. But Vaishali had been surprisingly nice about the whole thing. Apparently she had been toying with the idea of taking a sabbatical herself, and she wasn't sure if Mallika's flexible working hours would be acceptable to her replacement.

Feeling a bit like a fledgling, shoved out of its nest before it could fly, Mallika had emailed Darius, confirming that she'd be able to join Nidas in a month. He'd been travelling, and someone from his HR team had got in touch to figure out her salary structure and joining date. Darius hadn't even called her, and Mallika couldn't help feeling a little upset about it. And now that she was actually part of Nidas and about to start work, she was very nervous.

The sight of Venkat wasn't exactly inspiring either.

Short and squat and rather belligerent-looking, Venkat was as different from her previous boss as possible.

'We've set up an orientation for you with the team,' he was saying now as he ushered her into his room.

'Darius told me—' Mallika began, but Venkat interrupted before she could complete her sentence.

'Oh, Darius is a busy chap—he won't be able to take you through everything himself.' He peered at her owlishly. 'You do know he's moving out of the firm, right?'

Mallika drew in a sharp breath. A lot of things were suddenly falling into place. Darius's insistence that she join as soon as she possibly could. His asking Venkat to set up her induction plan instead of doing it himself. The lengthy meetings with the other directors, ostensibly to help her get to know them before she joined.

A black curl of disappointment started up in the pit of her stomach. He'd had multiple opportunities to tell her and he'd consciously decided not to. It felt like a betrayal, unreasonable though that was. Unconsciously, a large part of her decision to take the job had been based on the assumption that Darius would be around and that she'd be working closely with him.

Serve her right—trusting a man she hardly knew, she thought, squaring her shoulders and doing her best to keep Venkat from noticing how upset she was.

'He didn't tell me that he was moving out altogether,' she said crisply. 'Though I did get the impression that he'd be cutting off from this part of the business in a month or so.' She was determined to cover her disappointment with cool professionalism.

'Even less, if he has his way,' Venkat said, and an expression of bewildered loss crossed his face for an instant. 'It was a shock when he told me. We've worked together for years—we set up this business together—and out of the blue he tells me he's quitting. I still don't understand why he's doing it.'

Strongly tempted to find out more, Mallika bit down on her questions. It shouldn't matter to her where Darius was going or why.

'When you interviewed me *you* didn't mention that Darius was leaving the firm,' she reminded Venkat. 'Why did you assume I'd know now?'

He had the grace to look embarrassed. 'I couldn't tell you before you joined,' he said. 'Darius is a pretty big shareholder, and the news of his leaving isn't public yet. I thought he might have told you since—I got the impression you guys are pretty friendly.'

He took in Mallika's suddenly stormy expression and changed the subject in a hurry. 'Now, I thought I'd first introduce you to some of the key people in your team, and then you can start going through our current investment strategies. The team's brilliant—I've been working with them pretty closely for the last few months. I've put them on to a few good things as well. Of course now you're here you'll be in full control, but you can reach out to me whenever you want.'

As the day went by Mallika found herself feeling more and more confident. Venkat evidently valued her input, and his style of working wasn't as different from hers as she had feared.

She was packing up for the day when there was a knock on the door of her room. Assuming that it was the overzealous tea boy, who'd been popping up every half an hour, she said, 'Come in!' and continued stuffing files into her laptop bag.

It was a few seconds before she realised that the man in the room was about twice as large as the tea boy.

'Darius!' she said, her brows coming together in an involuntary frown as she saw him. 'I was wondering if I'd see you today.'

'I meant to come over in the morning, but I had one meeting after another. How was your day?'

'Good,' she said. 'I think I'm going to like working here.'

'Did Venkat manage to spend any time with you?'

'A lot,' she said drily.

Darius laughed. 'He believes in throwing people in at the deep end,' he said. 'But he's a great guy to work with. If you're done for the day d'you want to catch up over coffee? There's a decent café nearby.'

Mallika hesitated. She really wanted to confront Darius about him leaving, but her upbringing made her shy away from any kind of direct conflict.

Some of her indecision must have shown in her face, because he was beginning to look puzzled.

'Or some other day if you need to leave,' he said easily.

Mallika made up her mind.

'I need to get home, but I have time for a coffee from the machine down the hall,' she said.

Compromise—that was one thing she'd learnt early in life. And also that attacking issues head-on sometimes made them worse. She got to her feet and Darius followed her down the hall.

'On second thoughts, I'll have a soft drink,' she said, taking a can from the fridge next to the coffee dispenser. 'You can have that coffee if you want,' she said, gesturing at the mug Darius had just filled for her.

She picked up a second mug and half filled it with warm water from the machine before putting her un-opened can into it.

'It's too cold,' she explained as Darius raised his eye-brows. 'I'll leave it in the mug for a bit and then it'll be just right and I'll drink it.'

Darius's lips curved into a smile as he followed Mallika back to her room. She was wearing black trousers, a no-nonsense blue shirt, and extremely sensible shoes. The whole outfit looked as if it had been chosen to down-play her looks, but the most boring clothes in the world couldn't conceal the narrowness of her waist and the ath-letic grace of her walk. Quite contrary to the intended effect, the clothes made her *more* appealing—at least to him.

'Is Venkat involved in the day-to-day running of the fund?' she asked, perching herself on the edge of her desk and swinging her legs idly.

'Not really…' he said cautiously, and she gave him a quizzical look, 'Okay, he's *very* involved in it—but his area of expertise is sales. You won't be reporting to him, if that's your worry—all the directors report straight to the board.'

'Hmm…no, that isn't what was bothering me.'

She smiled at him, and Darius felt his heartbeat quicken in response.

'But tell me—is it true that he's interfered in some of the investment decisions the team have made in the past?'

It was very likely to be true. Darius had heard rum-blings from his team, but he hadn't paid much attention up till now. Mallika's pointing it out after being exactly one day in the job, however, hit him on the raw.

'He's talked to them about a few deals,' he said. 'I wouldn't go so far as to call it interference.'

'Maybe it wasn't brought to your attention, then,' she said, clearly unfazed by the sudden chilliness in his tone. 'But he's made some bad calls, and the fund's asset value has dropped. It'll take me a while to undo the damage.'

It was her air of knowing exactly what to do that got to him.

'I'd suggest you take a few days to understand the business properly first,' he said firmly, though he was feeling uncharacteristically defensive. 'Before you jump in with both feet and start undoing things.'

Mallika frowned. 'I thought the whole point of my being here was that I already know the business,' she said. 'I researched the fund before I even started interviewing with you guys, and it's obvious that you have problems. Logically, it makes no sense to wait to fix them.'

'There's a lot of stuff you wouldn't know from the outside,' Darius insisted. 'Venkat might have his…quirks, but not all the decisions he's made have been bad.'

She shrugged. 'Statistically speaking, even if you made decisions by rolling dice you would end up making some decent ones. But from what I can make out Venkat is superstitious, and his judgement is coloured.'

It had taken Darius months to realise that Venkat's superstitious side sometimes overruled his normally sharp business brain. Mallika had taken exactly one day to figure it out. She was extraordinarily perceptive and he felt slightly wrong-footed. *Again.*

What was this woman doing to him?

Mallika was leaning forward a little. 'Look, you hired me to run this fund,' she said. 'Not because you liked my face. So let me get on with my work. If I mess up you can play the hero and come in and rescue me.'

For a second Darius was tempted to tell her exactly how much he liked her face, but hard as it was he bit back the words. Being her colleague meant that he had to keep a certain professional distance. Speaking of which… Darius realised just how close he was to Mallika, and rolled his chair a few paces back. Unfortunately as soon as he started to speak again Mallika scooted her shapely butt closer to him once more, robbing him of his train of thought.

'You're right about Venkat,' he said, trying to sound as detached as possible. 'The whole superstition thing….' He hesitated a little while trying to find the right words. 'It's a little…'

'Kooky?' she supplied, putting her head to one side. 'Eccentric? Odd?'

'Unconventional,' he said. 'But it's not uncommon.'

'And it's unimportant too, I assume?' she said before she could stop herself. 'As far as you're concerned anyway. Because you're not planning to be around when the problems kick in.'

If she'd expected him to look guilty she was disappointed, because he threw his head back and laughed. 'I mightn't be around, but the fund's performance is still pretty damn important to me. I have a fair bit of my own money invested in it, and I don't fancy seeing it go down the tube.'

'I suppose I should be flattered,' she said drily. 'Here I was, thinking you'd given me the fund to run because you didn't care what happened to it.'

'And now you know I've put my life's savings in your hands,' he said. 'Who told you I was moving out? Venkat?'

'Yes,' she said.

'It's not supposed to be public knowledge yet,' he said. 'The board has asked me to stay on for a few months, and they felt it best that the rest of the firm be told I'm leaving only when it's a lot closer to my last day here.'

'Funny…Venkat assumed you'd already told me,' she said. 'Perhaps he thought it was only fair—given that you recruited me and everything.'

Darius leaned a little closer, his brow creasing. 'Are you annoyed that I didn't tell you?' he demanded, putting a hand under her chin to tip her face upwards. 'Even after what I just said?'

Mallika jerked her head away, trying to ignore the little thrill that went through her at his touch.

'Not annoyed…just a little…concerned,' she said, hoping her words would hide how much she longed to work alongside this charismatic man. 'There might be other things you omitted to mention. I pretty much took everything you said at face value.'

'Now, wait a minute,' he said incredulously. 'Are you suggesting I *lied* to you about the job? What makes you think that?'

'You weren't open at all,' she said. 'All this while you've let me think that you'd be around—that you were simply taking on something within the firm. If I'd known you were leaving…'

'You wouldn't have joined?' He looked quite genuinely puzzled. 'Why not? You seem like you have a handle on things already. My being here or not doesn't make a difference, surely?'

Darius was struggling to keep a smug smile off his face—he wasn't the only one who felt what was between them then.

Oh, but it does, Mallika almost said. The thought of working at Nidas without Darius was unsettling in a not very nice way, and she had to scramble to think of a logical explanation for her anxiety.

'I'm just wondering why you're leaving,' she said. 'I something's going wrong with the company… And I did discuss my working hours with you…'

His brow cleared immediately. 'Oh, the flexi-time thing?' he said. 'Don't worry about that at all—I've cleared it with the board. And give Venkat some time—he's a great guy to work with once you get past his superstitious streak.'

He was probably right—he'd worked with Venkat for years, after all, and she'd only met the man today. And she hadn't known Darius for very long either—there was absolutely no reason for the sinking feeling in the pit of her stomach when she thought about him leaving Nidas.

'Hmm….' she said. 'I think I'll get along well with Venkat—I'll have to. I'll need a lot of help from him for the first few months.'

'Will you?' he asked, feeling oddly jealous.

If Mallika needed help *he'd* have liked to be the one to provide it. For a few seconds before his rational side had kicked in he'd actually thought that she was upset because she'd miss him. Now he was left with an absurd feeling of being sidelined—just another stepping stone in Mallika's life.

Their timing was completely off, he thought ruefully. If he'd met her either a couple of years earlier or later he'd have tried to get to know her better—perhaps even acted on the growing attraction between the two of them. Right now it was completely out of the question. By the time they were no longer colleagues he'd be long gone.

'You still haven't told me why you're leaving,' Mallika said, and he blinked.

'Personal reasons,' he said, standing up to leave. 'Don't worry—the company's not about to go under.'

Mallika laughed at that. She had a particularly appealing laugh, Darius thought. It was as happy and uncomplicated as a child's, but it had a woman's maturity as well, and a sexy little undertone that was irresistible.

'That's reassuring,' she said, slipping off the desk to land on her feet right next to him.

Darius looked into her eyes and there was an instant of absolute connection that made his earlier thoughts irrelevant. A small part of his brain recognised how clichéd the moment was, and he was even amused. The rest of him was completely overwhelmed, and he kept on looking at her stupidly until she blinked and looked away.

'Goodness, look at the time!' she said, her voice slightly more high-pitched than normal. 'I really need to get going.'

'You haven't touched your drink,' he said, and she blinked at the can as if it had just materialised on her desk. 'I'll…um…carry it with me,' she said. 'What about your coffee?'

'I hate that stuff from the machine,' he said. 'Next time we'll go to a proper café.'

The way he said it made it sound like a promise he couldn't wait to keep.

'See you around, Darius,' she managed to squeak, before making a hasty exit.

The next time he saw her was a few days later, with over fifty other people in the same room. Venkat had called for an investor conference, and Mallika was the main presenter.

Darius came in late, slipping into the back of the room. He very rarely attended investor events, but Venkat had been unusually insistent, and he hadn't been able to resist the thought of seeing Mallika in top professional mode.

She was an impressive speaker—economical with words, but leaving her listeners with no doubt of her grasp over the subject. Slim and graceful in a raw silk printed sari, she exuded an aura of confidence and authority that was strangely attractive. Some people would probably think that it detracted from her femininity but, standing at the back of the room, Darius had to work hard to maintain a professional veneer.

She was quite something.

'She's brilliant, isn't she?' Venkat said, materialising next to Darius.

Mallika was answering a question raised by a grizzled investor old enough to be her father—and by the way the rest of the audience was nodding they were as impressed as Venkat was.

'It's been a while since we've held an event of this sort—it's bloody expensive, paying for the dinner and the booze, but it's worth it if we get the monies to come in. And people *are* interested—the market's looking up. We'll get a couple of hundred crores of investment after this event.'

'So does that mean you guys are doing perfectly well without me?' Darius asked, giving Venkat an amused look.

'We are,' Venkat said. 'Mallika's probably the best person you could have hired to replace you—in spite of all that flexible working rubbish. But, man, this place isn't going to be the same without you.'

The event wound to a close, and Mallika stepped off the dais to mingle with the guests. Venkat had been called back for the vote of thanks, and Darius stood alone at the back of the room, watching Mallika as she moved from one group of middle-aged men to the next, her smile firmly in place.

There were only a handful of women in the audience, and Darius noted that she spent longer with them, explaining something at length to one group and patiently allowing a much older woman to peer at the necklace of semi-precious stones she was wearing.

It was a while before the audience dispersed, most of them heading towards the buffet dinner.

Mallika's shoulders sagged a tiny bit, and the smile left her face as she walked towards the exit. It was as if she'd turnedt off a switch, changing from a confident, sparkling professional to a young woman who was just a little tired with life.

Darius waved to her, and she came across to him.

'I didn't see you come in,' she said. 'Did you just get here?'

'A while ago,' he said. 'I'm impressed, Mallika. You had everyone eating out of your hands.'

She shrugged. 'I've done this kind of event many times before,' she said. 'They're exhausting, but it's part of my job.'

'What do you find exhausting?' Darius asked.

'Talking to people,' she said. 'It's a strain. Everyone asks the same questions, and by the end of it I get so sick I could scream. Don't tell Venkat,' she added, looking up with a quick smile that lit up her face. 'He's planning a whole series of these events.'

'I was about to tell you that,' Darius said, a smile tugging at his lips. 'He's thrilled with the way you handled this one.' She made a little grimace, and a spurt of chivalry made Darius ask, 'Should I talk to him? He can handle the events himself—or one of the other fund managers could speak in your place.'

'The other fund managers aren't lucky for Venkat,' she said drily. 'I doubt he'll agree. Anyway, it's part of why you hired me, right?'

Darius nodded. It had been unprofessional of him to suggest he intervene, and he couldn't help admire Mallika's determination to do every part of her job well. Even when she obviously hated what she was doing.

It was intriguing, the way her ultra-professional mask slipped at times to betray her vulnerability. He had a feeling she didn't let it happen often, and all his protective instincts surged to the forefront whenever it did.

'Aren't you having dinner?' Venkat asked, popping up next to them. 'Or a drink? Mallika?'

She shook her head. 'I need to leave,' she said. 'My driver's taken the day off, so I've called a cab. The cabbie's been waiting for half an hour already.'

'Wouldn't it have been simpler to drive yourself?'

'I don't drive,' she said. 'I've tried learning a few times, but it's been an unmitigated disaster.'

'And you don't drink either! What a waste,' Venkat said sorrowfully. In his opinion, the best part of an event of this sort was the company-sponsored alcohol. 'Darius?'

Darius shook his head. 'I need to leave as well,' he

said. 'Got some people coming over. And I'm driving, so I can't have a drink either.'

Venkat looked ridiculously disappointed, and Darius laughed, clapping him on the shoulder.

'I'll take you out for a drink this Friday,' he promised. 'Come on, Mallika—I'll walk you to the lobby.'

Their event had been held in a rather exclusive mid-town hotel, and there were several other corporate events in full swing there. The banquet hall next to theirs was hosting an annual party, and the waiting area outside the banquet hall was dotted with entertainers. Jugglers in clown costumes, living statues, and even a magician or two.

Mallika paused next to a gigantic plastic sphere with a girl playing the violin inside it, and stared at it critically.

'What's the idea?' she asked. 'Why's the girl in the bubble?'

Darius shrugged. 'It's supposed to add a touch of the exotic,' he said. 'In the last party I went to of this sort they'd flown in a belly dancer from Turkey to dance for about ten minutes.'

'Ugh, what an awful job,' Mallika said, wondering which was worse—the few men who were openly leering at the blonde violinist in her low-cut green Tinker Bell dress, or the people who were walking past without even acknowledging her as a human being. 'I'm suddenly feeling a lot better about my own work.'

'No plastic bubbles?' Darius said solemnly as they went down the stairs that led to the hotel lobby. 'That *is* a significant upside, I agree. And wonderful colleagues to work with, perhaps?'

She giggled. 'Like Venkat?'

'Like *me*, I was going to say.' Darius held the door

open for her as they went out into the night air. 'But clearly I've not done enough to impress you yet.'

Mallika looked up at him. In the warm light pouring out from the lobby he looked incredible. His hair was slightly mussed, and a few strands fell over his forehead in sexy disarray. He'd come from work, but he'd taken off his tie and undone the top button of his shirt, and it was difficult to take her eyes off the triangle of exposed skin. And when she did it was only to lose herself in *his* eyes—dark and amused, with a hint of something that was disturbingly exciting.

'Consider me impressed,' she said lightly, and turned away to dig for her phone in her bag, ignoring the sudden movement he made towards her.

'What d'you mean, you've *left*?' she demanded a few minutes later, having finally got through to the cabbie.

She listened to what sounded like an incredibly complicated explanation, and sighed.

'He got another fare and went off,' she said. 'I'll have to ask the hotel to get me a cab.'

'Or I could drop you home?' Darius suggested.

'Isn't it out of your way?'

'Not terribly,' Darius lied. 'We'll take the sea link.' Dropping Mallika home would add forty-five minutes to his drive, but it was worth it.

'If you're sure, then,' Mallika said, heaving a sigh of relief.

It wouldn't be difficult getting another cab back, but the thought of the lonely drive home was singularly depressing. And, whether she admitted it to herself or not, the prospect of spending more time with Darius held a lot of appeal.

Darius handed his valet parking token to an attendant

and put a hand under Mallika's elbow as he steered her to one side. By Mumbai standards it was unusually chilly, and there was a strong breeze blowing. He felt Mallika shiver a little, and gave her a concerned look.

'Do you have a wrap or something?' he asked, and she shook her head, drawing the *pallu* of her sari around her shoulders.

'No, I didn't think it would be cold,' she said.

'And I've left my jacket in my car,' Darius said. 'All my life I've wanted to be chivalrous like in movies—put my jacket around a shivering girl's shoulders—and when I get the perfect opportunity…'

'You find you've forgotten the jacket?' she said, laughing up at him. 'Don't worry about it—I'm not likely to die of frostbite.'

'You could catch a cold, though,' he said, sounding quite serious. 'I'll take you back inside till the car comes up.'

Or you could put your arm around me, Mallika almost said. That would be another favourite Hollywood moment, copied faithfully by Bollywood in multiple movies. Even suggesting it was out of the question, of course, but oh, how she wished she could!

Before she could turn around, a slim woman with waist-length hair came up to them and tapped Darius lightly on the shoulder. A man followed her, a long-suffering look on his face.

'It's Tubby Mistry, isn't it?' she asked, after hesitating a little.

Darius looked around, his face breaking into a smile. 'Nivi! How are you doing?'

'It *is* you!' the woman said, giving a little squeal of delight before throwing herself into his arms.

The man, presumably her husband, gave Mallika a resigned look. Mallika smiled at him, though inwardly she was feeling absurdly jealous of the woman. It was particularly ironic, her turning up and flinging herself into Darius's arms just when Mallika had been wishing she could do exactly that.

'My goodness, I almost didn't recognise you,' Nivi said, stepping back after giving Darius several exuberant hugs and leaving a lipstick mark on his cheek. 'I spotted you when you were walking out of the hotel. You looked so familiar, but I just couldn't place you.'

'She thought you were a TV celeb,' her husband interjected, earning himself a reproachful look.

'You can't blame me for that—he's turned out so utterly gorgeous!' she said. 'You should have seen him in school! He was overweight and gawky and he wore a perfectly hideous pair of glasses. No girl would have turned to look at him twice.'

Her husband cleared his throat, jerking his head towards Mallika.

'Oh, I'm so sorry,' Nivi said, looking genuinely contrite. 'You don't mind, do you? I'm Nivedita. I knew Darius in school, and we've not met in years. I moved back to Kolkata, and I've lived there ever since. We only got here today, and he's the first person I've met from my old life.'

'You must send me some of his school pictures,' Mallika said promptly, and Darius groaned.

'Nivi, if you do anything of that sort I'll have to break that solemn blood oath you made me swear in school.'

'Blackmailer!' she said, giving him another affectionate hug. 'Don't you dare, Darius. Remember all the help I gave you for your Hindi exams?'

'Yes, well, I passed the exams, but I still can't speak a sentence without making mistakes,' he said, and Nivedita laughed.

'You'll learn the language some day,' she said. 'Okay, I'm off now—I can see the two of you are dying to be alone. I'll get in touch with you soon, Tubby.'

'It's our *karma*,' Darius said sadly once Nivedita and her long-suffering husband were out of earshot. 'Faces from the past popping up wherever we go.'

'It's happened exactly once for me—and that time it was a face from the present,' Mallika retorted. 'And Vaishali didn't start drawing up a list of my most embarrassing moments for the whole world to hear.'

'What can I say? Your past isn't as chequered as mine,' Darius said as he took his car keys from the valet parking attendant. 'Come on, let's go.'

'You said Nivedita swore you to a blood oath when you were in school,' Mallika said curiously after she got into the car. 'What was that about?'

'I caught her kissing our house captain,' Darius said as he manoeuvred the car out of a particularly complicated set of barricades at the hotel exit.

'Would that matter now? I'm sure her husband wouldn't be particularly shocked.'

'The house captain was a girl,' Darius said, grinning as Mallika's jaw dropped. 'Nivi was going through an experimental phase.'

'I suppose she finally decided that she preferred men,' Mallika said. 'Bit of a loudmouth isn't she? Were you really that hideous, or was she exaggerating?'

Darius sighed. 'I was a blimp,' he said. 'I weighed almost a hundred kilos and I wore glasses. My mother loved baking, and I loved eating. Luckily I managed to get into my school football team, and the coach made me run twenty rounds of the field every day before the others even turned up for practice. I was down to skin and bone in three months.'

'That explains a lot,' she said, and as he gave her a quizzical look went on, 'You're not vain about your looks. Most good-looking men act like they're doing you a favour by allowing you to breathe the same air as them.'

Darius, who hardly ever thought about his looks at all, felt absurdly flattered. He knew he was a lot more attractive now than he'd been in his schooldays, but he hadn't realised that Mallika liked the way he looked.

'So what happened to the spectacles?' Mallika asked. 'Contact lenses?'

'Laser correction,' Darius said. 'D'you realise you sound like you're interviewing me for a reality show?'

'Serves you right for having become so good-looking,' Mallika said.

They were heading onto the highway that connected North Mumbai to South, and she groaned as she caught sight of a sea of cars.

'We'll be here for ever!' she said. 'There's a new flyover being built, and three of the six lanes are blocked off.'

'If you'd told me just a little earlier I'd have taken a different route,' Darius murmured, edging the car into the least sluggish lane.

'They're all as bad,' she said, sighing. 'Anyway, at least we have each other for company.' There was a short pause after which Mallika said, 'Darius, can I ask you something?'

'Yes,' he said, though his eyes were still on the road. 'Ask away.'

'Where are you going to be working after you leave Nidas?'

She'd expected him to say that he'd got a better offer from a competitor, or perhaps that he was working on a new start-up. What he actually said came as a complete surprise.

'Nowhere,' he said, as casually as if it was the most obvious answer.

Mallika waited a bit, but when he didn't qualify his answer she said tentatively, 'What are you planning to do, then?'

He turned to give her a quick smile.

'Travel,' he said. 'And some volunteer work—but only after a year or so. For the first year I'm planning on Europe and Africa, perhaps a few months in China and Russia. I've made enough money to last me for several years—if it runs out I'm sure I'll find some way of making some more.'

'You're serious?' Mallika asked. 'I mean, I know people do that kind of thing in the West, but I've never heard of anyone in India quitting their job just to...*travel.*'

The way she said 'travel' was impossibly cute, as if it was a strange, slightly dangerous word that she was trying out for the first time—Darius found his lips curving automatically into a smile.

'I'm serious,' he said. 'Not planning to work for the next five years at least. After that... Well, I'll figure it out when I need to.'

Mallika sat silent for a few minutes, trying to digest what she'd just heard. Darius had struck her as a responsible, steady sort of a man—the last kind of man she'd have expected to leave his job and go wandering around the world on a whim. Showed how bad she was at reading people, she thought. Her own father had been careless to the point of being irresponsible, but this was the first time she'd met someone who was consciously and collectedly plunging into uncertainty.

'You don't approve?' Darius asked wryly as the silence stretched on.

She shook her head in confusion, 'It's not that,' she said. 'It's not my place to approve or disapprove—it just seems like such a drastic thing to do. I guess I don't understand why. I mean, you can travel on holidays, can't you? And what about your family?'

'My family understands,' he said. 'They're as crazy as I am, and they won't let a small thing like my being on a different continent affect the way they feel about me. And travelling on holiday isn't the same thing as being completely free, exploring and having adventures. Setting up Nidas was great, and I've loved that part of my life. But now that it's a success it's slowly becoming like any other large company. I don't find it as fulfilling as I did in the days when we were struggling to make a mark. I wasn't born to be a corporate suit.'

'Unlike me,' Mallika said with a little smile. 'I love the structure and safety of working for a large company.'

Her mother had set up a successful business of her own, but she'd hated the uncertainty and the ups and downs, and she'd taught Mallika to hate them as well.

Before he could reply her phone rang, and she frowned as she took the call.

'Hi, Aryan… Yes, I'm on my way back… No, I'm not coming that way. I'm taking the sea link… No, I can't, Aryan. I've taken a lift from someone, it's completely out of our way, and I'm exhausted.' There was a brief pause, and then she said wearily, 'Aryan, can't this wait till Saturday?'

Evidently it couldn't.

'Look, I'll do my best, but I'm not promising anything. Message me the specs.'

She stared out of the window unseeingly, and Darius hesitated a little before asking quietly, 'Everything okay?'

Mallika turned towards him. 'Yes,' she said with a sigh. 'My brother wants a new memory card for his camera. Actually for my camera—he's sort of taken it over, because I don't have time for photography any longer. I just got a little upset with him because he wants me to stop and buy it for him right now.'

'We can stop if you like,' Darius said, wondering why Aryan didn't go and buy the memory card himself. Maybe he was a little spoilt, and used to his sister running errands for him.

'No, it's fine,' Mallika said. 'I'll try calling a few stores and if they have it I'll get off at the nearest point and take a cab.'

'Assuming they're still open by the time we get to South Mumbai,' Darius said, indicating the traffic outside. 'It's already past nine.'

'So it is,' Mallika said.

Her phone pinged and she glanced down, laughing in spite of herself.

'He's figured out there's a shop that sells memory cards and is open till ten-thirty,' she said. 'And he's told the guy who owns it to wait until I get there.'

'Is it on the way?' Darius asked.

Mallika shook her head. 'No, it's in Worli. You can

drop me where the sea link ends and then you can go home. It'll save you some time. I can grab a cab.'

'I'll come with you,' Darius said, feeling unreasonably irritated with Mallika as well as with Aryan. 'I'm not sure how safe it is, you traipsing around on your own in the middle of the night.'

'It's perfectly safe,' Mallika said crisply. 'But if you're sure it's not inconvenient…' Here, her lips curved into a disarmingly lovely smile. 'I'd love it if you came along.'

'It's not inconvenient,' Darius said, and it took all his self-control not to lean across and kiss her.

Clearly Mallika didn't believe in the fine art of dissembling—if she wanted him around she came right out and said so, instead of pretending that she'd just feel safer if he came with her. It was an unusual and refreshing trait in a woman, and Darius felt himself fall just a little bit in love with her as he smiled back.

'Aryan isn't as spoilt as he seems,' Mallika said suddenly. 'He's got a bit of an issue with stepping out of the house.'

'His health?' Darius asked.

She shook her head. 'No, it's more of a mental thing. He was pretty badly affected when our parents died, but he didn't show it for a while. And then he started going out less and less, and now he doesn't step out at all. And he doesn't like people coming over, though he's usually okay talking on the phone. That time we went out for lunch and I had to leave—my aunt had come over to look after him and he refused to answer the doorbell. She thought something had happened to him, and she was so upset when she found out that he was perfectly okay—just not in the mood to open the door.'

She ground to a halt, wondering why she'd said so

much. Aryan and his peculiarities weren't a good subject for casual conversation.

'So that's why you need a flexible working arrangement,' Darius said slowly, a lot of things he'd found odd about Mallika clicking into place. 'I'm so sorry. I didn't realise that your parents....'

'They died in an accident,' she said hurriedly. 'It was more than two years ago. I don't talk about it much, but it gets more awkward the later I leave it.'

'I get that,' he said, and he looked as if he truly did.

Most people she told either looked awkward or felt terribly sorry for her and gushed over her—both reactions made holding on to her temper tough. Darius looked sympathetic, but not pitying.

'Car accident?' he asked, and she shook her head.

'Gas cylinder explosion,' she said, and he winced.

'That sucks,' he said. 'I'm sorry. Come on, the traffic's finally moving—let's go and get that memory card.'

He kept the conversation light until they'd picked up the memory card—the shop was in an unsavoury little lane, and his lips tightened a little as he thought of Mallika going there alone. He didn't say anything, however, answering her questions on his travel plans instead, and listening to her stories of a holiday in Switzerland that she'd taken with her mother.

It was the first time that Mallika had really opened up and talked, and Darius found his respect for her growing as he listened. She had obviously been very close to her mother, but she was handling her loss with dignity and restraint. Darius had been through his share of family problems, and he could catch the undertone of strain in her voice when she mentioned Aryan. But she didn't complain, and Aryan's name only came up in the context of a hilarious scrap she'd got into with an online clothing store when they'd delivered a set of women's underwear instead of the shirt Aryan had ordered.

Darius still got the impression that ever since their parents died she'd made Aryan the sole focus of her life, and that she felt deeply responsible for him.

They were almost at her flat when he asked, 'Have you tried taking Aryan to a doctor?'

'Several times,' Mallika said. 'Nothing's worked. You see, he needs to be interested in getting better. Right now, he doesn't want that. He seems happy as he is.'

Darius wished he could ask her if *she* was happy, but it was too personal a question, so he contented himself with giving her a light hug before she got out of the car. Her hair smelt of orange blossom and bergamot, and her slim arms were warm and strong around his neck as she hugged him back.

'Thanks,' she said as she straightened up. 'For dropping me home, and for listening to me chatter about things.'

She turned and went into her apartment block quickly, and she heard him start the car and drive away as she got into the lift. The lift man was off duty and the lift was empty—Mallika got in and pulled the old-fashioned door shut behind her before sagging onto the lift man's chair.

It had been a long while since she'd last talked about her family, and the conversation with Darius had brought the memories flooding back. For perhaps the hundredth time she wished she'd gone with her family to Alibagh that weekend.

It had been one of those totally pointless accidents— the kind that could have been avoided easily if only someone had been around at the right time. The cylinder of cooking gas had probably been leaking slowly for a while, but her mother hadn't smelt it because she'd had a cold. She'd picked up the lighter and clicked it on to light the gas stove, the way she did every evening—only this time there'd been a swooshing sound as the petroleum gas pervading the air had caught fire.

Her mother had screamed once, and the scream had brought her father rushing to the kitchen.

They hadn't stood a chance.

The wall of flame had hit the leaking cylinder, and the spare one next to it, and in the next second both cylinders had exploded, turning the kitchen into a blazing inferno. Aryan had been outside in the garden, but he hadn't been able to get anywhere near his parents. And Alibagh was a small, sleepy seaside town—it had been almost twenty minutes before a fire engine reached the house.

It had been in time to save the rest of the house, but far too late to save Mallika's parents. The firemen had told her later that both of them must have died within a few minutes of the explosion, and her only consolation was that at least it must have been quick.

She'd been in shock, but she'd managed to hold herself together long enough to let her relatives know, organise the funeral, and get her brother back to Mumbai. Then, when everything was done, and she'd been about ready to fall apart in private, she'd realised that something was seriously wrong with her brother.

CHAPTER FOUR

MALLIKA KNEW SHE was going to be at work late the next day. A neighbour had complained about Aryan's habit of taking photographs from the windows using a telescopic lens—apparently she thought he was spying on her. It had taken some time to soothe her ruffled feathers, and now Mallika had spent almost an hour trying to explain to Aryan that he couldn't go around peering into other people's houses.

'I was trying to take a picture of a crow on her windowsill,' he said. 'I mean, look at her—d'you think it's likely I'd want a picture of *her* taking up disk space?'

'She doesn't know that,' Mallika said, as patiently as she could. 'And that was *my* camera you were using without asking me. Aryan, look…things are tough enough without you trying to make them tougher. Be a little more considerate, will you? Please?'

He didn't reply, and she almost gave up. Another woman in her place might have lost her temper, or created a scene, but Mallika had had years of training from her mother. However upset she'd been, she'd always concealed her true feelings from the men of the family and soldiered on. For years she'd watched her mother deal with her grandfather and father, and with Aryan as he grew up—the other two men were gone now, and so was her mother, but Mallika found it difficult to shake old habits.

'I'll see you this evening, then,' she said. 'Make sure you eat your lunch, okay?'

He mumbled something that she couldn't catch.

'I didn't get that,' she said.

'I'm sorry,' he whispered, without looking up. 'I didn't mean to upset you.'

Mallika felt her heart twist painfully within her. Aryan was demanding, and sometimes troublesome, but he was very different from her father—and he was the only part of her family left to her.

She went across to him and patted his shoulder awkwardly. 'It's all right,' she said. 'Just be a little careful, *baba*. We can't afford to antagonise the neighbours.'

'I'll be careful,' he said, and looked up, his eyes pleading. 'Do you *have* to go to work?' he asked. 'Can't you work from home today?'

Mallika hesitated. She *could* work from home, but the last time she'd spoken to Aryan's doctor he'd told her that she should try and gently wean him from his excessive dependence on her. She hated leaving him when he'd asked her to stay—it filled her with guilt and worry. But she knew she had to do what was best for Aryan, to try and help him. He was her responsibility.

'I'll come back early,' she promised. 'Why don't you go downstairs and sit in the garden for a bit? Then when I come back we can try going for a drive. Wouldn't that be fun?'

Aryan's face clouded over and he shook his head. 'No,' he said.

Mallika sighed. She'd been trying for months to get Aryan to step out of the flat with absolutely zero success. 'Why, Aryan?' she asked. 'I know you're finding it tough without Mum and Dad, but you need to try and get back to normal. I'll be with you—we don't even need to go anywhere far…'

His grip on her hand tightened painfully. 'I just… can't.' he said, and she had to be content with that.

She couldn't push him any further. If he didn't want to get better she couldn't make him. Something had broken in Aryan when their parents died, and all her love didn't seem enough to set it right.

Her phone was ringing as she let herself into her room at work an hour later.

'Nidas Investments, Mallika speaking,' she said automatically as she picked up the phone without looking at the caller ID.

'Very businesslike,' a familiar voice said approvingly, and her mood was immediately lifted by several notches.

The scene with Aryan had left her feeling drained and helpless, but just the sound of Darius's voice made the world seem like a better place.

'I've called to ask you for some help,' he said. 'I'm looking for a flat to rent, and I'm kind of desperate now. Since you know the real estate business inside out…'

'Don't you have a flat of your own already?'

'It's a long story,' he said. 'I have a flat in the same building as my parents. My sister's moving back to India, and I offered it to her when I thought I'd be leaving Nidas this month. But now that the board's asked me to stay on for another three months I need a place to stay. Only it's difficult to get somewhere for three months—I'm okay with paying rent for six, but not too many people offer leases that short. I really liked a condo in Parel, but it got snapped up by the time I got around to making an offer.'

'That's a pity,' Mallika said, wondering what kind of flat Darius would like. You could tell a lot about a person from the type of home they chose, and she thought she could picture the kind he'd go for. Big, airy and luxurious, but in an understated way. 'Which building?'

He told her, and added, 'It was a great flat—really large living room, with a massive balcony and two bedrooms. But there are only a few flats in the building with that plan. The rest have normal-sized living rooms.'

'Yes, it's only the flats next to the fire refuge areas that have that layout,' Mallika said, chewing her lip thoughtfully. 'I know the building pretty well.'

She was silent for a few seconds, and Darius could hear her slow, careful breathing over the phone line.

'If you're really keen on a flat like that I might be able to get you one for three months,' she said. 'Reasonable rent, and you won't have to pay brokerage. But you'd need to keep the flat in good condition, be careful not to upset the neighbours and all that.'

'I'm keen,' he said, smiling slightly at her tone. 'And I'm housetrained.'

'Hmm…' she said, as if she was only partially convinced. 'Meet me in the parking lot at lunchtime—say at around one—and I can take you to see the flat. It won't take more than half an hour.'

'You mean today?'

'You were the one who said you were keen!'

'So I did.' Darius got to his feet. 'We'll take my car. See you downstairs at one.'

The building was only a couple of kilometres away, and Darius crossed his fingers as they drove through the gate.

He'd been trying to make the best of it, but living with his parents again after a gap of fourteen years was far more stressful than he'd anticipated. So far he'd found only that one place to rent that he'd liked, and he'd been seriously considering choosing one at random from the row of sub-par flats and service apartments his agent had lined up for him.

Mallika's suggestion was a godsend—even if the flat wasn't precisely the same layout as the one he'd initially chosen he was inclined to take it.

He glanced across at her. She was more casually dressed than usual—perhaps because she had no meetings to attend. A black top in some silky material clung lovingly to her curves, and he could see a tantalising hint of cleavage. Her trousers were well cut, and her shoes as sensible as always—the only dash of colour in her outfit was provided by a turquoise blue stole that matched her leather tote.

'You always carry a funky handbag,' he said suddenly as a security guard waved the car to a stop just inside the gate. 'But you wear sensible-looking shoes. Not seen too many girls do that—it's usually neither or both.'

She gave him a quick smile. 'I can't wear heels,' she said. 'Always trip and fall over. But I love bags, and I buy a new one almost every month. I'm surprised you noticed.'

She wasn't just surprised, she was also flattered he'd paid that much attention. Most men didn't notice anything about women's fashions beyond necklines and hemlines.

'I've grown up with a shopaholic sister,' he said, laughing. 'And every girlfriend I've ever had has been crazy about shoes and bags.'

Mallika wrinkled her nose a little at the thought of his girlfriends—she was sure he'd had several, and she found herself thinking negative thoughts about all of them.

The security guard came up to the car and Mallika had to get out and talk to him. Darius tapped the wheel idly as he looked out across the sprawling private garden that was one of the most attractive features of the building.

A tall man came out of the main entrance, and Mallika smiled at him, driving all thoughts of property prices out of Darius's head. The man put an arm around Mallika and gave her a hug that was halfway between friendly and proprietorial, and Darius felt an unfamiliar surge of jealousy as Mallika hugged him back. He knew that Mallika wasn't in a relationship, and it hadn't occurred to him that she might have close male friends. The thought was surprisingly unsettling.

'I have the keys,' Mallika said, sliding back into the passenger seat. 'There's parking for visitors at the back of the building. Take a left after the ramp… Left, Darius—*this* is your left.'

She tugged at his arm as he narrowly missed driving into a flowerbed and Darius grinned as he swung the wheel to the left. 'Sorry, I'm a bit directionally challenged,' he said. 'Especially when bossy women bark into my ear.'

'I'm not bossy!' Mallika protested. She'd let her hand linger on his arm a bit longer than strictly necessary, and now she squeezed it hard. 'Park by the wall. No, not behind the truck—there's more space behind that little red car.'

'Not bossy in the least,' Darius murmured, and she made a face as she got out of the car.

'I'm bossy only when the situation demands it,' she said, linking her arm through his. 'Come on, let's go see the flat.'

'Who was the man you were talking to outside?' he asked as they walked towards the building. 'The guy who gave you the keys? You seemed to know him pretty well.'

He sounded faintly jealous, and Mallika felt her mood improve even further.

'He's an old friend,' she said. 'We were at college together, and he worked with my mother for a while. He and his wife bought a place here last year, and they've been keeping an eye on the flat I'm taking you to.'

Darius nodded. It was ridiculous—it shouldn't matter to him in the least—but he felt a lot better now that he knew the man was married.

The lift man saluted when they got into the lift, and Mallika gave him a quick smile.

'Twentieth floor,' she said, and the man nodded.

'*Sahib* is going to stay here?' he asked.

'*Sahib* is going to figure out first if he likes it or not,' Mallika said. 'What do you think, Shinde? Will he like it?'

'*Sahib* will like it definitely,' Shinde said.

His expression suggested that *sahib* would have to be a blithering idiot not to like it, and Darius suppressed a smile. Mallika had an automatic air of command that Shinde was clearly not immune to—if she'd said that she was taking Darius up to the twentieth floor to persuade him to jump off it she would probably still have had Shinde's wholehearted support.

'It's a beautiful flat, madam,' Shinde added, giving

Darius a disapproving look as the lift doors opened at the twentieth floor.

Shinde was right—the flat *was* beautiful. The layout, of course, was excellent, with a living room that was huge by Mumbai standards, two respectable-sized bedrooms and a compact but very well-designed kitchen. Unlike the stark, unfurnished flat Darius had seen the last time he'd come to the building, this one was fully furnished—right down to elegant white leather sofas and sheer silver curtains with a blue thread running through them.

The colour scheme was predominantly blue and white, but lampshades and rugs made little splashes of vibrant colour. There were a couple of framed vintage Bollywood posters on one wall, while another had a collection of masks from across the country. The overall effect was one of laid-back luxury, and Darius could imagine a high-end interior designer working very hard to produce it.

'You can get rid of the posters and the masks, if you like,' Mallika said as she walked across the room to open the large French windows leading onto the balcony. 'And if you have furniture of your own we can get this put in storage.'

Darius followed her out onto the balcony. The flat overlooked a racecourse and the view was amazing. It was an unusually clear day, and the sea shimmered in the distance, the steel girders of the Bandra-Worli sea link providing a counterpoint to the expanse of blue water. The cars crossing the sea link were so far away that they looked like toys, but Mallika seemed unusually fascinated by them.

'Think of all those people driving from one place to

another, feeling ever so busy and important,' she said as Darius came to stand next to her. 'From here they look just like ants—completely insignificant. And if they look at us we'll look like ants to them too.'

Darius turned to face her, leaning his back against the balcony railing. There was a slight breeze ruffling her curls, and her eyes sparkled beguilingly as she smiled up at him.

'It seems to please you,' he said, laughing as he lifted a hand to tuck a stray curl neatly behind her ear. 'The insignificance of humanity in general and the two of us in particular.'

Mallika laughed, and her dimples deepened. Darius's fingers trailed to her cheek and he traced the line of her jaw, his thumb rubbing very close to her mouth. She went very still, but her large eyes held not even a hint of alarm as he bent down to brush his lips lightly against hers.

Her lips were soft and tempting, and they parted very slightly against his. He deepened the kiss, his arms going around her to pull her closer to him. She came willingly, her arms twining eagerly around his neck and her slim body fitting perfectly against his. Kissing her felt completely natural and wildly erotic at the same time, and it took a huge effort of will to finally stop.

He hadn't wanted to—it had been a last remnant of sanity that had prevailed before he could get completely carried away. It was too soon, he hardly knew her, and he was going away in three months. There were all kinds of things wrong with the situation. But the feel of her in his arms had been so right that stopping the kiss had been almost physically wrenching.

Mallika swayed slightly as he raised his head, and he put his hands on her arms to steady her.

'Wow,' she said softly, her eyes still slightly unfocussed. Then a sudden realisation of her surroundings seemed to hit her and she stepped back, running a slightly shaky hand through her hair. 'So, anyway,' she said, rushing into speech before he could say anything. 'You should probably look at the flat and…um…make up your mind. Whether you want to rent it or not. I'll wait here for you.'

'Or you could come and look at it with me?' he suggested, reaching out and taking her hand. She looked uncharacteristically flustered, and he could feel her pulse beating wildly in her wrist.

'Yes, of course,' she said, but she disengaged her hand from his before following him into the flat.

For a few seconds Darius wondered if he should ask her what was going on. The kiss had definitely not been unwelcome—he'd felt the desire surging through her body, and the urgency with which she'd returned it. Even afterwards, the way she'd looked at him had made him think that she wanted to take things further.

The change in her had been sudden—maybe she was just more conservative than she'd initially seemed and was trying to cover up her embarrassment. The temptation to repeat the kiss was huge, but Darius didn't want to crowd her.

It didn't take long for him to look the flat over, and he'd come to a decision by the time they were back in the living room.

'I'll take it,' he said. 'Any idea what rent the landlord's asking?'

She quoted a number that was around fifteen per cent lower than what his broker had quoted for the unfurnished flat he'd seen the week before.

'Are you sure?' he asked. 'Not that I'm complaining, but I was told that rents have gone up in the last few months.'

'There's been a market correction,' Mallika acknowledged. 'Not very major, though, and this building was overpriced to begin with. The landlord will be okay with the rent—she's…um…a little particular about the kind of person she gives the flat to.'

Darius looked around the flat. 'Whose is it?'

'Mine,' she said, and as he turned to look at her in surprise, she said, 'My mum bought up some flats in this building when it was still under construction.'

'When you say "bought up some flats"…?'

'Two,' Mallika said hastily. 'She bought two flats—one each for Aryan and me. The rates were lower when the project was first floated.'

Darius's eyebrows flew up. *His* family was reasonably wealthy, but buying a single flat in this building would use up at least half their life's savings. Buying two at a time was as inconceivable as sauntering off and buying a sack full of diamonds because you were getting them at a discount.

'Did she…um…do this kind of thing often?' he asked.

'Not really,' Mallika said, her voice guarded. 'Real estate is expensive.'

But between Aryan and her, they owned six flats in Mumbai, three in Bangalore and a farmhouse in Alibagh. It was a fact she usually tried to keep hidden—this was the first time she had voluntarily told anyone even about the flat they were standing in.

'Did the previous tenants leave just recently?' Darius asked, instinctively changing the topic. 'The flat looks as if someone was living in it until yesterday.'

Mallika shook her head. 'I got it furnished a year ago,' she said. 'Sometimes I just need a place to…to think in.'

'Most people do their thinking in the bathroom,' Darius said drily.

She flushed, wishing she'd kept her mouth shut. It was too much, expecting him to understand when he didn't know the first thing about her.

'I meant to rent it out eventually,' she muttered. 'I guess I got a little carried away, doing up the place.'

'Clearly you have more money than you know what to do with,' he said, sounding amused. 'Why d'you need a job?'

'To keep myself from going crazy,' she said.

And her voice was so serious that Darius felt she actually meant it.

CHAPTER FIVE

'THIS IS SO typical of a government office,' Darius said, glancing at his watch in annoyance. They were waiting in the property office to register his rent agreement—the appointment had been for seven in the morning, but it was already seven-thirty and the clerks hadn't yet turned up.

'It's always like this,' Mallika said, shrugging. 'Do you have morning meetings?'

He shook his head. 'No, but there's a ton of work I need to get done. And I thought I'd get started on the paperwork for my Schengen visa.'

'Stop thinking about it,' Mallika said, sliding down in her uncomfortable-looking moulded plastic chair and leaning her head against the back to look at the ceiling. 'We're here now. Let's talk about stuff until the clerks turn up.'

'What kind of stuff?' Darius asked, giving her an amused look.

Since the kiss in the flat they hadn't seen each other alone—Darius had been travelling, and after he'd come back Mallika had worked from home for a week. They'd agreed on the rental terms over email and, sensing that she needed some space, Darius hadn't suggested that they meet.

He glanced around the rather seedy office, with its broken furniture and *paan* stains on the walls where it had been chewed and spat out. It wasn't exactly romantic, but at least he was with Mallika, and she looked relaxed and pleased to be spending time with him.

"'Of shoes and ships and sealing wax,'" she said dreamily. "'Of cabbages and kings.'"

'*Alice in Wonderland*,' Darius said. 'It's from The Walrus and The Carpenter poem, isn't it?'

'Is it?' she asked. 'My dad used to keep saying it whenever I asked him what he was thinking about. I didn't realise it was a quotation.'

It was the first time she'd spoken about her father, though her mother figured prominently in her conversation, and Darius took it as a good sign. She was still looking up at the ceiling, as if she found something particularly fascinating in the stains and cracks.

"'*Paisa toh haath ka mail hai,*'" she said after a pause. 'My dad used to keep saying that too. "Money is like dirt on one's palms. Here one moment, washed away the next.'"

'He piled up one huge mound of it all the same, though, didn't he?' Darius said without thinking.

Luckily Mallika didn't seem offended. 'Actually, he lost money as fast as he made it,' she said, her mouth curving up into a wry grin. 'It was my mum who was the careful one.'

From her tone, it sounded as if she wished she could admire her mum for it, but couldn't quite bring herself to do so.

Sensing his enquiry, even though Darius hadn't said anything, she went on.

'She was into real estate,' she said. 'My mum. She started off as a real estate agent, but when the markets improved and my dad got back some of his capital she started investing in property herself.'

'Impressive,' he said.

She shrugged. 'I don't think she had much of a choice. My dad couldn't think of any way of making money other than the stock market. If she hadn't taken charge we'd have been out on the streets. Aryan and I were little kids when the stock market crash happened.'

'The Harshad Mehta one?' Darius remembered the crash, but it hadn't affected his life at all. His parents' money was all in fixed deposits and blue chip stocks, so the crash had made good dinnertime conversation—nothing else.

'Yes. My dad lost pretty much all the money we had. Not just his own money but his parents' as well. We used to live in my grandmother's flat in Malabar Hill, but she had to sell it and we moved to a tiny place in Kandivali. Even there, he could barely afford to pay the rent.'

'Must have been tough.'

She shook her head. 'It wasn't. When you're kids it doesn't matter, not living at a good address or having a car and a driver. My dad had more time to spend with us, and he made the whole thing seem like an adventure. He'd take us on bus rides to the zoo and to parks, and he'd invent games for the three of us to play… When I look back, it feels like the best time of my life. It was hell for my mum, though.'

It had been years later when she'd realised that her father had had a mild case of bipolar disorder. The whacky, fun Dad she remembered was the persona he'd taken on during his manic phases. When he'd been going through a depressive episode her mother had concealed it from Aryan and her, telling them that their father was busy at work when he'd locked himself up in a room for hours on end.

'Was that when your mum started up with the real estate thing?'

Mallika nodded. 'She'd been brought up in a rich family, but the dowry she brought with her went with everything else during the crash. And she was too proud to ask her parents for anything more.'

'Why real estate?'

'I guess because that was the only business she understood. Her father was a builder in Gujarat, and she knew how the industry worked. In those days there were very few women property brokers, and she was one of the first to figure out that wives play a huge role in deciding on a house. Most brokers ignored them, but whenever my mom met a couple who was trying to buy a house she went out of her way to understand what kind of layouts the woman liked, how big she wanted the kitchen to be. And kids—no one had heard of pester power, but she made sure she told them about the great play area downstairs and the guy who sold cotton candy across the street…'

'She sounds smart,' Darius said, thinking of his own mother. She was smart too, but she'd been a schoolteacher—selling anything at all was completely alien to her character.

'Yes…' Mallika sounded a little sad. 'But along the line she forgot to have fun or spend time with her family or relax. All she did was work hard and make money.

And every rupee she made had to either go into the bank or into property or gold. I probably have more gold jewellery than the Queen of Oman, even though I hate every piece of it.'

Darius gave her a quick smile. 'It sounds like a problem lots of women would love to have,' he said.

Mallika immediately wondered if she'd sounded too self-obsessed, too demanding and needy. It was difficult to explain the various things that had gone wrong in her family without mentioning stuff that she'd rather not talk about. Which begged the question—why the heck had she started moaning about her parents in the first place?

Giving herself a rapid mental slap, she straightened up.

'You're right,' she said. 'Perhaps some day I'll melt all the stuff down and make a dinner set out of it. I've always wanted to eat off a gold plate.'

'Or give it away to charity?' he suggested.

Mallika shook her head with a laugh. 'There's too much of my mum in me to actually give it *all* away. I do the usual annual donations to charities, and to a couple of religious trusts, but not much more.'

Used to people who claimed to do a lot more for society than they actually did, Darius found Mallika refreshingly upfront. He did a fair amount of volunteering, and he supported a small NGO financially as well, but it wasn't something he talked about much. He was beginning to understand the differences between them. Mallika craved stability, structure and security, whereas he longed for adventure, risk and new experiences that pushed boundaries and frontiers.

'What about *your* family?' Mallika was asking. 'What are *they* like?'

Darius grinned. 'They're a bunch of lunatics,' he said. 'Each one's nuttier than the next. Look—I think someone's actually arrived to open up the office.'

He was right—a surly clerk in a bright magenta sari was making a big show of opening a counter and ignoring the people who'd been queuing up for over forty-five minutes waiting for her.

Registering the agreement took around forty minutes—the last step involved putting their thumbprints onto the documents before signing them, and Darius grimaced as the clerk held out a stamp pad with purple ink to him.

'I thought you just took an electronic thumbprint?' he asked.

The clerk gave him a steely look. 'It's part of the procedure, sir,' she said severely.

Mallika suppressed a little giggle. Darius's thumb was now covered with bright purple ink, and he was looking at it with the kind of horror people usually reserved for maggots and slugs.

'Here, let me help,' she said, taking a pack of cleansing tissues out of her bag.

Darius eyed the packet. 'What're those?' he asked, clearly deeply suspicious of anything in pink packaging.

'Make-up-removing tissues,' Mallika said, taking his hand and beginning to rub the ink off his thumb.

They were out of the office and halfway down the dingy stairs, and there was a curious intimacy in the situation. Mallika took her time, her mouth puckering as she concentrated on getting the ink off. Darius stood still and watched her. The temptation to pull her close and kiss her was immense, but they were in a very pub-

lic place—and already they'd attracted curious looks
from a couple of people.

'Thanks,' he said, once she was done with scrubbing
his hand. 'Mallika, the other day in the flat...'

Mallika cringed inwardly. She'd behaved stupidly at
the flat, and she knew it. She was very thankful Darius
had left the topic alone so far—the reason for her behaviour was solid enough, only it was so incredibly embarrassing that she didn't want to talk about it.

'Yes?' she said.

'Did I upset you? Because you've been a little...dif-
ferent ever since.'

'I wasn't expecting it,' she said. 'And I've been feeling a little awkward—I'm sorry.'

She looked up at him, and for a second Darius forgot
what he'd been going to say as he looked into her lovely
brown eyes.

'I'm sorry if you think I crossed a professional line,'
he said after a bit. 'I kissed you on impulse—I wasn't
thinking straight.'

'I'm told that the best kisses happen on impulse,' she
said, so solemnly that he burst out laughing.

'Really? Who told you that?'

Mallika shrugged. 'I've forgotten,' she said. 'Anyway, whoever it was, they definitely would know more
about it than me.'

Darius gave her a curious look. She didn't come
across as being prudish or inexperienced—maybe she
meant that her previous lovers hadn't been impulsive.

There was a little pause as they walked out of the
building. Mallika was looking straight ahead, her lips
pressed tightly together. Embarrassing or not, she'd have

to tell him if she didn't want a repeat of what had happened in the flat.

They'd agreed to go back to the office together in Darius's car, and Mallika waited till they were safely inside before she said, 'It was the first time.'

He looked puzzled, as well he might—there had been enough of a pause for him to start thinking of something totally different—like national debt, or the future of the economy. Still, Mallika couldn't help feeling peeved at his not understanding immediately. She'd had to muster up a fair bit of courage to say it the first time, and having to repeat it was just piling on the embarrassment.

'It was the first time anyone had kissed me,' she announced, adding firmly, 'I'm warning you—if you laugh I'm going to have to kill you.'

It didn't look as if there was any danger of his laughing—his eyes widened slightly, and he switched the car engine off.

'You mean—ever?'

'Ever,' she said, wishing he wouldn't stare at her as if she was an alien with three heads and a beak. India was still pretty conservative—surely even in Mumbai it wasn't that unusual to have reached the age of twenty-nine without having been kissed?

Except clearly it was, because Darius looked completely gobsmacked. It took him a few seconds to find his voice, and when he did all he said was, 'Does that mean that you're…a…?'

'A virgin?' Feeling really cross now, Mallika said, 'Yes, it does. And I'm surprised you're asking. What kind of person would have sex and not kiss the person that they're…um…'

'Having sex with?' Darius supplied helpfully.

She glared at him, though that was exactly what she'd wanted to say. 'Anyway, so that was why I was feeling awkward,' she said. 'Can we go now?'

'In a minute,' Darius said, and then he leaned across and kissed her again.

Given that this was the second time it had happened, she should have been better prepared. But the kiss was so different from the first that she was left completely stunned. His lips barely grazed hers, and there was something tender, almost reverential in his touch. Unfortunately her long-dormant hormones weren't in the mood to be treated reverentially, and before she knew it her hands had come up to bunch in his shirt and pull him closer.

The kiss suddenly became a lot less tender and a lot more exciting. *Yessss!* her hormones said happily. *Got it right this time. Don't stop!*

She'd have probably gone with the flow, but catching sight of a large and interested audience of street children outside the car had a sudden dampening effect on Mallika. She pulled away abruptly, straightening her hair with unsteady fingers.

'Sorry,' she muttered. 'I got a bit carried away.'

'So did I,' Darius said, his voice amused. 'You have that effect on me.' Then her suddenly horrified expression registered, and he said, 'Are you okay?'

'Your shirt!' Mallika squeaked, and he looked down to survey his once spotless white shirtfront. Not only was it creased where Mallika had grabbed at it, the top button had popped off and her thumb had left purple ink stains all over it.

'I forgot to use the make-up remover on my own hands,' she said ruefully.

He laughed. 'I have a wardrobe full of white shirts,' he said. 'I won't miss this one.'

'I'll get you a new one,' she said. 'I'm so sorry—I'm a complete klutz when I get carried away.'

'Your getting carried away is worth ruining a shirt for,' he said, his smile warm and sexy as he put out a hand to lightly brush her curls back from her face.

She smiled back, though her heart was thumping at twice its normal rate.

'You're pretty amazing—you know that, right?' he said as he leaned across to kiss her again.

The second kiss was less explosive, but it made her feel cherished and incredibly desirable, and it was like stepping out into the sunlight after months of being locked in a cellar. The sensible part of her mind knew perfectly well that Darius was leaving in a few months, and that they had no future together. But somehow it didn't matter—what mattered was the feel of his strong arms around her and his firm lips moving against hers.

When he finally drew away she gave a little moan of protest.

'I know. I feel that way too,' he said regretfully, though his eyes were dancing with amusement. 'But we need to go—we're providing free entertainment to half the street population of Mumbai.'

He was right—the children had gathered closer to the car and were peering in curiously, and Mallika gave a little sigh.

'All right,' she said, though it felt as if she'd been pulled back to earth with a thump.

'There's a bike parked right in front of the car—I'll have to move it,' Darius said, opening the car door and getting out before Mallika could stop him.

The children followed to watch him, offering their help in shrill voices as he wrestled the locked motorcycle a couple of metres down the road. Mallika got out as well. This was the first time she'd seen Darius do anything…well…*physical*, and he was a treat to watch. He must work out often, she thought, admiring the muscles in his back and shoulders as he lifted the bike. And he was strong—the bike weighed a lot more than he did, and he made moving it seem absolutely effortless.

'Today's not my day,' he remarked as he handed the children a handful of loose change and walked back towards the car. 'First ink and then grease.'

Sure enough, his shirt now had a black grease stain on it.

'Give an old woman something…I haven't had a proper meal since yesterday,' a beggar woman whined from the kerb, and Darius gave her the rest of his change before sliding behind the wheel.

'Blessings on you and your pretty one,' the woman called out after them in Hindi. 'May you have a hundred handsome sons!'

'I like the sound of my "pretty one",' Darius said, sounding amused as Mallika spluttered in annoyance. 'Though having a hundred sons sounds a little impractical.'

'I thought you didn't understand Hindi,' she said crossly.

'Oh, I can get by,' he replied. 'Where to now? I need to get out of this shirt before I show up at work, but I can drop you there before going home to change.'

'You could come to my place,' Mallika suggested impulsively. 'It's nearby, and one of Aryan's shirts would fit you.'

Her body was still tingling in the aftermath of the kiss, and she wanted to keep Darius by her side for as long as she could. It was completely out of character for her to suggest such a thing, and it was reckless and spontaneous, but Darius's kiss had opened a door inside her that could not now be closed. She felt free, and she didn't want that feeling to end.

'Are you sure?' Darius asked.

Going to her place implied taking their kiss further, and he wasn't sure at all if that was a good idea. Kissing her had been on his mind for weeks now, and he hadn't been able to resist any longer. But he should have stopped once she'd told him she was a virgin. He had no intention of getting into any kind of long-term relationship—not at this stage in his life—and he couldn't imagine that Mallika was up for a casual fling.

'Sure that the shirt will fit?' Mallika asked, purposely misunderstanding him. 'It will—Aryan's skinnier than you, but he wears his shirts loose.'

She wasn't sure how Aryan would react to her bringing a man home—either he wouldn't even notice or he'd withdraw even further into his shell—but she found she didn't care. Her home had begun to seem like a prison to her. She loved Aryan to bits, and she felt responsible for him, but he seemed to be getting worse, becoming increasingly difficult to manage, and demanding more and more of her time.

The thought of taking Darius home was strangely liberating. She'd spent the last two years of her life mourning her parents and helplessly watching Aryan get worse. Her friends had gone through the usual ups and downs of relationships and heartbreak before settling down, but she'd listened to her ultraconservative mother and steered clear of men. And after the accident she had been so wrapped up in Aryan that she'd had no time for anyone else.

If she hadn't met Darius she probably wouldn't even have realised that she was living a half-life, and every instinct told her to make the most of the time she had with him. With her mother gone, her links with her conservative extended family had weakened, and she didn't really care what they thought of what she did. And right now she wanted to be with Darius more than anything else.

It took them less than ten minutes to reach her apartment complex, and Darius parked in a free spot outside the compound wall.

'Should I wait here?' he asked in a last-ditch attempt to keep his distance.

She shook her head. 'Better come with me,' she said. 'You'll need to try on the shirt. And I'll give you the keys to your flat too. Now that the paperwork's done, and everything, you'll probably want to move in this weekend.'

A neighbour coming out of the building looked a little surprised to see Darius, but Mallika gave her a sweet smile and swept him into the lift without stopping to talk. The neighbour had known her for years and was a notorious gossip. Mallika would bet her last rupee that she'd make an excuse to call or come over in the evening, with the sole purpose of finding out who Darius was.

The lift stopped on the third floor and Darius followed her to the door of her flat. She dug around in her bright blue tote for the keys—while Aryan was at home, there was only around a ten per cent chance of him opening the door if she rang the bell. Mostly, unless he'd ordered something for himself on the internet and was expecting it to be delivered, he didn't bother answering the door.

Mallika used her own keys to let herself in and out, and she'd got duplicates made for the cook and the cleaner.

Darius's clear, warm gaze on her made her fumble a little, but she finally got the door open, flushing a little as she ushered him in. He stopped as he stepped in, looking around the flat in surprise. He'd expected it to be done up in the same way as the flat he was renting—clean lines, lots of light and space. This flat, however, was crammed full of heavy furniture in some kind of dark wood. The upholstery was in shades of brown and maroon, and the oil paintings on the walls were depressing landscapes in dingy colours. Mallika herself seemed to have shrunk a little after stepping into the flat.

'We…um…usually take our shoes off before going into the house,' she said as she pushed the door open, slipping her own flat-soled pumps off and putting them on a rack just inside the door.

It was a common enough rule in conservative households, and Darius gave her an impish wink as he sat down on a bench next to the shoe rack and pulled off his shoes and socks.

'Sorry,' she said. 'My mum used to be very fussy about shoes in the house, and we've stuck to the rule even without her being around to yell at us.'

'It's a sensible rule,' he said, suddenly understanding why the house looked the way it did. She'd probably changed nothing after her parents had died.

He knew how much she hated any kind of pitying overture, so he didn't say anything, but his heart went out to her.

'I'll get the shirt—give me a minute,' she said, and went into a little corridor and knocked on Aryan's door.

There was no response, and after a minute she gave an exasperated little huff and went into the kitchen.

There was a little service area beyond the kitchen, and a pile of ironed clothes was lying on top of the washing machine. She took two shirts out of the heap and went back to the living room. Darius was still standing, and she held the shirts out to him.

'Here—one of these should fit,' she said. 'You can change in my room.'

Her room turned out to be at the end of the corridor, and unlike the intensely depressing living room it was painted a bright, clean white, with blue curtains and a turquoise bedspread. It was a cheerful room, and Darius felt a lot better as soon as he stepped into it.

'I'll find you a bag to carry your messed-up shirt in,' Mallika said as she shut the door behind her, and she went across to the small dressing table that occupied one corner of the room. 'Here you go.'

She handed him a medium-sized plastic bag and then went to sit on the bed, her eyes on him. The kiss earlier in the car had left her in a confused, half-aroused state so that she could hardly think straight. All she knew was that she wanted to kiss him again, and his suddenly formal attitude was making her feel so frustrated she could scream.

Darius caught her eye and started undoing the top button of his shirt.

Mallika was mesmerised. She couldn't move. 'Uh… maybe I should leave?' she eventually managed to say, but he laughed mischievously.

Darius continued to unbutton his shirt, a gently teasing smile on his lips, and Mallika knew she couldn't leave now. With a boldness that surprised her she slipped off the bed in one fluid movement and came up to him.

'I can help if you want,' she said softly, her hands going to the buttons of his stained shirt.

In the back of her mind Mallika was aware of a lifetime of duty, responsibility and conservative values. But faced with Darius, this beautiful man with his quiet strength, who challenged her but never tried to control her, she found herself responding with an uncharacteristically coy smile. This wasn't her, but it was the person she wanted to be—even if only for a little while. And it felt good…really good.

Darius stood very still as she undid the first two buttons, her hand slipping under the cloth to slide over his bare chest. Inexperienced she might be, but Mallika was very aware of what she was doing and the effect she was having on him. The height difference between them was only a few inches, and she leaned up to press her lips against his, her hands still busy with the buttons. Her tongue lightly teased his mouth, and finally that proved too much for Darius's self-control.

With a muttered oath, he pulled her into his arms, his mouth hard and demanding against hers. His shirt had fallen open, all buttons finally undone, and Mallika could feel his heart pounding under velvety hair-roughened skin.

Without quite knowing how she'd got there Mallika found herself lying on the bed, pinned under his heavy body as he began to kiss his way down her throat. Her hands knotted in his hair and she arched her body to get as close to his as she could without actually breaking skin. Her own clothes were in disarray, her top having ridden up to expose most of her torso, and the feel of his bare skin against hers was indescribably good.

They were probably a nanosecond away from having hot, messy sex on the bed when the sound of a door closing in another part of the flat made Darius jerk away from her.

'Damn, I'm so sorry,' he said.

His eyes were still hooded and a little unfocused as he groaned under his breath and wrapped his arms around Mallika to hold her tightly against his body.

'Bad timing,' he said softly as he dropped a kiss onto her forehead. 'I wish I'd met you a couple of years earlier, Mallika, before I decided to leave India.'

'You could delay going a little,' Mallika said, but she stopped trying to get the rest of his clothes off. She could feel the moment slipping away and she couldn't bear it. 'Or we could just be together until you leave.'

'It's not fair to you,' he said gently. 'Not that I wouldn't love to take this to…to a logical conclusion. I shouldn't have kissed you to begin with, and what happened right now was pretty inexcusable.'

Feeling frustrated, and a little hurt, Mallika sighed. He was right about their timing being completely off, and Mallika wished desperately that she *had* met him a few years earlier. Not that she was in the market for a serious relationship either, but at least they'd have had time to work something out. At least she could have explored all the new sensations and desires that were currently flooding her system. But it looked as if she was going to have to imagine where they might take her instead.

'Go latch the door and put on one of the shirts,' she said, pushing him lightly away.

He groaned reluctantly but got up, giving her an

opportunity to admire his perfectly toned torso as he shrugged off the shirt and put on a clean one. She'd been right—Darius was broader built and more muscular than Aryan, but the shirt fitted perfectly. And the colour suited him. So far, she'd seen Darius only in white or cream formal shirts. This one was a dark blue, and set off his golden skin and jet-black hair perfectly.

'Looking good, Mr Mistry,' she said as he bundled up his old shirt and shoved it into the plastic bag. 'Time for a cup of coffee before you go?'

Darius nodded and Mallika slid off the bed and headed for the kitchen, hastily rearranging her clothes into some semblance of normal.

'Black or with milk?' she asked.

'Black, but with plenty of sugar,' he said.

He took a minute before following her out—his body had reacted with indecent haste to her kisses and he wanted to be sure he was fit to be seen before he left the room. Once he was sure he had everything under control, he tucked the shirt in, gave himself a cursory look in the mirror and strode out.

Mallika was tapping a foot nervously on the floor as she spooned instant coffee powder into two mugs. Her frustration at having to stop was turning into an irritation with everything around her—especially Aryan, who'd disturbed them by slamming his door shut.

'D'you want to grab something to eat before we leave?' she asked Darius when he walked into the kitchen.

It wasn't food he was thinking about just then, but he shrugged. 'A sandwich or something,' he said. 'I'm not particularly hungry.'

She handed him his coffee and went to the fridge.

'I'm sure I can figure something out. The cook will have made lunch for Aryan…I'll just need to see if there's enough for all of us.'

'Mally, do you know where my camera is?'

Darius had built up a mental picture of Aryan, and the reality was so different from the weedy, sallow-looking youth he'd imagined that he blinked in surprise. The resemblance between brother and sister was so close that they could have been twins if not for the obvious differences of gender and age. If anything, Aryan was better-looking than Mallika, and other than his skin being a little pale there was nothing to indicate that he hadn't been out of doors in months.

Mallika had turned at the sound of his voice, and she said curtly, 'It's in my room. And you're not getting it back until you promise to stop taking photos from your window.'

'I promise,' he said. 'Can I have it back now?'

'I'll tell you in the evening,' she said. 'Say hello to Darius, Aryan.'

Aryan's brow furrowed a little as he turned.

'Hello, Darius,' he said slowly, and it was difficult to tell if he was being sarcastic or not. His brown eyes, disconcertingly like Mallika's, flicked over Darius, stopping a little to take in the shirt.

'I lent him one of your shirts,' Mallika said. 'His got ruined by ink and grease—long story. Have you had lunch?'

'Fruit and some milk,' Aryan said. 'There were only oily *parathas* for lunch.'

'Those'll do for us,' Mallika said, locating the *parathas*

and sliding them onto two plates with a little heap of pickle on each. 'Here you go, Darius.'

Darius took the plate. Their hands touched briefly, and a slight blush suffused Mallika's face. Aryan gave her a thoughtful look, but he didn't say anything.

Mallika looked up at him. 'Did you get any work done today, Aryan?' she asked.

'Lots,' he said, stretching like a cat, his mouth curving into a boyish smile that was surprisingly charming. 'The market's very active today.'

'Hmm, I saw the alerts,' Mallika said as she finished her last *paratha*. 'Be careful, though, it'll be very volatile until the elections. Shall we go, Darius? Venkat's probably tearing his hair out—I was supposed to submit a report to him before lunch.'

Aryan watched them leave, an indefinable expression in his eyes. There was clearly a lot going on beneath the surface with Mallika's brother that Darius could only guess at.

'See you around,' Darius said as he brushed past him to get to the door. 'I'll get the shirt cleaned and sent back to you in a couple of days.'

'See you,' he echoed.

His voice was perfectly cordial, though Darius got the impression that Aryan was happy to see him go. It was an odd set-up, and he felt desperately sorry for Mallika, living in that depressing flat with only her reclusive brother for company.

'Aryan works?' Darius asked as they got into the car. He didn't want to talk about what had just happened between them, and felt that Mallika was thinking the same.

'Stock-trading,' Mallika said. 'He inherited the knack from my father and he's doing quite well. Unlike my dad, he knows how to take calculated risks, so he makes money.'

'And your dad?' Darius said eventually.

She shrugged. 'Made a fortune one day—lost it the next. He let his gambling instincts take over too often.'

There hadn't been any photos in the house, Darius realised suddenly. That was what had seemed out of place. The flat was like a museum—all that expensive heavy furniture and dark draperies—with no personal touches at all. No photographs, no tacky souvenirs from foreign trips, no sign that anyone actually *lived* there.

'What did you think of him?' Mallika was asking. 'Aryan, I mean. It's been a while since he met anyone. He doesn't go out, and the only people who visit us have known him for years. I was wondering how he comes across to someone who's met him for the first time.'

'He didn't talk much,' Darius said cautiously. 'It's not that uncommon to be a bit of a hermit at that age, is it?'

'"A bit of a hermit"?' she repeated, and laughed shortly. 'That's a good description.'

He got the sense that she wanted to say more, but she seemed to think better of it and began talking about work instead. Darius felt a strange sense of frustration—not all of it physical. There was something elusive about Mallika…a quicksilver quality that made him feel he was never quite sure of where he was with her.

The admission that he was the first man she'd ever kissed had shaken him up—it was the first indication he'd got that she felt more for him than she'd shown. As for his own feelings—he knew he was already in way too deep to walk away at this point. In addition to wanting her so badly that it hurt, he needed to talk to her, find out what made her tick.

CHAPTER SIX

'NOT THIS WEEKEND. Aryan needs me around,' Mallika said.

She'd tried talking to Aryan again about getting help—it was eight months now since he'd last stepped out of the flat—but she hadn't got anywhere. And he'd been even more distant since he'd met Darius, talking even less than usual and not coming out of his room except for meals. She was really worried about him—afraid he would become so reclusive that she would lose him completely.

'I really want to see you,' Darius said, his voice dropping an octave.

She felt a pleasurable heat curling through her body. And this was in reaction to just his *voice*. A mental image of him shirtless and super-hot intruded, and she squirmed.

'I want to see you too,' she whispered back. 'It's just that this weekend is a bit…tough. I need to figure a few things out.'

As she put the phone down she noticed Aryan at the door, looking at her. It was impossible to gauge how much he'd overheard, and he didn't say anything—just walked off to the dining table.

A surge of annoyance left her cheeks warm and her pulse racing—she badly wanted to meet Darius, and Aryan was one of the main reasons she'd said no. But it seemed a rather pointless sacrifice when it didn't seem to be helping him.

She obsessed over it for a while, before she came to a decision. Her aunt wouldn't mind coming down and being with Aryan for a bit—heaven knew she deserved to have a life of her own. For a minute she wondered what her mother would have thought of her decision and her nerve almost failed her. Her mother had been courageous and independent, but she'd also been rigidly conventional—which was partly why she'd ended up being deeply unhappy all her life. She'd have hated the thought of what Mallika was about to do. But she was gone anyway, and Mallika had her own life to live and her own choices to make.

Picking up her phone, she typed out a quick text.

Are you still free this weekend? Might be able to meet you on Saturday.

Her text arrived in the nick of time—Darius was just about to promise an elderly aunt that he'd drive her to visit a friend who lived around thirty kilometres away.

'Next Saturday instead,' he told his aunt firmly.

The last time he'd driven Auntie Freny to meet a friend she'd insisted on leaving home at nine in the morning, and had subsequently proceeded to party till three the *next* morning.

'*Dikra*, this time you can have a drink too,' Auntie Freny said cajolingly.

Darius promptly felt as if he was six again, being promised a chocolate if he was good.

'Last time, *ni*, you had to drive, no? This time we can stay overnight—just pack some clothes.'

'Next Saturday,' Darius said, and gave his aunt an affectionate hug.

'Some girl you're going to meet—don't think I don't know.'

His aunt made a surprisingly nimble grab for his phone, and Darius managed to whisk it away only just in time.

Balked of her fun, Freny shook her head at him sorrowfully. 'Never do I get to meet these girls. Get married and settle down, *dikra*, this is no time for flirting and having fun. Our race is dying out! I went to the Parsi *panchayat* last week and...'

'And they told you that unless I got married and fathered fifteen children I'd be responsible for the end of the Parsis?'

Aunt Freny gave him an exasperated look. 'No, I met an old friend with a really nice daughter who'd be perfect for you. If you just met her once you'd give up this crazy idea of travelling around in all kinds of strange places, away from your family. Should I call my friend?'

'Thanks, but no thanks,' Darius said firmly. 'I'm perfectly capable of finding a girlfriend of my own if I want one.'

'Freny, he doesn't *want* to marry and settle down,' his mother said tartly as she walked into the room. 'If he did, he wouldn't want to go traipsing across the world like this.' She caught Darius's suddenly stricken look and added in a gentler tone, 'Relax, I'm not trying to make you feel guilty. You've done everything you can for this family, and you deserve a few adventures for yourself.'

Finding something to wear for a date when you possessed a sum total of zero remotely suitable outfits shouldn't have been difficult, but it was.

Mallika grimaced as she surveyed her clothes. She had several shelves of cotton tunics that she teamed with jeans when she went out to indulge her photography hobby, two formal business suits, a couple of silk *churidaar kameez*, and half a dozen saris. Dozens of loose cotton T-shirts…

Even the 'remotely suitable' outfits were beginning to look unusable—one of the tops had a mark on it, and the other two hung loose on her slim frame. Evidently she'd lost weight and not realised it.

Beginning to feel a little desperate, she took everything out of the wardrobe, in the hope that something suitable would surface. Buying new clothes to go out with Darius would be taking the concept of trying too hard to a completely different level…

Perhaps she could wear a silk *kameez* over jeans and pretend that she was going for an arty look.

At the back of the wardrobe, a little patch of flame-coloured matt silk caught her eye. *Ah, right.* That was the dress that an old college friend had given her, evidently not realising that Mallika never wore dresses or skirts.

Tugging the dress from its cellophane wrapping, she shook it out and held it against herself. There was a reason why she avoided anything that showed her legs—there was a narrow, but very visible scar from a bicycle accident that ran up her left leg from mid-calf to knee.

'If it scares him off it's probably a good thing,'

she muttered to herself as she pulled the dress on and smoothed it over her hips.

It should have looked hideous. The colour was anything but subtle, and it was a while since she'd last worn a dress. But the fabric clung softly to her curves, outlining the soft swell of her breasts and emphasising her perfect waist. The hem was asymmetrical, and it hid part of the scar—but she found the scar itself was nowhere as scary as she remembered it being. Her legs were long and shapely, and the scar was barely noticeable.

The dress was probably not suitable for a simple date, but once she'd seen how she looked she didn't feel like taking it off.

'You're looking nice,' Aryan informed her as she stepped out of her room.

Her eyes flew up to his in surprise. She hadn't expected him to come out of his room to see her off. Still less had she expected him to notice what she was wearing.

Feeling the excitement drain out of her, she said tentatively, 'Thanks. Um…are you sure you'll be okay with *mausiji*?'

He nodded, and when she didn't look convinced gave her a crooked smile. 'I'm alone at home when you go to work,' he reminded her. 'Go ahead—I'll be fine today.'

Aryan probably hadn't intended it, but she felt inordinately guilty as she stepped out of the flat. She did her best to work from home whenever she could, but she did end up having to go to the office at least two, sometimes three days a week. Aryan never liked being left alone in the flat, and ever since she'd changed jobs he'd been more on edge—staying in his room and skipping meals if she wasn't around to force him to eat.

Darius was waiting in his car at the end of the lane, and she half ran the rest of the way to reach him.

He leaned across and unlocked the door, giving her a quizzical smile as she slid in, half out of breath. 'Are the Feds after you?' he asked.

She laughed. 'No—worse, I have the snoopiest neighbours in the universe. So, what are we doing today?'

He'd planned lunch and a movie, but one look at Mallika in her flame-coloured dress had driven everything out of his head—all he could think of was taking her home and making slow, delicious love to her.

'Whatever you want,' he said slowly. 'I've booked tickets for a movie, and a table at a restaurant. But most of all I want to talk to you. We left a lot of things unfinished the last time we met.'

His eyes met hers, and it was as if she could read what he'd been thinking a second ago.

'You've moved into the Parel flat, haven't you?' she asked, and he nodded. 'And have you managed to set up your home theatre system yet?'

He nodded again, and she broke into a smile so bright and alluring that he could hardly tear his eyes away from her face.

'Let's go there then,' she said. 'Watch an old movie, order takeaway…talk.'

'Right,' he said, his throat suddenly dry. 'Sounds like a plan.'

Predictably, watching a movie was the last thing on their minds as they tumbled into the flat fifteen minutes later. Darius had pretty much broken every speed limit in town, getting them there, and they were barely inside the flat before Mallika was in his arms, kissing him so eagerly that it took his breath away.

'Slow down,' he said softly, smoothing her hair away from her face. 'We have all the time in the world. And I really do think we should talk.'

It took everything he had not to whisk her straight into the bedroom, but it was important that they laid some ground rules before taking things further.

She sighed and pulled away from him. 'What's there to talk about?' she asked. 'You're leaving in a few months and I'm stuck here.'

'I know,' he said. 'Logically, we should stay away from each other—but that's not happening, is it?' It looked as if she wanted to interrupt, but he went on, 'It's mostly my fault—I've been trying to convince you to meet me. If you want me to, I'll stop.'

'I don't want you to stop,' Mallika said, her voice low. 'Look, I can't commit to a long-term thing either, but I haven't felt like this about anyone ever before. I haven't wanted to do this with anyone before. Maybe it's just physical attraction, but I…I dream about you. And when I'm with you I can't seem to stop myself from…from…'

Touching you, she wanted to say. *Kissing you and wanting to make love to you all night long.* The words didn't come, though—and already she'd said more than she'd meant to.

Darius's expression had changed. Maybe he thought she was throwing herself at him. She quickly tried to dispel the thought.

'I can't marry while I still have Aryan to look after,' she said. 'Until I met you I used to stay away from men and concentrate on work. It was much easier that way.

Only with you I've not been able to stick to the rules I made for myself.'

Mallika took a deep breath. She'd never had such a conversation with a man before, and she had to screw up her courage to get the next words out.

'So I was thinking—maybe I should just forget about the rules for a bit. Do what *I* want for once—with someone who wants it just as much as I do.'

Darius leaned closer to her, capturing both her hands in his. 'Mallika, I don't want to take advantage,' he said. 'I'm crazy for you, but the last thing I want to do is hurt you in any way.'

'You won't,' she said, her eyes meeting his steadily. 'I know you'll leave, and I'm okay with it. I just…' Her voice quivered a bit, but she steadied it with a visible effort. 'I haven't really been able to let go and do what I want. *Ever.* When I was in school and college I was studying hard all the time, because that was the way my mother wanted it. Even when I started working I stayed away from parties and men. She was trying to protect me because she'd had such a tough life herself. By the time I figured out that the world wasn't that bad after all, she was dead. And I had Aryan to look after.'

Darius's eyes were sympathetic now, and she felt she couldn't bear it.

'While you're here, let's be together,' she said, making her voice as upbeat and cheerful as possible. 'And once you need to go we'll separate—with no regrets. How does that sound?'

'Like the last bit's going to be damn tough,' Darius said honestly. 'I'm finding it difficult enough to be objective right now. I don't know what it'll be like three months from now.'

'If we're lucky it'll wear off by then,' she said.

He had to laugh. 'If we're lucky,' he repeated, tracing a line down the side of her face with one hand and watching her quiver in response. 'But—just so that you know—even if we're perfect together I'm not going to stay. I need a clean break from my current life, and that's important for me. More important than anything else.'

'Relax, I get that,' she murmured. 'If you like we'll get the legal team to draft a set of disclaimers for you! I'm not looking for a happy ending, here—just a few weeks of fun.'

'Right,' he said.

There was an awkward moment while they stared at each other, both unsure of what to do next, then Darius muttered something and swept her into his arms, his lips hot and insistent against hers. Mallika melted against him, but a few minutes later, as his hands went to the zip on her dress, she made a little sound of protest and Darius pulled back.

'Are you okay?' he asked, his mouth against her throat.

She nodded her head. 'Yes,' she said decisively. 'Just go a little slower. I'm…nervous.'

The admission shook him more than he would have cared to admit and he changed his touch, skimming his hands over her skin as gently as if she was made of spun glass.

It was only when she made a little sound in her throat and pressed her hips hard against his that he let his lips become a little more urgent, his hands more demanding…

Much later, Mallika raised her head lazily from Darius's shoulder and surveyed the room. Her dress lay in a tangled heap near the foot of the bed, next to his jeans, and the rest of their clothing was strewn around the room. It was a miracle that they'd made it to the bed and not ended up making love on the living room sofa or on the floor.

'That was good,' she said.

'Just *good*? I must be losing my touch,' he murmured, running a finger lightly down her arm. She shivered in reaction and he grinned, twisting her around to kiss her. 'Did I hurt you?' he asked, more seriously.

She shook her head. 'I'm a little sore, but I guess that's to be expected. And I hate to spoil the mood, but I'm starving after all that exercise. Any chance of getting something to eat?'

'We'll have to order in,' Darius said. 'The sum total of food available in this house is one apple and a box of biscuits.'

'I'll take the apple,' she said, turning and burrowing closer to him.

'I have some takeaway menus in the kitchen,' Darius said. What do you feel like eating?'

'I'm not sure,' Mallika said with a sigh. Lying in Darius's arms felt so good she wouldn't move at all if her stomach weren't rumbling.

'Did you live here ever, Mallika?' he asked. 'Before you decided to rent the flat out?'

The place had a sense of having been lived in, despite its pristine state.

'I wanted to move here when my parents died,' she said. 'Our old place reminds me of them every minute I'm in the flat. But Aryan wasn't keen, and now I can't leave him there by himself.'

'That's understandable,' he said.

There was a brief pause as Mallika cuddled up closer

to him and nibbled playfully at his shoulder. She responded enthusiastically when he pulled her in for a hard kiss, but after a bit twisted away from him.

'I'm really, really hungry,' she said. 'Can we order food first?'

Darius groaned and picked up the first of the menus. 'Here you go,' he said. 'I can see I'm much lower in your priority list than lunch.'

Mallika took the menu and gave him a conciliatory little kiss. 'You're *much* more important than lunch,' she assured him. 'I just want to get lunch out of the way so that I can concentrate on you.'

The thought of her concentrating only on him made it difficult for Darius to think straight, but he leaned back and watched Mallika as she went through the menu.

'*Tandoori roti, daal tadka* and *aloo jeera*,' she said. 'What about you?'

'I think I'll have the chicken *sagawala*,' he said, mentioning the first thing he'd noticed on the menu. 'Or, no—you're vegetarian. I'll have the same stuff you're having.'

'I'm okay with you ordering chicken as long as I don't have to eat it,' Mallika said. 'But it's *saagwala*—not *sagawala*.'

Darius frowned. 'What's the difference?'

'*Saagwala* means that it's made in a spinach sauce,' she explained patiently. '*Sagawala* means that the chicken is a blood relative.'

'Seriously?'

'Seriously.'

He looked impressed. 'There's more to this speaking Hindi thing than meets the eye,' he said. 'Maybe you should give me Hindi lessons.'

'Maybe I should,' she said, dimpling as she tossed the menu back to him and went to get a glass of water.

Darius used his cell phone to order lunch, and once he was done wandered back to the bedroom. He lay down and stared at the ceiling. In spite of it being Mallika's first time, the sex had been mind-blowing, and he could hardly stop a goofy grin from spreading across his face at the thought of how good it had been.

Mallika came back into the room a few minutes later, still swathed in the bed sheet. She perched on his side of the bed and looked at him thoughtfully. Darius was sitting up now, his bare chest on display as he gave her a slow smile—and he looked so heartbreakingly perfect that for an instant she forgot the lines she'd been rehearsing in the kitchen.

Impulsively, she leaned across and kissed him, but pulled away when he tried to take her into her arms. Losing her head once a day was enough—it had been amazing, unforgettable, but now she needed to be sensible.

'This is going to be complicated,' she said. 'We should talk.'

CHAPTER SEVEN

'I AGREE,' DARIUS SAID. 'I think ground rules are a very good idea.'

'So that we don't end up making a mess of things,' Mallika continued. 'I mean, you'll be going away, so it doesn't matter so much for you, but I don't want to have to deal with unnecessary gossip.' She thought for a moment, and went on, 'Plus it'll be difficult for me if Aryan finds out. He's very fragile right now—even more so than usual.'

'We don't need to tell him,' Darius said, reacting to the last sentence first. Her expression changed and he added hastily, 'Or anyone else. What's next?'

He looked so tempting, standing there with his shirt still partly unbuttoned and his hair rumpled after making love, that Mallika felt like abandoning the list of rules and going back to bed with him.

Sighing, she turned away and walked to the window. 'Gossip is only part of it,' she said. 'We should probably be careful not to…um…get too close—like talk about our lives too much and all that. Keep it limited to the physical stuff.'

Darius nodded again, a little more slowly this time. What she said made sense, but it made him think that she was perhaps more emotionally affected than she said she was. It sounded as if she was trying to build up walls so that she didn't get hurt when he left.

'What else?' he asked, beginning to wonder if this had all been a huge mistake.

He was a lot more experienced than her, and he should have foreseen the complications that would occur if they slept together. He couldn't get tangled up in something that would make him question his travels. He needed this…he *deserved* this—it had been his goal for so many years and now it was within touching distance. He wouldn't give it up—not again.

'We should…um…be together only in the evenings,' she said. 'I'll come to you.'

That would set some boundaries, she thought. Ensure that she didn't throw herself at him at all hours. And she'd make sure she went to him only on the days that she'd been working from home, so Aryan wasn't alone for more than a few hours.

He nodded again, and she said. 'Just one more thing. I have a lot of stuff going on right now, so while I'd love to meet you as often as you want to it probably won't be possible.'

This was beginning to sound a bit clinical, thought Darius. He understood that Mallika was only trying to protect herself, and goodness knew the rules certainly worked in his favour, but it made him feel concerned that she had already got in over her head.

'Problems with Aryan?' Darius asked, and his voice was so gentle that Mallika felt suddenly very close to tears.

'Yes,' she said. 'He doesn't like me leaving him at home and going out.'

Darius moved to stand behind her, his arms coming around her to pull her gently against him. He would agree to the rules, of course, but he would have to stay on his guard. After all, rules could always be broken.

'Maybe I could help?' he suggested. 'If nothing else, I could take your mind off everything that's bothering you.'

Mallika turned abruptly and buried her face in his chest. 'It isn't so simple,' she said, her voice muffled against his shirt.

'It could be,' he said, his breath stirring her hair. 'Think about it.'

'I should go now,' she said, without looking up. It's getting late and Aryan's alone. My aunt will have left by now.'

For a few seconds Darius felt like telling her that Aryan was a grown man and capable of taking care of himself for a few hours. But he bit the words back. Mallika clearly felt responsible for her brother, and making snide remarks about him wouldn't help matters. Also, he trusted her judgement—if she said her brother wasn't fit to be left alone for long periods she was probably right.

But he was feeling incredibly frustrated—Mallika had got to him in a way no woman had before, and her determination to stay emotionally unattached bothered him more than he would have expected.

'I'll drop you home,' he said, but she shook her head again.

'I'll take a cab.'

'Stop being stubborn about it,' he said. 'Even if someone sees us, we can tell them you're my landlady.'

She nodded obediently, and Darius tipped her face

up so that she was forced to look right into his laughing eyes.

'Come on, landlady,' he said teasingly. 'Let's get you home.'

Perhaps it would have been easier if Darius had taken her rules at face value, Mallika thought a few weeks later. She slipped into Darius's flat almost every alternate evening, and the sex was as hot and passionate as it had been the first time. But Darius didn't seem content with that—she'd expected that he would stay away from her when they weren't actually sleeping together, but he was doing quite the opposite.

'People know that we're friends,' he said. 'It'll seem far more suspicious if I stop talking to you at work than if we continue to hang out together.'

And so, in public, he'd assumed the role of a friend—one who wanted to spend as much time with her as possible. Every couple of days he'd call to suggest meeting up for coffee or a movie—if she said no he'd laugh and suggest an alternative date. Or he'd bully her into admitting she needed a break and take her out anyway.

Once he'd bought tickets for a stand-up comedy show and told Venkat that she needed to leave work early to participate in a personality development exercise.

Venkat had asked suspiciously, 'What's wrong with her personality?'

He'd said, 'Her sense of humour could do with some work—she takes life way too seriously.'

And Venkat, who wouldn't have recognised a joke if it had walked up and hit him on the nose, had agreed with him and forced her to go.

Another time he'd booked both of them onto a heritage walk across the old parts of South Mumbai, which had ended at an open-air music festival at the Gateway of India. The music had been a crazy jumble of jazz, blues, fusion and rock, and Mallika had had the time of her life.

Afterwards, they'd wandered through Colaba and had dinner at a little tucked-away Lebanese café. They'd talked for hours and hours about music and travel and books, and hadn't realised how late it was until they'd been the last people in the café, with the owner waiting patiently for them to pay their bill and leave.

When she'd got home Aryan had been waiting for her, his eyes large and accusing in his pale face, and she'd resolved never to stay out so late again.

The next few times Darius had asked her out she'd made excuses and stayed at home, playing Scrabble with Aryan, or just sitting in his room with a book while he pored over his laptop screen.

Today, Darius was on the phone insisting she get up at this unearthly hour in the morning to go with him to Sewri. A flock of migratory flamingos stopped at the Sewri mudflats for a few weeks every year on their way from Siberia, and Darius was appalled to hear that she'd lived in Mumbai for her entire life and never seen them.

'Darius, I can't,' she protested. 'I've just woken up, and I need to get breakfast for Aryan. And I need to go to my Alibagh house for a few hours in the afternoon. I can't come.'

And I can't be with you and pretend to be friends without wanting much more, she said silently to herself. It was time she put her foot down and made sure they stuck to the rules. She was new at this, and she could feel herself starting to fall for him, to rely on him being a part of her life. She didn't want to get hurt, and of course there was Aryan to consider.

'I'll stop at a café and fetch something for Aryan's breakfast,' Darius said easily. 'And we'll be done with the flamingos by ten—I'll drop you to the ferry after that.'

'I don't want to leave Aryan alone for that long,' she said. 'My aunt can't come over today—she's got a *puja* prayer ritual to go to. And I'm a little tired.'

She'd woken up with a bad headache, and the thought of the Alibagh trip was depressing. The little beach villa was where her parents had died—she'd not been able to bring herself either to sell it or rent it out, and it had been lying vacant for the last two years. It had been repainted after the accident, and there was a caretaker who kept the house clean and tended the lawn, but she'd visited it only four times in the last two years. Now there was a leakage problem and she had to go.

'We can go tomorrow, then,' Darius said. 'Or next week, if you like.'

Mallika sighed, and then said abruptly, 'Darius, why are you doing this?'

'Doing what?' he asked innocently.

'You know what I mean,' Mallika said.

She got up and closed the door to her room, to make sure that Aryan couldn't overhear her.

'Look, we're doing what we said we would—having a fling before you go to Alaska or Mongolia or wherever. But you're also doing this "just good friends" routine. I'm not sure if it's fooling anyone, and it's definitely confusing the hell out of *me*. It just…doesn't make sense.'

'It does to me,' he said. 'I really like you. I like being with you—in bed and out of it. And, maybe I'm wrong, but it feels like you don't have any close friends—not people you can be yourself with.'

'So you feel *sorry* for me?'

She probably hadn't meant to sound bitter, but it came out that way and Darius winced. He hadn't wanted to have this conversation so soon—and definitely not over the phone. What she'd said about never having had a chance to have fun and do what she wanted had struck a chord with him. He'd never had the kind of problems she had, but he understood the need to break loose and he'd been doing his best to help.

Quite apart from that was the fact that he actually loved every minute he spent with her—but he tried not to think about that too much. He knew that their spending time together like this was dancing on the edge of what their rules allowed, but somehow he couldn't stop himself.

'Not sorry, exactly,' he said. 'I just think that you're young and you have your whole life ahead of you—it's a little early to be cooping yourself up at home and only coming out when you need to go to work. You said it yourself—you want to go out and have fun, do all the things you missed doing when you were younger.'

'I might have said it, but it's not practical to think only about myself,' she said. 'I have a brother with problems, remember?'

'I know,' Darius said.

She didn't mention Aryan often, but he had now got a fair idea of what she was dealing with there. He gritted his teeth before plunging ahead.

'But I don't think you can solve his problems by locking yourself away as well. He needs professional help, and the sooner you get it for him the better it'll be for both of you.'

'Perhaps *I* need professional help as well, then,' Mallika said. 'Because I can't see my way to dragging him to a doctor when he refuses to go. And I can't stop caring about him or looking after him.'

'There's always a way out,' Darius said. 'It's just not obvious because you're so closely involved.'

'Maybe I don't want a way out,' she said softly, the hopelessness of the entire situation striking her anew. 'I'm not like you, Darius—I can't just walk away from my family without a backward glance.'

There was a long pause, and then Darius asked, 'Is that what you think I'm doing?'

'Well, isn't it?' she countered hotly. He had pressed her buttons and now her blood was up. She was spoiling for a fight. 'Your parents are old, and there's your grandmother, and your aunt—you're just leaving them to fend for themselves, aren't you?'

'My sister's here,' he said, wondering why he was even bothering to justify himself.

He hadn't talked to Mallika about his family much—their rules forbade it, after all—so it wasn't surprising that she was jumping to all the wrong conclusions. Still, her words stung, and he couldn't help thinking they'd been right about keeping their relationship superficial. Their approach to life was so different that they didn't have a hope of ever fully understanding each other.

'That's not the same thing,' Mallika was saying. 'She's got kids and a husband, hasn't she?'

Shirin was in the process of divorcing her husband. That was another thing Darius had never told Mallika, and this was definitely not the right time. Suddenly his plans for a glorious morning with Mallika had turned into an ugly argument and he coulnd't wait for it to be over.

'Mallika—' he said, but she interrupted him.

'I'm sorry,' she said. 'This isn't any of my business, and I'm getting a bit too emotional about it. I miss my own parents and I can't understand you leaving yours behind while you go off to discover yourself, or whatever. So I'm not being rational, and I've probably said a bunch of things I shouldn't have.'

Her voice was shaking a little, and Darius felt his anger dissipate as quickly as it had flared up.

'It's all right,' he said. 'You're right, in a way. But my family and my decisions don't have anything to do with the situation you and Aryan are in. I really do want to help, Mallika. Don't keep pushing me away.'

'I'm not,' she said. 'It's just…very tough talking about him with anyone. Even you. It feels like I'm betraying him. And I love spending time with you, but I feel guilty every minute because I know he needs me more than you do.'

There was a longish pause, after which Darius spoke. 'I can understand that,' he said slowly. 'But what about what *you* need?'

'I don't know, Darius, but I do know that I have to put him first. That's what you do when it comes to family— you don't just go off and leave them to it.'

Family would always be her priority, but as she began to calm down she realised how harsh that must have sounded to Darius. It had been a long and tiring week, and Aryan's moods and ingratitude had pushed her over the edge. A weak, but insistent part of her kept saying that she should apologise and do whatever he wanted, but she squashed it firmly.

Luckily, before she could say anything, he said, 'All right, then. I guess I'll see you around the office next week.'

His voice was remote and expressionless, and Mallika just got to say a brief goodbye before he cut the call.

She put the phone on her bedside table and flopped back into bed to stare at the ceiling. It was all very well to tell herself that she'd get over Darius in a bit—right now she felt as if she'd succeeded in cutting her heart out with a rusty knife. He had been genuinely trying to help her, to connect with her better, and she'd said some unforgivable things to him. No wonder he'd sounded as if he never wanted to see her again.

She tried to focus on Aryan instead. Darius wasn't the first person to say that he needed professional help, though he'd said it far more bluntly than most. Mallika had done her best to shield her younger brother from the aftermath of their parents' death, but he'd actually been there when the accident had happened. He'd escaped completely unharmed, but since then he'd been a shell of his former self.

Mallika and he had been close when they were growing up, but despite her best efforts she hadn't been able to get him to talk to her about what was wrong. And the more she tried to draw him out, the more silent he became.

The only time Aryan seemed really happy was when he was in front of his laptop, staring at the flickering screen as he traded stocks and moved money around from one set of investments to another. He had inherited just the right mix of talents from his father and mother to be a formidable trader, and he had almost doubled the money they had inherited from their parents over the last year.

Aryan lived most of his life online—he worked online and bought everything he needed on various websites and had it delivered to the flat. They had a cook and a cleaner, and of course he had Mallika for anything else. He no longer needed to go out at all.

After a while, she had stopped pushing him to talk, and that had had the result of making him more and more dependent on her. He tried to stick as close to her as he could whenever she was at home, and messaged her constantly when she was at work. Mallika sometimes found herself wishing he'd leave her alone—he was as demanding as he'd been when he was three and had toddled behind her everywhere like a pudgy little shadow.

Mallika sighed as she got out of bed. There were little sounds coming from the kitchen that indicated that Aryan was awake and foraging for breakfast. She'd forgotten to order groceries the day before, and there wasn't any ready stuff that he could eat. She'd need to make him some *upma* or something before she got ready and left to catch the eleven o'clock ferry to Alibagh.

There was a long queue for the ferry at the Gateway of India and Mallika joined it, cradling her bright green tote in her arms. The sun was beating down uncomfortably on her head and she wished she'd thought to wear a hat in addition to the sunglasses that she'd perched on her nose.

The glasses served the dual purpose of saving her eyes from the sun as well as concealing quite how puffy they were. Post-breakfast, with a morose and monosyllabic brother, she'd gone to her room and had a good cry.

It hadn't done much for her looks, but at least she felt a lot calmer than she had in the morning.

'Excuse me, would you mind keeping my place for me in the queue for a few minutes?' the woman in front of her said. 'My son wants an ice cream, and if I don't get it for him right now he'll whine for the entire hour that we're on the ferry.'

'No, I won't,' the pudgy youngster standing next to her said indignantly.

He had a pronounced accent which Mallika couldn't quite place—it wasn't American, but it was close.

'You promised me an ice cream last week and I didn't whine when you didn't buy it, did I?'

'Of course you did,' his slightly older sister chimed in.

Their mother groaned. 'Can it, both of you,' she said. 'Do you want ice cream or not?'

'Want ice cream,' both of them said firmly.

The woman turned back to Mallika. 'Sorry,' she said. 'They're at a terribly argumentative stage. So—is it okay if I leave the queue for a minute?'

'Yes, of course,' Mallika said.

'Of course it's okay if you *leave*,' the girl said scornfully. 'The point is, will she let you back in the line when you come back?'

'I will,' Mallika promised, her lips twitching slightly. The girl was around nine, dignified, knobbly-kneed and totally adorable.

'Thank you so much,' the mother said with evident relief, grabbing her children's hands. 'Come on, people.'

Mallika gazed after her as she walked towards the ice cream vendor, holding a child's hand in each of her own. She had a slight twang to her accent as well, and there was something about her that was vaguely familiar.

The queue had moved quite a bit before the woman came back, breathless and clutching ice cream bars in each hand.

'Oh, thanks,' she said in relief as Mallika waved to her. 'Here—I forgot to ask you which flavour you'd like. So I got chocolate and vanilla both—you take the one you like and I'll have the other.'

'You shouldn't have,' Mallika said, taking the chocolate bar gratefully. 'But thank you so much—it's so hot I feel like I'm about to melt.'

'It'll be more pleasant on the boat,' the woman said. 'Come on, now, kids—be careful on the stairs or you'll slip and fall in the water.'

'Papa would have carried us if he was here,' the boy grumbled.

His sister glared at him. 'Well, he isn't, so *manage*,' she said fiercely. 'Whine-pot.'

'Cry-baby,' the boy retorted. 'Mud-face.'

'Muuuummm...' the girl said.

'Be *nice*, people!' the woman snapped.

'I can carry you, if you like,' Mallika offered. 'Your mum's got too many bags to handle.'

The boy looked as if he wasn't sure which was worse—being carried in public by a *girl*, or having to walk down the stairs on his own. His evident fear of heights won over, and he held his chubby arms up to Mallika.

'I wish Papa was here,' the boy said defiantly once she'd picked him up, and Mallika wondered where their father was.

'He divorced us,' the girl said in a fierce whisper to her brother. 'Stop whining or I'll punch you in the face.'

Their mother sighed. 'So much for being dignified

and discreet,' she said, and gave Mallika an artificially bright smile. 'I'm so sorry you're being subjected to this.' In a whisper, she continued, 'My husband ran away with his secretary a few months ago and we're still trying to deal with it.'

Under the smile she looked tired and defeated, and Mallika's heart went out to her. 'Men can be pigs,' she said quietly once they were all on the ferry. 'I'm sorry— it must be tough for you.'

'I'm thrilled to be rid of the cheating bastard, actually,' the woman replied in an undertone as they climbed to the upper deck behind the kids. 'But it's tough on the kids. If he'd given me a choice I might have actually stayed with him to keep them happy. As it turned out he didn't, so here we are—back in India.'

'Where were you before this?'

'Canada,' she said. 'But I'm happy to be back with my family.' They had reached the upper deck, and the woman looked around. 'Are you in the A/C section as well?' she asked.

Mallika shook her head. 'I prefer the sea breeze,' she said. 'See you in a bit.'

She took a seat towards the front of the ferry, where she didn't have to look at other people, and leaned her head gratefully against the cold guard rail. She'd loved these ferry rides to Alibagh when she was a teenager. Aryan had still been a kid then, and he'd used to run around madly while Mallika stood near the railing, soaking in the sun and the sea breeze.

Even in those days she'd been more of an outdoor person than Aryan was—he'd preferred the lower deck, and after a few arguments their mother had started buying two tickets for the upper deck and two for the lower, so that they didn't fight.

Mallika cast a glance towards the air-conditioned cabin where the woman and her kids had gone. *'I might have actually stayed with him to keep them happy...'* It sounded so terribly sad, when the woman was clearly happier without her husband.

Mallika wondered whether her own mother would have been happier without her father. She'd definitely been more than capable of taking care of herself, but their extended family was extremely conservative. Maybe she'd stayed so that she didn't have to be cut off from them. Or maybe she'd not wanted to separate Aryan and Mallika from their father.

She still felt guilty when she thought of how much trouble they'd given their mother during their growing up years. It had only been when she was in her late teens that Mallika had begun to understand why her mother worked so hard and was so grim and serious most of the time. And even then she'd not known the full story.

As she'd told Darius, her father had lost most of his money in the stock market crash of the eighties—what she hadn't realised for many years was that her mother had been supporting the family ever since. When she'd found out she'd been more sympathetic, but she still hadn't been able to understand why her mother couldn't loosen up a little…be a little more fun.

Her attention was attracted by the girl and her mother coming out of the air-conditioned cabin. The girl's face was distinctly green.

'I'll be all right on my own,' she was telling her harassed mother. 'You go inside and be with Rehaan.'

'I'm not leaving you here on your own,' the mother said. 'Are you still feeling pukey?'

'Not that much,' the girl said, pushing her way through the crowded deck to come and stand next to Mallika by the railing. 'It's better in the breeze.'

'Seasick?' Mallika asked, and the woman nodded.

'The sea's really choppy, and it's a bit disorientating inside the cabin. Rehaan's refusing to come out. I should have just stayed home instead of trying to take these two out for a weekend break.'

'I'll be okay on my own,' the girl insisted.

'I can keep an eye on her, if you like,' Mallika offered.

The woman laughed. 'You know, this is the part I love about being back in India,' she said. 'It feels like being part of one big family. I'm Shirin, by the way, and this is Ava.'

'Pleased to meet you,' Mallika said, grinning back at her. 'So, if you like, you can leave Ava with me and go be with Rehaan.'

'He'll be all right on his own for a bit,' Shirin said, and lowered her voice a little. 'It's Ava I worry about—it's not as safe for a girl as it is for a boy, and I don't know how to explain that to her. And I'd die before I admit it to her, but I'm feeling a bit seasick as well.'

They were both silent for a while, watching Ava as she waved to a flock of seagulls following the ferry.

Ava was too engrossed in the seagulls to hear them, and Mallika said impulsively, 'I don't mean to be intrusive, but you said that you'd have stayed with your husband for the sake of the kids—it's not worth it. You'll be much happier on your own.'

Shirin turned to look at her, raising her brows a little. 'Sounds like you're speaking from personal experience.'

'Sort of,' Mallika admitted.

She'd never spoken about this before, and confiding in a stranger wasn't the kind of thing she normally went in for. Still, there was something about Shirin that made Mallika want to talk to her.

'My dad had affairs,' she said. 'Many of them. My mum put up with them—I guess she didn't have much of a choice—but me and my brother didn't understand why she was unhappy most of the time and we tended to blame her a little. My dad was fun, only he wasn't around much—it was only when I was in my teens that I figured out that he was a pathetic excuse for a husband.'

'No wonder you don't have a high opinion of men,' Shirin said. 'Is your dad still like that?'

'He died in an accident,' Mallika said. 'Along with my mum.'

'Oh, my…' Shirin said sympathetically. 'That sucks.'

Mallika nodded. There was something oddly familiar about Shirin's reaction, but she couldn't put her finger on who she reminded her of.

'Anyway, what I was trying to say is that your kids might be a bit upset now, but it's better for them to be growing up with you.'

'That's good to hear,' Shirin said. 'Most of the time I'm sure I'm doing the right thing, but sometimes I wonder. The kids miss their dad, and they miss Canada, and I'm not really sure how I'm going to manage.'

'Where do you work?' Mallika asked.

'I don't,' Shirin said with a sigh. 'I sponge off my brother. But I'm planning to start once I get the kids settled in school.'

Mallika wondered for an instant what it would be like to have a brother she didn't have to worry about, then shook herself. Aryan might be a bit of a liability, but she wouldn't swap her own life for Shirin's for anything.

'Older brother?' she asked, for the sake of something to say.

'No—younger,' Shirin said. 'I used to make his life hell when he was a kid, but he's—without exaggeration—the best brother a girl could have.'

There was a little pause, and then she went on.

'My parents offered me a place in their flat, but it was impossible to manage. They're old, and set in their ways, and the kids drove them crazy. My brother had a flat in the same building and he's turning it over to me.'

'Has he moved out already?' Mallika asked, though she already knew the answer.

It had taken a while for the penny to drop, but she'd finally realised why Shirin seemed so familiar. She didn't look much like Darius—she was petite and sharp-featured—but some of her mannerisms were just like his, and their smiles were identical.

'Yes, he's rented a hideously expensive place in Parel,' she was saying now. 'He says he's enjoying being on his own, but I still feel terribly guilty. Anyway, he's going overseas in a few months—some complicated "finding himself" kind of journey. I'm happy for him, but I'll miss him like crazy.'

And so will I, Mallika thought to herself, feeling suddenly very shallow and stupid.

It hadn't even occurred to her to ask Darius *why* he'd given his flat to his sister. All this while she'd thought Darius was being callous about Aryan, not realising that he took his responsibilities as a sibling quite as seriously as she did.

'Are your parents okay with your brother going away?'

she asked, the words slipping out before she could help herself.

Shirin nodded. 'He's wanted to do it for as long as I can remember, and he planned his trip a couple of years ago,' she said. 'He's had to cancel it twice already—once because Dad had a heart attack, and a second time because I'd come back to India to have my second baby. Our grandmother fell down and broke pretty much every bone in her hip around the same time, and poor Darius was saddled with looking after all of us *and* paying the medical bills. Luckily he was minting money by then, so the bills weren't a problem, but he went crazy trying to look after everyone at the same time. It doesn't help that we're a bit of an eccentric family too... Anyway, this time hopefully he'll get away before one of us does something stupid.'

Rehaan stuck his head out of the cabin, and Shirin hurried towards him while Mallika tried to get her disordered thoughts back on track. This didn't really change things. If anything, it underlined the fact that she wasn't suited to be with a man like Darius even if he had been ready for a relationship.

Any other woman would have tried to find out about his family—*she* was so hung up about her own that she'd avoided the subject of his completely. From what Shirin had said, Darius was as unlike her father as he could be—he was responsible and trustworthy. And she'd made all kinds of assumptions about him that were totally untrue. Worse, she'd accused him of not caring for his family—and he hadn't even defended himself.

Shirin waved to her as they got off at the jetty, and Mallika saw them get into a car that had the logo of an expensive resort printed on the side. Alibagh had been a sleepy little seaside town during her growing up years, but in the last decade high end hotels and villas had gone up all around the place. Property prices had rocketed as well, and her mother's decision to buy a bungalow there had been more than vindicated.

It took her most of the day to get a contractor to commit on the money and the time it would take him to get the leakage in the Alibagh house fixed. It didn't turn out to be as expensive as she'd feared, but she'd need to make a few more trips to the house over the next few weeks.

She grimaced at the thought. Even now she couldn't bring herself to go into the kitchen and cook a meal for herself, and she ended up sitting in the living room and eating the packed lunch she'd brought with her.

It was ironic, she thought—after all the grief and heartache he'd caused her mother, her father had finally died trying to save her from the fire. If there was an afterlife, perhaps her mother had forgiven him. Mallika still couldn't bring herself to do so.

The weeks after her parents' death would have been horrific enough without having to deal with her father's mistress. She was a virago of a woman, out for all that she could get, and finally Mallika's father's impecuniousness made sense—all this while he'd been supporting her on the side.

Mallika's mother had known, and she'd been careful to make sure that all her investments and the property she'd bought were either in her own name or in her children's. Even so, there had been a bitter battle to hold on to Mallika's grandparents' flat, which her father had inherited, and his mistress had done all she could to claim a share of it. Finally, when she hadn't been able to take any more, Mallika had paid her off—she didn't regret the money, but the experience had left her very bitter.

Once she'd sorted everything out with the contractor and the caretaker, and made advance payments to the workers, Mallika headed back to the jetty. There was just about time for her to catch the last ferry out, and she settled herself into a corner seat with a sigh. She hadn't been able to stop thinking about Darius all day, and impulsively she pulled out her phone and dialled his number.

The phone rang a few times, but Darius didn't pick up and she dropped it back into her bag. Calling him had been a stupid idea anyway—he was probably out partying with his friends.

Feeling suddenly very lost and alone, she shut her eyes and tried not to think about him. The images kept coming, though, and she had to blink very hard to stop tears from welling into her eyes. Damn Darius—he was proving far more difficult to forget about than she'd thought.

CHAPTER EIGHT

IT WAS PAST eleven when Darius finally got back home. He'd gone to the tennis court in his building to see if he could catch a game, and he'd run into an ex-colleague who was now a neighbour. They'd played a couple of gruelling sets, after which they'd walked down to a nearby bar to watch a football match over beer and chicken wings. His ex-colleague was a cheerful, sporty sort of man who didn't go in for deep thinking—he was the perfect companion to take Darius's mind off Mallika.

Once he was back in the flat, though, the morning's conversation replayed itself in his head. He was able to be a little more objective now, and he could see things from Mallika's point of view. She was going through a tough time with Aryan, and she wasn't yet over her parents' death—she couldn't be blamed for not wanting to complicate her life by getting into a relationship with a man who was about to go away for who knew how long.

He'd left his phone in the flat, and picked it up now to see three messages from his sister. Shirin had taken the kids out for a weekend on the beach, and while she said it had got off to a rocky start they seemed to be fine now.

He smiled as he read through her quirky messages

about the kids' reactions to the hotel and the pool—and the last message read: Hired a babysitter and am now off to the spa!!!

He was still smiling as he scrolled through the list of calls he'd missed, and his expression stilled as he saw the call from Mallika. Damn, she'd called over four hours ago—she must have thought he was purposely avoiding talking to her.

He glanced at the time—too late to call her back, but he could text her. They both used the same mobile chat app, and he checked her status. It said she was last on at ten twenty-five p.m., which wasn't that long ago.

Hey—sorry I missed your call, he typed. Had forgotten my phone was at home.

Mallika reached out for her phone as it pinged. She still kept in touch with a few school friends through mobile chat—most of them lived overseas now, and she was used to getting texts at odd hours from them. But this time it wasn't Naina or Kirti messaging about their latest boyfriends...

No worries, she typed. I just wanted to apologise for being so rude when we spoke in the morning.

The reply was almost instantaneous.

I'm sorry too. I shot my mouth off a bit.

Cool, so we're quits.

Mallika thought a bit and added a smiley.

How was Alibagh?

Not bad. I got most of my work done. Guess what—I met your sister on the ferry on the way out.

She took the ferry? I thought she was taking the speed-boat!

Must have changed her mind. She's really nice, by the way. And so are the kids.

She didn't mention meeting you! I saw her messages a minute ago.

We just had a random conversation. I figured out she was your sister from something she said.

You didn't introduce yourself?

No L wasn't sure if she'd know who I was.

I've talked about you. No details, though.

Thank heaven no details.

Mallika typed the words, even though she felt flattered that he'd spoken about her at home.

She's my older sister—what d'you expect?

The text was quickly followed by another.

Can you talk? Texting feels a bit teenagerish…

Teenagers don't type full words. Can't talk L A's a light sleeper and his room's right next to mine.

There was a pause of a couple of minutes, as if Darius was deciding how to respond.

OK, got it.

Will the flamingos still be there tomorrow?

Guess so.

Can we go?

Guess so.

Mallika stared at the phone in frustration. The problem with texting was that she couldn't figure out whether he wanted to see her or not—*Guess so* was as vague as it got. She was about to type a message when his chat window popped up again.

Should I pick you up?

Can meet you there. But no pressure, seriously, if you don't want to go.

Isn't that my line?

It was—this time I'm the one who's asking you to come!

I want to see you. The flamingos are incidental.

They agreed on a time, and Mallika put her phone back on her bedside table, feeling strangely euphoric.

Mallika took a cab to Sewri the next morning. She'd arranged to meet Darius at the path that led to the mudflats, and her body was thrumming with nervous energy—she had to take several deep breaths to calm herself before she got out of the cab.

The cabbie gave her a jaundiced look as she fumbled in her wallet for change. 'Should I wait?' he asked. 'You won't get a cab back from here.'

Mallika shook her head and handed him the fare. 'No, I have a ride back.'

'I can wait anyway,' the man said. 'In case whoever you're meeting doesn't turn up.'

Goodness, she hadn't even thought of that! What if Darius didn't come?

She spotted him as soon as she'd dismissed the thought as ridiculous, and her breath caught in her throat. He looked achingly familiar and wildly desirable at the same time.

'He's here—you don't need to wait,' she muttered to the cabbie, and got out of the cab, standing stock-still as Darius came up to meet her.

He was wearing a dark blue open-necked T-shirt over jeans, and he looked good enough to eat. It took a significant effort of will not to throw her arms around him.

'Hello,' she said shyly—but she didn't get any further. Darius put an arm around her and pulled her against his side in a surprisingly fierce hug.

'Good morning,' he said. 'Come on, let's go.'

There was an ancient shipwreck at the beginning of the mudflats that gave the best view of the flamingos.

There were people milling around, and Darius took his arm away from her shoulders to help her up the rickety ladder.

'I can manage,' Mallika said, but just at that instant her foot slipped a little and she had to cling onto him for support.

'I'm sure you can,' he said soothingly. 'I just feel like holding your hand for a bit.'

Put like that, she could hardly say no, and the ladder *was* rickety…with a thirty-foot drop to the mud below.

The flamingos were amazing—flocks and flocks of them, perched among the mangroves that grew out of the sludgy mud. They were a bright salmon-pink, and they were showing off a little—taking off and swooping back onto their perches in little groups. Some of them were busy looking for food, and a guide nearby was explaining their migratory habits to a bunch of serious-looking kids.

'Did you ever bring Ava and Rehaan here?' Mallika asked, cuddling in a little closer to Darius. Public displays of affection weren't normally her thing, but she could hardly bear to keep her hands off him.

He nodded. 'Last week,' he said. 'I hear Shirin confided in you quite a bit on the ferry yesterday?'

Mallika looked up in surprise. 'Is she back?' she asked. 'I thought they were away for the weekend?'

'She called this morning,' Darius said. 'Thanks for pepping her up. She's going through a bit of a guilt trip, keeping the kids away from their dad.'

'I figured that,' Mallika said slowly.

If Shirin had relayed their conversation to him, she'd probably told him what Mallika had said about her own family.

Feeling suddenly a little vulnerable, she leaned her

head against his arm and said, 'When you told me she'd moved back to India I didn't realise she was going through a divorce.'

'I guess we didn't talk about her much,' he said, even though he'd consciously *not* told her. She had enough problems of her own without him moaning about his family to her as well, and they had agreed not to talk too much about personal family matters.

'I'm sorry about all I said yesterday,' Mallika said. 'I made a lot of assumptions about you that were completely wrong.'

'It doesn't matter,' he said quietly. 'It was as much my fault as yours—it was natural that you jumped to a few wrong conclusions.'

'*Very* wrong conclusions,' she said, her mouth twisting into a wry smile. 'From what Shirin said, you've done far more for your family than I've ever done for mine.'

'And I'm now escaping from them,' he said, holding up a hand when she began to protest. 'It's true,' he said. 'Not exactly the way you thought it was, but it's true all the same. They've come to depend on me a lot over the last few years. My mother says she's fine with me leaving, but I know what she'd really like is for me to marry a nice Parsi girl and settle down in Mumbai for the rest of my life. Shirin would like me to hang around and be a father figure for my niece and nephew. And my father would like me to join his golf club and start taking an interest in fine wines.'

It was the most Mallika had ever heard him say about his family, and it took her a few seconds to absorb it fully. 'It all sounds rather overwhelming,' she admitted.

'It is,' he said. 'I love my family a lot, and if they really needed me I'd cancel my travels for a third time without a single regret. But with Shirin around I think they'll be fine.'

'I'm sure they will,' Mallika said, wanting more than anything to remove the slight uncertainty lurking in his eyes. 'You should go—especially since it's something you've wanted to do for so long.'

'It's bigger than me, in a way,' he said, and laughed slightly. 'This whole need to go out and see the world. Shirin says it's inherited—some ancient Persian wanderlust gene that's skipped a few generations.'

'Maybe she's right,' Mallika said, reaching out to take his hand.

There was a tinge of sadness in her voice as she thought of how different the two of them were. His family sounded like the kind she'd always longed for and, while she understood his motivations a lot better now, she knew that she wouldn't have taken the same decisions in his place. She craved stability and was comfortable with the conservative values of a traditional family, whereas Darius wanted to break out, challenge himself and push boundaries.

He helped her down the ladder, and once they were on dry land again turned her to face him.

'Want to come over?' he asked, and she nodded, her throat suddenly dry.

There was no mistaking his meaning—and there was also no point bringing up the rules again. Their attraction was too strong to fight, and the most she could hope for was that it would die away after a while without doing too much damage.

Neither of them spoke during the short drive to his flat, their heightened anticipation too intense to allow for casual conversation. Mallika found that her knees were trembling just a bit as Darius unlocked the flat and let her in.

She had barely stepped inside when he bolted the door and turned to take her into his arms.

'Welcome back,' he murmured against her mouth, and then there was no room to talk any more as a tide of pure unadulterated desire overtook both of them.

'What next?' Darius asked many hours later. 'I guess a few of the rules just went out of the window.'

'I guess,' she said, trailing her hand slowly down his chest.

She didn't want to think about practical stuff right now, and Darius's question had brought her back to reality with a bump.

'We can take each day as it comes, can't we?' she asked. 'I mean, some of those rules I made were downright silly.'

'I agree,' Darius said, and it sounded so heartfelt that both of them burst out laughing.

Mallika pressed herself closer to him. With her slim, pliant body and sparkling, naughty eyes, Mallika was almost impossible to resist, and Darius bent his head to capture her lips under his.

'You know, Shirin really liked you,' he said.

'I liked her too,' Mallika said, feeling absurdly flattered.

Darius reached out and tucked a stray strand of hair behind her ear.

'I think it's time for you to meet the family,' he said musingly.

Mallika looked up in alarm. 'Whose family?' she asked.

'The Prime Minister's,' Darius said. 'Whose do you think? Mine.'

'I thought we'd agreed not to tell them!' Mallika said.

'We did. You're going to be my scary colleague-cum-landlady. Shirin's guessed, but to my parents you'll be just one more among my many admirers. Come on, I'd like you to meet them—they're a little crazy, but they're fun.'

Mallika couldn't bring herself to say no—she still didn't know *why* Darius would want to take her home, though.

'Aunt Freny's going to be there as well,' he told her. 'You'll like her.'

'What should I wear?' she asked.

'I've no idea,' Darius said. 'We'll be going from work, so regular office gear should be fine. My parents aren't particular.'

Particular or not, Mallika felt devoutly grateful that she'd dressed up a little when she met Darius's perfectly groomed mother the next day. All of five feet tall, she was like a Dresden figurine with her pink cheeks and carefully styled snow-white hair. She gave Mallika a polite kiss on the cheek, her flowery perfume enveloping them as she ushered Mallika and Darius into the room.

'Papa Mistry, this is Darius's landlady,' she announced, and Darius's father peered short-sightedly at her.

'She looks too young and too pretty to be a landlady,' he said firmly. '*Now* I know why Darius didn't want to live here any more.'

'He didn't want to live here because this place is like

a mausoleum,' Aunt Freny grumbled. 'Or a madhouse when those kids of Shirin's turn up. Little devils.'

'Don't you dare call my grandchildren names,' Mrs Mistry said, her eyes narrowing dangerously. 'They're perfectly angelic if you know how to handle them.'

'With a pair of long-handled tongs,' Aunt Freny muttered.

Mrs Mistry pretended not to hear her. 'Do sit down, child,' she said to Mallika. 'How do you take your tea? One cube of sugar? And milk?'

The tea tray had a tea cosy on it with a fat little teapot inside, and a tiny jug of milk with a bowl full of sugar cubes next to it. Mallika looked curiously at Mrs Mistry as she poured the tea. She'd seen tea served so elaborately only in British period movies on TV—real, live people drinking it this way was a novelty. Her own mother had always just boiled everything together and then strained it into cups.

'So you met Darius at work?' Mr Mistry asked, leaning forward curiously. 'This is the first time he's brought a girl home.'

'The first time this month,' Aunt Freny said promptly, and Mallika dissolved into laughter.

Aunt Freny was adorable—Mallika's own relatives tended towards the stiff and formal, and she wished she'd had someone like Aunt Freny around when she was going up.

'Freny is our *enfant terrible*,' Mr Mistry said indulgently. 'Tell us about what you do, Mallika. Darius said you work in real estate investments? How did you end up there?'

He seemed genuinely interested, and he knew far more about real estate than most people did.

Shirin trooped in with her children when they were halfway through the conversation, and Rehaan promptly clambered onto his grandfather's lap.

'Where's Great-Granny?' he demanded.

Mr Mistry turned to his wife. 'Is Mummy still asleep?' he enquired.

'No, I'll go and call her,' Mrs Mistry said, and a few minutes later a tiny, very frail-looking old lady emerged from somewhere inside the house.

Darius got up to help her to a chair. 'Meet my grandmother,' he said to Mallika. 'She was an army nurse during the Second World War.'

The elder Mrs Mistry was alert and very garrulous. But with the children running around, and Shirin keeping up a parallel conversation on school admissions, poor Mallika could hardly understand what she was saying, and after a while she gave Darius an appealing look.

'Darius, you should take Mallika out dancing instead of making her sit with us old folks,' Aunt Freny said.

'I used to love dancing when I was a girl,' Darius's grandmother said wistfully. 'My Rustom used to waltz so well.'

'He used to step on everyone's toes,' the irrepressible Aunt Freny said. 'And sometimes he got the steps wrong. But he looked good—I'll give you that.'

'Darius, I'm coming to your building on Saturday,' Ava announced. 'To swim in the pool.'

'You're very welcome,' Darius said. 'I won't be there, but don't let that stop you.'

'Why can't you swim in the club, *dikra*?' Mrs Mistry asked, shooting a quelling look at Darius.

'Because the club pool is full of old hairy men,' Ava said. 'Can I just say—*ewwwww*?'

'Men *should* be hairy,' Mrs Mistry said. 'Not too much, but all these models and actors nowadays with waxed chests—they look terrible. What do you think, Mallika?'

Completely thrown by the sudden appeal for her opinion, Mallika floundered. 'I…uh…I guess it's fashionable nowadays.'

'Darius doesn't wax his chest,' Rehaan volunteered. 'I saw him in the pool last week and he's got hair. Not the orang-utan kind—just normal.'

'Thank you, Rehaan,' Darius said, getting to his feet. 'And on that note I think we should leave. People who aren't used to our family can handle us only in small doses.'

'If you mean Mallika, I think she's made of sterner stuff,' Shirin said, giving Mallika a friendly smile.

'Do you like orchids?' Aunt Freny asked abruptly.

Mallika nodded, and Freny reached behind her chair and produced a flowering orchid in a small ceramic pot.

'This is for you,' she said, handing it to Mallika with a firm little nod. 'Don't overwater it, and make sure it's not in the sun.'

Mallika took the orchid, and as Darius looked all set to leave she stood up as well, and followed him to the door.

'It was really nice meeting all of you,' she said, giving the four generations in the room a comprehensive sort of smile.

'It was lovely meeting you too, *dikra*,' Mrs Mistry said warmly. 'Darius, you must bring her again.'

'Yes, sure,' he said drily, but he was smiling as he bent down to kiss his mother.

He waited till they were in the car before turning to her and raising his eyebrows.

'Well? Did they scare you?'

She laughed and shook her head. 'They were fun,' she said.

And so they were—but she wasn't sure why Darius had decided that it was the right time to introduce her to his family. After all, he was going away, so what they had couldn't go anywhere.

Back at Darius's flat, she shut the front door behind her and leaned against it, her eyes dancing as she looked at him.

'I need to refresh my memory,' she said. 'Exactly *how* hairy is that chest of yours?'

CHAPTER NINE

'ONE OF MY schoolfriends is coming from the US this Friday,' Darius said a few days later. 'We haven't met in years, so I've invited him to stay with me over the weekend. Shirin and a few other people are coming over for dinner on Saturday. Would you like to come?'

Mallika hesitated. She'd insisted that Darius still did not tell his parents the truth about them, the way she'd not told Aryan or any of *her* relatives, but Shirin had guessed anyway—and meeting a few people for dinner trumped not seeing Darius at all for the entire weekend.

'Okay,' she said. 'D'you need help planning the dinner?'

'No, I'll outsource everything,' he said. 'There's a friend of mine who does catering for Parsi weddings. I'll just ask her to manage it.'

'Catering… Exactly how many people are you inviting?'

'Around twenty-five or so, I thought,' Darius said, not noticing Mallika's horrified expression. 'The living room's big enough to hold that many, and if it isn't they can go and stand on the balcony.'

The intercom rang and he went to answer it, leaving Mallika to deal with her panicky reaction to meeting twenty-five of Darius's friends all at once. She always felt shy in large groups—while not agoraphobic, like Aryan, she still preferred meeting a maximum of three or four people at a time.

Darius came back after a short conversation—presumably with the security guard who screened visitors at the main gate.

'I bought a painting last week and it's on its way upstairs now,' he said. 'I was hoping I'd get a chance to show it to you before I left for Delhi again.'

Nidas had recently taken over a smaller firm, and Darius was travelling to Delhi almost every week to manage the merger of the two companies' assets. It was stressful, and Mallika knew he didn't enjoy the trips. She hoped it was because they took him away from her and the small amount of time they had left together...

'I didn't realise you had to go this week as well,' she said. 'When's the takeover going to be complete?'

'At least another two months,' Darius said, sighing as he pulled her close. 'It's crazy. There's so much to do. But it's a big acquisition for Nidas, and in the long term it will make a big difference to our share value. It's just a difficult process right now—especially since the need for greater efficiencies means some of their staff are being let go.'

He was silent for a while, and Mallika hugged him back without saying anything either. It was the first time he had touched her seeking comfort, she realised—so far everything had been about sex. In a way she felt closer to him this way than when they were making love, and it was an odd sensation.

The doorbell rang, and he let her go to open the door.

The painting was carefully packaged in layers of bubble wrap, and Darius had to use a knife to get it out.

'What d'you think?' he asked as he knelt to prop the painting against the nearest wall.

The painting had appealed to him the minute he'd seen it, tucked away in the corner of a little art gallery he patronised. A mass of swirling colours, it managed to capture exactly the feel of an Indian market—you could almost smell the spices and feel the dust and the heat.

Mallika looked at the signature at the bottom right-hand corner. 'This is a good example of the artist's work,' she said, sounding impressed. 'It would have been a brilliant investment if you'd bought it a few years ago.'

'I bought it because I like it,' Darius said, a puzzled look on his face. 'It isn't an *investment*.'

'That's a good reason as well,' Mallika said, sounding amused. 'I'm sorry—I guess I've been working on investments too long to remember that people sometimes buy expensive things just because they like them.'

'Different perspectives,' he said, laughing as he got back to his feet.

He came closer and slid his hands around her waist, making her shiver with longing.

'Stay for dinner?' he asked, nuzzling the most sensitive part of her neck.

'I can't,' she said regretfully. 'I need to get back home.'

'Stay this once,' he said, pulling her closer, and they kissed once more—a long, drugging kiss that left her with trembling knees and a blind desire to tug his clothes off and spend the rest of the day making love on the living room floor.

'Aryan…' she said.

Darius groaned. 'He'll be okay just this once,' he said. 'We've never spent a night together, Mallika, and I'm leaving soon—we mightn't get another chance.'

Put like that, she found it almost impossible to say no, and after another half-hearted protest she messaged Aryan to let him know that she was staying over at a friend's home.

It was around four in the morning when Mallika woke up with a start. She didn't know what exactly had woken her, but her pulse was pounding as if she'd just finished a gruelling race. Next to her, Darius muttered something in his sleep and put a heavy arm around her, pulling her close to his magnificent chest.

Gingerly, Mallika stretched a hand out to the bedside table to pick up her phone. Perhaps the message tone had woken her—she wouldn't put it past Aryan to be messaging her to come home quickly, or perhaps to pick up some exotic computer accessory on her way home.

The screen was blank, however, and there were no messages at all other than one from her bank offering her 'never before' rates on a loan. Puzzled, she checked the signal—it was at full strength, so that meant Aryan hadn't messaged her at all.

'Darius,' she whispered, and he woke up, blinking a little as the light from the mobile phone display hit his eyes.

'Something wrong?' he asked, sitting up as he took in her expression.

'There's not a single message from Aryan,' she said weakly, realising how stupid she sounded as soon as the words were out of her mouth.

Thankfully, Darius immediately understood what she was trying to say.

'Have you tried calling him?'

'He might be asleep,' she said, and to his eternal credit Darius reached across and put his arms around her.

'Do you want me to take you home?' he asked softly, and she nodded.

There were very few cars on the road, and it took less than ten minutes to drive to her flat. The watchman was asleep, and the lift had been switched off, so they had to climb the stairs to her flat. Mallika's knees were trembling by the time she got to the right floor and unlocked the door.

'Should I wait outside?' Darius asked.

She shook her head. 'Stay in the living room,' she said. 'I'll just check on Aryan—hopefully he's fine and I've dragged you all this way for nothing.'

But he wasn't fine.

When Mallika tiptoed into his room she found him lying stock-still in bed, his eyes wide open and feverish. For a few seconds he didn't seem to recognise her, and she sagged onto her knees in relief when he blinked and said, 'Mally...'

'Are you okay?' she asked.

He shook his head. 'I have a headache,' he offered.

She reached out to touch his brow. 'You're burning up,' she said, trying to keep the worry out of her voice. 'I'll get you a paracetamol...maybe you'll feel better after that, okay? Why didn't you call me?'

'I fell in the bathroom and hit my head. I'm not sure where my phone is.'

Mallika clicked on the light—sure enough, there was a huge purpling bruise on his forehead.

'Is he all right?' Darius asked softly as she came out.

She shook her head. 'I don't think he's eaten a single meal since yesterday,' she said. 'And he's got a raging fever. He's also fallen down and hurt his head.'

'I'm so sorry,' he said quietly. 'I shouldn't have pushed you to stay. Is there anything I can do?'

She shook her head angrily. 'It's not your fault,' she said, almost to herself. 'It's mine—for even imagining that I could have a life of my own. Will you get me some biscuits from the kitchen, Darius? I need to make sure he eats something before I give him a paracetamol.'

He nodded, and she went to the medicine cabinet to try and locate the pills. There were only three left in the blister pack, and she popped one out. Darius came back with the biscuits and a glass of water, and she carried them into Aryan's room.

'Eat these first, and then swallow the medicine with the water,' she said.

'I'm not hungry,' Aryan whispered.

Suddenly her control snapped. 'I don't *care*!' she said. 'I stay away for one night and you don't even take care of yourself! Sit up right now and eat—if you don't want me to call an ambulance and get you put in hospital.'

It was the first time she'd ever shouted at him and Aryan sat up in shock, blinking woozily as he took the biscuits from her. Mallika felt horribly guilty, but at least he ate them silently before swallowing the medicine.

'Try and sleep now,' she said, tucking him back into bed. 'I'll call Dr Shetty as soon as it's morning.'

'Stay with me,' Aryan mumbled, reaching for her hand as she got up, but she pulled away.

'I'll be back in a minute,' she said, and went out to Darius.

'I'm so sorry I dragged you out like this,' she said wearily. 'I should have just come home last night.'

'Do you need me to go and fetch a doctor?' he asked.

She shook her head. 'I'll call our family doctor in the morning,' she said. 'I think he'll be okay till then.'

'Right,' Darius said. 'I'll see you when I'm back from Delhi, then—okay?'

She nodded, and he dropped a quick kiss on her forehead before letting himself out.

'He's got an infection. His immunity levels have dropped, staying indoors like this,' the doctor said as he prescribed a course of antibiotics over the phone. 'I'll try to come and see him in a couple of hours, but if he doesn't start leading a normal life this is going to happen more and more often.'

'How's he catching an infection, then, if he isn't going out?'

'From *you*,' he said. 'You work, don't you? *You're* carrying the infections home, but because your immunity levels are normal you're not catching them yourself.'

She spent the next two days nursing Aryan. The doctor visited him, as he'd promised—he'd known both Mallika and Aryan since they were children, and he was as worried about him as Mallika was.

Aryan didn't react as the doctor spoke to him—he'd slipped back into silent mode, and he stared passively at the ceiling while the doctor tried to explain the harm he was doing himself by his self-imposed house arrest.

'The quicker you get him to a good psychiatrist, the better,' Dr Shetty told Mallika when she took him aside to ask what she should do. 'I can treat his physical symptoms, but I can't do much about his mental state. And you're just making it worse by humouring him.'

Perhaps he was right, Mallika thought wearily as she went back inside to persuade her brother to eat something and take his medicine. Perhaps she *was* making her brother worse. Only there was little she could do if he refused to see a psychiatrist—it had been difficult enough persuading him to see Dr Shetty.

She tried to get a psychiatrist to come and meet Aryan, perhaps by pretending to be a friend of hers, but that wasn't the way they operated, apparently. Or at least the reputable ones didn't, and she didn't want to trust Aryan to a quack.

'I mightn't be able to come for dinner on Saturday,' she told Darius when he called one evening.

'Won't Aryan be okay by then?'

'He's over the worst, but he's still a little weak—and he's still not eating properly.'

'Can't one of your relatives stay with him? That aunt of yours who lives nearby?'

'He doesn't want anyone else around,' Mallika said. 'I'm so sorry, Darius.' She was very tired, and her voice shook a little.

Darius immediately softened.

'I'm sorry too,' he said gently. 'Take care. I'll be back from Delhi tonight, and I'll come across and see you on Sunday.'

Mallika was too exhausted to tell him not to come—anyway, Aryan had probably figured out by now that she was dating him. And she wanted to see Darius badly. He'd become the one sane, stable thing in her world, and she knew she was growing horribly dependent on him.

'Are you going out?' Aryan asked on Sunday morning.

It was obvious why he'd asked—Mallika had changed the ancient T-shirt and tracks she normally wore at home for a peasant blouse and Capri pants, and she'd brushed her hair into some semblance of order.

'No,' Mallika said shortly. 'A friend's coming over, and I don't want to look like something from a refugee camp.'

'Is it that Parsi friend of yours? Cyrus, or something?'

'Darius,' she said.

Aryan didn't reply, and she felt a surge of annoyance sweep over her. She'd spent the last few days waiting on him hand and foot—he hadn't bothered to thank her, even once, and now he was behaving as if she didn't have the right to invite a friend over.

Hot words bubbled up to her lips, and she was about to say something when Aryan spoke again.

'Your hair looks just like Mum's when you tie it back like that,' he said, and suddenly Mallika felt tears start to her eyes.

She'd inherited her riotously curly hair from their mother, but while her mum had always carefully brushed her curls into a tight bun, she'd always kept hers short.

Darius gave her a brief kiss, full on the mouth, as he strode into the flat. 'For you,' he said, handing her a box of expensive-looking chocolates. 'How's Aryan doing?'

'He's much better,' she said, taking the chocolates from him. 'Thank you so much.'

He grinned at her. 'You don't need to be so formal,' he said. 'We missed you yesterday—especially Shirin. She's been dying to meet you again.'

'I wish I could have come,' Mallika said regretfully. 'I couldn't leave Aryan alone, though.'

'I'd have been all right on my own,' Aryan said petulantly, walking into the room, his eyes hostile as he looked at Darius. 'Hello,' he said, nodding briefly at him before sitting down on the sofa.

'She was worried about you,' Darius said as he settled his tall frame into the chair opposite Aryan. 'You were quite ill, weren't you?'

The boy looked a little thinner than the last time Darius had seen him, but otherwise he seemed perfectly healthy. And more than capable of looking after himself for one evening.

'I'm better now,' he said, his eyes dark and resentful. 'I can manage on my own if I have to. Anyway, she's hardly at home—whenever she can, she goes away without telling me where she's going.'

The unfairness of it took Mallika's breath away, and she could only stare at Aryan speechlessly.

Darius took one look at her, and took over the conversation. 'I think your sister stays with you for as much time as she can,' he said. 'She can't work from home *every* day, can she?'

Aryan bit his lip, but didn't reply.

Mallika jumped in to dispel the suddenly awkward silence. 'Which would you prefer? Tea or coffee?'

'Tea's good, thanks,' Darius said, and she got up to make it.

'Aryan...?'

'You should know by now that I don't drink the stuff,' he muttered.

Darius frowned.

'Did you have an argument with your sister?' he asked quietly once Mallika had left the room.

Aryan said nothing, but his eyes widened a fraction.

Darius leaned forward. 'I don't think that's the way you normally speak to her,' he said. 'She's completely devoted to you, and she wouldn't be if you were that rude all the time.'

For a second it looked as if Aryan would burst into speech, but then he got to his feet and left the room without a word. A door shut somewhere inside the house, and Darius assumed that he'd gone back to his room. He exhaled slowly, standing up and running a hand through his hair. He very rarely lost his temper, and the sudden surge of anger he'd felt had surprised him as much as it had upset Aryan.

He made his way to the kitchen, where Mallika was pouring tea into two delicate china cups. She looked up at him and smiled, and he felt immediately guilty.

'Sorry—did Aryan leave you alone?' she asked. 'His social skills are a bit basic.'

'I think I sent him away,' he admitted, leaning against the doorway. 'I didn't like the way he spoke to you and I called him out on it. It's not the kind of thing I normally do, but he got under my skin.'

He'd expected Mallika to be annoyed, but she just handed him his teacup, her brow furrowed in thought.

'What did you say to him?' she asked.

He told her, and she shrugged.

'That's pretty mild,' she said. 'Our family doctor spoke to him for a good fifteen minutes yesterday— I'm not sure Aryan even registered what he was saying.'

'How long are you going to manage like this?' Darius asked softly, his hand going out to caress her cheek. 'You need to have a proper life of your own—it just isn't fair to you.'

Mallika went into his arms, burying her face in his

chest. 'I don't know,' she said. 'I need to sit down and have a proper talk with Aryan—maybe I'm reading him all wrong, hovering over him when he could do with some space.'

'It's worth a try,' Darius said, bending down and brushing his lips lightly against hers, making her quiver with need. 'Will you be able to get away for a while in the afternoon? Varun really wanted to meet you.'

For a few seconds Mallika couldn't remember who Varun was. Then she realised he meant the schoolfriend who'd come over from the US.

'At your place?' she asked.

'Yes,' Darius said. 'I'm going down to his hotel to collect him—I'll see you in a couple of hours, okay?'

After Darius left, Mallika went and knocked tentatively on Aryan's door. There was no reply, and she knocked once more before pushing the door open. Aryan was in bed, his face turned towards the wall, and she went in and sat next to him.

'Are you feeling okay?' she asked, putting a gentle hand on his shoulder.

He flipped over onto his back—an abrupt movement that threw her hand off.

'Are you going to marry that guy?' he demanded.

Mallika took a deep breath. Clearly she'd been wrong about the conversation with Darius having had no effect on her brother.

'He's just a friend, Aryan,' she said. 'I'm not planning to get married for a long, long while. Perhaps never.'

Aryan stared at her, his eyes stormy. 'Because of me?' he asked.

She shook her head. She couldn't lay all the blame

at his door, however much she wanted to. 'Because I think I'd make a rotten wife,' she said, a little sadly. 'Don't worry about it, Aryan. Concentrate on getting better. Once you're back on your feet, maybe we could try going out together. Maybe for a walk to Hanging Gardens. Remember how much you used to love going there as a kid?'

'I don't want to go out,' he said, sounding like a truculent kid. 'You don't need to fuss over me, Mally. I'll go when I want to.'

'When will that be? You heard what the doctor said. You're making yourself ill like this.'

'I don't care,' he said, turning away from her again. 'And if I do get ill you can leave me here and go wherever you want. I'm not forcing you to hang around and look after me.'

'You're not,' Mallika said calmly. 'I feel like looking after you because you're my brother and I love you, even though you're perfectly obnoxious at times.'

Aryan didn't react, but when she got up to go he stretched out a hand and held her back without turning around.

Mallika sat down again, reaching across to smooth his hair off his brow.

'I do too,' he muttered under his breath.

She leaned closer. 'You do too, what?' she asked.

'I love you too,' he said, the words so indistinct that she had to strain to hear them. 'And I'm sorry if I'm obnoxious. It's just so hard without Mom.'

His breath hitched in his throat, and Mallika's heart went out to him. They had never been a very demonstrative family, and this was probably the first time she'd told her brother that she loved him since they'd both reached adulthood. Maybe that was part of the reason he was this way—he'd been only twenty-two when their parents had died, and it had to have been tougher on him than her.

'I miss her too,' she said softly.

Aryan said something under his breath that she couldn't hear at all.

'What was that, *baba*?' she asked.

He said in a whisper, 'It was my fault.'

'What was your fault?'

'The accident,' he said. 'I smelt the gas leak when I went into the kitchen to fetch some water. But I forgot about it and I didn't tell Mom.'

'You *knew* about the leak?' Mallika said blankly.

This had never occurred to her. She'd berated herself so many times for not having gone down to Alibagh with the rest of the family—if she'd been around she'd have gone into the kitchen with her mother and smelled the leak. The only reason her mother hadn't noticed was because she'd had a bad head cold and had completely lost her sense of smell. Her father, of course, never stepped into the kitchen, and normally neither did Aryan.

'I've been wanting to tell you ever since,' he said. 'I can't stop thinking about it.'

'Why didn't you tell me?' she demanded, but deep, dry sobs were racking his body now and he couldn't answer.

Mallika got up from the bed, too worked up to stay still. The last two years had been hellish. She still wasn't over the shock and grief of losing both parents together. Almost every day she wished she could have done something to make her mother's life easier—if she'd known about her father's unfaithfulness she'd at least have been more understanding with her mum. Every teenage tantrum she'd thrown had come back to haunt her, and every time she'd taken her father's side in an argument now seemed like a betrayal of her mother.

She looked at Aryan, huddled up on the bed. Aryan had always been petted and spoilt. Her mother had expected Mallika to grow up fast and shoulder responsibilities as soon as she could, but she'd been far more indulgent with Aryan. Her father had been equally indulgent with both, but it had been quite evident that he had valued his son over his daughter.

'Did you tell Dad about the leak?' she asked suddenly, but Aryan was already shaking his head.

'I didn't realise it was serious,' he said in a flat little voice. 'It was only when I heard her screaming... And by then it was too late to do anything.'

He'd been in the garden, Mallika remembered, studying for his college exams. She'd always felt terrible for him—actually being there and unable to help. A lot of her subsequent indulgence towards him had been because she'd thought he was dealing with the trauma still.

'I'm sorry,' Aryan said, his eyes pleading with her. 'I'd do anything to undo what happened...but I can't.'

'I know,' Mallika said. 'I know. I just wish...'

There were so many things she wished—that Aryan had raised the alarm, that he'd at least told their father... The accident hadn't been his fault, but the fact that he could have prevented it made it seem even more tragic than it had before.

Aryan bit his lip, tears welling in his eyes, and Mallika suddenly remembered him as a child, toddling around the kitchen one day and getting underfoot until her mother had picked him up and sat him on the kitchen counter. Mallika had protested at the unfair treatment—*she* never got to sit there—but her mother had laughed and picked her up as well, dancing around the kitchen with her to the tune of an old Bollywood song playing on the radio while Aryan laughed and clapped his hands.

It was one of the very few memories of her childhood she had where her mum was happy and smiling.

'Mum wouldn't have wanted you to torture yourself like this,' she said, going to Aryan. 'It was an accident, and we can't undo any of it. Come here.'

She held out her arms and Aryan crawled into them, hugging her back surprisingly fiercely.

'I'll try to be less of a pain from now on,' he said. 'I wish I'd told you earlier…but, Mally—you don't know how difficult it's been.'

'I can imagine,' she said. 'But it's behind us now. Let's try and get you sorted out.'

For the first time Aryan seemed amenable to the thought of getting help, and Mallika used the opportunity as best as she could. After an hour of coaxing and cajoling she'd managed to get him to agree to going with her to a psychiatrist, and she heaved a sigh of relief. Hopefully things would take a turn for the better now that she knew exactly what was bothering Aryan.

It was only when she went to fetch her phone to make an appointment that she noticed all the messages and missed calls from Darius. Her mouth dropped open in dismay—it was past six, and she'd agreed to meet him and Varun at four.

Fingers trembling a little, she dialled his number.

'I'm so sorry—' she said when he picked up.

'It's all right, Mallika, you don't need to apologise,' he said, sounding resigned. 'Is Aryan okay?'

'Yes,' she said. 'I should have called. I'll explain when we meet, but I really couldn't have come.'

'I understand,' he said. 'I'll see you around at work tomorrow, then.'

Darius was frowning as he put the phone down, and Varun raised his eyebrows. 'You've got it bad, haven't you?' he said.

Darius smiled reluctantly. 'Is it that obvious?'

'Pretty obvious,' Varun said lightly. There was a brief pause, and then Varun said, 'So what are you going to do about it?'

Darius shrugged. 'Nothing,' he said. 'I'm out of here in a few weeks, and I don't know when I'll be back. There's no point trying to do anything about it. In any case, she isn't interested in anything serious either.'

'You could be wrong about that,' Varun murmured.

Darius shook his head. 'I'm not,' he said, but he wondered if it was true.

There were times when he'd thought Mallika was close to admitting that she cared for him, but something seemed to hold her back. Perhaps the same thing that held him back—the realisation that they wanted very different things from life. He was going away, and for Mallika Aryan would always be her first priority.

'If you really care about her there's always a way,' Varun said.

Darius laughed. 'You sound like a soppy women's magazine,' he said lightly, trying not to show how much the words had affected him.

He *did* care about Mallika—in fact, there was a real

risk of his being completely besotted by her. But he couldn't give up his adventures—not when he was finally free to go.

Maybe there *was* a way, and all he had to do was convince her that it would work.

CHAPTER TEN

'I'M SORRY ABOUT YESTERDAY,' Mallika said guiltily. 'Aryan was very upset, and I completely lost track of the time.'

'Don't worry about it,' he said. 'I understand. Is Aryan okay now?'

'Yes,' she said, and before she knew it she was telling him what had happened. 'I think he'll be better now,' she said. 'The guilt was eating him up, and he hadn't told anyone.'

'Poor chap.' Darius's expression was sympathetic. 'That's one hell of a burden to be carrying around. But you're right—if he's talking about it, it's a turn for the better.'

'Let's see how it goes,' Mallika said.

She was being careful not to sound too optimistic, but it was clear to Darius that she was much happier than she'd been in weeks.

'In any case, I'm feeling a lot better about leaving him on his own now. There was a time when I was scared he'd actually harm himself…he was behaving so oddly. Anyway, let's not talk about Aryan—how was your weekend with Varun? Did you guys have a good time?'

'The best,' Darius said, thinking back to his last conversation with Varun. This was probably a good time to bring it up with Mallika, only he wasn't sure how to begin.

'You look very serious,' Mallika said teasingly. 'What are you thinking about so deeply?'

'Not thinking, really. Just…wondering.' He'd meant to lead up to the subject slowly, but his naturally forthright nature made it difficult.

'Wondering about what,' she asked. 'Global warming? Cloud computing? How to save the euro?'

He grinned in spite of himself—Mallika was so often serious that she was irresistible in a lighter mood.

'Nothing quite so earth-shattering,' he said. 'I was thinking about us.'

Her smile faltered a little, and she said, 'Oh…' before making a quick recovery. 'Serious stuff?'

'Well, kind of.' He reached across and took her hands in his. 'Mallika, I know you've had a lot to deal with since your parents died, and I don't want to put you under pressure. But I was thinking—perhaps we don't necessarily need to split up when I leave.'

'Not split up?' she repeated stupidly.

He leaned forward, his expression serious and intense. 'Come with me,' he said. 'If not for the whole trip, at least for part of it.'

Mallika stared at him as if he had suddenly gone crazy. 'What about my job?' she said. 'Aryan?'

'We'll work that out,' he said. 'You can take some time off—I'll square it with Venkat. And Aryan will be fine for a while—especially since it sounds like he might be on the mend now. I'm not asking you to come immediately, if that doesn't work for you. Take some time to settle him properly…maybe ask a relative to be with him. But you need to get away perhaps even more than I do.'

It was an incredibly tempting thought. Being alone with Darius, far away from the problems and complications of her day-to-day life.

Darius meant a lot to her, and if she'd been a little less cynical about life and relationships she'd have fancied herself in love with him. He was committed and caring, and so incredibly hot that she could hardly keep her hands off him. Any other woman would have kidnapped him by now and forced him to marry her—she must be certifiably insane to let the thought of splitting up even cross her mind.

He was still looking at her, the appeal in his eyes almost irresistible, but she slowly shook her head.

'I don't think it would work,' she said slowly. 'I'm not saying I don't want to, but it just makes more sense to end this before it gets too complicated.'

'Mallika…' He took a deep breath. 'How d'you *really* feel about me?'

'I like you,' she said, stumbling over the words a little. 'You make me laugh when I want to cry. You're honest and straightforward, and I can trust you with every secret I have. When you look at me I feel like I'm the most beautiful girl in the world—you're probably the best thing that ever happened to me.'

'I can sense a *but*,' he said softly, though he gripped her hands a little harder.

'But I'm not sure I'm the best thing that ever happened to *you*,' she said in a rush. 'I'm not good for you, Darius. We shouldn't drag this out.'

'And what made you arrive at that conclusion?' he asked.

'We're completely different,' she said. 'You're a straight-forward guy—everything's simple for you—you know exactly what you want. If you feel like doing something, you go ahead and do it. If you like someone, you tell them. If you don't understand what they want, you ask. Things are a lot more complicated for me. Especially when it comes to love and relationships. My parents had the most messed-up marriage ever, and the thought of anything serious or long-term makes me want to run.'

It was probably the most direct conversation they'd ever had, but Darius was beginning to have a bad feeling about the way it was going.

'So we're different?' he said. 'That doesn't mean it can't work. And we're not in the same situation as your parents—we're not even planning to get married.'

Mallika sighed. 'I know,' she said. 'But it isn't just about us being different, or about my parents, Darius. Aryan's better, but I don't think I can leave him for a long while. And I'm not sure if I believe in long-distance relationships. It'll be torture for me, and it might end up being a drag on you. What if you meet someone else? For that matter, what if *I* meet someone else when you're away?'

Darius took a deep breath. 'I'm just saying that we have a good thing going and we don't have to split up when I leave. If either of us meets someone we like better, we can deal with it when it happens.'

'It won't work,' she said unhappily. 'It might be years before you come back—what's the point of trying to drag things out? We'll just make each other unhappy, and when we do split up we'll hate each other. I don't think I could bear that.'

Darius took her by the shoulders and turned her to face him.

'Mallika, do you know how many reasons you've given for not coming with me?'

Mallika shook her head.

'Five,' he said. 'Or maybe six—I lost count after a while. Sweetheart, no one needs five reasons not to do something. One or two are usually enough. Maybe you're overthinking this? For once you should just go with what your heart tells you.'

'I stopped listening to my heart years ago,' she said wryly.

She hadn't been making up the reasons—they were all there, buzzing around like angry bees in her head, and the more she thought about them, the more confused she got.

'Okay, so let's do something less drastic,' Darius said.

He was still holding her by the shoulders, and he pressed on them lightly to make her sit down opposite him.

'Why don't you take a couple of weeks off and come with me for the first leg of my trip at least? We could spend some more time together. Aryan should be fine.'

But she was already shaking her head. 'I don't want to,' she said flatly.

Darius just didn't seem to understand, and she was done with trying to explain herself.

'I left Aryan for one night, and you saw what happened to him.'

'Yes—he had a breakthrough! Maybe the start of his recovery,' Darius countered.

Mallika clenched her teeth. He just wasn't getting it.

'If you want to spend more time with me, shouldn't

you stay here, instead of asking me to go with you? I have a perfectly good reason to want to stay here. Why should I leave my brother to traipse around after you just because you've got some quixotic notion in your head?'

Darius inhaled sharply as a whole lot of things suddenly fell into place for him.

'So *that's* the reason,' he said quietly. 'You're scared because I'm doing something that's a little unconventional and you don't know how to deal with it. All this stuff about not wanting to get into anything long-term is hogwash.'

'I'm not a risk-taker,' she said. 'So you're right—it bothers me. And if we're still in a relationship when you leave I'm not sure I'll be able to handle it.'

'Right,' he said, his expression tight and angry. 'So we stick to the original plan, then? It's over when I leave?'

'That would be best, I think,' she said.

She was so close to falling in love with him that she couldn't bear the thought of dragging out the end—pretending that they could sustain a long-distance relationship. There was only heartbreak at the end of it, but she couldn't bear to see him so upset either.

'Darius?' she said. 'I know you've tried to explain it many times, but *why* do you need to go?'

His expression relaxed a little and he said, 'I thought I *had* explained it. There's just so much more to life than this—so much to learn, so many places to explore, so many things to do… I don't want to wake up one day and discover that I've wasted most of my life. The world is such a big place, and I've only seen one small corner of it. I want to explore, have adventures, challenge myself—really see what I'm made of.'

'Right,' she said. 'I hear what you're saying, but I

guess my brain's just wired differently. I like the comfort of what's familiar...of doing what's expected of me.'

'It's wired just fine,' he said, reaching out to twine a lock of her hair around his fingers. 'I suppose I'm the one being unreasonable, asking you to stick with me when I'm not offering anything concrete in return.'

'It's not that,' Mallika said, and when he didn't reply, she added, 'I can't handle uncertainty, that's all. If it helps, I'm crazy about you.'

Darius's eyes darkened in response.

'How crazy?' he asked, and she pressed her body against his, nibbling at his throat and tugging his shirt out of his jeans to slide her hands over his hot bare skin.

'Moderately crazy,' she whispered. 'Actually, make that extremely crazy.'

He was moving against her now, lifting her so that her body fitted more snugly against his, and unbuttoning her top to get access to her pert, full breasts.

'I guess crazy will have to do for now,' he said, and she gasped as he finally got rid of her top and laid her down carefully on the nearest sofa. 'But I'm not going to give up on you.'

'I'll be moving out of the flat in a couple of days,' Darius said over lunch a few weeks later. 'The board's agreed to let me leave Nidas a little early.'

Mallika stared at him in dismay. While she was sticking to her decision, she hadn't realised how much it would hurt when he actually left. Unconsciously, she'd got addicted to him—to seeing him every day, hearing him laugh, running her hands over his skin and putting her lips to his incredibly sexy mouth.

Sometimes she thought that agreeing to go with him

for part of his trip would be worth the inevitable heart-ache—then all her old demons would came back to haunt her and she'd change her mind again.

'When are you leaving Mumbai?' she asked.

'Four weeks from now,' he said. 'But I thought I'd spend the last month or so with my parents and Shirin—just to make sure everything's settled for taking care of them while I'm away.'

Who's going to take care of me? Mallika felt like yelling at him, but she knew there was no point, so she tried to look as unconcerned as possible.

'Do you need help with moving?'

He hesitated. 'Not really. It's mainly clothes and some kitchen things—I'll be leaving most of it with Shirin anyway.'

'Finished packing?'

'No, I'll start tomorrow,' Darius said, wondering if he was being a colossal idiot.

He knew Mallika cared for him, and that if he pushed just a little harder he'd be able to break through her defences. But he'd planned for years to take this time off just for himself, with no work or family responsibilities, and he knew he'd regret it all his life if he stayed. And Mallika hadn't even *tried* to understand why he felt the way he did. If he stayed for her he knew he'd resent it—and her—after a while, and that would be the end of any kind of relationship.

He was halfway through packing the next day when the doorbell rang. Straightening up from the carton he was taping shut, he wiped a hand across his forehead. It was a hot day, and the number of cartons was growing alarmingly—he seemed to have collected a fair amount of junk in the few months that he'd lived in the flat.

'Oh, good, you're here,' Mallika said when he opened the door. 'I was worried you'd have already packed up and left.'

She was wearing skin-tight jeans and a peasant-style top that showed off her slender neck and shoulders, and Darius stood staring at her for a minute, his mouth growing dry with longing. Over the last few days he'd told himself over and over again that their relationship no longer made sense. He'd more or less bullied Mallika into giving it a shot, but now that his departure was imminent keeping the pressure on just wasn't fair. To either of them.

Wordlessly, he stood aside to let her into the flat. A whiff of her citrusy perfume teased his nostrils as she walked past and he bit his lip. Good resolutions were all very well, but he was only human.

Mallika stopped in the middle of the living room. 'Oh…' was all she said as she took in the cartons neatly lined up in rows and filling more than half the room.

'Shouldn't you have hired professional packers?' she asked. 'Do you have any help at all? Or are you trying to handle this on your own?'

'On my own,' he said. 'A lot of these are books and CDs—they take up more space than you'd think.'

But she wasn't listening to him any longer—her mouth was turning down at the corners and she put her arms around him abruptly, burying her face in his shoulder. 'I wish you didn't have to go,' she said, her voice muffled against his shirt. 'I'll miss you.'

'I'm leaving the country, not dying,' he said drily, though all he wanted to do was tip her face up and kiss her and kiss her, until there was no space for conversation or thought.

'Yes,' she said. 'But we won't have a place to be together for the next month. Unless....' She looked at him, her face lighting up. 'Oh, how silly—why didn't I think of it before? This flat'll be empty, won't it? I won't rent it out, and we can meet here whenever we want.'

Darius shut his eyes for a second. Mallika probably had no idea of what she was doing to him. All his life he'd prided himself on his decisiveness and self-control—it was only when he was with Mallika that he turned to putty.

'Don't leave India right away,' she said, stretching languorously on the bed a couple of hours later. 'Stay on in Mumbai for a few more weeks. You can start your self-discovery thing here just as well as in any other country.'

He shook his head, smiling at her. 'It won't work.'

She cuddled a little closer to him, pulling the sheet up to her chin. 'Don't move all your things, then,' she said. 'I'll cancel the lease agreement, so you won't need to pay rent, but you could come back to stay here whenever you want.'

Darius caught her close, pressing his lips to her forehead. 'Sweetheart, I need to do this *my* way,' he said. 'I need to work some things out, and I need a little space.'

The words stung far more than he'd meant them to, and he saw Mallika bite her lip to keep it steady.

'That's odd,' she managed finally, her tone as light as she could make it. 'I didn't have you pegged as someone who really got the concept of space.'

He gave her a wry grin. She had him there, and he

knew it. 'Perhaps you were right,' he said. 'Perhaps I never should have pressured you in the beginning.'

Mallika stared at him, a nasty, icy feeling gripping her heart. She'd been so close to telling him that she'd changed her mind—that she'd found she cared for him and wanted to give a long-distance relationship a shot. The last thing she'd expected was Darius himself having a change of heart.

'So you're saying that this is it?' she said, her voice still deceptively light. 'We don't stay in touch after today?'

'Something like that,' he said, and she nodded, not trusting herself to speak any more.

After a few seconds she slid out of bed, keeping the sheet wrapped around her as she collected her clothes from the floor.

'Be back in a minute,' she said, and slid into the bathroom.

For a few minutes she could only stare at her face in the mirror, feeling mildly surprised that it looked just as it usually did. Then, after splashing some water on her face, she quickly put on her clothes and flushed the toilet to account for the time she'd spent.

When she came out of the bathroom she looked as if she didn't a have a care in the world. Unfortunately Darius wasn't around to notice, and her lips trembled a little as she saw that he was already dressed and back to his packing.

'Got a lot to finish?' she asked, after watching him dump a big pile of clothes into a suitcase.

He shook his head. 'Another fifteen minutes or so. I'm sorry—I need to get this stuff done and then get back home. My mother has organised a family gathering and I promised I'd be there.'

She sat down on the bed, looking at him thoughtfully. One of the things *her* mother had repeatedly dinned into her head was to act with dignity. '*Apni izzat apne haath*— your dignity is in your own hands.' That had been one of her favourite sayings, along with, 'No one will respect you unless you respect yourself.'

'You should head off soon, then,' she said, getting to her feet with a brightly artificial smile on her lips.

It cost her every last ounce of willpower, but she walked across to him and leaned up to kiss him lightly on the lips.

'It was really good while it lasted,' she said. 'Thanks for putting up with all my whims and *nakhras*. Have a good life.'

'Mallika…' he said, and something indefinable flickered in his eyes.

She stepped back quickly, before he could touch her.

'I'll see you, then,' she said. 'Some time. Deposit the keys with the watchman, will you?'

And, leaving him standing in the bedroom, she hurried out of the flat, waiting till she was in her car before allowing a few hastily wiped away tears to escape.

CHAPTER ELEVEN

'I'M GOING OUT,' Aryan said.

He sounded oddly defiant—as if he expected Mallika to object.

It was almost a month since she'd broken up with Darius, and it had been tough. She missed him so badly that it hurt, and only the highest levels of self-control had stopped her from calling him.

Aryan hadn't said anything, but he'd been unusually well-behaved—probably sensing that she was very close to breaking point.

'Out?' she asked. 'Where?'

'Um…I thought I'd get a haircut. And maybe buy a couple of shirts.'

She should have felt pleased—Aryan was a lot better, but except for his trips to the doctor he'd stepped out of doors only once, for a walk around the garden with her. Wanting to go somewhere on his own was a first. He still ordered his clothes on the internet, and paid a local barber to come to their home and trim his hair once a month, and she couldn't figure out what had prompted the sudden decision to go to the shops on his own.

'D'you need the car?' she asked, trying to stall for time while she gauged his mood.

Aryan shook his head. 'Not today,' he said. 'I'll walk down Warden Road and get what I need. But if you could spare it for some time on Saturday that would be great?'

Feeling completely at sea, Mallika nodded. 'Yes, of course. You can have it for the full day, if you like.'

'I'm meeting someone,' Aryan volunteered after a brief silence. 'A…um…a girl. She's from Bangalore, and she's going to be here for a few days. I got to know her online,' he added a tad defensively as Mallika gaped at him.

'Figures,' Mallika muttered, once she'd got her breath back.

While she'd been obsessing about her little brother's lack of social interaction he'd gone right ahead and acquired an online girlfriend. Served her right for being so presumptuous, thinking he needed her help to get back to a normal life.

An unpleasant thought struck her, and she said, 'Aryan…?'

'Yes?'

'This girl—just checking—she's real, right? Not computer-generated or a…a…fake persona or something?'

Aryan laughed—a full-bodied, boyish laugh that made him look years younger. 'She's real, all right,' he said. 'I've video called her a few times, and I've done basic checks on her online profile. She's a computer engineer, and she's training to be a hacker. An *ethical* hacker,' he added hastily as Mallika choked on her tea. 'She's hired by corporates and governments to identify possible security breaches in their systems.'

'She sounds lovely,' Mallika said, wondering what kind of 'basic checks' one did on a prospective girlfriend. Finishing her tea, she got to her feet. 'Are you inviting her home?'

'I might,' Aryan said cautiously.

Mallika knew she had been a bit on edge ever since she'd broken up with Darius and Aryan was probably testing her mood. She turned her back to him now, and rinsed her tea cup with unnecessary vigour.

'You okay with me meeting her?' he asked.

'Yes, of course,' Mallika said, turning towards him with an overly bright smile on her lips. 'It's a good thing—you getting to know more people.'

She kept the smile plastered on her face until he left the flat, and then let out a huge sigh and flopped down onto the nearest sofa.

It was a relief, having the place all to herself to be miserable in. Aryan wasn't an intrusive presence, but he was around all the time, and sometimes she wanted to give full rein to her misery. Maybe scream and throw a few things, dignity be damned. She'd thought of going to the flat that Darius had vacated, being by herself for a few days, but it was too closely linked to him.

She'd gone back once, to get it cleaned and cover up the furniture, and the first thing she'd seen on walking in was the huge painting of a spice market that Darius had bought. He hadn't taken it with him, and it was still occupying pride of place on the living room wall. Walking closer to it, she'd noticed a little note stuck to the frame. *'Leaving this for you,'* it had said. *'Love, Darius.'*

It was the *'Love, Darius'* that had done it—she'd burst into tears, standing right there in front of the painting, and the skilfully etched heaps of nutmeg and chillies and cardamom had blurred into random blotches of colour.

Once she'd stopped sobbing she'd locked up the flat and never gone back.

Sighing, Mallika buried her face in her hands. She'd finally admitted to herself that she loved Darius, and that letting him go had been one of the stupidest things she'd ever done. She should have worked harder at their relationship instead of endlessly obsessing about her own troubles. But it was too late now—Darius had made it quite clear that he wanted a clean break.

After a while she pulled herself together and went out for a jog in a park near the sea. It had been a while since she'd last run, and she found the rhythm soothing—the steady pounding of her feet on the track helping her push everything to the back of her mind at least for a little while.

She stopped only when she was completely exhausted and the sun had begun to set. And when she got home she was so tired that she flopped into bed and sank into a blessedly dreamless sleep.

'It's the *annual party*!' Venkat said, in much the same tones that an ardent royalist might say, *It's the coronation*!

Strongly tempted to say *So...?* Mallika raised her eyebrows.

'You can't *not* come,' he said, looking outraged. '*Everyone* will be there.' He brightened up at a sudden thought. 'Darius will be there—he's still in town, and he's made an exception. We haven't told him, but we're holding a little surprise farewell for him at the end.'

Which was exactly the reason why she didn't want to go—but she could hardly tell Venkat that.

'I'll come,' she said. 'But I'll need to leave early. I have some relatives over.'

Well, Aryan *was* a relative, so technically she wasn't lying. And she could think of several things she would rather be doing that evening.

As it turned out, Darius was the first person she ran into when she walked into the party. *Of course*, she thought, giving herself a swift mental kick. She should have landed up there after nine, when the party would have been in full swing, said hello to Venkat and slipped out. Now she was terribly visible among the twenty or so people dotting the ballroom.

Darius found himself unable to take his eyes off Mallika. She was simply, even conservatively dressed, in a full-sleeved grey top and flared palazzo pants. The top, however, clung lovingly to her curves—and it didn't help that he knew exactly what was under it.

'Looking good,' he said, and her lips curved into a tiny smile.

'Thank you,' she said primly, hating the way her heart was pounding in her chest.

The people around them had melted away as soon as they saw Darius and Mallika together—even a blind man would have sensed the strong undercurrents to their conversation.

'Not too bad yourself,' Mallika added, just to prove that she wasn't shaken by his proximity.

It was true—in jeans and a casual jacket worn over a midnight-blue shirt Darius was breathtakingly gorgeous. His hair was brushed straight back from his forehead, and his hooded eyes and hawk-like features gave him a slightly predatory look. He'd lost weight in the last month, and his perfectly sculpted cheekbones stood out a little.

'Venkat said you mightn't come,' he said.

She shrugged. 'I don't like formal parties,' she said. 'But he made a bit of a point about it. So I thought I'd hang around until a quarter past eight and then push off.'

Darius glanced at his watch—it was barely eight, and most of the Nidas staff hadn't even arrived yet. In previous years the party had continued till three in the morning. While a few people had left earlier, even then, an eight-fifteen exit would set a new record.

'Do you really need to leave?' he asked. 'Dinner won't be served before ten.'

'I'll eat at home,' she said, giving him a quick smile. 'I'm not too keen on hotel food in any case.'

There was a brief pause, and then they both started speaking together. Somehow that broke the awkwardness, and when Darius laughed Mallika smiled back at him.

'You go first,' he offered.

'I was just asking how your parents are,' she said. 'And Shirin and the kids.'

'They're fine,' Darius said. 'Though my mum's taken to bursting into tears every time we talk about me leaving. It's driving my dad nuts.' His smile was indulgent, as if he was talking about a child and not a sixty-year-old woman. 'And Shirin's doing well. Her divorce hasn't come through yet, but we're hoping it'll happen by the end of the year. She's coping, the kids have settled and she's started looking for a job.'

'That's all good news, then,' Mallika said, smiling warmly at him.

He felt his heart do a sudden flip-flop in his chest.

'Yes,' he said stiltedly. It was tough enough, having to pretend that she was just like any other colleague. Having to actually stand here and carry on a superficial conversation was proving to be incredibly difficult.

'I'll…um…circulate a bit, then,' she said, indicating the half-full room. 'Now that I'm here I should say hello to as many people as I can before slipping out.'

He nodded, about to tell her that he'd like to see her before she left when the lights went out quite suddenly. A loud popping sound followed by the smell of burning plastic indicated a short-circuit.

Mallika stopped in her tracks as people around her gasped and exclaimed. A few women giggled nervously and Darius came to stand next to her, his features barely discernible in the dim light.

He took her arm and swivelled her around a little. 'Maybe you should wait till the lights are back on before you walk around and talk to people.'

'No, I'll just go now,' she said. She hated the dark, and the people milling around were making her nervous. 'I have a torch on my cell phone—hang on, let me put it on.'

The light from the torch was surprisingly strong, and he could see her quite clearly now, her brow furrowed in thought.

'Damn,' she said. 'This thing's running out of charge. I must have taken dozens of calls during the day, and I forgot to charge it before I left.'

'I'll walk you to the exit,' Darius said, taking her arm.

She thought of protesting, but her whole body seemed to turn nerveless at his touch—following him obediently seemed to be the sensible option.

'Shouldn't they put on a back-up generator or something?'

'They won't if it's a short-circuit,' he said. 'There's a risk of fire. Here—I think this is a shorter way out.'

He led her down a corridor that to Mallika looked exactly like the one she'd been in earlier. This was deserted, though, and it opened into a little *faux* Mughal courtyard with a small fountain in the centre. The fountain wasn't playing, but the pool of water around it shimmered in the faint light coming from the streetlights outside the hotel.

At that point the light coming from her phone flickered and the battery died. Mallika made a frustrated sound and shoved it into her bag. 'I can't call my driver now,' she said.

'D'you want to use my phone?'

'That would be very helpful,' she said drily. 'If only I remembered his number.'

'We'll page the car, then,' he said. 'Do you remember the car's number?

'Sort of,' she said. 'It has a nine and a one in it.'

'That helps,' he said gravely. 'Driver's name?'

'Bablu,' she said, so triumphantly that he laughed.

'We can page Bablu, then,' he said. 'That's assuming the paging system is working.'

She grimaced. 'I didn't think of that,' she said. 'Which way's the exit, anyway?'

He pointed to some glass doors opposite the ones they'd used to enter the courtyard.

'That way,' he said. 'Though we might as well sit here for a while. There's a bench over there, and it'll more pleasant outside than inside the hotel with no air-conditioning.'

She followed him to the bench, and he brushed a few leaves off it before they sat down. 'It's so quiet here,' she said. 'You'd hardly think we were in the middle of Mumbai.'

'The walls cut off the noise,' he said. 'But you can tell you're in Mumbai, all right. Look up—you can't see a single star because of the pollution.'

Mallika laughed. 'You're right, I can't,' she said. 'I should have known you'd burst my little fantasy.'

Darius went very still next to her. 'Why d'you say that?' he asked finally.

She flushed, thankful he couldn't see her in the dark. The words had slipped out, but she *had* been thinking of the happy bubble she'd been living in when they were still dating.

'It was just a stray remark,' she said, wishing he wasn't so perceptive. 'I didn't mean anything by it.'

'I think you did.'

'And I'm telling you I didn't!' Her voice rose slightly. 'Can't you just leave things alone, instead of digging around and trying to make me say more than I want to?'

'I'm sorry,' he said quietly, putting a hand over hers. 'I'm not trying to upset you.'

Mallika jerked her hand away. It was a childish gesture, but she was very near tears, and soon a few drops did escape and roll down her cheeks. She didn't wipe them off, hoping he wouldn't notice in the dark.

Of course she should have known better—Darius immediately leaned closer.

'Are you crying?' he asked, sounding so worried and concerned that her tears rolled faster.

'Of course not,' she said, trying to sound dignified and totally in control.

Unfortunately a little sniffle escaped, and Darius muttered something violent under his breath and swept her abruptly into his arms.

'Mallika—don't,' he said, trying to kiss the tears off her cheeks while simultaneously smoothing her curls away from her face. 'What's wrong? Is it something I did?'

Mallika fought for control and jerked away from him finally, scrubbing at her cheeks with her hands.

'It's all right,' she said. 'Moment of weakness. All better now.' She was feeling hideously embarrassed—crying all over an ex-boyfriend was the ultimate dumped woman cliché.

'It's *not* all right,' he said firmly. 'I know we're not together now, but I care about you still, and I'm not going away until you explain what's wrong.'

'*What* did you say?' Mallika asked, so stunned that she could hardly get the words out coherently.

'I'm not going away until I find out why you were crying,' he said.

'Before that, you dimwit!'

'We're not together now?'

'No, no—*after* that!' Mallika said, sounding outraged.

'I care about you still?' he asked, puzzled and amused in equal parts now.

'Yes, that's it,' she said, relieved that he'd finally got it right. 'Did you mean it?'

'Yes,' he said slowly. 'But you already know that.'

'You never told me!' Mallika said through gritted teeth. 'How the *hell* was I supposed to know?'

It was still dark, and Darius couldn't see her face, but he could sense the anger coming off her in waves. For the first time since he'd met her that evening he began to think that there might be some hope after all.

'Why else do you think I kept on trying to make it work for us?' he asked gently. 'Even when you kept sending me away?'

'I don't know!' she said. 'I thought it was general cussedness or something! And you lost interest as soon as your travel visas came in!'

He should have been annoyed at that, but right now what she was *not* saying was more important than what she was.

'I *do* care,' he said gently. 'In fact, I think I've been in love with you for a while now—only I kept trying to make myself believe that I was confusing attraction and affection with love. It was only after we split up that I realised how much I love you, and by then it was too late to do anything about it.

'You utter *idiot*,' she breathed.

He frowned. 'Does that mean…?'

'Of course it does,' she said, grabbing him by the shoulders and managing to shake him in spite of his bulk. 'I've been in love with you ever since you took me to meet your family that day. But after that you started to back off, and I didn't know what to think! I wanted to—'

What she'd wanted was lost as his arms came around her, crushing her against his chest.

'I've missed you,' he said, his lips hot and urgent against hers. 'God, so much.'

Mallika kissed him back just as hungrily, her hands gripping his shoulders as if she'd never let him go again. It felt so *right*, being back in his arms—she felt completely alive for the first time since he'd left.

'I missed you too,' she said, when she was able to speak. 'I'd think of calling you every single day, and then I wouldn't because I didn't want to seem desperate.'

'You couldn't have been more desperate than me,' he said wryly. 'I've been an idiot, Mallika. I was so sure I was doing the right thing.'

'By breaking up with me?' She shook her head, sounding confused. 'If you were in love with me, how could it possibly be the right thing?'

'I didn't know you cared for me too,' he said, tracing the delicate line of her jaw with one finger. 'It felt like I was forcing myself on you sometimes. Not physically,' he added as she made a sudden movement of protest. 'But you wanted to keep things light—and there I was, talking about long-distance relationships and making it work, when you clearly didn't want to listen… And you were obviously so uncomfortable with me giving up my job and leaving Mumbai that I thought the best thing to do would be to call a halt.'

'I've thought a lot about that,' Mallika said, sliding a hand up his chest to rest right against his heart. 'I think I finally do understand why you want to get away from the rat race—why you need to break away from what's expected of you.'

'So will you come with me?' he asked, capturing her hand in both of his and dipping his head to kiss it. 'At least for a while?'

The hidden lighting in the courtyard came on as if on cue, and he could see that her lovely lips were curled up slightly in a smile.

'I'd love to,' she said. 'Not right away—you should have the first few months to yourself, to do what you originally planned, and Aryan still needs me around— but I'll spend every bit of leave I get with you. And once you're back we can figure out what we should do.'

'Get married,' Darius said, and when she instinctively

pulled back he didn't let her go. 'I know all the reasons you have for not marrying,' he said. 'But if you think about it none of them hold if we're in love with each other.'

'I'm scared of marriage,' she admitted. 'Scared that things will go wrong and we'll end up being unhappy like my parents were. Even if we love each other now.'

'We'll be fine,' Darius said. 'Trust me.'

And suddenly Mallika knew that she did. She trusted Darius completely and absolutely, and she wanted to spend the rest of her life with him. Marriage still scared her, but she'd have plenty of time to get used to the idea.

'I love you,' she said softly. 'And you're right. We can make it work. Together.'

EPILOGUE

'*A GHAR JAMAI*—that's what these Hindustanis call men who marry their girls and move in with them,' Aunt Freny said with relish. 'That's what you're going to be. Not that we're not happy you're back. This gypsy-type living for a year might have been fun for you, but it drove all of us mad with worry. Hopefully once you marry you'll stay put. And as you've had your honeymoon before the wedding…'

'Freny!' Mrs Mistry said in awful tones.

Darius had been back for a month, tanned and leaner than he'd been when he left, but otherwise unchanged. Mallika had left Nidas and spent the last three months with him, travelling around Europe. After the wedding they would move into Mallika's flat in Parel, and then they had plans to set up a small company to aid NGOs with improving the infrastructure in rural areas.

'We're still going for a honeymoon, Aunt Freny,' Darius said mildly. 'It's just that it'll be in the villages around Mumbai.'

'It's his wedding day—you leave him alone, Freny,' Mrs Mistry said warningly as Freny geared up to retort. 'Come here, *dikra*, your collar's just a little crooked.'

Darius ignored her. 'Mallika's here,' he said, his eyes lighting up.

Aunt Freny snorted. 'Your son's a son until he gets a wife, et cetera, et cetera,' she said to Mrs Mistry. 'Though in your case your daughter really does seem set to be with you all her life!'

Luckily Mrs Mistry wasn't paying attention either, and she didn't hear Aunt Freny.

Mallika was walking in on Aryan's arm, dressed in a perfectly lovely red brocade sari with a heavily embroidered deep-red veil draped over her head. Her arms were loaded with gold bangles, and she wore a heavy gold *kundan* necklace around her slender neck. For the first time in years her curly hair was parted in the middle and tied back in a demure chignon, and she wore a red *bindi* in the centre of her forehead.

Darius was still gazing at her, spellbound, when she stumbled a little. She was quite close to him now, and he caught her by the shoulders to steady her.

'High heels,' she said, making a little face and laughing up at him. 'My aunt insisted.'

'You look lovely,' he said, meaning it.

She blushed a little. 'I don't feel like myself,' she said. 'If I could, I'd get married in my work clothes.'

'You'd look just as lovely,' he said, bending down to kiss her.

There was a collective indrawn breath from Mallika's side of the family, while Darius's smiled indulgently.

'Come on—let's get this show on the road,' Aryan said. 'Stop looking into each other's eyes, people.' His newly acquired, now *off*line girlfriend elbowed him, and he said, 'What? They'll miss the *muhurat* and Auntie Sarita will have a fit!'

It was a simple registered wedding, in spite of Mallika's interfering aunt's insistence on a traditional wedding sari and the actual signing happening at an auspicious time. Once they were done, both bride and groom heaved a sigh of relief.

'Any chance of us being allowed to skip the reception?' Darius asked hopefully.

His mother glared at him. 'Absolutely not,' she said firmly. 'How can you even suggest it, Darius?'

'Because I want to be alone with my wife,' he said in an undertone.

Mallika smiled up at him. 'We have the rest of our lives together,' she said, and he smiled back, putting an arm around her and pressing his lips to the top of her head.

'So we do,' he said softly as she slipped an arm around his waist and leaned in closer. 'Did I happen to mention how much I love you, Mrs Mistry?'

'You did say something about it,' Mallika said thoughtfully. 'But it wasn't all that clear. Could you explain it a little more clearly, please?'

* * * * *

Perhaps he should end this interview here and now.

He'd opened his mouth to do just that when she opened her eyes, gave a little wriggle in the chair, and—*wham!*

An image zig-zagged across his brain—a picture of Imogen Lorrimer, standing up to wriggle her way right out of that navy skirt, shrug off the jacket and slowly unbutton the pearl buttons of her white shirt. Before shaking that dark hair free so it tumbled to her shoulders, then sitting back down on that damn red chair and crossing her legs.

A hoarse noise rasped from his throat. What the hell…? *Why?* Where on earth had *that* come from?

It was time to get a grip on this interview—*and* the conversation. A sigh escaped her and for a second his gaze focused on her lips. Hell, this was *not* good. 'Never Mix Business and Pleasure' was a non-negotiable rule.

Dear Reader

I *so* enjoyed writing this book—hey, Montmartre, Paris, and a yurt in the Algarve…what's not to enjoy?

But most of all I loved writing about Imo and Joe—they became totally real to me even while they drove me nuts as they fought the idea of love all the way.

Imo wanted to play it safe and Joe wanted to play by the rules. So when the sparks began to fly in the bedroom *and* out they—and I—were thrown in at the deep end.

I hope you enjoy seeing what they did about it!

Nina xx

BREAKING
THE BOSS'S RULES

BY

NINA MILNE

MILLS &
BOON

Published in Great Britain 2014
by Mills & Boon, an imprint of Harlequin (UK) Limited,
Eton House, 18-24 Paradise Road, Richmond, Surrey, TW9 1SR

© 2014 Nina Milne

ISBN: 978-0-263-25329-0

Harlequin (UK) Limited's policy is to use papers that are natural,
renewable and recyclable products and made from wood grown in
sustainable forests. The logging and manufacturing processes conform
to the legal environmental regulations of the country of origin.

Printed and bound in Spain
by Blackprint CPI, Barcelona

Nina Milne has always dreamt of writing for Mills & Boon®—ever since as a child she discovered stacks of Mills & Boon® books 'hidden' in the airing cupboard. She graduated from playing libraries to reading the books, and has now realised her dream of writing them.

Along the way she found a happy-ever-after of her own, accumulating a superhero of a husband, three gorgeous children, a cat with character and a real library…well, lots of bookshelves.

Before achieving her dream of working from home creating happy-ever-afters whilst studiously avoiding any form of actual housework, Nina put in time as both an accountant and a recruitment consultant. She figures the lack of romance in her previous jobs is now balancing out.

After a childhood spent in Peterlee (UK), Rye (USA), Winchester (UK) and Paris (France), Nina now lives in Brighton (UK), and has vowed never to move again!! Unless, of course, she runs out of bookshelves. Though there is always the airing cupboard…

Other Modern Tempted™ titles by Nina Milne:

HOW TO BAG A BILLIONAIRE

**This and other titles by Nina Milne
are also available in eBook format
from www.millsandboon.co.uk**

For my parents, for believing in me.

PROLOGUE

Dear Diary

My name is Imogen Lorrimer and my life is in a less than stellar place right now.

For a start there is every possibility that my temporary new boss is about to fire me. His name is Joe McIntyre and, just to really mess with my head, he has taken to appearing in my dreams.

Naked.

Last night was particularly erotic. I won't go into detail, but we were in his office and let's just say various positions were involved...as were varying bits of office furniture...glass-topped desk, red swivel chair...

Obviously I know this is thoroughly unprofessional and utterly inappropriate.

In my defence he is gorgeous.

Think sexy rumpled hair—dark brown, a tiny bit long, with a few bits that stick up. Think chocolate—the expensive kind—brown eyes. Think a strong but not too dominant nose. A long face, with a sculpted jaw and clearly defined chin. Oh, and a body to die for—Joe McIntyre is a long, lean fighting machine.

Problem is, however much I appreciate the man in my dreams, the real live clothed version of Joe McIntyre is a ruthless corporate killing machine. He is a troubleshooter who has been called in to overhaul Langley Interior Design and we are all in danger of losing our jobs.

In fact there is every chance he will fire me on the spot tomorrow—especially given my recent screw-up.

I cannot let that happen. I cannot afford to lose my job. Not on top of everything else.

To be specific I am:

Homeless—my scumbag boyfriend, Steve, of three years has just dumped me for his ex—Simone—and thrown me out of the flat we shared. So I am currently living with my BFF—and, whilst I love Mel like the sister I never had, I can only sleep on her pull-out bed for so long. I think I'm cramping her style.

Heartbroken—Steve ticked all the boxes on my 'What I am looking for in a Man' list. I thought he was The One.

Broke—I blew my savings on a romantic holiday for Steve and me. And, unbelievable though this may sound, he is now taking Simone. How humiliating is that?

It's no wonder that I am fantasising in my dreams. My real life sucks.

Time for some ice cream, methinks!

Imogen x

CHAPTER ONE

JOE MCINTYRE LEANT back in the state-of-the-art office chair and picked up the CV from the glass-topped desk.

Imogen Lorrimer. Peter Langley's PA for the past five years.

She of the raven-black hair and wide grey-blue eyes.

Faint irritation twanged Joe's nerves; her looks were irrelevant. 'No Mixing Business and Pleasure'. That was an absolute rule. Along with 'One Night Only' and 'Never Look Back'. From *The Joe McIntyre Book of Relationships*. Short, sweet and easy to use.

Joe gusted out a sigh as his eyes zoned back to his emails. Leila again. Shame the manual didn't tell him how to deal with a blast-from-the-past ex-girlfriend from a time he'd rather forget. But this was not the time to open *that* can of worms—his guilt was still bad enough that he had agreed to attend her wedding, but there was no need to think further about it. Right now he needed to think about this interview.

Imogen Lorrimer had snagged the edge of his vision the moment she'd entered the boardroom two days before, when he'd called an initial meeting of all Langley staff. He'd nodded impatiently at her to be seated and been further arrested by the tint of her eye colour as she'd perched on her chair and aimed a fleeting glance at him from under the straight line of her black fringe. For a fraction of a second he'd faltered in his speech, stopped in his tracks by eyes of a shade that was neither blue nor grey but some-where in between.

Since then he'd stared at her more than once as she scuttled past him in the corridor, dark head down, clearly reluctant to initiate visual contact.

But he was used to people being nervous around him. After all he was a troubleshooter; people knew he had the power to fire them. A power he used where necessary—had in fact already used that morning. So if firing Imogen Lorrimer would benefit Langley Interior Designs he wouldn't hesitate. However attractive he found her.

As if on cue there was a knock at the open office door and Joe looked up.

Further annoyance nipped his chest at the realisation that he had braced himself as if for impact. Imogen Lorrimer was nothing more than an employee he needed to evaluate. There was no need for this disconcerting aware-ness of her.

For a second she hesitated in the doorway, and despite himself his pulse-rate kicked up a notch.

Ridiculous. In her severely cut navy suit, with her dark hair pulled back into a sleek bun, she looked the epitome of professionalism. The least he could do was pretend to be the same. Which meant he had to *stop* checking her out.

'Come in.' He rose to his feet and she walked stiffly across the floor, exuding nervous tension.

'Mr McIntyre,' she said, her voice high and breathy.

'Joe's fine.' Sitting down, he nodded at the chair oppo-site him. 'Have a seat.'

Surely a simple enough instruction. But apparently not. Astonishment rose his brows as Imogen twitched, stared at the red swivel chair for a few seconds, glanced at him, and then back at the chair. Her strangled gargle turned into an unconvincing cough.

Joe rubbed the back of his neck and studied the apparently hypnotic object. As might be expected in an interior designer's office, it was impressive. Red leather, stylish design, functional, comfortable, eye-catching.

But still just a chair.

Yet Imogen continued to regard it, her cheeks now the same shade as the leather.

Impatience caused him to drum his fingers on the desk and the sound seemed to rally her. Swivelling on her sensible navy blue pumps, she stared down at the glass desktop, closed her eyes as though in pain, and then hauled in an audible breath.

'Is there a problem?' he asked. 'Something wrong with the chair?'

'Of course not. I'm sorry,' she said as she lowered herself downwards onto the edge of the chair and clasped her hands onto her lap.

'If it's not the chair then it must be me,' he said. 'I get that you may be a bit nervous. But don't worry. I don't bite.'

Stricken blue eyes met his as she gripped the arms of the chair as though it were a rollercoaster. 'Good to know,' she said. 'Sorry. Um…I'm not usually this nervous. It's just…obviously…well…' Pressing her glossy lips together tightly, she closed her eyes.

Exasperation surged through him. This was the woman Peter Langley had described as 'a mainstay of the company'. It was no bloody wonder Langley was in trouble. Perhaps he should end this interview here and now.

He'd opened his mouth to do just that when she opened her eyes, gave a little wriggle in the chair, and—*wham!*

An image zigzagged across his brain—a picture of Imogen Lorrimer, standing up to wriggle her way right out of that navy skirt, shrug off the jacket and slowly unbutton the pearl buttons of her white shirt. Before shaking that dark hair free so it tumbled to her shoulders, then sitting back down on that damn red chair and crossing her legs.

A hoarse noise rasped from his throat. What the hell...? *Why?* Where on earth had *that* come from?

It was time to get a grip of this interview—*and* the conversation. A sigh escaped her and for a second his gaze focused on her lips. Hell, this was *not* good. 'Never Mix Business and Pleasure' was a non-negotiable rule. His work ethic was sacrosanct—the thought of jeopardising his reputation and ruining his business the way his father had done was enough to bring him out in hives.

So this awareness had to be nixed—no matter how inexplicably tempting Imogen Lorrimer was. His libido needed an ice bath or a night of fun. Preferably the latter—a nice, relaxed, laid-back evening with a woman unconnected to any client. Someone who could provide a no-strings-attached night of pleasure.

In the meantime he needed to concentrate on the matter in hand.

What had Imogen said last? Before she'd frozen into perpetual silence.

'It's just...obviously...what?' he growled.

Imogen caught her bottom lip in her teeth and bit down hard; with any luck the pain would recall her common sense. If it were logistically possible to boot herself around the room she would, and her fingers tingled with the urge to slap herself upside the head.

Enough.

She had had enough of herself.

It was imperative that she keep her job. For herself, but also because if she were here she could do everything in her power to make sure this man didn't shut Langley down.

Peter and Harry Langley had been more than good to her—the least she could do was try to ensure this corporate killing machine didn't chew up their company and spit it out.

Instead of sitting here squirming in embarrassed silence over last night's encounter with a fantasy Joe McIntyre.

Time to channel New Imogen, who fantasised over gazillions of hot men and didn't bat an eyelid.

She moistened her lips and attempted a smile.

Brown eyes locked with hers and for a heartbeat something flickered in their depths. A spark, an awareness—a look that made her skin sizzle. The sort of look that Dream Joe excelled in.

Then it was gone. Doused almost instantly and replaced by definitive annoyance, amplified by a scowl that etched his forehead with the sort of formidable frown that Real Joe no doubt held a first-class degree in.

Straightening her shoulders, she forced herself to meet his exasperated gaze. 'I apologise, Joe. The past few weeks have been difficult and the result was an attack of nerves. I'm fine now, and I'd appreciate it if we could start again.'

'Let's do that.' His words were emphatic as he gestured to her CV. 'You've been Peter's PA for five years—ever since you came out of college. He speaks very highly of you, so why so nervous?'

OK. Here goes.

There was no hiding the fact that she'd screwed up and, given that Joe had been on the premises for two days, there was little doubt he already knew about it. So it was bite the proverbial bullet time.

'I'm sure you've heard about the Anderson project?'

'Yes, I have.'

Stick to the facts, Imogen.

'Then you know I made a pretty monumental mistake.' Her stomach clenched as she relived the sheer horror. 'I ordered the wrong fabric. Yards and yards of it. I didn't realise I'd done that. The team went ahead and used it and the client ended up with truly hideous mustard-coloured curtains and coverings throughout his mansion instead of the royal gold theme we had promised him.'

A shudder racked her body as she adhered her feet in the thick carpet to prevent herself from swivelling in a twist of sheer discomfort on the chair. 'Mistake' was not supposed to be in the Imogen Lorrimer dictionary. To err was inexcusable; her mother had drummed that into her over and over.

'It was awful. Even worse than...' She pressed her lips together.

His eyes flickered to rest on her mouth and a spark ignited in the pit of her tummy.

'Even worse than what?' he demanded.

Nice one, Imogen. Now no doubt Joe was imagining a string of ditzy disasters in her wake.

Tendrils of hair wisped around her face as she shook her head, sacrificing the perfection of her bun for the sake of vehemence. 'It doesn't matter. Honestly. It's nothing to do with work. Just a childhood memory.'

Joe raised his dark eyebrows, positively radiating scepticism. 'You're telling me that you have a childhood disaster that competes with a professional debacle like that?'

He didn't believe her.

'Yes,' she said biting back her groan at the realisation she would have to tell him. She couldn't risk him assuming she was a total mess-up. 'I was ten and I came home with the worst possible report you could imagine.'

Imogen could still feel the smooth edges of the booklet in her hand; her tummy rolled in remembered fear and sadness. *Keep it light, Imogen.*

'Having lied through my teeth all term that I'd been doing brilliantly, I'd pretty much convinced myself I was a genius—so I was almost as upset to discover I wasn't as my mum was.'

The look of raw disappointment on Eva Lorrimer's face

was one that she would never forget, never get used to, no matter how many times she saw it.

'Anyway…' Imogen brushed the side of her temple in an attempt to sweep away the memory. 'I had the exact same hollow, sinking, leaden feeling when I saw the mustard debacle.'

Joe's brown eyes rested on her face with an indecipherable expression; he was probably thinking she was some sort of fruit loop.

'But the point about the Andersen project is that it was a one-off. I have never made a mistake like that before and I can assure you that I never will again.'

Whilst she had no intention of excusing herself, seeing as the word 'excuse' also failed to feature in her vocabulary, she had messed up the day after Steve had literally thrown her onto the street so his ex-girlfriend could move back in. She'd reeled into work, still swaying in disbelief and humiliation. Not that she had any intention of sharing *that* with Joe; she doubted it would make any difference if she did. She suspected Joe didn't hold much truck with personal issues affecting work.

Panic churned in her stomach. The Langleys wouldn't want Joe to fire her. But Peter was in the midst of a breakdown and Harry was stable but still in Intensive Care after his heart attack; neither of them was in a position to worry about *her*.

Leaning forward, she gripped the edge of the desk. 'I'm good at my job,' she said quietly. 'And I'll do anything I can to help keep this company going until Peter and Harry are back.'

Including fighting this man every step of the way if he tried to tear apart what the Langley brothers had built up.

For a second his gaze dropped, and his frown deepened before he gave a curt nod.

'I'll bear it in mind,' he said. 'Now, let's move on. According to Peter this is a list of current projects and obligations.' He pushed a piece of typewritten paper across the desk. 'He doesn't seem very sure it's complete and he referred me to you.'

Imogen looked down at the list and tried to focus on the words and not on Joe's hand. On his strong, capable fingers, the light smattering of hair, the sturdy wrists that for some reason she wanted so desperately to touch. Those hands that in her dreams had wrought such incredible magic.

Grinding her molars, she tugged the paper towards her. 'I'll check this against my organiser.' She bent at the waist to pick up her briefcase. And frowned. Had that strange choking noise been Joe? As she sat up she glanced at him and clocked a slash of colour on his cheekbones.

Focus.

Imogen looked at the paper and then back at her organiser. 'The only thing not on here is the annual Interior Design awards ceremony. It's being held this Wednesday. Peter and Graham Forrester were meant to attend.' She frowned. 'Could be Peter forgot. Or he's changed his mind because the client can't make it. Or he's too embarrassed to face everyone.'

Joe's forehead had creased in a frown and his fingers beat a tattoo on the desk—and there she was, staring at those fingers *again*.

'Tell me more about it.'

'It's a pretty prestigious event. We won in the luxury category for the interior of an apartment we did for Richard Harvey the IT billionaire. He commissioned us to create a love nest for his seventh wife.'

Joe's brows hiked towards his hairline as he whistled. '*Seven?* The man must be a glutton for punishment.'

'He's a romantic,' Imogen said. 'You've got to admire that kind of persistence.'

'No.'

'No, what?'

'No, I *don't* have to admire it. It's delusional. Sometimes dreams have to be abandoned because they aren't possible.'

Easy for him to say—it was impossible to imagine a lean, mean corporate machine having *any* dreams.

'Some dreams,' she agreed. 'But not all. I truly believe that if you persevere and try and you're willing to compromise there is a person out there for everyone.'

After all, she had no intention of giving up finding a man to match her tick list just because she and Steve had gone pear-shaped.

'Richard has just had to try harder than most. And,' she added, seeing the derisory quirk to his lips, 'he and Crystal are very happy—in fact they are in Paris, celebrating their meetiversary.'

'Excuse me?'

'The day they met a year ago. Richard has whisked her off to Paris for a romantic getaway. That's why they can't attend the awards. I hope Richard and Crystal get to celebrate *decades* of meetiversaries.'

'Good for you. *I* hope to show Richard that we value the award we won for decorating his apartment. So, tell me more about the project. Who worked on it?'

'Peter, Graham and me. Peter often lets me get involved with the design side of things as well as the admin stuff.'

Joe's brown eyes assessed her expression and his fingers continued to drum on the desk-top. 'How involved were you on the project?

'I designed both bathrooms.'

'Could you show me?'

'Sure.'

Trepidation twisted her nerves even as she tried to sound calm. Maybe Joe would use this to make his final decision on her job. Or was it something else? There was something unnerving about his gaze; she could almost hear the whir and tick of his brain.

'I'll get the folder.'

Once she'd pulled the relevant portfolio from the filing cabinet at the back of the room she walked back to the desk.

Placing the folder carefully on the glass top, she leaned over to tug the elastic at the corner. *Whoosh*—an unwary breath and she had inhaled a lungful of Joe: sandalwood, and something that made her want to nuzzle into his neck.

No can do. Newsflash, Imogen: this is not a dream— it's for real.

She needed to breathe shallowly and focus—*not* on the way an errant curl of brown hair had squiggled onto the nape of his neck but on demonstrating her design talent.

'The spec was to create something unique to make Crystal feel special.'

'Tough gig.'

'I enjoyed it.'

Back then she'd been living in Cloud Cuckoo Land, absolutely sure that Steve was about to propose to her, and throwing herself into the spirit of the project had been easy. She had enjoyed liaising with Richard over the plan and ideas—loved the fact that the flat was to be a wedding surprise for his wife.

'These are the bathrooms.'

She pointed to the sketches and watched as he flipped through the pages.

'These are good,' he said.

His words vibrated with sincerity and she felt her lips curve up in a smile, his approval warming her chest.

'Thank you. The hammock bath is fab—big enough for two and perfect for the wet room.'

Imogen and Joe, lying naked in the bath... Just keep talking.

'I went for something more opulent for the second bathroom. All fluted pillars and marble. With a wooden hot tub, complete with a table in the middle for champagne.'

Her breath caught in her throat. *Imogen and Joe, playing naked footsie... Move on, move on.*

'And this was my *pièce de résistance*. I managed to source sheets threaded with twenty-two-carat gold for the bedroom.'

Oh, hell. Time to stop talking.

Closing the folder, she moved around the desk, willing her feet not to scurry back to the dratted chair.

'Anyway, Graham can take you through the rest of the project.'

'Not possible.'

'Why not?' Imogen studied Joe's bland expression and the penny clanged from on high. 'Have you *sacked* Graham?'

Joe shrugged. 'Graham no longer works for Langley.'

'But...you can't do that.' Outrage smacked her mouth open and self-disgust ran her veins. How could she possibly fantasise over a man who could be so callous?

He raised his eyebrows. 'I think you'll find I can.'

'Graham Forrester is one of the best interior designers in London. He's Peter's protégé. Why would you get rid of him?'

'That is not your concern.'

Her hands clenched into fists of self-annoyance. She'd let herself relax, been *pleased* that he had approved of her work. Taken her eye off the fact that he had the power to take Langley apart.

'Graham is my friend and my colleague. I went to his wedding last month. He *needs* this job. So of course it's my concern. And it's not only me who will say that. *Everyone* will be concerned. We're like a family here.'

'And that's a good thing, is it?' His tone was dry, yet the words held amusement.

Anger burned behind her ribs. 'Yes, it is.' A wave of her hand in the air emphasised her point. 'We're the interior design version of *The Waltons*. And sacking Graham is the equivalent of killing off John-Boy.'

His lips quirked upwards for a second and frustration stoked the flames of her ire. He could at least take her seriously.

'You *have* to reconsider.'

The smirk vanished as his lips thinned into a line. 'Not happening, Imogen.'

'Then I'll…'

'Then you'll what?' he asked. 'I think you may need to consider whether your loyalty lies with Graham Forrester or with Langley.'

'Is that a threat?'

'It's friendly advice.' Rubbing the back of his neck, he surveyed her for a moment. 'Peter described you as an important part of the company—if you walk out to support Graham, or undermine my position so I'm forced to let you go, the company will lose out.'

Dammit, she couldn't let Peter and Harry down—however much she wanted to tell him to shove his job up his backside. If she were still here maybe she could do something to prevent further disaster…though Lord knew what. Plus, on a practical note, she couldn't add unemployment to her list of woes.

'I'll stay. But for the record I totally disagree with you letting Graham go.'

'Your concerns are noted. Now, I need you to reinstate Langley's presence at the awards ceremony. We're going.'

'What?' Imogen stared at him. '*You* can't possibly mean to go.'

'Why not?'

'Because it will look odd for Graham not to be there. And you being there is hardly going to send out a good message; it's advertising that Langley is in trouble.'

He shook his head. 'It's *acknowledging* that Langley is in trouble and showing we're doing something about it. The head in the sand approach doesn't work.'

The words stung; she knew damn well from personal experience that the head in the sand approach didn't work. 'My head is quite firmly above ground, thank you.'

'Good. Then listen carefully. Whether you believe it or not, I am good at my job. Me being at these awards will re-assure everyone that Langley is back on its feet and ready to roll.' He leant back and smiled a smile utterly devoid of mirth. 'So we're going. You and me.'

Say what? Imogen stared at him, her chin aiming for her knees.

Joe nodded. 'You worked on the project, you liaised with the client—it makes sense.'

CHAPTER TWO

IMOGEN PACED HER best friend's lounge, striding over the brightly flowered rug, past the camp bed she was currently spending her nights on, to the big bay-fronted window and back again. 'Makes sense!' She narrowed her eyes at Mel and snorted. 'Makes sense, my…'

Mel shifted backwards on the overstuffed sofa, curled her legs under her and rummaged in her make-up bag. 'Imo, hun… You need to calm down. Joe is in charge and you have no choice.' Holding up two lipsticks, she tilted her blonde head to one side in consideration. 'It may even be fun.'

'Fun?' Imogen stared at her, a flicker of guilt igniting as her tummy did a loop-the-loop of anticipation. 'Fun to spend two hours working late with Joe and then going to an awards ceremony with Joe. That's not fun. It's purgatory.'

Mel raised her perfectly plucked eyebrows. 'Imo! Imo! Imo! Methinks you protest too much. Methinks you fancy the boxers off the man.'

There was that fire of guilt again. How could she be so shallow as to have the hots for such an arrogant, ruthless bastard?

'Youthinks wrong,' Imogen said flatly. 'And why are you looking at me like that?'

'A) Because you couldn't lie your way out of a paper bag and B) because I'm hoping you aren't planning to go to the awards ceremony looking like that.'

Imogen looked down at herself. 'What's wrong with

this? I wore this to a big client dinner with Steve a few months ago.'

'Exactly.'

'What is that supposed to mean?'

'Imogen, sweetie. That dress is *dull*. It's grey and it's shapeless and it's boring. It's how Steve liked you to dress because he was terrified you would run off—like Simone did.'

'That's not true. I chose this dress because…' She trailed off. 'Anyway, it will have to do. In fact with any luck no one will notice me. I mean, it's wrong to go to the awards ceremony when Graham did most of the work.'

Mel frowned. 'It sounds to me like you did your fair share. Plus, Graham can't go because he doesn't work for Langley any more. Plus, you said that Joe said he would still be credited.'

'Humph…' Damn man had an answer to everything.

'So you are going to this ceremony to display to the world that Langley is alive and flourishing. If you go dressed like that everyone will think Langley is on its last legs and you've bought a dress for the funeral.'

'Ha-ha!' Imogen exhaled a sigh as she contemplated her best friend's words. Mel knew all there was to know about clothes, and she had a point. 'OK. How about my little black dress with…?'

'It's more big black bin-bag, Imo. I have a way better idea. You can borrow one of *my* dresses.'

'Um…Mel. You know me. I really, really don't want to be…'

'The focus of attention? Yes, you do. And I've got the perfect outfit. Wait here a second.'

Imogen exhaled a puff of air—of course she wanted to do the right thing for Langley, but she knew Mel, and her friend's fashion taste was nothing like hers. Imogen's taste was more…

More what? In a moment of horror she realised she didn't know. In all her twenty-six years she'd always dressed to please others.

Eva Lorrimer had had very firm ideas about what a young girl should wear, and at her insistence Imogen had obediently donned plain long skirts and frilly tops. It had seemed the least she could do to make her mum a little bit happy. Plus, anything for a quiet life—right?

Then Steve… Well, was Mel right? *Had* she let him dictate what she wore? Steve had always said he hated women who flaunted or flirted when they were in a relationship. He had told her how Simone had always done exactly that. So she'd worked out what he approved of and what he liked and taken care to shop accordingly. Because it had made her happy to make him happy. Plus, anything for a quiet life—right?

Mel waltzed back into the room. 'What do you think?'

Imogen starcd at the dress Mel was holding up. If you could even call it a dress. For the life of her she couldn't work out how she would get into it, or where all the lacy frou-frou would go, or even how it could even be decent. The only thing that was clear was the colour—bright, vibrant and sassy.

'It's very…red.'

OK. It wasn't what *she* would choose. But if she had the choice between something in her wardrobe chosen by her mum or Steve and something chosen by Mel, right now she was going with Mel's choice.

'I'll wear it.'

Mel blinked. 'Really? I was prepared for battle.'

'Nope. No battle. Though you may have to help me work out how to put it on.'

'I'll do better than that—I'll lend you shoes and do your make-up as well.'

'Perfect. Thanks, sweetie. You're a star.'

Surprise mixed with a froth of anticipation as to what this New Imogen would look like.

An hour later and she knew.

Staring at the image that looked back at her from the mirror, she blinked, disbelief nearly making her rub her eyes before taking another gander. Her mother would keel over in a faint, Steve's lips would purse in disapproval— and Imogen didn't care. She looked....*visible*.

'You look gorgeous. You look hot. Joe McIntyre won't know what's hit him.'

'I'm not doing this for Joe.'

Liar, liar, pants most definitely on fire.

Squashing the voice, she gave her head a small shake. The butterflies currently completing an assault course in her tummy were nothing to do with Joe.

'I'm doing it for Langley.'

Mel dimpled at her. 'You keep telling yourself that, Imo,' she said soothingly. 'Have fun!'

Joe glanced around the office and gusted out a sigh. Not that there was anything to complain about in the surroundings; he'd sat in far worse than this mecca to interior design and it hadn't bothered him. The problem was that wherever he was sitting he'd never had this level of anticipation twisting his gut.

Irritation stamped on his chest. Anticipation had no place here. The awards ceremony would go better for Langley if Imogen Lorrimer were there. She had worked on the Richard Harvey project, knew many of the people who would be there, so it made sense for her to attend.

Joe snorted and picked up his cup of coffee. Listen to himself. Anyone would think he was justifying his decision because he had an ulterior motive in taking Imogen. When of course he didn't. Or that he was looking forward to taking Imogen. Which was ridiculous. The woman couldn't stand him, and he had the definitive suspicion that she was planning some sort of rearguard action against him in the hope that he'd change his mind about Graham Forrester.

She was probably running a Bring Back John-Boy Campaign.

Yet in the past two days he had more than once, more than twice, more than…too many times…found himself looking for Imogen or noticing her when there'd been no need to. Caught by the turn of her head or a waft of her delicate flowery perfume.

Exasperation surfaced again and he quelled it. Just because her appearance had somehow got under his guard it didn't mean there was a problem. He knew all too well the associated perils of letting personal issues into the boardroom. That was what his father had done and the result had been a spiral of disaster—a mess bequeathed to Joe to sort out.

So there was no problem. All he had to do was recall the grim horror of working out that his family firm was bankrupt and corrupt. Remember the faces of the people he'd been forced to let go, the clients whose money had been embezzled.

Enough. The lesson was learnt.

His computer pinged to indicate the arrival of an email; one glance at the screen and he groaned. *Another* email from Leila. Every instinct jumped up and down—he was no expert on the intricacies of relationships, but he was pretty damn sure it wasn't normal for an ex to suddenly surface after seven years, invite him to her wedding and then email him regularly to give him advice he hadn't asked for.

Resisting the urge to thump his head on the desk, he looked up as the door rebounded off its hinges and Imogen entered.

No. She didn't enter. It was more of a storm… A vivid

red tornado of gorgeous anger headed straight towards him and slammed her palms down on the glass desk-top.

'Something wrong?' Joe asked, trying and failing to ignore the sleek curtain of hair that fell straight and true round her face and down past her shoulders to the plunging V of her dress. Surely there was more V than material?

Continuing his look downward, he took in the cinched-in waist and the flouncy skirt that hit a good few centimetres above the knee. Her legs were endless, long and toned, and ended in a pair of sparkly peep-toe sandals.

Stop looking. Before you have a coronary.

He tugged his gaze upward to meet a fulminating pair of grey-blue eyes.

'Yes, there *is* something wrong.'

Her breath came in pants and Joe clenched his jaw, nearly crossing his eyes in an attempt to remain focused on her face.

'I know I shouldn't say anything. I know I shouldn't put my job on the line. But I've just come from seeing Harry and Peter in the hospital and they told me that you've got rid of Maisey in Accounts and Lucas in Admin. How could you? It's *wrong.*'

The fury vibrating in her voice touched a chord in him, aroused an answering anger to accompany the frustration and self-annoyance already brewing in his gut.

'No, Imogen, it isn't wrong. It's *unfortunate.* Streamlining Langley is the only way for the company to survive. I'd rather a few people suffer than the whole company collapse.'

She huffed out air and shook her head, black hair shimmering. 'But don't you care?' she asked. 'It's like these people are just numbers to you.'

The near distaste in her eyes made affront claw down his chest. 'I do my very best to minimise the number of people I let go and I certainly don't take any pleasure in it.'

She stood back from the desk and slammed her hands on her hips. 'You don't seem to feel any pain either.'

Her words made him pause; sudden discomfort jabbed his nerves. It was an unease he dismissed; feeling pain sucked, and it didn't change a damn thing. This he knew. Hell, he had the whole wardrobe to prove it. So if he'd hardened himself it was a *good* thing—a business decision that made him better at his job.

Aware of curiosity dancing with anger across Imogen's delicate features, he shrugged. 'Me sitting around crying into my coffee isn't going to enable me to make sensible executive decisions. I can't let sentiment interfere with my job.'

'But what if your executive choices hurt someone else?'

'I don't make choices to hurt people.'

'That doesn't mean they don't *get* hurt. Look at Graham. I happen to know he has a large mortgage, his wife is pregnant, and now you've made the choice to snatch his job from under his feet. Doesn't that bother you?'

'No.' To his further exasperation he appeared to be speaking through clenched teeth. 'The bottom line is I do the best for the company as whole. Overall, people benefit.'

'Have you ever watched *Star Trek*?'

Star Trek? Joe blinked. 'Yes, I have. My sisters are avid fans.' Repeats of the show had been a godsend in the devastating months after their parents' death; Tammy and Holly had spent hours glued to the screen. Blocking out impossible reality with impossible fiction.

'Joe? Are you listening to me?'

'For now. But only because I am fascinated to see what pointy-eared aliens and transporters have to do with anything?'

'You know how it works—they *say* they believe in sacrificing the few for the many. But they don't really mean it—somehow in real life they end up knowing that it's wrong and they go back to rescue one person, risking everyone, and everything is OK.'

Was she for real? 'The fatal flaw in your reasoning is right there. *Star Trek* isn't real life. It's *fiction*.'

'I get that—but the principle is sound.'

'No. The principle sucks. If you run around trying to please everyone, refusing to make tough choices, then I can tell you exactly what happens. Everyone suffers.' He'd got another wardrobe to prove *that*. 'In real life Kirk would go down, and so would the *Enterprise*.'

'That is so...'

'Realistic?'

'Cynical,' she snapped. 'I don't understand why you can't see reason. The main reason Langley is in difficulties is because of Harry's ill health. He's the one who understands finance. Peter doesn't. Once Harry's on his feet everything will go back to normal. Surely you should be taking that into consideration? Trying to think of some way to salvage everyone's jobs.'

The jut of her chin, the flash of her eyes indicated how serious she was, and although he had no doubt his decisions were correct, it occurred to him that it was a long, long time since anyone had questioned him, let alone locked phasers with him. Apart from his sisters, anyway...

It was kind of...exhilarating.

Even more worrying, his chest had warmed with admiration: Imogen was speaking out for others with a passion that made him think of a completely different type of passion. His fingers itched with the desire to bury themselves in the gloss of her dark hair and angle her face so that he could kiss her into his way of thinking.

For the love of Mike... This was so off the business plan he might as well file for bankruptcy right now.

Curving his fingers firmly round the edge of his desk, he adhered his feet to the plush carpet and forced calm to his vocal cords. 'My job is to make sure that Harry has a viable company to come back to. I am not out to destroy Langley. That's not how I operate.'

'That's not what your reputation says.'

Disbelief clouded her blue eyes with grey and the disdain in her expression caused renewed affront to band round his chest.

'Imogen, there are some companies that even I can't salvage. But if you study my track record you will see that most of the companies I go to sort out get sorted out. Not shut down. My reputation is that I'm tough. I'll make the unpopular decisions no one wants to make because they let sentiment and friendship cloud their perspective. I don't.'

A small frown creased her brow. 'So you're telling me you're cold and heartless but you get results?'

'Yes. Peter and Harry wouldn't be able to let Graham go. I can. They, you and Captain Kirk may not like my methods, but I *will* save Langley.'

Annoyance at the whole conversation hit him—talk about getting overheated. Who did he think he was? The corporate version of the Lone Ranger? He'd spent the better part of the past half an hour justifying his actions, and he was damned if he knew why. Anyone would think he *cared* about her opinion of him.

'Now, can you please sit down so we can get some work done?'

At least that way the bottom half of her would be obscured from sight and his blood pressure would stay on the chart.

Imogen dropped down onto the chair. Joe's words were ringing in her head—and there was no doubting his sincerity. So, whilst she saw him as the villain of the piece he saw himself as the hero.

She chewed her bottom lip—was there any chance that

he was right? Then she remembered Harry Langley's pale face, blending in with the colour of his hospital pillow. His slurred voice shaking with impotent anger as he vowed to put things right.

She thought of the size of Graham's mortgage, his pride that his wife could be a stay-at-home mum if she wanted… of Maisey's tears when she'd phoned her on the way here from the hospital…

All those people suffering because of the man sitting opposite her.

Yet a worm of doubt wriggled into her psyche. His deep voice had been genuine when he'd spoken of the necessity of his cuts, the bigger picture, his desire to save Langley.

But, hell, that didn't mean she had to *like* him. Nonetheless…

'Imogen.'

His impatient growl broke into her reverie.

'Did you hear a word I said?'

'Sorry. I was thinking it must be hard to always be seen as the villain,' she replied.

'Doesn't bother me.' A quizzical curve tilted his lip. 'You starting to feel sorry for me now?'

'Of course not.'

The idea was laughable; Joe McIntyre didn't need sympathy. He needed to be shaken into common sense and out of her dreams.

'Well, tonight we need to at least call a truce. You acting as though I am some sort of corporate monster will do more damage to Langley than I can. So you need to play nice.'

Wrinkling her nose in a way that she could only hope indicated distaste, she nodded. Instinct told her a truce with this man would be dangerous, but he was right: they could hardly attend the award ceremony sparring with each other.

'As long as you know I am playing. As in pretending.'

'Don't worry,' he said, his voice so dry it was practically parched. 'Message received, loud and clear. The truce is temporary. Now, can we get on with it? I've ordered a taxi to take us to the hotel at seven, and I want to go through Peter's client list with you before then.'

An hour later Imogen put her pen down. 'I think that's it,' she said.

Flexing her shoulders, she looked across at him. Big mistake. Because now she couldn't help but let her gaze linger on the breadth of his chest under the snowy-white dress shirt and the tantalising hint of bare skin on show where he hadn't bothered doing up the top buttons.

Looking up, she caught a sudden predatory light in his brown eyes. A light that was extinguished almost before she could be sure it had been there, but yet sent a shiver through her body.

'You've done a great job.' Pulling at the sheaf of paper she'd scribbled on, he glanced down at her notes.

'Thank you. I'll type those up for you first thing tomorrow. The notes indicate what each project was, how many times they've used us, and a few personal bits about them. Not *personal* personal, but...'

Babble-babble-babble. One probably imagined look and she'd dissolved into gibberish.

'Things that show I'm not delivering the same spiel to each client,' he said. 'Exactly what I need.'

He stared down at the paper and cleared his throat, as if searching for something else to say. Could he be feeling the same shimmer of tension she was?

'So...according to this, you've done a lot of actual design work.'

'Er...yes... I told you I help out.'

'I didn't realise how much. Why haven't you put all the project work you've done on your CV? Or, for that mat-

ter, why haven't you put things on a more formal footing?
I'm sure Peter would agree to sponsor you so you could
go to college.'

'That's not the way I want my career to go.'

It was a decision made long ago. What she prized above
all else was security—a job she enjoyed, but not one that
would rule her life. She'd seen first-hand the disastrous
consequences of a job that became an obsession, and she
wasn't going there.

'Why not? You've got real talent and great client liaison
skills. Everyone I've spoken to so far has only had good
things to say about you—even Mike Anderson.' He nodded at the paper. 'From everything you've written there,
it seems clear they'll all be the same.'

Imogen couldn't help the smile that curved her lips as
she savoured his words, absorbed them into her very being.
'Everyone? Even Mike Anderson? For real?'

'For real.'

He smiled back and, dear Lord above, what a smile it
was. Instinct told her it rarely saw the light of day—and
what a good thing *that* was for the female population. Because it was the genuine make-your-knees-go-weak article.

The moment stretched, the atmosphere thickening
around them, blanketing them...

'So what do you think?' Joe asked.

'About what?' *Focus, Imo.*

'Changing career? Within Langley if it remains a viable option. Or elsewhere.'

Forcing herself to truly concentrate on his question,
she let the idea take hold. New Imogen Lorrimer—wearer
of red dresses and trainee interior designer. *Yeah, right.*
There was no version of Imogen who would leap out of
her comfort zone like that.

And she was fine with that. More than fine. The whole
point of a comfort zone was that it was *comfortable.*

'Not for me, thank you. I'm very happy as I am.'

End of discussion; there was no need for this absurd urge to justify herself.

Glancing at her watch, she rose to her feet and pushed the chair backwards. 'Look at the time. I need to get ready before the taxi gets here.'

An audible hitch of breath was her only answer, and she looked up from her watch to see dark brown eyes raking over her. Without her permission her body heated up further—a low, warm glow in her tummy to accompany the inexplicable feeling of disappointment at a decision she knew to be right.

'You look pretty ready to me,' he drawled.

Was he flirting with her? Was she dreaming?

An unfamiliar spark, no doubt ignited by the sheer effrontery of the dress, lit up a synapse in her brain. Hooking a lock of hair behind her ear, she fought the urge to flutter her eyelashes.

'Is that a compliment?'

'If you want.'

There was that look again—and this time she surely wasn't imagining the smoulder. Even if she had no idea how to interpret it.

'It's also an observation.'

As he rose to his feet and picked up a black tie from the back of his chair Imogen gulped. Six foot plus of lean, honed muscle.

'So,' he continued, 'seeing as you had a bathroom break a quarter of an hour ago, my guess is that you're avoiding this discussion. True or false?'

Mesmerised, she watched his strong fingers deftly pull the tie round his neck before he turned and picked his jacket up.

'False…' she managed.

Right now she needed to get away from the pheromone onslaught—she *wasn't* avoiding the discussion. Much…

'If you say so.' Slinging the jacket over his shoulder, he headed towards her. 'And, Imogen? One more thing?'

'Yes?'

Oh, hell—he was getting closer. Why weren't her feet moving? Heading towards the door and the waiting taxi? Instead her ridiculous heels appeared superglued to the carpet as her heart pounded in her ribcage. A hint of his earthy scent tickled her nostrils, and still her stupid feet wouldn't obey her brain's commands.

His body was so warm…his eyes held hers in thrall. Hardly able to breathe, she clocked his hand rising, and as he touched her lower lip heat shot through her body.

A shadow fleeted across his face and he stepped backwards, his arm dropping to his side.

'Don't forget to smile,' he said.

CHAPTER THREE

IMOGEN DUCKED INTO a corner of the crowded room, needing a moment to breathe after an hour of smiling, socialising and being visible. The set-up was gorgeous—worthy of the five-star hotel where the event was being held. Glorious flower arrangements abounded, in varying shades of pink to fuchsia, layered with dark green foliage. Chandeliers glinted and black-suited waiters with pink ties appeared as if by magic with trays of canapés or a choice of pink champagne and sparkling grapefruit juice.

Surreptitiously she slipped one foot out of a peep-toe, six-inch heeled shoe. Flexing it with relief, she let her gaze unerringly sift through the crowds of beautiful professionals, slip over the fabulously decorated room, heady with the fragrance of the magnificent spring flower centrepieces that adorned each table, and found the tall figure of Joe McIntyre.

If it really was Joe and not some sort of clone.

Because ever since they'd walked through the imposing doors of the hotel Joe had undergone some sort of transformation. It had been goodbye to her taxi companion, Mr Dark and Brooding, and hello Mr Suave as he networked the room, all professional charm and bonhomie, not a single frown in sight.

But worst of all had been his closeness, the small touches as he'd propelled her from person to person, dispensing confidence in Langley and an insider knowledge of interior design that was impressive.

Little surprise that he had gathered a gang of female groupies who were now hanging on to his every word adoringly.

'What's wrong, Imo? That's a pretty hefty scowl. Contemplating the man who'll bring Langley down?'

Shoving her foot back into her shoe, Imogen turned and plastered her best fake smile to her face. *Great!* The man she'd been avoiding all night: head of IMID, Langley's chief competitor.

'Evening, Ivan. How are you?'

'I'm fine. Bursting with health. Which is more than can be said for poor old Harry and Peter. How *are* they?'

Imogen's skin crawled as Ivan Moreton's grey eyes slid over her with almost reptilian interest. Ivan had no principles or scruples, and had engaged in so many underhand schemes to undercut and undermine Langley that she'd lost count.

His methods were unscrupulous, but legal. So to hear him stand there, full of spuriously concerned queries as to Peter and Harry made her blood sizzle. Especially when he looked as though he could barely stop himself from rubbing his hands together in glee.

'Firmly on the road to recovery, thank you, Ivan. I'll be sure to tell them you were asking as a further incentive to get them back into the office.'

To wipe that smug smirk off your face.

'If, of course, they have an office to return to,' Ivan said, with a wave in Joe's direction. 'Could be that Mr McIntyre will have sold it off.'

'Joe wouldn't do that.' Imogen clamped her lips together; had there been a note of *hero-worship* in her voice? Please, no...

Ivan's eyebrows rose. 'Don't be deceived by those rugged looks, Imo. Joe McIntyre will do what it takes. Though even *he* makes mistakes. You see, Graham Forrester now works for me—and he's one very angry designer. Imagine offering him a salary cut. Graham said he's never been so insulted in his life.'

Imogen blinked as she tried to process that little snippet of information.

True, Graham couldn't afford a salary cut—but Peter had given Graham his first break, shown faith in him, showered him in pay rises. Shouldn't loyalty count for something? At least enough for Graham not to feel insulted and maybe not go straight to Langley's biggest competitor?

Or perhaps everyone else in the world got it except her? Were all capable of making executive decisions without sentiment?

Imogen took a step backwards, uncomfortably aware that whilst she had been thinking Ivan had stepped straight into her personal space. Enough so that now the coolness of the wall touched the bare skin on her back. If he came any closer, so help her, she'd either punch him on the nose or—better yet—take a step forward and pinion him with her heel.

'Joe won't be selling off the offices because there will be no need to,' she stated. 'Langley is still alive and kicking—and hopefully we'll be kicking *your* sorry behind for a long time to come.'

'Dream on, Imo. But I like your style.'

His cigarette-infused breath, tinted with alcohol, hit her cheek and she turned her face away.

'When I buy Langley out I'll put in a special bid for you.'

Ewwww. No one would thank her for creating a scene, but enough was enough. Imogen lifted her foot.

'Sounds like you need to be talking to *me*, Ivan.'

Imogen expelled a sigh of relief as she heard Joe's drawl, and then she looked up and saw the glint of anger in his eyes. She spotted the set jaw and something thrilled inside her.

Get some perspective, Imo.

For a start she was quite capable of looking after herself, and had had a perfectly good self-defence plan. Plus, Ivan was planning a Langley buy-out—*that* was what she needed to be thinking about. Instead of going all gooey because Joe was being protective.

The interior designer spun round and held his hand out. 'Joe. My friend. How are you doing? Imogen and I were just—'

'I can see exactly what *you* were just doing, Ivan, and I'd appreciate it if *you* didn't do it again.'

Ivan's grey eyes flicked from Imogen to Joe. 'You calling dibs, my friend?'

Imogen gave a small gasp. *Please let it have sounded like outrage, not hope.*

'No.' Joe stepped forward, his lips curling in a smile that held no mirth whatsoever. 'But if you want to talk about Langley deal with me. Not anyone else.'

The interior designer gave a toss of his dyed blond hair and stepped backwards. 'I'll do that. I'll get my PA to call your PA and set something up. I'm *very* interested in a buy-out.'

With that he turned and walked away.

'You OK?'

'I'm fine.' Imogen waved away his look of concern. 'Ivan Moreton is a sleazebag, and if you hadn't turned up he'd have been on his way to A&E with a stiletto through his foot.'

This time Joe's smile was real, and Imogen's stomach rollercoastered, all focus leaving the building.

'It's time for the presentations,' Joe said.

So not the moment to discuss the impossibility of an

IMID buy-out; plus, it would best to do that out of Ivan's range.

'I'll text Richard.'

'Why? What happened to the romantic Parisian get-away?'

'Nothing. He wants to show his support so I've arranged for him to be video conferenced in.'

'Great idea? Yours?'

There was that warmth again at his words... She needed to stop being so damn needy of people's approval. Just because praise had been a rarity in her childhood it didn't mean she had to overreact to it.

'Thanks,' she said, as coolly as she could, and quickly bent over her phone to hide the flush of pleasure that touched her cheeks.

A minute later her phone vibrated and she glanced down at it and blinked. Read the words again and gave a small whoop under her breath.

'Good news?'

'Yup. Look. That's Richard. He and Crystal have bought a place in Paris and they want us to pitch for the job of doing it up.' She continued reading. 'He wants us—you and me—to meet him in Paris on Friday.'

Joe and Imogen off to Paris. Be still her beating heart.

Polite applause broke out around them as the first speaker mounted the podium.

'That's excellent news. You'd better book some tickets on the Eurostar, then.'

Was that all he had to say? Was she the only one all of a flutter here? Of course she was. After all she was the one with the dream problem.

Turning away from him, Imogen stared resolutely at the speaker and tried to focus on his words. For the rest of the evening she would focus on interior design. *Not* on the man sitting beside her.

* * *

'Paris?' A pyjama-clad Mel stared at her in sheer disbelief. 'You are going to *Paris* with Joe McIntyre?'

'Yes.' Imogen snuggled back on the sofa and cradled her mug of hot chocolate. 'Ironic, really. I practically begged Steve to take me there, but he wouldn't. Said it held too many memories of Simone.'

She took a gulp of hot chocolate and pushed away memories of just how much time she had spent choosing a cruise that didn't contain any locations holding any memories of Simone. There was *real* irony for you. Because right this minute now Steve and Simone were on that luxury cruise, paid for with *her* hard-earned money, creating new memories.

'I'd rather go with someone hot like Joe than Steve,' Mel said musingly.

'That's plain shallow,' Imogen said. 'Heat level isn't everything in a man, you know. There are other attributes that are way more important.'

The sort of traits *she* looked for in a partner: kindness, stability, loyalty, security. More irony—how had she misjudged Steve so badly?

Mel shook her head, blonde curls bobbing. 'Not if you're on a jaunt to Paris.'

'It's not a *jaunt*. It's a business trip. We're not even staying overnight. Joe is out of the office tomorrow, I'm meeting him at St Pancras Station on Friday late morning, then we're coming back straight after our meeting.'

'*Tchah!* Why don't you book the wrong tickets by "mistake"? Then you could end up staying in a romantic hotel and...'

'I'd end up fired.'

Though for one stupid, insane moment her imagination had leapt in... She could see the hotel silhouetted on the Parisian horizon...

Imogen drained her mug. 'I'm for bed.'

'Oh!' Mel gave a gasp. 'I was so gobsmacked by Paris I forgot to tell you. Your mum called—she said it was urgent. Not *that* sort of urgent,' she added hastily, seeing panic grip her friend as she imagined the worst. 'But she did say you needed to ring her back, no matter what time it was.'

Imogen sighed. This wasn't what she needed right now, but Eva Lorrimer hated being made to wait.

Grabbing her mobile phone from the floor, she dialled her mother. 'Hey, Mum. It's me.'

'Finally.'

'Sorry. The awards ceremony finished late.'

'I only hope you going means you'll keep your job, Imogen. You make sure you impress Joe McIntyre. *Somehow.* Good PAs are two a penny, and now you've managed to lose Steve you will need to support yourself and—'

'Mum. Mel said it was urgent?' Surely reciting all Imogen's shortcomings couldn't be classed as imperative at past midnight. Even by Eva's standards.

'It *is* urgent. Steve has proposed to Simone on that cruise he's taken her on. They're getting married.'

Breath whooshed out of her lungs; surely this was some sort of joke. 'How do you know?'

'Clarissa rang me with the news.'

Better and better—Imogen bit back a groan. Clarissa was Steve's mother and one of Eva's old schoolfriends. If you could call her a friend. No doubt she had rung up to gloat.

'It's all over social media too,' Eva continued. 'Simone even put out a message thanking you for providing such a wonderful setting.'

Excellent. Now she'd be a laughing stock to everyone who knew her. Humiliation swept over her in a wave of heat that made her skin clammy.

Eva gusted out a sigh. 'That could have been *you* if you'd played your cards right. *You* could have a man to rely on—a man to support you and keep you secure. You should have done more to keep him, Imogen.'

Like what? She'd done everything she could think of to make Steve happy. Obviously she'd failed. Big-time. Steve himself had told her that she wasn't enough for him.

But instead of the usual self-criticism a sudden spark of anger ignited in the pit of her stomach. The bastard had actually proposed to another woman on the cruise *she* had paid for using her hard-earned savings. What would he do next? Send her the bill for the engagement ring?

'Actually, Mum, maybe I'm better off without him.'

'Steve was the best thing that ever happened to you, Imogen. Yes, I'd have preferred a fast-track banking career for you, but the next best thing would have been marrying a man with one...'

As Eva's voice droned on Imogen ground her molars and waited for the right moment to intercede.

'Mum. I understand how you feel.' That her daughter had let her down yet again. 'But I'm exhausted. We'll talk more tomorrow.'

Imogen disconnected the call and resisted the urge to bang her head against the wall.

Joe glanced at his watch, and then around the busy Victorian-style St Pancras station. Men and women tapped onto tablets, sipped at coffee or shopped in the boutiques. But there was no sign of Imogen. Where the hell *was* she?

Ah. There she was: striding across the crowded lounge, briefcase in one hand, cup of coffee in the other, dove-grey trouser suit, hair tugged up into a simple ponytail.

'Sorry I'm late,' she stated as she came to a halt next to him.

Joe frowned; her tone indicated not so much as a hint

of sincerity. In fact it pretty much dared him to comment. Imogen seemed… He glanced at her coffee cup as she tugged the lid off. Full. Yet she seemed wired—there was a pent-up energy in the tapping of her foot, an unnecessary force as she dropped her briefcase onto a chair.

'No problem. We've still got three minutes till we need to board.'

'Good.' She took a gulp of coffee. 'Then I have time to grab a *pain au chocolat*. Get myself in the mood.'

Because what she *really* needed right now was sugar on top of caffeine.

Joe swallowed the words. As a man who had brought up twin sisters, he knew exactly when it was best to keep his opinions to himself.

Clearly something had happened in the day and a half since he'd last seen her. But equally clearly Imogen's private life was nothing to do with him.

So he was *not* going to ask her what was wrong; he was going to stick to business.

Focusing on her back, he followed Imogen through the departure lounge to the ticket barriers, where they were smiled through by a svelte member of Eurostar staff. They moved along the bustling platform and onto the train.

He waited until she'd tucked her briefcase next to her and sat down opposite him, her eyes still snapping out that 'don't mess with me' vibe.

'So, could you brief me on our meeting with Richard Harvey? Has he told you anything about the project at all?'

'Nope. All I know is that it's a place in Paris. He's also said he's giving Graham a chance to pitch for it as well, because it seems only fair.' She frowned. 'My guess is Graham got on the phone and guilted him into it with a sob story about how you had brutally thrown him out.'

Joe raised his eyebrows. 'I thought you agreed with him?'

'I do, but…' Her slim shoulders lifted in a shrug and her

eyes sparked. 'If you must know Graham rang me yesterday, and he was really vindictive. Not only about you but about Peter too—and that's not fair. It's not as though *Peter* sacked him. And even *you* offered him a reduced salary.'

'You told me yourself about his mortgage and his wife; you can't blame him for accepting a more lucrative offer and now being loyal to Ivan.'

'I can blame whoever I like for whatever I like.'

Joe blinked at the sheer vehemence of her tone.

'Anyway,' she went on, 'Ivan is an out-and-out toad.' The description brought a small quirk to his lips until she said, 'And you aren't going to let him buy out Langley, are you?'

Damn. He'd hoped she'd forgotten that, but maybe this was why she was on the warpath.

'That's not something I can discuss with you.'

'But…you can't be seriously thinking about it. It would kill Harry off.'

'If a buy-out is offered I have to consider it.'

She opened her mouth as if to argue but inhaled deeply instead. 'OK. Fine. Clearly you don't have a better nature to appeal to, so tell me what I can do to help avert a buy-out.' Her fingers encircled the plastic table's edge and her nose wrinkled in distaste. 'Because I'd rather starve in a ditch than work for Ivan.'

He could hardly blame her; a sudden wave of aversion washed over him at the very thought. Irritation with himself clenched his jaw. If the buy-out was best for Langley that was the road he'd take. Full stop.

'That will be your choice. My decision will be based on what's best for Langley as a business.'

Eyes narrowed, she tapped a foot on the carriage floor. 'If we win this Paris project will that make Langley safe from Ivan?'

'Depends on the full extent of the project. But, yes, it would help.'

'So you're fully on board with going all out to win it? You haven't already decided that the buy-out is the way to go?'

Joe resisted the urge to roll his eyes. Why didn't she get that the decision was nothing to do with her?

'Can we drop the subject of the buy-out and concentrate on winning the Richard Harvey project? What else can you tell me about Richard and this meeting that will help our pitch? Is he bringing wife number seven?'

'Yes. I've told you her name is Crystal—and obviously don't make a big deal of her being number seven.'

Joe snorted. 'Well, gee, Imogen—thanks for the advice. *My* plan was to ask for a rundown of each and every wife along with a view of the wedding albums.' He gusted out a sigh. 'I'll happily avoid the entire topic of marriage.'

Imogen shook her head. 'Richard likes talking about marriage. Like I said, he's incurably romantic—which I suppose is why he's bought a place in Paris. As far as he is concerned he has finally fulfilled his dream—he's found The One. So probably best *not* to share your "dreams should be abandoned" theory.' Her eyes narrowed. 'Even if I'm beginning to wonder if you're right.'

'Me? Right? Wonders will never cease.' Curiosity won out over common sense. 'What brought that on?'

Opening her mouth as if to answer, her gaze skittered away as she clearly thought better of it and shook her head. 'You know, the daft dreams we have when we are young. I once thought I'd become an artist—had some stupid vision of myself in smock and beret, sketching on the streets of Paris or attending the Royal Academy, studying the masters in Italy, exhibiting in Rome—' She broke off. 'Absurd.'

Yet the look in her eyes, the vibrant depth of her tone, showed him that the dream had been real.

Lord knew he could empathise with giving up a dream. For a second he was transported back to a time when the world had truly been his oyster. He could smell the sea spray, taste the tang of salt in his mouth, feel the thump of exhilaration as he rode a wave. The incredible freedom, the knowledge that he would win the championships, would get sponsored, would…

Would end up dealing with bereavement, loss and responsibility.

Whoa. There was no point going there, and guilt pronged his chest because he had. The decisions he had made back then had been the right ones and he had no regrets about making them. His sisters had needed him and nothing else had mattered. Then or now.

Shaking off the past, Joe focused on Imogen—on the dark tendrils of hair that had escaped her ponytail and now framed her oval face. On the blue-grey of her eyes, the straight, pert nose and lush, full lips.

'So what happened to those dreams?' he asked quietly. Had they crashed and burned like his?

Picking up her cup, she rested her gaze on his mouth. 'Common sense prevailed. Bills need to be paid…security needs to be ensured. Starving in a garret sounds very romantic, but in real life I like my food too much. So I ended up opting for a PA role. I'm more than happy with that.'

Coffee splashed onto the table as she thunked the cup down, the black droplets pooling on the plastic. Instantly she grabbed a napkin to absorb the liquid.

For a moment Joe was tempted to argue. She didn't look that happy to him. But that really was nothing to do with him.

'Good,' he said instead. 'If you think of anything else to do with Richard let me know. Anything that could give us the edge.'

'I can tell you more about him, if that would help. He's

very generous—almost too much so. He likes throwing his money around and it can come across as a bit in your face, or as if he's showing off. But it's not like that. I think he thinks he has to buy friendship. Reading between the lines, I think he had a pretty rotten childhood. So, yes, he's generous. On the flip side of that he *does* have a bit of a chip on his shoulder, and that can make him take offence easily. He's also a touch eccentric—there's a story about how he actually locked three rival advertising executives in a room together and gave them an hour to come up with a snappy slogan. Said he was fed up with long meetings and endless presentations and statistics.'

Joe drummed his fingers on the table. Clearly the two of them had got on—that would be an advantage. What else could they use?

'Have you been to Paris before?' he asked.

'Nope.'

'Has Graham?'

A frown creased her forehead. 'I'm not sure… Oh, yes, actually he has.' An indecipherable expression flitted across her features. 'He proposed to his wife atop the Eiffel Tower.'

Was it his imagination or was there a quiver of bitterness in her voice?

'Is that the sort of thing that will impress Richard Harvey?'

'Yes, but I don't think there's much we can do about that. Unless, of course, you…?'

'No. I've never proposed to anyone in Paris.'

For a second the memory of his one and only proposal entered his head and he couldn't prevent the bone-deep shudder that went through him. The humiliation of being on bended knee, Leila's look of sheer horror, the violin faltering to a stop in the background… *Whoa. Not going there.*

'But,' he said. 'I *do* think we need to do something to impress Richard. Something that will appeal to his eccentricity more than a lengthy proposal.'

'Such as…?'

'What time are we meeting him?'

'Six p.m.'

Joe looked at his watch. 'So we'll have a few hours when we get there. Let's go to Montmartre.'

Confusion furrowed her brow further. 'Why?'

'Because it will appeal to Richard's sense of the romantic as well. We can tell him we've soaked in the ambience, walked the streets of a place where great art has flourished. And…' He shrugged. 'For a few hours you can live your dream.'

The words sounded way too significant.

'I'll even buy you a beret.'

Live your dream.

Imogen followed Joe across the bustling train station, revelling in the sound of French being spoken around her and inhaling the aroma of croissants and baguettes that was being emitted from patisseries and *boulangeries*. No matter what, she wasn't going to let Steve's actions spoil the next few hours and her chance to see a bit of Paris.

The chance to *live her dream.*

Oh, God. Her eyes snagged on the breadth of Joe's back as he strode through the crowds He had no idea what he was suggesting; if she lived her X-rated dreams she'd be arrested.

Her head whirled as a flutter of nerves rippled her tummy, her thoughts running amok as they made their way through the bustle of the Métro.

Joe hadn't so much as flirted with her, and yet…there was something. Something in the way his eyes rested on her that sent a shiver through her. Something…just something that was making her overheated imagination leap and soar.

Something that was mixing with the anger at Steve that continued to burn inside her...something that was making her want to be different.

Deliberately, she reached up and pulled the pins out of her hair, ran her fingers through it so that it rippled free to her shoulders. She felt Joe stiffen by her side, saw his hand clench around his broad thigh. Astounded by her own daring she oh, so casually allowed her leg to brush against his, revelling in the solid muscle. Then surprise shot out a tendril as a tremor ran through his body.

What if...what if Joe was *attracted* to her? Even a little bit?

Stop it, Imogen.

That way lay madness. Joe McIntyre was a ruthless businessman and her temporary boss. Moreover he was responsible for sacking her friends and colleagues. Worst of all he was considering a buy-out by Ivan Moreton. Joe McIntyre was the enemy, and she'd do well to remember it.

'Our stop,' he said.

They emerged into the late summer sunshine and Imogen tipped her face up and let the rays warm her. It was glorious, and the feel of the cobblestones through her sensible flat navy pumps seemed to send Parisian history straight to her very soul.

Glancing up at Joe, she wondered if the surroundings were affecting him. Somehow he looked different—his mouth a touch less grim, his whole body more relaxed. His sleeves were rolled up and her eyes snagged on his forearms and she gulped. A sudden crazy urge to capture his toned muscular glory on canvas touched her. Montmartre—home to so many artistic greats—must be getting to her.

'OK. Where first?' Joe asked.

She swivelled to look at the imposing outline of the Sacré Coeur, looming on the Paris skyline in its sugar-white beauty. Considered the cemetery where so many artists were buried. Then there were all the shops, the *tabacs*, the boutiques, the Moulin Rouge, the…'

Yet right now all she could focus on was Joe.

Think, Imogen. Focus.

'Let's get lost in the alleyways—randomly explore. And I've heard of a wonderful fabric shop that is here some-where—maybe we'll find that. Richard would appreci-ate that. If we can I'd love to go the Sacré Coeur as well.'

'Sounds like a plan,' he said as he tugged his dark blue tie off and shoved it into his jacket pocket, then freed the top button of his shirt.

To reveal the bronzed column of his throat.

Licking suddenly parched lips, Imogen knew they had to get moving before she threw her arms around him and pressed her lips to the warmth of his skin. Yet the danger-ous attraction tilted through her, urging her to throw cau-tion to the wind. Be shocking, be different.

Make a total arse of herself.

Any minute now Joe was going to sense how she was feeling, see her quiver with desire, and then mortification would consume her. She'd made enough of a fool of her-self over Steve to last a lifetime.

'This way,' she said brightly, and plunged into an al-leyway, barely aware of the bright colours and bustling crowds.

The key was to keep talking until she'd got her head on straight. Dredging her brain for any information she had on Montmartre, she kept up a flow of conversation. 'Such an amazing place… Did you know there are so many art-ists who lived and worked and are buried here…? Not only artists… Have you heard of Dalida…? Iconic singer…but so tragic… Amazing how many artists are tragic, really…

My father was a big fan of Degas…and Zola… Isn't it so wonderful to be here…? I really feel we are getting the real Montmartre vibes—'

'Imogen.' Joe's deep voice broke into her words. 'Are you OK?'

'Of course. I'm just making conversation.'

'I think you'll find you're making a monologue,' he said.

'Yes, well. It's so super…'

Super? Really, Imogen?

'To be here. We're getting the real Montmartre vibes. I guess I'm a little overexcited.'

'Hardly surprising, really,' he said, and now his rich voice was laced with amusement. 'This is definitely the essence of Montmartre, all right.'

'Huh…?'

Foreboding raised the hair on her arms as she looked round. Oh, crap. Crap. Crappity-crap. Garish neon signs vied with more artistic depictions, but it was abundantly clear exactly where they were.

The entire street was filled with sex shops.

CHAPTER FOUR

NOW WHAT?

Soon enough she'd be able to boil a kettle on her cheeks—not that a kettle would be easy to come by in a sex shop.

This was the stuff of nightmares; they couldn't just have found a street full of museums, could they? Or artists sketching people? Oh, no! Or this couldn't have happened when she was with Mel. Or on her own. With *anyone* other than Joe McIntyre.

Her nerves jangled with irritation as he looked round with an interest he didn't even bother to hide before turning his gaze back on her.

Damn the blush that still burnt her cheeks, and damn her prudish upbringing that had left her believing that sex was something dangerous.

Not that she blamed her mother; Eva Lorrimer had fallen prey to lust and then fallen pregnant—an event that had thoroughly derailed her life. She'd ended up married to a penniless artist she'd had nothing in common with—a man she'd considered beneath her socially and intellectually whom she had never forgiven. Any more than she'd forgiven herself.

Little wonder she'd drummed into Imogen the need never to let herself be dazzled by looks or taken in by 'the physical side of things'. Her mother would have hustled her out with here, hands over her eyes. But Eva wasn't here.

Plus it was ridiculous, really—this insane feeling of awkwardness. Looking round, it was more than clear to her that no one else was embarrassed. Couples strolled with their arms wrapped round each other's waists, stopping to look into windows. A group of women whose pink bunny rabbit outfits indicated that they were without doubt on a hen party laughed raucously, the noise carrying on the afternoon air. Chic single women, debonair single men, groups of chatting tourists all smiled, sauntered on completely at ease. Whereas *she* stood here like some prim and proper maiden from Victorian times.

The amused look that Joe gave her didn't help one bit, ruffling her self-annoyance into a desire to…to…to what? Kick him. *Very mature, Imo.*

'I take it you didn't plan on visiting this particular bit of the district.'

'No.'

'Come on, then. I think if we double back down that alleyway there we should hit a *different* type of shop and then it shouldn't be difficult to find the Sacré Coeur.'

Imogen hauled in a breath and stiffened her spine. 'Now that we're here I think we should check one out.'

Joe's brown eyes glittered with surprise and something else—perhaps a flash of discomfort. *Ha!* Maybe he wasn't as man-of-the-world as he appeared to be.

'You sure?'

Double *ha*! She was right. His body was ever so slightly rigid and his voice had a hint of clenched jaw and gritted teeth about it.

So now she knew that he was feeling awkward too, the sensible thing to do would be to get the hell off this street. *Sensible.*

The word grated on her soul.

She was sick of being sensible. She had oh, so sensibly picked an oh, so sensible man—using her über-sensible tick list—and look where it had got her. Well, stuff it. Sensible Imogen could take a hike. Not for ever, but just for a while. Temporary New Imogen was going to take over and things were going to be different.

The unfamiliar spark of rebellion took hold and took over her vocal cords.

'Of course I'm sure. Why shouldn't I be? There's nothing wrong in having an interest. A *healthy* interest in... you know...' Imogen closed her eyes in silent despair. Had she said that?

'I do know,' he said, and suddenly the atmosphere thickened. The buzz of French chatter, the sound of the church bells all dimmed. Everything faded and all Imogen was aware of was the look in Joe's eyes as he stepped towards her. So close that she could smell that tantalising male aroma, the underlying sandalwood. So close that if she lifted a hand she would be able to place her fingers on the width of his chest and feel the beat of his heart.

Whoa!

They both stepped back at exactly the same second and Imogen gave a slightly shaky laugh, horribly aware that her legs were feeling more than a touch jellified.

Joe rubbed the back of his neck and his face was neutralised, all emotion cleared. 'Lead the way,' he said.

Joe knew this was a bad idea; he was having enough issues keeping his attraction for Imogen leashed. Entering through the portals of a sex shop with her probably wasn't going to help—not so much because of the merchandise but more because he sensed that Imogen was bubbling with...*something*. She had been all day and certainly was now; there was undoubtedly an emotional maelstrom brewing and he wasn't at all sure he wanted to be caught up in its wake.

'This one,' Imogen said, pointing towards a large well-lit store that looked like an emporium or even a supermarket.

Joe followed her through the doors into the spacious

shop and nearly crashed straight into her back as Imogen came to an abrupt halt. Moving next to her, he glanced down at her and saw her eyes widen, but before he could say anything a shop assistant crossed the floor.

In his forties, the man had a discreet charming smile, dark blond hair and an urbane manner. *'Bonjour,'* he said courteously. *'Anglais?'*

Joe nodded. *'Oui, monsieur. Je parle français, mais—'* He broke off. Maybe Imogen did speak French. 'Do you speak French?' he asked.

A shake of her head served as her answer; evidently the merchandise was still rendering her speechless.

The man smiled. 'It is not a problem,' he said. 'I speak English. My name is Jean and I am here to help. Is there anything in particular the two of you are looking for? Something to spice up—?'

Imogen's head snapped round. 'We aren't together.'

'Apologies. You just have the look of—'

'Colleagues,' Imogen intercepted. 'We are here to… research…for a friend…who is…um…writing a book on erotica.'

Jean swept his gaze over them. 'I comprehend completely,' he said, his voice smooth. 'You are enquiring for a friend. Many people do that. So, you must let me show you around to make sure your…friend…gets a proper overview of passion. I shall show you items that can enhance pleasure.'

Joe felt a shudder run through Imogen's body and wondered what she was thinking. Was she imagining herself in the throes of passion—? Oh, hell—*her* thoughts weren't the problem here. His, however, were. Images branded his retina. His body wasn't interested in anything that this shop could offer—his body knew that all it needed was Imogen's touch. In fact any enhancement and he'd probably go up in flames.

So perhaps a guided tour was preferable to walking round just with Imogen.

'*Merci*, Jean. Much appreciated.'

'This way.' Jean stepped forward.

'Why did you agree?' Imogen whispered.

'Why did you say we were researching for a friend? If that were true we would *want* a tour.'

No way was he explaining *his* need for a chaperon.

'Now, here we have the lingerie. Come closer—touch… feel.'

Jean motioned to Imogen and after a second's hesitation she stepped forward and fingered the deep midnight-black confection. 'Oh…'

Joe bit back a groan at her reaction. Her gasp was soft, yet so appreciative as her slender fingers stroked the material.

'It's so sensual,' she murmured. 'Is it pure silk or…or a mixture?'

For a second Jean looked surprised, and then his face cleared. 'Ah, you are a woman who likes texture and feel. This is a blend of silk and satin, but we also have other fabrics. Cashmere…soft suede. Perhaps for you the blindfold would be a good thing?'

Imogen dropped the lingerie and jumped backwards. 'Um…I'm not sure…'

But Jean was in full swing as he led them inexorably over to a section that was devoted to an extensive range of blindfolds. 'You see, to be deprived of sight lifts the anticipation and allows the other senses to come into play.'

The audible hitch of her breath, the flush that tinged her high cheekbones, told Joe all he needed to know. Imogen was wondering exactly what it would be like to be blindfolded—and, heaven help him, *he* wanted to be there when she explored that particular fantasy.

'I am sure,' Jean said smoothly, 'that your friend would be interested in this.'

'Friend?' Imogen flushed even redder and then nodded. 'Yes, absolutely. This is all very helpful. Isn't it, Joe?'

There was a certain part of his anatomy that would undoubtedly disagree.

Her elbow in his ribs prompted his vocal cords and demonstrated exactly how close they were standing. 'Yup. Our friend will be very interested in all this.'

Jean beamed. 'Then let's keep going. Down here is the costume aisle. You have the nurse costumes, the superhero, the…'

Aisle followed aisle, until finally Jean came to a halt. 'So this has been helpful?'

Joe stepped forward. 'Amazingly so. Thank you, Jean.'

'We'll be sure to recommend our friend visits here,' Imogen chimed in.

Minutes later they exited the shop, and Joe inhaled the Parisian air as they started walking in the late-afternoon sun, heading towards the Sacré Coeur.

Imogen stared down at the ground as she walked, presumably shell-shocked by the mass of information she had accrued.

'I can't believe we did that,' she said.

Neither could he. What had he been thinking? Checking out a sex shop was hardly a work-related activity, however he spun it. Time to regroup.

'Let's stop for coffee and check out a map to find that fabric place you mentioned.'

'OK. Good idea.'

He led the way into a small café and sat down at a scarred wooden table. A few minutes later, espresso in one hand and a map in the other, he expelled a sigh of relief. Control restored.

Until he glanced at her, took in the way she twirled a tendril of hair round her finger as she gazed at him almost speculatively.

'What?' he said.

'I'm not sure I can ask,' she said.

He snorted. 'We just spent half an hour in a sex shop with a man extolling the virtues of a Power Stallion vibrator. Right now you can ask me anything.'

She stared at him for a moment and her lips tipped up in a smile. 'I wish you could have seen your face when he said it still wasn't quite the same as the real thing.'

He grinned. 'I imagine my expression was pretty much a mirror image of yours when he explained what a g-wand does.'

Imogen giggled—a full-on, proper fit of giggles—and as he watched her features scrunch up in mirth he couldn't help himself. A sudden chuckle fell from his lips and developed into laughter. The kind that came straight from the belly. The sort of laughter he hadn't experienced for a while—not since his sisters had taken off travelling.

'I can't believe it really happened,' Imogen said breathlessly. 'Poor Jean. We should have bought something, really.'

Lord—she looked so beautiful when she laughed. Her face was so alive, her dark hair highlighted by the sunshine filtering through the window. An intense spike of desire pierced his chest, and the urge to lean across the polished wood of the table and cover her delectable mouth with his own was almost overwhelming.

Gripping the edge of the table, he forced himself to remain still, all inclination to mirth gone.

Her blue-grey eyes met his and her laughter ceased abruptly.

The silence thickened and her lips parted as her breathing quickened. Joe's brain was scrambled. Conversation—he had to find something to say before sheer momentum tilted him towards her.

'So, what were you going to ask?'

Imogen blinked, as if his words were reaching her through a haze of desire. 'It doesn't matter. Really.'

'No, go ahead.' Surely she grasped that they *had* to talk—use their lips to form words, not anything else.

'All those things in the shop… Do you think they're important in a relationship?'

OK. This wasn't the topic he'd been hoping for. Damn it, couldn't she have been wondering about the weather, or French politics, or his opinion on the socioeconomic state of Britain or something?

'Would you like your girlfriend to come home dressed as Wonder Woman, wielding a whip?' she continued.

'I don't have a girlfriend.' As answers went it was a cop-out, but as questions went hers hadn't exactly been social chitchat.

'Hypothetically?'

'Not hypothetically either. I'm not really a relationship type of guy.'

'So you're celibate?' Imogen raised a hand to her mouth as pink stained her cheeks. 'Hell. Sorry. I really did *not* mean to say that.'

'Don't worry—and, no, I'm not celibate. I just don't do relationships.'

'So what *do* you do? One-night stands only?'

For a moment he was tempted to duck the question, but a strange defensiveness tightened his grip around his coffee cup. 'Yes.'

'Oh. So, then…um…would you mind if your bedroom partner was into all that stuff?'

'I wouldn't have a problem exploring the idea of using some of the things Jean showed us, but I certainly don't expect or want all my bedmates to come accessorised with a whip or a latex uniform.'

'But would you *prefer* a partner who wanted to explore those ideas?'

'If we're going to have this conversation—' and heaven only knew why they were '—then I need to know why we're having it.'

'It's…' For a second she stared down at her coffee. 'Research.'

'Research for what?'

'I was wondering if I should…well…maybe pick up a few items from Jean's arsenal.'

'That's something you would need to discuss with *your* bedroom partner.'

'Given my current bed partner is a cuddly rabbit that's seen better days, that's probably not going to work. That's why I'm asking you. For a general opinion.'

'I don't think turn-ons can be boiled down into a general formula, Imogen. Everyone's rules of attraction are different.'

Imogen sighed. 'I guess I've just never thought that sexual attraction was particularly important in a relationship.'

Joe frowned. How could a woman so clearly made for the bedroom think sexual attraction was unimportant?

'That probably explains the rabbit situation,' he said.

Clearly not the right thing to say.

Imogen's eyes narrowed. 'You're saying I'm single because I don't believe sex is the be-all and end-all to life?'

'I'm saying sexual attraction is a key component to a relationship.'

'What makes *you* an expert? You just said you don't do relationships.'

'I don't. But I *do* do sexual attraction, and I can vouch for it being an important thing.'

'Sure. But there are other things that are way more important. Kindness, loyalty, shared goals, a sense of humour, being good parent material. They all rate way higher than sexual attraction on my tick-list.' Her voice vibrated with absolute belief.

'Tick-list?' *She had a tick-list?* 'You have an actual, for real list of requirements? Manly chest? Sizeable bank balance? A yen to walk down the aisle.'

He was honest-to-God fascinated.

'Chest size irrelevant,' she said.

Though he couldn't help but notice her gaze linger on his pecs with perhaps a hint of regret.

'Moderate rather than sizeable savings account to demonstrate that security is important to him. And, yes, I need him to be pro marriage. And kids. I want financial security and whilst I'm happy to share my salary I need a partner who pulls their weight.' Her voice had a steely ring Joe usually heard in a corporate boardroom not a bedroom. Any minute now she'd give him a PowerPoint presentation. 'I want a man who wants children, who will be a wonderful dad who puts his children before himself.'

'So what do you do? Sit every eligible man down, ask for a copy of his bank statement and make him write an essay on his opinion of a white picket fence?'

'Of course not.' Against the odds her eyes narrowed further. 'But, yes, I do need to know whether we have long-term compatibility. So of course I do an assessment.'

'You don't think that's a bit clinical?' To say nothing of a touch kooky.

'No more clinical than only having one-night stands to serve a bodily function.'

The disdain in her voice touched a nerve.

'A one-night stand is about way more than bodily functions.'

'If you say so...'

Her nose wrinkled in distaste and defensiveness rose within him.

'I do. It's about passion and chemistry and spark.'

He allowed his gaze to linger on her mouth, heard her breath catch in the slender column of her throat.

'When the scent of the other person turns you on, when the idea of touching them becomes consuming, when all you want to do is pull them into your arms and kiss them.'

Her tongue snaked out to moisten the bow of her lips and his willpower snapped. Maybe he could show her what she was dismissing with such contempt.

'A bit like now,' he growled.

And in one movement he hitched his chair around the curve of the wooden table and cupped her jaw in his hands, expelled a sigh at the silken texture of her skin beneath his fingers. He ran his thumb over the fullness of her lower lip, saw the quiver run through her body.

As he covered her lips with his own, Joe was dimly aware that this was a bad, *bad* idea—but then Imogen's taste, her scent, her warmth eradicated all vestige of thought. All he wanted was to plunder the softness of her coffee-scented lips as they parted to allow him access.

Her tongue tentatively stroked his, and as she moaned into his mouth he was lost. He tangled his fingers in her smooth glossy hair as she twined her arms around his neck; her fingers brushed his nape and desire jolted through him.

'Closer,' she murmured, and he slid his hands over her shoulders and down, spanned her slender waist and pulled her onto his lap.

Who knew how long they remained, lips locked, lost in sheer pleasure? Until the clink and clatter of plates, the whir of the coffee machine penetrated his brain. What the hell was he doing? Melded against someone tantamount to being an employee. Someone whose job he had the power to take. Someone who could be trying to influence him to protect not just her own job but other people's as well.

Hell and damnation.

Pulling backwards, he broke the kiss and she gave a small mewl of protest, her eyes pools of desire clouded with confusion.

Her breathing as ragged as his, she scrambled off him and stood, one hand gripping the table for support. 'I...I...'

Joe hauled in air and willed his pulse-rate to slow down and his brain to move into gear. Imogen did not look like a woman out to seduce him for gain; she looked as shell-shocked as he felt. Surely that couldn't be simulated?

Regardless... 'That was a mistake,' he said flatly.

Yet she looked so damn desirable still, with her hair dishevelled, her lips swollen from his kiss, that it took all his willpower to remain seated.

Chill, Joe. It was a kiss. One kiss. Even if it had been the kiss of all kisses it was not a deal-breaker. 'Never Mix Business with Pleasure' was still Rule Number One.

Yes, he'd erred; he'd let the line between professional and personal fuzz. Given Imogen a few hours to live the dream, agreed to visit a sex shop, shared laughter, discussed sex. Time to redraw that line in permanent marker. Of the fluorescent kind.

'A mistake that we need to put behind us.' He glanced at his watch. 'We've got a couple of hours. Let's put them to good use and visit some places that will impress Richard Harvey.' As opposed to a sex shop.

Imogen nodded, tugged the edges of her jacket together and smoothed down her trousers, visibly pulling herself together. 'I think we should find the fabric shop, visit the cemetery and go to the Sacré Coeur.'

'Done.'

Imogen walked up and up and up the calf-wrenching steps towards the top of the glorious domed cathedral. She welcomed the pain—welcomed even more the legitimate reason for her heart to pound against her ribcage.

As the sun struck the blinding white of the travertine walls she was dazzled—not just by the rays but by the sheer dizzying possibilities of life.

She knew how she *should* be feeling: thoroughly ashamed with herself. She'd kissed a man who was her boss, her enemy, the wrecker of her friends' and colleagues' lives. Joe had spoken the truth: the kiss *had* been a mistake.

But it had also been earth-shattering. She'd never experienced one like it and her body still fizzed with the sheer joy of it. Apparently lust trumped principles. But who would have thought a kiss could be so incredible? How could she regret a kiss like that?

Apprehension prickled her skin. *Take care, Imo.* Perhaps this was how her mother had felt all those years before—beguiled by Jonathan Lorrimer's looks and charm. And look what had happened there.

Not that Joe was remotely charming, nor making any attempt to beguile her. In fact he appeared to have erased the kiss from his memory banks.

Their whole trip around the fabric store and their entire tour of the museum had been achieved civilly enough—Joe had asked intelligent questions about the fabrics, observed the paintings in the museum with genuine appreciation—but gone was the man who had laughed with her and wreaked such magic with his kiss. *This* man was the consummate professional, with his tie back round his neck as if that could restore professional equilibrium.

Currently Imogen would have settled for any sort of equilibrium. Even now the nape of her neck tingled. Every molecule of her body was hyper-aware of the strength of him just behind her on the narrow stairway as they approached the summit.

Her breath caught as she looked down over the awe-inspiring vista of Paris. The Eiffel Tower jutted above the rooftops of thousands of differently shaped buildings, all glinting in the late-afternoon sun. It made her feel dizzy, different, infused with wonder.

'It's incredible…'

'Yes.'

Had his gaze lingered on her face for a heartbeat before he'd turned to stare out at the panorama?

Ridiculous. He was talking about the view, for heaven's sake! She had to get some perspective. They'd shared a kiss. Big deal. Now they had to return to normal. Joe equalled Big Bad Boss. Imogen equalled Employee. She needed to concentrate on her job.

'Have you seen it before?' she asked. There. Perfect. Normal civil conversation.

'Yes.' As if realising the brevity of the syllable, he continued, 'I came with my sisters once.'

'Really?' It was strange to imagine Joe in family mode.

'Really.' A smile touched his lips—a genuine one. 'I'm not sure they appreciated the glory of the scenery. They were fourteen and more interested in the glory of French boys.'

His lips pressed together, as though he regretted sharing even that much personal information.

A glance at his watch and, 'We need to go.'

Guilt prodded her as she scuttled after him through the tourist crowd. She'd completely lost track of time—hadn't given work a single thought since they'd got on the Métro. All she'd thought about was Joe. Oh, and sex. In conjunction.

As their taxi screeched and sped through the Paris traffic Imogen squeezed her hands into fists and focused. The hours for living the dream were over and it was time to concentrate on reality and the need to wow Richard. If only her body would stop with the snap, crackle and pop…

The taxi glided to a stop and she climbed out, stood on the pavement whilst Joe paid the driver. The street teemed with chicly dressed chattering women and casually dressed men. Elegance mixed with gesticulation and passion, and for a minute Imogen wished with all her heart that she was in Paris with a lover.

Joe.

Delusional, Imo.

'Let's go,' she said, and they wended their way through the throng into the warmly lit interior of a bar.

Small and intimate, its tables glowed golden in the muted light from retro lamps and the candles that dotted the embrasures in the wax-dripped wall.

A bar curved down one side of the room, behind which there was a bewildering array of bottles and an old-fashioned cash register that evoked images of a Paris of decades before. The soft strains of jazz filled the evening air, reminding Imogen of the sheer thrill of being in the romantic capital of the world.

'Over here.'

Peering through the throng, Imogen spotted Richard and Crystal sitting in a corner booth, a pitcher of delicate pink liquid on the table in front of them.

Happiness was evident in the glow of their smiles, the linking of their fingers as they both rose to their feet. Richard looked younger than she remembered, his salt-and-pepper hair longer, his whole stance more relaxed.

No doubt that was Crystal's influence. In her late thirties, she radiated a serene timeless beauty and her glance at her husband was soft with love. For them Paris was a truly romantic getaway, and envy tugged at Imogen's heartstrings.

Forcing a smile to her face, she stepped forward and greeted the couple, introduced Joe.

'Good to meet you, Joe,' Richard said. 'Sit—order whatever you like. On me. I recommend the Vieux Carré cocktail. Cognac, sweet vermouth, rye and Benedictine, with a dash of Angostura bitters.'

'Sounds good to me,' Joe said.

'Me too,' Imogen agreed.

Once they were seated, with their drinks in front of them, Richard smiled at Imogen. 'Isn't Steve accompanying you on this trip? I thought you'd take advantage of the chance for a romantic getaway?'

Next to her Joe stiffened for a second, his movements jerky as he picked his glass up.

'Maybe give him the opportunity to pop the question if he hasn't already, eh?'

Mortification encased her body as her cheeks heated to no doubt a tomato-red. Memories came of how she had gushed to Richard about her belief that she and Steve were so suited, so compatible, so together.

She had been truly delusional.

Now she would have to admit that Steve had left her for his ex and was going to marry her. Well, call her a great fat fibber but she couldn't do it—couldn't bear to see the pity in Richard Harvey's eyes.

'He couldn't make it,' she said, ignoring the snap of Joe's head, sure she could feel his look boring through her temple.

'That's a real shame,' Crystal said. 'We were hoping to meet him.'

Richard turned to Joe. 'Did *you* bring a significant other half with you?'

'No. *I'm* a single man.'

The older man sighed, and then shrugged. 'Then I suppose the best thing will be for you both to stay in the apartment.'

Huh? The words of confession Imogen had been preparing withered on her tongue. Trepidation tiptoed down her spine as she picked up her glass and forced herself to sip rather than gulp.

'What apartment would that be?' she managed.

Richard smiled. 'Well, as you know, Crystal and I have

bought a place in Paris and want it done up. I could go to someone over here, but I'd prefer to use either you or Graham. So I've come up with a plan.'

Oh, hell; this plan was going to be a Harvey Humdinger—Imogen just knew it.

'Sounds intriguing,' Joe murmured.

'I've rented two romantic Parisian apartments,' Richard explained. 'One for Graham and his wife and one was meant to be for Imogen and Steve—though now it's for you two. You stay there tonight. Then on Monday morning I want a two-page proposal on how you would design the interior of a four-bedroom, three-bathroom Parisian apartment. I'll make my decision based on that.'

'How does that sound?' Crystal asked.

'That sounds like a challenge Langley will be more than happy to accept,' Joe said.

Come on, Imogen. She could do the whole gibbering wreck thing later. Right now wasn't the time.

Raising her glass, she summoned a smile that she could only hope denoted calm, professional confidence. 'I'll drink to that.'

'Excellent,' Richard said. He reached into his pocket and pushed a set of keys across the table. 'Here are the keys to 'Lovers' Tryst.'

Of course. What else could it be called?

Joe and Imogen—off to Lovers' Tryst for the night. Dear Lord.

Panic bubbled in her tummy, and yet a thoroughly misplaced anticipation strummed her veins.

CHAPTER FIVE

IMOGEN SWEPT A sideways glance across the limo that Richard had insisted they use and shifted on the seat, nerves jangling. Joe's whole body pulsed with contained anger and had done ever since they had said their goodbyes to Richard and Crystal. It wasn't her fault that Richard had come up with this mad idea, so she could only assume that his irritation was at the situation—not her.

Sod it. The brooding silence was getting old. 'So,' she said brightly, 'isn't it generous of Richard to say he'll pay for any clothes and things that we need to purchase? And to have booked us a table at one of the poshest restaurants in Paris?' She glanced down at herself. 'Do you think this is all right to wear to eat in a French restaurant? Probably not.'

'It doesn't make any difference to me whether you wear a sack,' he said, the words rasping in the regulated air of the limo. 'So don't waste your time or Richard's money on a seduction outfit.'

'What?' Confusion tangled her vocal cords. 'I don't understand.'

'I don't like being played, Imogen.'

'Still not with you.'

'I don't trade business favours for sexual ones.'

'*Excuse* me?'

'The kiss.'

Her neck cracked as she swivelled on the plush leather seat to face his grim expression. The dusk had harshened the angles of his face further. 'Are you for real? You think that was for *business* reasons?'

'You wouldn't be the first to try it. You said yourself you would do anything to save Langley. Maybe you're hoping to persuade me to drop the buy-out plan, give your friends their jobs back.' He leant back against the padded leather. 'So if you had seduction plans for later cancel them.'

'Believe me, Joe, I'd rather seduce...' Hell she couldn't think of anyone low enough. 'Ivan...'

'Maybe that's your plan B. Though I can't help feeling sorry for that poor sap of a boyfriend you've got at home, waiting to propose. The man who satisfies your crazy tick-list. Does Steve *know* you go round kissing people in cafés? Sitting on their laps and—'

'Stop!'

Imogen wondered if it were possible to explode with rage. If so, she damn well hoped she took Joe with her. Anger ignited, heated her veins. How *dared* he?

'You arrogant, stupid schmuck! For your information, Steve and I split up six weeks ago.'

He snorted. 'More lies, Imogen? Why didn't you tell Richard?'

'Because I felt such a damn fool. I raved about Steve to Richard, about him being The One. I was too embarrassed to admit I was wrong.'

As the limo glided to a stop outside a shopping mall tears of sheer rage and mortification threatened. How could Joe tarnish a kiss that had made her blood sing and her head spin? Made her feel attractive and desirable and wanted? Palliated the sting of Steve's parting words?

Now it turned out he believed she had engineered that kiss because she was a gold-digger, a spy or a cheat. Good grief—if she wasn't so furious she'd laugh. Because one thing she knew: Joe had been just as much into that kiss as she had.

'I think you're forgetting something, here. That *you* kissed *me*!'

'Imogen…'

'Just leave it, Joe.' She shoved the car door open, nearly tumbling the chauffeur over as he waited to open the door for her, and set off across the car park, her rage spiking further as she marched, feet pounding the tarmac, and realised he wasn't damn well even going to follow her.

Fine.

Anger heated her veins, seethed and simmered as her brain formulated a plan.

She'd show him. She'd show him exactly what he was missing. There wasn't a cat's chance in hell she'd seduce him, but she was damn well going to make him wish she would.

Sanity tried to point out that maybe Joe had been a little misled by the fib she'd told Richard. But that wasn't the point! He could just have *asked* her before jumping to such insulting, stupid conclusions.

An hour later Imogen stared at her reflection, relieved that rage still buoyed her because she knew otherwise there was no way in heaven or hell she would be able to carry this off.

The dress was…outrageous. In a good way. It managed to scream seduction whilst hollering elegance. Black see-through gauze featured, fluttering to mid-thigh and covering her chest, whilst allowing tantalising glimpses of the black corset-like bit underneath. Shells striped the dress in a fun, flirty line, and the whole look was complemented by the strappiest high-heeled shoes imaginable. Delicate leather lines crisscrossed her feet, cool and seductive against her skin.

'*C'est magnifique!*' the sales assistant exclaimed, clapping her hands together.

'*Merci bien.*'

To her own surprise she didn't feel even a smidgeon of self-consciousness as she walked through the mall. Instead she fizzed with a sheer intoxicating vitality, every sense heightened and fuelled by the attention she garnered.

Joe was leaning back against the limo, arms folded, the breadth of his shoulders somehow accentuated by the length of the car. His white shirt had been swapped for a black one, with the top button undone to reveal a triangle of tanned skin that tantalised her gaze. He was intent on his phone screen, and a frown slashed his forehead.

Anticipation whispered in her stomach as she neared him and he looked up. The temptation to punch the air at his expression nearly overwhelmed her but she restrained it. Instead she savoured every second of his dropped jaw, every shade of heat that glittered in his brown eyes as they swept over her, lingering in appreciation as he stepped towards her.

Her brain gave out conflicting orders—*step towards him, move backwards, turn and run*. Grinding her molars, she adhered her stilettoed feet to the tarmac of the car park and faced him. He was so close she could smell the tang of masculinity, the scent of arousal. Her muscles ached with a need to reach out and touch him, to trace a finger along that V of skin, to unbutton his shirt and…

No! The plan was to show him what he was missing— not to offer herself up on a plate, thereby confirming all his insulting, overbearing assumptions.

'You ready for the restaurant?' she asked, keeping her voice casual with a supreme effort of will. 'I figure it will be pretty upmarket, so I want to look my best. You never know. As you're not available I may get lucky and find some loaded French sex god to seduce instead.'

She slapped her palm to her forehead.

'Oh, yes. I forgot. I'm *not* here with some cunning plan

to seduce anyone. I'm here to work. To come up with a proposal for Richard and Crystal.'

Joe stepped backwards, leant against the car and raised his eyebrows. 'You can hardly blame me for jumping to the conclusions I did.'

'Wrong. I can *totally* blame you. You could have asked first. You know—like, *Imogen, I'm a bit confused. Who is Steve?*'

'OK.' Folding his arms, he met her gaze. 'Imogen, I'm a bit confused. Who is Steve?'

'I told you. He is my *ex*-boyfriend. I am a free agent, and that kiss earlier wasn't about me being out to get anything or me being unfaithful to anyone.'

'So what *was* it about?'

'You tell me.'

His heated gaze swept over her body and then he straightened up, the glint in his eyes doused. 'It was a moment of insanity,' he said. 'And I apologise. For being so unprofessional. How about we put the whole episode behind us and move forward? Truce?'

What could she say? His voice was sincere, his gaze direct. 'Truce,' she agreed.

The twitch of his lips was a surprise as he gestured towards her. 'I take it that dress was chosen with the express purpose of torturing me?'

'Absolutely. Is it working?'

'Yes.'

Why, oh, why did he have to smile? A devastating smile sinful enough to make her hair curl. Oh, God. Perhaps this whole idea hadn't been so brilliant after all—especially as Joe wasn't playing the part she'd allotted him. Her tummy churned as she tried to work out what the hell was going on. Wondered if Joe had any idea either.

He opened the limo door for her and she slid inside, pulling her stomach muscles in so as not to so much as brush against him before scooting all the way across the leather seat.

Clamping her knees together, she shoved away the realisation that short and see-through, whilst effective, was also…well, short and see-through. From somewhere she had to muster the light sabre of professionalism. Hadn't she said she was here to work? Now would be an excellent moment to do exactly that.

'So,' she said. 'What do you think about Richard's idea of a two-page proposal?'

'I think you were right. Richard Harvey is a touch eccentric. But his idea has its merits. We'll have a quick decision for the minimum outlay of time.' He paused. 'I do realise he's thrown you in at the deep end, though. I'm thinking about calling Belinda off a project so that she can come and look at the apartment.'

Joe's words were as effective as a bucket of ice, dousing elation in reality. How stupid was she? It hadn't even occurred to her that *she* wouldn't be the one to put together the proposal. Forget stupid and substitute nonsensical. Her job at Langley was as a PA—sure, she'd dabbled in interior design, but Belinda had proper qualifications and expertise and was the obvious choice to go up against Graham.

Richard had asked for her presence, but he hadn't specified that Imogen worked on the proposal. She was just a point of contact and she should have realised that herself. If she hadn't been too busy living in some sort of fantasyland.

All too aware of Joe's gaze on her face, she looked out of the window, not wanting him to read the hurt or the sheer embarrassment that was no doubt etched there, relieved when the limo pulled to a stop.

'I'll text Belinda from the restaurant.'

It was all for the best. Did she *really* want the responsibility of going up against Graham? Having to face Peter's disappointment and the knowledge that she'd let Langley down if or rather *when* she didn't succeed? Far better to stay ensconced in her comfort zone.

'She's perfect for the proposal.'

Tension pounded Joe's temples as he followed Imogen into the restaurant and nodded automatically at the *maître d'*, who swooped towards them majestically, his gold-braided jacket a perfect fit with all the grandeur of the baroque theme.

Not that Joe cared about the gold and gilt that abounded, or the ornate mirrors on the stone walls, or even the wrought-iron chandeliers that glinted with the ambience of wealth.

Right now he was too busy questioning the swirl and whirl of emotions that Imogen had unleashed inside him. Anger at himself rebounded against a small and unfamiliar sense of panic. There was the ever growing problem of their attraction, not helped by the tantalising torment of her dress. But worse than that was the way his chest had panged at the quickly veiled hurt in her eyes when he'd suggested Belinda.

Realising that the *maître d'* still hovered, he shook the thought away. 'We have a reservation. Made by Richard Harvey,' he said.

The *maître d'* smiled his dignified approval and gestured to a black-suited waiter with a gold tie. 'This is Marcel. He will look after your table. Marcel, please take Miss Lorrimer and her companion to the table Mr Harvey requested for them.'

Joe gave in to temptation and placed his palm on the small of Imogen's back to steer her, his flesh tingling with warmth and an unexpected sense of possession. Just what he needed—more unfamiliar emotions that didn't make sense.

He eyed the table and further misgivings tingled his already frazzled nerve-endings. The table was… The word *intimate* sprang to mind. The kind of table for lovers, not colleagues—the type where you sat at adjacent angles so your knees pressed together, so it was easy to place your hand on your partner's thigh, indulge in a little footsie. The handy pillar would allow or even encourage canoodling.

He suddenly remembered that the gleaming candlelit table had been originally intended for *Steve* and Imogen.

Bloody wonderful.

Marcel seated them and then beamed. 'Mr Harvey has made a selection for you, but he's asked me to tell you first in case you have any allergies.'

Joe allowed the list of exquisite dishes to wash over him; the only relevant thing here was the length of the damn menu. They would be here for *hours*. On the other hand that might well be better than whatever Lovers' Tryst had to hold.

Right now it was time to get a handle on the situation, get a grip of said handle and start steering. Whatever the menu, this was a business dinner.

'That sounds fine. But I'll stick to water rather than wine.'

'It sounds *incredible*,' Imogen interpolated. 'Please make sure that you let Mr Harvey know how much we appreciate all this. And water for me as well, please.'

The waiter bowed, turned and glided across the restaurant floor, leaving them alone. No, not alone. Yet despite the fact that the restaurant was full, and the hum and buzz of conversation filled the air, Joe had the ridiculous impression that he and Imogen were in their own private space.

Imogen darted a glance at him and then reached down for her bag. 'I'll try Belinda now.'

'Is that what *you* want to do?' he asked, rubbing the back of his neck.

A frown creased her forehead as she moistened her lips. 'It makes sense.'

As he forced himself not to linger on her glossy lips it occurred to him that *nothing* made sense—and that was the problem. She'd got him so damn distracted that he'd let the personal and the business line fuzz. *Again*. He couldn't tell whether he wanted Belinda to come and look at the apartment because it was best for Langley or because Belinda would provide them with a chaperon. Didn't know if he wanted to allow Imogen to do the proposal because that was the right thing for Langley or because he wanted to assuage the hurt that had flashed across her eyes.

Enough.

Time to apply logic.

'I'm not sure it does,' he said as he drummed his fingers on the snow-white tablecloth. 'The impression I got was that Richard wants *you* to do it. I also believe that you understand how his mind works. We're up against a time limit. And Belinda is flat-out on other projects.'

There was a pause as she looked down at the bread roll she was crumbling into tiny pieces. 'But I'm a PA. I have no qualifications in interior design—or advertising and marketing.'

'But this is coming up with a concept. Isn't that exactly what you did for Richard's bathrooms?'

'Well, yes. But that was after we'd won the contract. And if Peter hadn't liked my ideas he'd have nixed them. There's a whole lot more riding on this.'

'Is that what's scaring you?'

Her fingers stilled, her head coming up as her eyes narrowed. 'It was your idea to bring in Belinda.'

Joe shook his head. 'I acknowledged that Richard was asking you to take on a lot and said I was *thinking* about bringing Belinda in. I haven't made a decision.'

'Oh.'

'So, do you think you can pull this off?'

She hesitated, her features creased into worried lines as she manoeuvred the crumbs into a line. 'It's just such a big responsibility. What if I let you down?'

Watching the play of light over her features, he was gripped by the urge to reassure her, to tell her that of *course* she wouldn't, to reach out and cup the delicate curve of her jaw.

Instead, 'There are no guarantees, Imogen. It's the risk you take. For what it's worth, I think you have a better shot at it than Belinda.'

'You do? You think I can pull this off?'

'Yes.'

'For real?'

'For real.'

Her face lit up and her lips curved in a genuine smile that constricted his lungs.

'I've seen your work and I've seen your rapport with Richard. I think that's key. So, yes, I think you can do it. But if you feel more comfortable calling in Belinda that's fine too.'

With a swoop of her hand she swept the crumbs into a small pile and nodded. 'I'll do it. And I'll give it my very best shot. I promise.'

Joe lifted his glass as relief trickled over him—they were back in *business*. His gut told him that using Imogen was the right decision.

'It's a plan,' he said.

'Thank you…'

Leaning forward, she placed a hand on his forearm, her touch sparking awareness. A citrus burst of shampoo, a tendril of black hair tickled his nose as she placed her lips in a fleeting caress against his cheek.

'For believing in me.'

CHAPTER SIX

BIG MISTAKE. FROM the second she slanted her body so close to his Imogen knew she might as well be juggling dynamite. His toned forearm tensed under her fingers and as her lips brushed the six o'clock stubble of his jaw need shivered through her.

The sensible thing to do would be to pull away, but the urge to nuzzle his skin, to take the opportunity to inhale that Joe scent, was nigh on overwhelming. Adrenalin swept through her tummy in a wave—this man wanted her as much as she wanted him, he believed in her, and he was so damn close that suddenly it seemed mad to fight this attraction. In this second she couldn't even remember why they were.

His body stilled, and then with a murmured curse he pulled back. 'Jeez, Imo. You are messing with my head.' He shoved his hands through his hair and nodded towards the centre of the restaurant. 'We're in public—in Richard Harvey's favourite restaurant. When Richard asks Marcel how we enjoyed our meal I'd like Marcel *not* to say we spent it in a clinch.'

Heat flushed her cheeks as she tried to quell the elation. She was messing with his head—who would have thought it? But...

'You're more than right. Here isn't the place. But—' She broke off as Marcel approached the table with a genial smile.

'Here we have a selection of dishes. The *amuse-*

bouches. Lemon, nuts, grapefruit and celery in a potato net. Haddock soufflé. And tuna in squid ink. Along with the best baguette in Paris.'

'It looks fabulous, Marcel. *Merci*.' Her words were spoken on automatic. Not even the scrumptious aroma that wafted up from the plate could distract her from the buzz her body radiated, the tingle of her lips where she'd brushed his cheek.

Once Marcel had gone, she met Joe's gaze.

'We have a problem,' he said. 'So I suggest we have a look round this apartment and then book separate rooms— preferably on separate floors—in a local hotel.'

'What about Richard? Staying there is part of his plan.'

'I'll come up with a reason if he asks. I doubt he will. The important thing will be the proposal. Whatever it is going on with us, I think distance is the key solution.'

'Or we give in to it.'

The words were blurted out without thought, spring-boarded to her brain from her instincts.

His body stilled and then he shook his head. 'No. Bad idea. We work together so that is not an option.'

'I get that—and, hell, I'd normally agree. But in this case the business is done. You've already made a decision about the proposal. And I swear to you I will give it my all. I am excited about the opportunity to do this for Langley. But I'm not propositioning you out of gratitude or because I want anything else.'

'So why *are* you propositioning me?'

'Because I've never felt like this before. And once, Joe—just once in my life—I want to succumb to lust. To say sod the rules. Not to be sensible. For one night.'

Hell, it wasn't too much to ask, was it? That for once she could ride the wave and not do the right thing? Sure, there was a part of her brain that was covering its eyes, unable

to look, *shocked* by the sheer effrontery of this version of
Imogen Lorrimer. But, damn it, she was going to ignore it.

'That's what you do, isn't it? One-night stands?'

'I thought they weren't your thing.' Joe picked his glass
up and put it back down again, his eyes dark with desire.

Her lungs seemed to have forgotten how to function;
breathing was problematic. 'I've changed my mind.'

A moment's pause during which his brown eyes bored
into her expression. 'You're sure? One night? No strings?
Because I can't offer anything else, Imogen.' He raised
his hand before she could protest. 'I don't mean job-wise.
I mean emotionally or time-wise. I don't tick your boxes.'

'One night is all I want as well, Joe. I'm not in the
market for a relationship right now.' She needed time to
regroup, update her tick-list. 'I've just come out of one.
Plus—' She broke off. There was no need to explain to
Joe that she didn't trust this whole insane attraction, that
she would never risk letting it control her. That was the
beauty of a one-night stand. 'I promise you this is all about
the sex.'

A long moment and then he gusted out a sigh, his expression unreadable, before he smiled—the toe-curling,
hair-frizzing version. 'Then let's eat and get out of here.'

How was she supposed to eat? Her appetite for food
had legged it over the horizon long ago. All she wanted
to savour right now was Joe; her nerves stretched taut
with need.

But somehow she made it through the exquisite com-
bination of tastes: the bite and tang of roast lobster fla-
voured with lemon and ginger, the intensity of a seafood
bisque complemented by seaweed bread. But all the time
she was oh-so aware of the solid thickness of Joe's thigh
next to hers, the pressure of his knee under the table, the
plane and angle of his strong jaw, the way the chandeliers
glinted over the dark spikes of his hair.

The promise in his eyes made her tummy swirl in anticipation. Until finally—*finally*—they had eaten the last bite of a superbly light pistachio soufflé, had exchanged compliments with Marcel and could exit the restaurant.

Imogen welcomed the cool evening breeze on her face, though she couldn't help a small shiver as it hit her sensitised skin. Without speaking Joe shrugged off his jacket and placed it round her shoulders. Warmth encased her inside and out.

'Thank you.'

His hand clasped hers in a firm grip. 'No problem. The apartment isn't far.'

'Good. I'm…' *Burning. Yearning. Desperate.*

He looked down at her. 'Me too,' he said, with a sudden low chuckle that rippled into the breeze and tugged her lips into an answering smile.

Half-walking half-running, they wended their way along the pavement.

'It should be just down this alley,' he said, already digging in his pocket for the keys.

They reached a navy blue wooden door—he shoved the key into the lock and thrust the door open.

And came to an abrupt halt.

She could see why: the room they had stepped into was…*sumptuous*. Decadent. Luxurious. With warm red walls, rugs and throws that begged to be touched, deep crimson and gold curtains that would cocoon the room and its occupants against the outer world.

Then she saw the mural on the wall directly opposite the door.

A man and a woman entwined together, their naked bodies sinuous and beautiful. The pose intense, passionate, vivid.

Imogen swallowed, and then moistened her lips to relieve her parched mouth as her awareness of Joe further heightened. But with awareness came worry, and a sudden shyness tensed her body. What if she didn't come up to scratch? Surely this apartment was meant for women who were more…more beautiful, experienced, sexy?

Then Joe moved behind her, his body heat warming her as his fingers massaged her shoulders.

'You OK?' he murmured.

'My heart is beating so damn hard it's like I'm consumed—and yet I'm scared that I'll mess this up.'

Disappoint you.

'Not possible.'

His fingers continued to wreak their magic and she wriggled in sheer appreciation.

'But if you've changed your mind…'

A last lingering doubt snaked through her brain and she quashed it ruthlessly. This was her chance to experience something she might never experience again. Yes, lust was dangerous—but it was a danger she was fully aware of and had no intention of falling prey to.

As for the risk of disappointing Joe… Every molecule in her body told her that they'd work it out. This was *her* night and she'd regret it for ever if she didn't take it.

'No. I haven't changed my mind.'

'Good,' he growled as his hands slid to her shoulders, glissaded down to her waist.

He nuzzled her neck and at the touch of his lips she shivered, arched to give him better access. As she did so her gaze fell on the mural and she saw it in a new light— a picture of two normal people who were following their instincts, engaged in something natural and beautiful.

The realisation sent a thrill through her, and suddenly she needed to see Joe—see the man who was already giving her such pleasure.

As if he felt the same he stood back and turned her, so she was flush against the hard plane of his chest. The light scent of sandalwood mixed with sheer Joe assaulted her senses. Imogen looked up at him and her breath caught in her throat at the sight of the raw desire that dilated his pupils.

Standing on tiptoe, she looped her arms round his neck, buried her fingers in the thick brown hair. Joe's broad hands curved round her waist and his mouth covered hers. Imogen savoured the tang of pistachio and the flavour of mint leaf as his tongue swept the bow of her mouth and she parted her lips. Sensations rocketed through her as his tongue stroked hers, sliding and tangling and tormenting, and she matched him stroke for stroke.

She pushed against him, desperate to be closer, for more, pressing heavy breasts against his chest. His hands plunged down from her waist to cup her bottom, and she moaned into his mouth as momentum built and strummed inside her.

Breaking their kiss, he stepped backwards and sank down onto the deep crimson sofa, pulling her onto his lap, the strength of his thighs hard under hers.

Her clumsy-with-need fingers fumbled at the buttons of his shirt and tugged the silken black edges apart. Then *finally* she touched his skin, ran her hands over his packed chest.

Joe found the zip of her dress and tugged it down in one deft movement, gliding the gauzy material over her shoulders and down her arms, freeing her breasts.

'Jeez…' he breathed. 'You are gorgeous, Imogen.'

His large hands cupped her breasts and as he circled her standing-to-attention nipples. Imogen arched backwards in ecstasy. Then in one smooth movement he lifted her off his lap and laid her down on the expanse of the sofa.

'I need to see all of you,' he said roughly as his hands pulled her dress down.

Lifting her hips, she felt the material slide down and

off into a pool on the floor, followed by the lacy wisp of her knickers.

Joe's heated gaze glittered over her. 'So beautiful…' he murmured

Imogen allowed her gaze to run down his body, saw the impressive bulge that strained the zipper of his trousers. A quiver of anticipation thrilled through her.

'Joe?'

'Yes.'

'I think you need to take your clothes off. Things seem to be a little out of balance at the moment.'

'Your wish is my command, beautiful.'

In one lithe move he stood on the plush carpet and shucked off trousers and boxers to stand before her in glorious naked splendour.

Unfamiliar exultation shimmered over her that he could be so aroused by her body. Propping herself on her elbows, she let her gaze absorb every glorious millimetre of him— the light sheen of his sculpted torso, the ripped abs, the thick muscular thighs—and she shivered, imprinted the memory on her brain.

He smiled at her. 'Seen your fill?' he asked with a delectable quirk of his eyebrow.

'I could look at you for hours.'

It was nothing but the truth, and the knowledge that she'd love to draw him, to try and capture his arrogant male beauty on paper, crossed her mind. *No way, Imo.*

Instead, 'But I can think of other things to do right now.'

'As I said, your wish—'

'Then come here,' she said.

CHAPTER SEVEN

JOE PULLED THE fridge door open and welcomed the stream of cold air that hit him as he inspected the contents. As he'd suspected there was everything he needed for an impromptu midnight picnic—he wouldn't expect anything less from Lovers' Tryst. And he wanted Imogen to know that she deserved champagne and caviar and strawberries and cream, even if they weren't sensible.

Though the real reason he was here in the kitchen wasn't only food and drink—he needed a moment to regroup. The past hour had been sensational, and yet his body still hummed with desire. As if it was greedy to make the most of every hour of this night.

But he wanted this to be special for Imogen—more than just for the sex. Her words from the restaurant echoed in his ears. *'Because I've never felt like this before. And once, Joe—just once in my life—I want to succumb to lust. To say sod the rules. Not to be sensible. For one night.'* There had been wistfulness in her voice, along with the certainty of what she wanted—and it had called to something in him.

Convinced him to just once break a rule. There was no harm in it. Imogen had been right—he'd made the decision to let her run with the proposal and that decision had been made with no ulterior motive in mind. They were here for a night. From tomorrow morning it would be all about work, and soon he would leave Langley and move on. Rules Two and Three were still in place. 'One Night Only'. 'Never Look Back'.

The thought brought a certain relief as he loaded a tray and pushed the fridge door closed. He exited the kitchen and made his way down the corridor to the bedroom.

Breath whistled between his teeth as he took in the opulent splendour. An enormous circular bed with a curved wooden barred headboard dominated the floor and mirrors mastered the wall space.

Imogen sat cross-legged on the bed, dressed in a thick white towelling robe. 'It's a little unnerving to see myself from all angles,' she said. She gazed at the tray and her face lit up. 'I can't believe I'm saying this, but I'm ravenous.'

'It's all the exercise,' he said as he stepped forward and lowered the tray onto the bedside table. 'Champagne?'

'Yes, please.'

Minutes later they had plates balanced on their laps and a glass of bubbles in their hands.

'Thank you for this. It's incredible,' she said. 'I can safely say I've never eaten caviar in bed at midnight before. I've never eaten caviar at all.' The glance she swept at him was a touch shy. 'I thought one-night stands were just about the sex.'

Her words sent a small cold shock straight to his chest; when had he ever contemplated a midnight picnic before?

'No need for thanks. All I did was open the fridge.' *But you went looking*, a small voice pointed out. 'Seemed a shame to waste the contents.'

Imogen paused, a caviar-spread cracker halfway to her lips. 'Don't sweat it, Joe,' she said. 'I meant what I said. I don't want any more than a one-night stand. I'm just happy that it's turning out to be a definite once-in-a-lifetime experience.'

Since when had he been so readable? 'So you still don't believe in one-night stands?'

Her slim shoulders lifted in a small shrug. 'I can't see the point in them.'

'Really? Then I must have done something wrong.'

For a second she looked discomfited, her lips forming the cutest circle, and then she chuckled. 'You know damn well you did everything completely right. But it wouldn't feel right to do this on a regular basis. Like I said, I want a lot more than sex from a relationship and I won't risk getting blindsided by lust.'

'I thought we did pretty good on the lust front. Don't you agree?'

'Yes.' Her lips curved up in a sudden sweet smile. 'This has been totally amazing. But in a long-term relationship there are other things that are way more important.'

'Fair enough. But why not go for it all? Security, shared goals *and* great sex.'

Imogen blinked, as if the idea had never even occurred to her as a possibility, and then she shook her head and sipped her champagne. 'Honestly? I think a dynamite attraction would fuzz my brain and my perspective. I don't want physical desire to affect how I think and reason, or cause me to make stupid decisions. I've seen how that works out. My mother married my father because she fell in lust—and, believe me, their marriage is *everything* I don't want mine to be.'

The vehemence in her voice twanged a chord of empathy in him. 'Yet they've stayed together, haven't they?'

Perhaps Imogen knew the answer as to why two unsuited people stayed together despite every reason in the world to separate. An image of his own parents came to his mind and he felt the familiar gnarling of emotions in his gut. Frustration, confusion, anger, bewilderment.

Max and Karen McIntyre—good-looking, rich and devoted to each other. Or so they had appeared to Joe. Because he'd seen what he'd wanted to see or what they'd wanted him to see? Little wonder that he'd been sent to boarding school—he could only imagine the strain the pretence must have cost his parents.

'Yes,' Imogen said. 'They have. I think it's because in some dreadful way they've become codependent. So used to the shouting and the arguments and the bitterness they can't imagine leaving. They've made a mess of it and I don't want that—I certainly don't want that for my children. So I think I'll stick to my tick-list and keep sexual attraction off it. It's not a big deal.'

Given her earlier responsiveness, her sheer uninhibited enjoyment, that was hard to believe. And anyway... 'Don't take this the wrong way, but clearly the tick-list didn't work with Steve.'

'Noooo. But the principle is still sound. All I need to do is amend the list to make sure I avoid men who are still hung up on a previous girlfriend.' A small sigh escaped her lips. 'You'd think that would have been obvious, wouldn't you? Instead I was sure I could be the one who'd help him get over her—be there for him, build up a relationship. *Hah!*'

Joe frowned as he considered her words. 'You're telling me Steve left you for his ex?'

'Yup. It's even worse, in fact.' Her hands clenched round a fold of red sheet.

'What happened?'

Jutting out her chin, she gazed at him almost defiantly, her blue-grey eyes daring him to feel pity. 'I gave Steve tickets for a cruise for his thirtieth birthday a few months ago. He took Simone instead of me and proposed to her on the cruise. They're getting married in a couple of months.'

'For real?'

'I don't think you could make that up.'

'Well, I'd like to say I'm sorry. But I'm not. The man sounds like an absolute tosser and you're way better off without him.'

Imogen's lips curved up in a sudden smile. 'So no sympathy?'

'Nope.' He topped up their glasses and raised his. 'I think it's more a cause for celebration. To a new start.'

The chime as crystal hit crystal was oddly significant, and as if feeling it Imogen wriggled backwards to lean against the graceful curve of the headboard.

Shaking away the emotion, Joe took her empty plate from her. 'You done?'

'Yes.'

'Good. Because I have some excellent ideas for what to do with the strawberries and cream.'

She moistened her lips. 'Care to share?'

'Oh, yes. I have every intention of sharing. Now, come here. And drop the sheet.'

Batting her eyelashes at him in an exaggerated fashion, she pushed the sheet down in one fluid movement. 'Your wish is my command,' she murmured, and the hot rush of desire swept away all other thoughts.

Imogen opened her eyes and for a heartbeat confusion fuzzed her brain—until the twinge of hitherto unused muscles brought back a flood of glorious memories. Memories that culminated in finally falling asleep wrapped in Joe's arms, her cheek nestled against the smattering of hair on his chest.

Rolling over, she realised her only bedmate now was the finger of light that filtered through the slats of the blinds to hit the rumpled, cold red sheet.

A sense of bereavement socked her, and Imogen gritted her teeth. *No!* The night was over and waking up naked in bed together was not the way forward for the professional day ahead. Joe at least had had the sense to realise it.

Yet how could she erase those memories that still buzzed through her veins and exhilarated her body. Surely she wouldn't be human if she didn't regret the bone-deep knowledge that she'd never plumb the depths of lust as deeply again? For the first time ever she truly understood exactly how her parents might have got carried away by a tornado of passion. How they might have believed that if their bodies were so in tune so must their minds be.

Well, Imogen knew differently, but it was probably just as well not to put that knowledge to any further test.

So…no regrets. Instead it was time to haul herself out of bed and start to concentrate on work.

Entering the bathroom, she did her very best to look at it with the eye of an interior designer.

But how could she when her skin tingled as it relived the memory of leaning back against those glittering mirrored tiles, water jetting down, Joe soaping her, his muscles under her fingers smooth, hard, delectable as she returned the favour. The memory made her dizzy her and she clenched her hands around the cool edge of the sink.

Come on.

Lists. That was the way forward. As she showered she focused on the minutiae of the bathroom. Mirrored tiles, wet room, scented candles, exotic shampoos…

Shower over, she tugged her hair into a ponytail, pulled on the simple jeans and striped T-shirt she'd purchased the day before and pushed the bedroom door open.

This was fifty shades of awkward—and her nerves tautened as she approached the kitchen. The aroma of strong coffee tickled her nostrils as she entered and walked across the marble floor to the open French doors.

She put one hand to the side of the door for balance as she took in the scene.

Joe sat at a circular wrought-iron table—damp from the shower, hair spiked up, jeans and navy T sculpting the toned strength of a body she knew by heart. There was a cup of coffee in front of him, his laptop was up and running, his phone was to his ear. So gorgeous… The temptation to grab him by the hand and drag him back to the bedroom had her tightening her grip on the doorjamb.

Moving on. Maybe she should concentrate on the exotic plants that hid the patio from the street, on the hum of traffic, the sunlight striping the verdant leaves. Anything but Joe.

He nodded as he spoke. 'May the best man win. I'll see you on Wednesday.'

He dropped the phone onto the table and suddenly Imogen knew she couldn't face him just yet.

Coffee. The world would come into focus with the help of caffeine.

Hurriedly she turned and headed towards the coffee machine. She just needed a minute to regroup—*breathe in, breathe out and repeat*—then, coffee cup in hand, she headed outside to join him.

Joe was intent on his laptop, his conversation over, a frown creasing his forehead.

'Morning,' Imogen said, and foreboding weighted her stomach. Joe looked formidable—a far cry from the man she'd had a midnight picnic with in bed.

'Good morning.'

Fighting the urge to turn and run, Imogen forced her unwilling legs forward, pulled out a chair and sat down.

What now? For the first time since they had entered the apartment Imogen wondered if she had screwed up monumentally by sleeping with Joe. 'Um…'

His gaze was unreadable, his expression unyielding as he looked across the table at her, and Imogen felt the heat of embarrassment curdle her insides. This was not the expression she'd wanted to see.

Come on, Imo. What did you expect? The night was over and Joe was back in ruthless businessman mode—there was no reason for him to look at her with warmth.

Yet surely what they had shared last night had to mean *something*?

'So how does this work?' she blurted out. 'This is uncharted territory for me. I don't know the etiquette of the morning after. What usually happens?'

'Breakfast and goodbye.' He picked up his coffee cup. 'Unfortunately not an option in this case.'

'Unfortunately?' Hurt crashed into anger and created fury.

For a second she thought she saw emotion flash across his face, and then the guard was back up, his jaw set, the outline of his mouth grim.

'Come on, Imogen, let's be grown-up about this. I could write a whole tick-list of my own with reasons why last night should not have happened.' He closed his eyes and grimaced. 'I can't believe I said that. I meant a list—not a tick-list.'

Imogen forced herself not to flinch. She'd shared something important with him last night about her parents' disastrous marriage and her need for a tick-list, and now he was mocking her.

'I'd rather have a tick-list than some sort of cold, emotionless relationship avoidance criteria.'

A sigh gusted through the air as he pushed his chair back over the paved stones. 'And this is exactly why last night was a mistake. We need to work together—not sit here trading *emotional* insults.'

Imogen opened her mouth and then closed it again, focusing on the backdrop—the terracotta pots and the mosaic patterns of the outdoor tiles

Joe was right. This was about Langley. About keeping Langley safe from Ivan Moreton by winning the Richard Harvey project.

Imogen frowned as Joe's earlier words echoed in her ears. *'May the best man win. See you on Wednesday.'*

'Who were you on the phone to earlier?'

His fingers drummed a tattoo on the table. 'Ivan Moreton.'

'You're going to see Ivan Moreton on Wednesday?'

'Yes.'

'But…'

'But what?'

There was no quarter in his voice or expression; any minute now she'd see icicles form as he spoke.

'Did you think last night would affect my buy-out decision?'

'No!'

What *had* she thought? She'd foolishly, erroneously, stupidly thought the man she'd shared a bed and so much more with last night wasn't capable of selling off the company to a douchebag like Ivan Moreton.

Cold realisation touched her with icy fingers—she'd done the thing she'd sworn she wouldn't. Let lust—the way Joe had made her *body* feel—affect her judgement. Joe had never claimed to be Mr Nice Guy—Imogen had repainted him to suit herself. Just because he could make her body achieve the heights of ecstasy, she'd rewritten his personality.

Idiot. Idiot. Idiot.

Shame coated her very soul when she remembered how she'd spilled her guts about tick-lists, her parents' marriage, Steve and Simone. And what had he shared in return? Zilch—a great big zip-a-dee-doo-dah zero. Humiliation jumped into the mix. Maybe he hadn't even been listening—maybe all his women experienced the urge to confide in him post-orgasm and he just tuned them out until he was ready for the next round.

'Well?' he rasped.

'I have no expectations of you whatsoever.' Hauling in breath, she dug deep, located her pride and slammed her shoulders back. 'There is no need to worry that last night will make any difference at all to us working together.'

She'd made a monumental error and slept with the enemy—forgotten her work obligations and where her loyalty lay. It was time to make up for that. So she'd use what he'd given her—channel the fizz and the buzz, take the memories and turn them into creative vibes.

'*I* care about Langley and I will create a kick-ass proposal that will beat Graham's hands-down. And, yes, I do hope that influences your decision about selling out to Ivan Sleazeball Moreton.'

His email pinged and he glanced down at the laptop screen. For a second Imogen saw irritation cross his face.

'Trouble?' she asked. As long as it wasn't anything to do with Langley she damn well hoped that it was.

'Nothing I can't deal with.' He lifted his gaze. 'So, any ideas yet?'

'Give me a ch—' Just like that an idea shimmered into her brain, frothed and bubbled. 'Actually, yes, I do.'

He gestured with his hand. 'Go ahead. I'm listening.'

Imogen hesitated—right now she didn't even want to share air space with the guy, let alone tell him her idea. But, as she had so spectacularly forgotten last night, Joe McIntyre was the boss.

'I need to show Richard and Crystal that Langley can create an apartment that is essentially French—a place that combines fantasy and reality, a place where they can feel at home and on holiday all at the same time. A home with a sexy edge, with glitz and glamour, but somewhere to feel comfortable. For example—look at this kitchen. It's very minimalist…not really the sort of kitchen you could imagine cooking in. So I'd design a kitchen that conveys the chicness of croissants and coffee, the sexiness of caviar and champagne, but also the hominess of cooking a romantic boeuf bourgignon together. Then on the proposal I'd sketch all those elements.'

To her own irritation she realised she was holding her breath, waiting for Joe's opinion. *Please just let it be a need for the professional go-ahead. Nothing more.*

His fingers tapped on the wrought-iron of the tabletop as he thought.

'Sounds good. Come up with an idea like that for each room and I'll come up with a cost mock-up. Let's get to work.'

CHAPTER EIGHT

'Done.' Imogen dropped the charcoal pencil onto the sheened mahogany Langley boardroom table and blew out a sigh. Exhaustion made her eyelids visibly heavy, and dark lashes swept down in a long blink as she reached for her cup of coffee. 'Here.' She pushed the piece of paper towards him. 'If you hate it don't tell me.'

Joe shook his head. 'I haven't hated anything yet.'

Far from it—over the past two days Imogen had produced some truly exceptional sketches. Perplexity made him frown yet again at her genuine inability to see her own talent. Instead doubt often clouded her vision and caused her to chew her lip in a way it was nigh on impossible not to be distracted by.

Not that he had given even the whisper of a hint of said distraction. After the sheer stupidity of his behaviour in Paris he'd made sure to keep to strictly professional boundaries. As for Imogen—once she'd got immersed in the project it had been as if she'd entered a world of her own.

'I know you haven't. But I'm worried neither of us can see straight any more—we're too knackered.'

She had a point; they'd worked round the clock. They'd worked in the apartment, worked on the Eurostar and come straight to Langley, where they'd set up shop. Grabbing only a few hours' shut-eye on the boardroom sofa.

'And,' she continued, 'this last room is pretty crucial— the master bedroom is meant to be the *pièce de résistance*.'

Full marks to her, he thought. Although a flush tinged

the angle of her cheeks, her voice and gaze were steady. Yet he knew she must be remembering their own bedroom interlude. He glanced down at the sketch and his heart thudded as images filtered across his brain. Imogen had taken the bedroom at Lovers' Tryst and delivered to it her own unique twist. No longer circular, the bed seemed suspended in the air.

'It's a floating bed,' she said. 'It's different and romantic. I know it may be more expensive, but...'

'I'll check.'

'No!' Her face paled as she nodded at the clock. 'Look at the time.'

'It's eleven.'

'Eleven *p.m.*'

'Oh, hell.' The impact of her words hit Joe with a sucker punch. 'Richard said first thing Monday morning and it's an hour until midnight. Do you think we need to get this over there now, rather than at nine a.m.?'

'I think Richard is quite capable of disqualifying us if we don't meet the exact letter of his instructions.'

'So we'd better get it couriered across right now. I'm on it. You get it packaged. We'll email it across as well.'

Anger spiked inside him, along with a surge of adrenalin—he should have spotted that midnight trap right from the get-go. Instead of pondering over Imogen's lack of self belief. Instead of interspersing working flat-out with his fight to sever the bonds of attraction that had him so distracted.

Imogen nodded and raced across the boardroom, and he pulled his phone out of pocket—this proposal would get to Richard Harvey on time if it killed him. No way would he let Langley down—that would *not* be acceptable. If he didn't know a courier service would get it there more quickly he'd take it himself.

Fifteen minutes later Imogen stared at him, worry painting creases on her forehead. 'It *will* get there, won't it?'

'Yes. I've used Mark before—he whizzes round London faster than the speed of light. And Richard's offices aren't that far away. Plus, we know the email made it. So we're covered.' He nodded. 'Well spotted, Imogen.'

'I should have thought of it before,' she said. 'But now I'm worried we've sent a proposal that's not as good as it could be. I thought we had a few more hours to polish it.'

'Don't be so hard on yourself. I didn't think of it at all.'

'You don't know Richard as well as I do.' She paced the room, long jean-clad legs striding the length of the boardroom table. 'I *want* this contract.'

Her smile was tremulous, and for an insane moment he wanted to pull her into a hug, slide his hand down her back and utter soothing words. Shock rooted him to the deep-pile carpet that covered the boardroom floor and he tried to school his features into professional support mode.

'So do I. I promise you it's a damn fine proposal and it's got a really good chance. You couldn't have done more than you did.'

'Huh. That's what I used to tell myself after exams. *You've worked really hard, Imogen, maybe this time you haven't messed it up.*' Her hand covered the slight curve of her tummy. 'Ugh. It makes me feel queasy.' Pressing her lips together, as if to stop the flow of further information, she resumed pacing.

Her words triggered a memory of Imogen in his office just a week before, telling him about her ten-year-old self bringing a report home and her mother's disappointment. He recalled her words in the Michelin-starred restaurant, her fear of undertaking the proposal, and a pang of understanding hit him.

Instinct prompted the words he had used so many times with his sisters. 'You have given this your all and no one can ask more than that. Including yourself. If we don't win this proposal you haven't let anyone down.'

'That's easy for you to say,' she said, coming to a stop in front of him 'If I lose and Graham wins there's a bigger chance you'll sell Langley to Ivan. For you that's just business—another day on the job. But for me… I will have let Peter and Harry down. They will be devastated, and in their state of health that will have a knock-on effect. And I will always wonder if I should have called Belinda in.'

He shifted backwards slightly—not a good plan to have the lush curve of her breasts in his line of sight. 'That was my call, and no matter what happens I stand by that decision. You are taking too much on yourself. Both Peter and Harry have seen this proposal and they love it.'

'That doesn't guarantee I'll win. And if I don't, Langley is one step further to ending up in Ivan's hands. That's a fact, isn't it?'

To his own surprise Joe felt a prod of guilt, even as he forced his features to remain neutral. No way could he let emotional reasoning affect a business decision.

'Yes.'

'There you go, then. *My* responsibility. My bad if it goes wrong.' Her hair shielded her expression as she continued her relentless striding across the room.

He rose and strode towards her, blocked her path as she paced. 'Stop.'

This was important enough that he would force himself to ignore the way her delicate scent enveloped him, would allow himself to get close to her.

'It will *not* be your fault if Langley ends up in a buy-out situation. You will *not* have let Peter down—or Langley. Promise me you get that.'

Her chest rose and fell, her blue-grey eyes were wide as she stared up at him, and suddenly he felt all kinds of a fool. What was he doing, overreacting like this? If only she wasn't so beautiful—ink-stains, smudged eyes, creased T-shirt and all.

Stepping backwards, out of temptation's way, he forced himself to sound casual. '*I* will be making the decisions as to Langley's future—no matter what happens you can absolve yourself from blame. In fact I'll provide you with a life-size photograph of me and a set of darts. How's that?'

'It sounds like a plan.'

A thoughtful frown creased her brow—almost as if she were trying to figure something out. *Join the club.*

'Joe?'

'Yes?'

'I'll still be throwing those darts, and I'm still a bit of a wreck, but…you've made me feel better. Thank you.'

'No problem.' Embarrassment still threatened and he shrugged it off. 'In the meantime, if you want to head home now I'll call you a taxi.'

Imogen shook her head. 'I don't think I'll be able to sleep—I'm too wired on coffee and adrenalin. And what if Richard gets back to us now? I'll stay here—but you don't have to stay as well.'

As if he'd leave her in a deserted building at this time of night. Hell, call him old-fashioned, but he wouldn't leave *any* woman in that situation. Anyway…

'I want to hear Richard's decision too.'

It was no more than the truth—he did want Langley to win this bid as a stepping stone on its way to recovery. And he did also want to be with Imogen when the verdict arrived—to see her lips curve into her gorgeous smile if they won or to offer comfort if they hadn't. That was fair enough. They'd worked incredibly hard for this proposal— had bonded *professionally.*

'Why don't you order a pizza? I don't think we remembered to eat today.'

'Sounds like a great idea,' she said.

His tablet pinged to indicate the arrival of an email. He glanced down and supressed a groan. Leila again. This was now officially out of hand and he had no idea what to do about it.

'Your mystery caller again?' Imogen asked. 'The one who makes you sigh every time you get an email?'

Nearly choking in an attempt to inhale a puff of air, he shook his head. 'She's *not* a mystery caller.'

For a nanosecond Imogen's shoulders tensed, and then she turned the movement into a shrug. 'If she isn't mysterious why don't you tell me who she is?' She hesitated. 'It may help to talk about it.'

'No.'

He regretted the curtness of the syllable as soon as it dropped from his lips, but the thought of explaining the Leila situation in full had moisture sheening the back of his neck.

With an expressive upturn of her palms she rolled her eyes. 'Fair enough. It was just a thought. I'll go and order the pizza.'

Joe watched her as she picked up the phone and then dropped his gaze to the email. Incredulity descended, causing him to reread the words in the hope that he'd got it wrong. *Now what?*

His gut informed him that he was seriously mishandling Leila, his actions being dictated by the sear of guilt. His eyes veered up to Imogen—could it be time to acknowledge that he needed some help, here? Every bone in his body revolted at the idea, but as he read the email again panic roiled in his stomach.

There was no choice—he couldn't afford to mess this up and, like it or not, he was way out of his depth.

Imogen placed the order, trying and failing not to watch Joe. It didn't look as if the email was giving him joy. In fact she was pretty sure he'd groaned—and she didn't think it was because she'd ordered him an extra-hot pepperoni, double on the chillies.

His mystery woman was none of her business. Joe had made that more than clear and he was right. It was personal stuff, and she and Joe had already got *plenty* up close and personal. Heaven knew what impulse had even made her offer to help—perhaps it had been the way he had clearly wanted to help *her*?

Tucking her phone back into her jeans pocket, she marched over to him, pulled out the seat opposite and plonked herself down. 'Pizza won't be long.'

'Great.' Thrusting his hand through his already spiky hair, he inhaled audibly. 'Um...now I've read the email, if you're still up for that offer of help, I could do with a little feminine insight.'

Surprise made her raise her eyebrows; it must be bad, because it was clear from the way he had squeezed out each word that the request had been made with total reluctance.

'You *are* a little pale about the gills.'

'I'm feeling a little pale about the everywhere.'

Imogen flicked a glance at Joe's screen and curiosity bubbled to the surface. 'OK, then. Tell me how you can use a female point of view and I'll give it a shot.'

Joe gestured at the email. 'The mystery woman is Leila. She's an ex-girlfriend from seven years ago. I hadn't heard from her since the split, then three weeks ago she emailed me an invitation to her wedding. Which is less than two weeks from now. You may have read about it—her fiancé is Howard Kreel.'

Imogen blinked. 'Your ex-girlfriend is Leila Wentworth? The woman who is engaged to the son of one of the planet's richest men?'

She and Mel and most of the country had discussed the wedding, marvelling over Leila's blonde beauty and the entire rags-to-riches Cinderella story, with an element of superhero thrown in. Howard had rescued Leila in an alleyway, where she had been on the verge of being robbed, and their relationship had grown and flourished from there—to the point where now they were planning a three-day wedding extravaganza in the Algarve.

'Wow.'

'Yeah, *wow*.' The sarcastic inflexion was accompanied by a lip-curl.

Obviously Joe was less than entranced by the prospect. In which case...

'It is kind of weird that she has asked you, but maybe she has literally invited everyone she has ever known. If you don't feel comfortable my advice is not to go.'

Difficult to believe he hadn't worked that out for himself.

Joe shook his head. A faint colour touched his cheekbones and a shadow fleeted across his eyes. 'There's more to it than that. It's...' He drummed his fingers on the table. 'I need to go.'

'Why?'

'It doesn't matter why.'

'Even though you don't want to?'

Impossible to believe that Joe would attend any function he didn't want to. Confusion along with a hint of foreboding threaded through her tummy.

'I don't have a problem going. The problem is that Leila has started sending me emails on a daily basis.'

'Saying what?'

Joe expelled a sigh, and for a moment he looked so bewildered she felt an irrational misplaced urge to lean over and smooth the creases from his forehead.

'Saying how important love is and how I must learn to embrace it—how important it is to find the person of your dreams. Pages and pages of it.'

'So how have you replied?'

'I tell her that my life is very happy as it is, but thanks for the advice. But the emails keep on coming.'

The woman sounded unhinged—which begged the question: why was Joe going along with her?

'I'm not getting this. What happened to being ruthless? Tell her to get knotted and say that you have your love-life perfectly under control.'

'I can't do that.' Joe shifted in his seat, discomfort clear in the set of his jaw and in the frown that slashed his forehead. 'This is important to her—I just need to figure out why.'

Realisation dawned with a sense of inevitability that stuck in her craw. Joe was hung up on an ex-girlfriend. What was it about her that attracted men who held ten-foot torches for old lovers?

'You OK?' Joe asked.

'I'm fine.'

What else could she say? All she'd wanted from Joe was a great night between the sheets. He'd given her that—it made no difference if he'd harboured feelings for an ex whilst he did so. Yet somehow… Damn it, it did. Bad enough that he regretted the night—now the attraction was even further sullied. But that wasn't Joe's problem. It was hers. She'd offered her insight and she'd make good on that.

'Absolutely fine. What did today's email say? Obviously she's upped the ante or you wouldn't need my input.'

'Today's email informs me that Leila has lined me up with a series of potential girlfriends because she wants me to—' he hooked his fingers in the air to indicate quote marks '—"find true love and embrace the peace and inner tranquillity that this true love will bring".' He snorted and pushed away from the table. 'Little wonder I'm a bit green about the gills.'

Imogen frowned—why on earth would Leila want to

set Joe up with a friend of hers? Come to that, why was she so worried about Joe's love life?

Joe exhaled a sigh. 'No way do I want to face a line-up of women, all trying to bring me to a sense of inner tranquillity. Come to that, it would hardly be fair to them. I'm not on the looking-for-love market.'

'Just don't go. That way the line-up can't get you.'

'It's not that's simple, Imogen.' He tipped his palms in the air. 'If Steve and Simone ask you to their wedding will you go?'

'That's different.'

'Why?'

'For a start my mum and Steve's mum are friends—or at least they went to school together. So no doubt my parents will go, and Mum will want me to go so that everyone can see that I'm OK. And Steve and I were together only recently—we share lots of mutual friends and I guess I'll want to show them that I'm not licking my wounds somewhere. So it's a matter of parental pressure and pride. That's not the case for you.'

'But it is important to you that everyone thinks you're OK?'

'Well, yes…'

'It's important to me to see that Leila is OK. And I need her to believe that *I* am OK.'

The words shouldn't hurt as much as they did—yet each one impacted her chest with meaning. Joe was still in love with Leila, but he was willing to stand aside and watch her go to her true love. Leila knew Joe still loved her and was doing her best to get him to move on. Any minute now Imogen would need a bucket.

'If it's important to Leila that you find love then I guess you'd better find a woman, fall in love and take her to the wedding.'

Then perhaps as a finale everyone could watch a herd of flying pigs perform a musical.

'Don't be sil—'

Joe broke off, leant back in the stylish boardroom chair, and surveyed her with a thoughtful expression that set alarm bells off in her mind. The last thing she wanted was for Joe to suspect her state of mind—hell, she wasn't sure she understood it herself yet. She just knew she was sick and tired of hearing about men and their love for their exes. Been there. Done that. And it was getting old.

To her relief the intercom buzzed to herald the arrival of the pizza.

Joe lifted a hand. 'Just give me a second. I'll grab the pizzas.'

'OK.'

Imogen had no intention of taking this conversation further. Joe would have to figure this one out on his own. Maybe he should storm the wedding and declare his love. After all, surely he wasn't the sort of man to stand aside and let the love of his life marry someone else without a fight.

It was nothing to do with her. Yet the insidious feeling of *yuck* still made her skin clammy. It seemed every which way she was doomed to being second-best.

CHAPTER NINE

JOE HANDED SOME money over to the pizza delivery boy and balanced the boxes on both hands as he strode back to the boardroom, his brain whirring as he analysed his idea from all angles.

He pushed the door open and glanced round. Imogen sat at her laptop, intent on the screen, her hair hiding her expression from him, body tilted away from the door.

'Pizza's up.' Joe walked to the other end of the boardroom, put the boxes on the table and lifted the lids.

Twisting away from the screen, she narrowed her eyes and stared at the pizza.

Joe frowned. 'Has Richard called? Is something wrong?'

There must be some reason for her obvious withdrawal.

'Nope and nope.'

'Come on, Imo.' Two sisters had taught him exactly when *nope* meant *Yes—I'm really pissed off.*

'I'm fine.'

'Great. Then would it be OK if we keep talking?'

Pulling out a slice of pizza, he took a bite.

'Mmm...'

She gave a roll of her eyes and an exasperated sigh that blew her fringe upwards...but she rose from her seat and headed over with the instinctive grace that he loved to watch.

She picked up the box. 'There's nothing to talk about. You asked for my advice. I gave it. You won't listen to it. Topic closed.'

'I've got a proposition for you.'

'For *me*?' Eyebrows raised, she halted in mid turn away from the table.

'Yup. You come to Leila's wedding with me and I'll come to Steve's wedding with you.' He allowed his lips to quirk upwards in his most persuasive smile.

'That's a joke, right?'

'Nope.' He tilted his palms upward. 'It's the perfect solution.'

'I wasn't aware *I* had a problem.'

'Think about it, Imogen. You said you wanted to go to Steve's wedding and show everyone you're over him. What better way than to take a man with you? You can present me however you like. As a man you're enjoying a wild, uninhibited affair with or as a boyfriend—either way, it should give everyone the message that you're over him.'

'I may have a bona fide date of my own by then. Either a sex god or the perfect man.'

'Maybe you will.' The idea was not one he wanted to contemplate or encourage. 'But most likely you won't.'

Her eyes narrowed. 'Why's that?'

'Because it's going to take you at least a year to find a man who ticks all the boxes on your list. That or a miracle.'

'Really?' Her voice would have created ice in a desert.

'Anyway, the point is you can help me and I can help you. You come to Leila's wedding and you'll be showing people you're *already* over Steve. In style.'

For a second he thought he had her, and then she shook her head and redirected that laser look at him.

'So I can help you *how*, exactly?'

'It's simple. I take you, we pretend to be in love—that will make Leila believe I'm OK and I'll be safe from the line-up of women.'

It was genius. As long as he ignored the small voice

that pointed out that it would mean spending three days *and nights* with Imogen Lorrimer.

Not a problem. After all, they had already had one night together—he'd already broken Rule One. It was inconceivable that he would break Rule Two. Even if Imogen wanted to—and he was damn sure she didn't.

'So I'll be camouflage?'

There was an edge to her voice that indicated Imogen was failing to see the mastermind qualities of the idea. But he really couldn't see her issue. It had been her suggestion that had sparked the idea in the first place.

'Yes.'

She slammed the pizza box down on the table with a thunk. 'Can you not see how insulting that is?'

'Insulting to whom?'

'*Me!*'

Joe stared at her; her blue-grey eyes sparkled with anger and her hands were clenched into small fists. 'How do you figure that?'

'You really can't see it, can you? I stupidly told you about Steve and Simone, but you still don't get it.'

'So why don't you calm down and explain it?'

'Fine. You—' a slender finger was jabbed towards his chest '—still love Leila. You don't want Leila to know you're holding a torch the size of the Empire State Building for her but, believe you me, it's obvious—and she knows it. If I come with you everyone will watch you mooning over Leila and feel sorry for me for being second-best. Or however far down the list I come in your table of one-night stands. So, thanks—but no thanks. I am *not* coming along to be an object of pity.'

Anger that Imogen would believe he was such an insensitive jerk clawed at his chest. 'That is the most stupid analysis of the situation imaginable.'

'*Hah!* Face the truth. You are nothing more than an insensitive arrogant bastard with his head up his bum. Well, you can find some other sucker. Hell, seems like I've been second-best or not up to scratch all my life. I'm not doing it again. No freaking way!'

His vocal cords appeared to have stopped working in the face of her torrent of words. Before he could find so much as a syllable her phone buzzed.

Tugging it out of her pocket, she looked down at the screen and the angry flush leeched from her skin. 'It's Richard.'

Joe raked a hand over his face and attempted to locate his professional business head. 'Pick it up. And put him on loudspeaker.'

Imogen hauled in an audible breath, pressed a button and lifted the phone. She wrapped one arm around her stomach and said, 'Hi, Richard. Imogen speaking.'

Looking down, Joe realised his knuckles had whitened as he grasped the table edge—he couldn't remember the last time a business deal had mattered this much to him.

Imogen rocked to and fro on the balls of her feet, her face scrunched into creases of worry, and Joe felt his anger dissipate—to be replaced by a deep, almost painful hope that they'd won this proposal.

'I'm grand.' Richard's voice boomed. 'Thank you for your proposal. Crystal and I have discussed it, and Graham's, and…'

Joe watched as Imogen caught her lower lip in her teeth, felt his gut lurch in sympathy.

'Yours came in more expensive…'

Her shoulders slumped and Joe rose to his feet, striding around the table to take the phone, see if he could negotiate.

'But we absolutely loved the premise so we've decided to go with you.'

'*Yes!*'

He could feel the grin take over his face as he heard the words, saw the smile that illuminated Imogen's features as the conversation continued.

'Th...thank you so much, Richard. Absolutely. Yes. I'll get a contract across to you as soon as the office opens for business.'

Dropping the phone onto the table, she fist-pumped the air before doing a twirl—he could almost see the elation fizzing off her and it made his chest warm.

'Congratulations. You did good.'

'*We* did good. They loved it. I mean *really* loved it. You heard Richard—he said the idea was inspirational and that the sketches made him feel like he was living and breathing France. He also said that the proposal was balanced by a sensible and realistic budget that showed him we'd done our homework. *We* gave better value for money *and* showed a much better understanding of what they wanted.'

Another twirl and she ended up right next to him, so close that her delicate flowery scent assailed him. So close all he had to do was reach out and...

Her eyes widened as she looked up at him—and then she jumped backwards, shaking her head.

'I...I...need to let Peter and Harry know, and—'

'It's one a.m., Imogen. Best to wait until morning.'

'Of course... Um...well, thank you, Joe. I truly mean that.'

One long blink and then she smoothed her hands down her jeans, the rise and fall of her chest distracting him as she breathed deeply. Once, twice, thrice.

'Sorry I got a bit heated earlier. I hope that you work it out with Leila and the wedding goes all right.'

'Whoa. Not so fast.'

'What do you mean?'

'I mean we hadn't finished our conversation. I thought you'd just hit your groove, in fact.'

'Yes, well… Probably a good thing we were interrupted. Before I screeched along in my groove and got myself fired.'

Affront panged inside him. 'I wouldn't fire you because of a personal argument.'

Her nose wrinkled in obvious disbelief. 'Um…good to know. But as far as I am concerned the topic is over.'

'Think again. I am *not* still in love with Leila.' The idea was laughable, even if he didn't feel like cracking so much as a smile. 'You will *not* be seen as second-best.'

Imogen huffed out a sigh. 'It's not going to fly, Joe. You're kidding yourself if you truly believe you're not carrying a flaming torch for her. There is no other explanation. No girlfriend since Leila. Just one-night stands. An aversion to relationships. Going to her wedding to make her happy. Wanting her to believe you're OK. Willing to lie and undergo an elaborate charade rather than say no to her.'

For a second, shock had him bereft of speech—he could see exactly why Imogen had added up two and two and got approximately a million. But now what? It wouldn't be easy to convince her of her utter miscalculation without telling her a lot more than he wanted to share.

Joe drummed his fingers on his thigh as he weighed up just how badly he needed Imogen's cooperation. Damn it—he couldn't come up with a better solution to the whole Leila issue than to take Imogen to the wedding.

Bottom line: he needed her on board.

Though it was more than that—truth be told, he didn't want to feature in Imogen's brain as a man hung up on his ex. The idea of being lumped together with a git like Steve left an acrid tang. If he wanted to bring utter honesty to the table he could see that Imogen was hurt, and that made his skin prickle in discomfort.

So he would have to tell her the truth.

'I'm not holding a torch for Leila. Truth is, I owe her.'

'Owe her what?' Imogen's brow creased.

Guilt panged inside him at his past behaviour; discomfort gnawed his chest at the thought of the man he had been. *Come on, McIntyre. No truth...no lifeline at the wedding from hell.*

'Leila and I met nine years ago at uni.' A lifetime ago. 'We started going out.'

The cool surfing dude and the hot surfer chick. Tension shot down his spine.

'Then two years later my parents died in a car crash.'

Imogen stilled, her eyes widening in shock as she stretched her hand across the table. He let it lie. He needed to focus on getting the facts out—there was no need for sympathy along the way.

'Joe. I am so sorry. I had no idea. I can't even imagine what that must have been like. But it must have been devastating for you. For you all. Your sisters...'

'It was a difficult time.' Not that he had any intention of going into detail; the lid was not coming off *that* buried box of emotions. 'For me, for the twins, and for Leila as well.'

Imogen frowned. 'Difficult for Leila how?'

'I made it difficult. I had to grow up fast and I put pressure on her to do the same.'

'The twins?'

'Yes. It got complicated. Holly and Tammy were eleven; I was twenty-one.' Twenty-one with a promising surfing career ahead—not exactly parent-equivalent material. 'There were no relatives on the scene so Social Services intervened, questioned whether I could look after them or whether they would be better off in care.' The taste of remembered fear that his sisters would be wrested from him coated his throat. 'Obviously there was no way I could let them go but...that was tough for Leila to understand.'

Imogen scrunched up her nose in clear disapproval. 'So Leila jumped ship?'

'Yes. No discredit to her. She was twenty-one as well—she didn't want to settle down and raise two grieving, rebellious pre-teens who didn't even like her.'

Her shoulders hitched in a shrug. 'Hmm... Call me dim, but I don't get how that makes you owe her?'

'Because I didn't take her ship-jumping very well. I was desperate for us to stay together.'

He'd been a mess of confusion, frustration, fear and anger as he'd watched the life he'd thought he had unravel—as he'd realised everything he'd believed his parents to be had been an illusion. The idea that everything he'd thought he and Leila had was another fantasy had been hard to get a handle on.

'I thought love should conquer all and a woman should stand by her man. I believed that being in a stable relationship would help me in my case for winning custody of the twins.'

Her blue-grey eyes held an understanding he didn't merit.

'That seems more than reasonable, Joe. You must have been terrified and grieving and shocked. You needed your girlfriend's support.'

'Unfortunately I wasn't exactly firing on all cylinders, so I wasn't at home to reason. First I proposed marriage.' He gave a small mirthless laugh as he remembered his frenzied planning and his clumsy stupidity. The candlelit dinner, the violins, the ring bought with scraped-together money he'd ill been able to afford. 'Leila refused to marry me and I... Well, I reacted badly.'

Imogen rose and walked round the table to sit beside him, placed a warm hand over his and held on when he tried to pull away.

'Save your sympathy. Believe me, I don't deserve it. I

made Leila's life hell. I couldn't let it go. I begged, threatened, hounded her. I tried character assassination tactics and I made wild promises. The works.' Shame seared his gut, along with the bitter memory of his abject neediness. 'In the end she threatened me with a restraining order and I forced myself to back off before the custody case went down the pan. So, you see, I do owe her.'

Imogen's hand tightened over his. 'You're being pretty hard on yourself. You were in a bad place then, coping with a lot of emotions.'

'That didn't give me the right to stuff up someone else's life.'

'That's plain dramatic.'

'I wish. Leila has invited me to her wedding because her therapist has recommended it so she can have closure and truly move on in life with her husband. Turns out she's been racked with guilt all these years and it's prevented her from forming relationships. Even now she's had to work extremely hard in therapy to believe herself worthy of love.'

'Joe, this all sounds a bit screwy to me. Wouldn't it be more sensible for the two of you to meet up in private, not at her wedding? Talk it through?'

He rubbed the back of his neck. 'Apparently her wedding is symbolic for both of us. She's the injured party here—I'll do whatever it takes to help her to find closure. I did send her a letter years ago, to apologise and let her know I'd won custody of the twins. I guess she never got it. I guess I should have tried harder to make amends. But, whichever way I look at it, the least I can do is go to the wedding. Not because I have any feelings left for her but because I owe her. Question is: will you come with me?'

There was a million-squillion-dollar question if ever there was one. Could she survive three days in the Algarve with

Joe? Forget days—what about the nights? What about the posing-as-loving-girlfriend factor?

Emotions swirled round Imogen's stomach and questions whirled around her brain. Overriding everything was the instinct just to say yes. Because her heart was torn by what Joe had told her and the tragedy he'd gone through. Because her chest warmed with admiration for the way he had fought to look after his sisters, his decision to take on a responsibility far beyond his years. And because she was damn sure Leila wasn't as injured as all that—something was off…she was sure of it.

But somehow she had to retain perspective.

She released his hand and picked up a piece of pizza—more for show than out of hunger. 'I'm not sure lying to Leila is the way forward. You'd be better to talk it all through.'

A barely repressed shudder greeted this suggestion—she'd swear his gills had paled further.

'Wouldn't work. I've tried for the past three weeks to convince her I'm perfectly happy as I am and that she has no need to feel bad. I've got nowhere. Leila needs to see me gallop off into the sunset to my own Happy Ever After.'

Maybe he had a point—talking to Leila did sound pointless. She seemed determined to see things her way. Mind you, so did Joe—he seemed unable to see that his behaviour, whilst not right, had been motivated by grief.

'Fair enough. But why me? There must be women queuing up to go with you—especially to the wedding of the decade. You could take anyone.'

'I don't want to take *anyone*—I want to take you.'

Her heart skipped a beat. 'Why?'

'Because I don't exactly have a list of women I can ask to pose as my girlfriend. And if I hire someone I risk them going to the press—this wedding is big news. I trust you not to do that.'

There was a daft, puppy dog aspect of her that pricked up its ears at any approval. Gave his words a significance they didn't have. The man was her boss and he had the power to make or break Langley. To give him credit, she knew he wouldn't use that to sway her decision—but there was every chance he'd sack her if she ran round betraying him to the press. Hell, she wouldn't blame him.

'Imogen? Yay or nay?'

Think, Imo.

It was a stupid idea for so very many reasons. Such as…

'What about Paris?'

His face shuttered: features immobile, eyes hard. 'What about Paris?'

'Won't it be…awkward?'

'Nope. The past few days have been fine, haven't they?'

Only because they'd become so immersed in work that somehow the awkwardness, the anger and the coldness of the morning after had thawed. Even then 'fine' was probably an exaggeration. Because to her own irritation, her own self-contempt, despite her absorption in work desire had strummed, *flared*, clenched at her tummy muscles with each accidental brush of his hand.

She had managed to keep her cool, not betrayed that desire by so much as a glance, but even so three days and nights in Joe's company would be akin to taking up fire-eating as a new career without any training. It wasn't just stupid—it was crazy.

'Yes. But you're proposing we act as a couple at a wedding. It's a bit different from working together in a boardroom.'

'It won't be a problem.'

As if just because he said so it would be so.

'I've never broken my One Night Only rule and I have no intention of starting now. You were pretty clear that you didn't want a repeat performance either. We agreed one night; we've had one night. I can't see an issue.'

Yet for a fraction of a second his gaze skittered away as he rubbed his neck—and there was the hint of a tic pulsing in his cheek.

Curiosity rippled inside her, along with a thread of sympathy. 'Is your rule because of what happened with Leila?'

Joe snorted. 'Spare me, Imogen. My relationship decisions have nothing to do with Leila or our split. One-night stands suit me because my priority is my sisters. The last thing they need is me introducing anyone into our circle who may not remain in it. But celibacy isn't my chosen option. Equally I have no desire to hurt anyone. One night means there's no time for hopes to be raised or for a relationship to be a possibility.'

'Oh.' That all made perfect sense, and yet... 'How old are your sisters now?'

'Eighteen.'

His face softened and his lips tilted up into a smile of affectionate pride that touched her.

'They're off travelling for a year. Holly has a place lined up at uni and Tammy wants to get straight into the job market. She's already landed a job in television—' He broke off and shook his head. 'Sorry—you don't want to hear about the girls.'

'Actually, I do,' Imogen said. 'It sounds like you've done a marvellous job, and it's wonderful that you've encouraged them to follow their dreams.'

Live the dream.

Moving on fast... 'But now they're eighteen they won't be so affected by you having a relationship longer than a night with someone.'

'I know that. But now it's about what *I* want—and I don't want the hassle or the commitment of a relationship. I love my sisters, and I'll always be there for them, but right now I'm going to kick back and see what it's like to be not just fancy-free but footloose as well.'

That made perfect sense too—he'd had his twenties turned upside down, been emotionally and fiscally responsible for two grieving young girls. Of course he would avoid further commitment like the avian flu. Yet she couldn't help but wonder if he had been more affected than he realised by Leila.

'Anyway… What's your decision? Three days in the Algarve at the wedding of the year? Surrounded by sunshine and the rich and famous? Showing Steve and Simone and the world that Steve is a dim and distant memory?'

When in doubt, eat pizza.

As she chewed Imogen tried to think. Every sensible bone in her body told her to scream *aargghhh* and run the hell away. But she couldn't—she wasn't made that way. Joe might be a ruthless corporate machine, but it turned out he was a human being too. A man who had undergone tragedy and stepped up to the plate to take on a responsibility beyond his years. Her heart ached for him—for the loss of his parents and all the attendant consequences.

Plus, for reasons she couldn't fully fathom, the thought of abandoning him to the wedding—the thought of him being pursued by a line-up of women on the catch for him—had her teeth on edge. There was also the consideration that this wedding would garner publicity, and she'd be less than human if she didn't want to cock a snook at all the people pitying her for Steve's defection.

So what was holding her back, really? Fear that she'd rip all his clothes off? That wouldn't happen. She'd learnt her lesson in Paris—realised that lust truly was dangerous and that all her theories were bang on the nail.

Joe didn't tick any boxes on her tick-list and as such he was off-limits.

'I'll do it,' she said.

His lips curved up into a smile that creased his eyes and flipped her tummy.

'Provided we have separate rooms.' No need to test her resolve too much.

'Separate beds. Apparently I have been allocated a twin room in a villa. Leila and Howard are paying for everything for all their guests. I think separate rooms would defeat the purpose of the whole charade.'

'Fair point.'

Joe reached for his tablet. 'I'll email Leila. Explain that I met you recently and it was love at first sight. We spend three days making sure she believes we've fallen for each other. She swans off into the sunset with full closure achieved.'

It all sounded so simple, and yet a faint flicker of foreboding ignited inside her.

'This calls for a celebration,' Joe stated, and strode across the boardroom to the fridge. 'I bought a few bottles of champagne so the office could celebrate if we won the proposal. I think a toast is in order right now.'

Minutes later he handed her a glass of sparkling amber liquid and clinked his glass against hers. Only then did she realise the sheer error of letting herself get so close.

His sculpted chest was just millimetres from her fingers. His warm scent ignited a deep yearning. Images strobed in her brain. Paris. Champagne. Naked Joe. Naked Imogen.

His eyes darkened, his powerful chest rose and fell, and she wondered if his heart was pounding as hard as hers. Then his jaw clenched as he stepped backwards and raised his glass.

'To the Harvey project,' he said. 'And to the Algarve.'

CHAPTER TEN

IMOGEN STARED OUT of the window of the aeroplane and tried to relax. Before her muscles cramped from the strain of keeping the maximum distance from Joe. Why couldn't she focus on the glorious blue of the sky and the wisps of cotton wool cloud? As opposed to the glory of the toned body scant millimetres from her own and the wisps of ten days' worth of dreams that clouded her brain.

Ten days during which she had managed to avoid him at Langley—relieved that he had held a lot of meetings off site, relieved that he'd spent a lot time closeted with Peter and Harry, walking them through the changes he'd made.

Maybe this hadn't been the world's best idea after all. Mel thought she'd lost the plot *and* her marbles, but Imogen had assured her she was in no danger. The irony wasn't lost on her that she had been sucked into helping another man with his ex-girlfriend issues. But Joe wasn't Steve and the situation was different. Imogen wasn't interested in Joe—he had no long-term relationship potential and she certainly didn't trust this damned attraction that had her practically squirming in her seat.

'So,' he said. 'Peter tells me that the Paris apartment is going well?'

'Yup.' This would be the *other* reason why she'd been avoiding Joe. 'Gosh. Look at that cloud. It looks a bit like a dragon, don't you think?'

'Nope.' He turned his torso so that he faced her and didn't so much as glance out of the window. 'He also said that despite my interim report recommending that you work on the project you've refused.'

'That's right.' Realising she'd folded her arms across her chest, she pushed down the absurd defensiveness and met his gaze full-on. 'There's no need. Peter is so excited by Richard's apartment he's back on form, and he and Belinda are working flat-out. Harry is back part-time and keeping an iron fist on finance, just as your report stated. Plus, there's been an awful lot of admin work to do—especially with all the new procedures you've recommended. So I appreciate your suggestion but I've decided that isn't the way forward for me. From now on I'm a PA and nothing more.'

An ominous frown creased his brow. 'Why?'

'Because…'

Because her time with Joe had terrified her on all sorts of levels and she'd run screaming back into her comfort zone and barricaded all the doors.

'I want to concentrate on streamlining my job properly. Also I need to focus on other aspects of my life. Like finding a place to live, thinking about my future.'

The future she had been in danger of forgetting. The nice, safe, secure one with her tick-list man.

His lips tightened and his eyebrows slashed into the start of a scowl.

'Anyhoo,' she said brightly. 'All in all it has been a very busy few days, so I think I'll catch some sleep.'

As if.

But at least closing her eyes put an end to the conversation. It had been tough enough to explain her decision to Peter—almost torturous not to get involved in the project itself. But her resolve had been bolstered when she'd heard Belinda on the phone to her husband, explaining night after night that she had to work late, seen her harassed expression when her child-minder had let her down. All a timely reminder of what could happen if you let a job take over your life. That was not for her.

Forcing herself to breathe evenly and remain still, Imogen kept her eyes firmly closed for the seemingly endless remainder of the journey. Relief arrived when the plane finally began its descent and she could legitimately stretch her cramped muscles.

'Nice rest?' Joe asked, a quirk of his lips expressing scepticism.

'Lovely, thank you.' She could only hope her nose hadn't stretched a centimetre or so. 'I can't believe I'm in the Algarve!'

Still hard to believe even when they descended the steps and a definitely non-British sun kissed her shoulders with glorious warmth as they headed for the airport terminal.

Once they had successfully negotiated passport control, customs, and collected their luggage Imogen looked round. 'What happens now?'

'According to my email from the very efficient wedding planner there will be a car to take us to the villa.' Joe glanced round. 'There we go.'

Following the direction of his finger, Imogen saw a man in a chauffeur's cap and suit holding up a card emblazoned with. 'Leila and Howie's guests'.

As they approached they saw a few others headed the same way. Imogen eyed them, a lump of doubt forming in her tummy. 'They look very glam,' she whispered. 'I'm not sure I'll fit in.'

Joe shrugged. 'And that's a problem because…?'

Before she could answer they had reached the chauffeur, whose name-tag identified him as Len.

'Joe McIntyre and Imogen Lorrimer.'

Len scanned his list and then shook his head. 'You're down for a different car.' He glanced round and pointed. 'Luis will be looking after you.'

'Senhor McIntyre—Senhorita Lorrimer?'

Imogen smiled at the young man who beamed at them as he pushed an overlong lock of dark hair from his forehead.

'I am Luis. I am one of the wedding planners and I will do my best to answer any questions you have about the timetable and I will deal with all your requirements. But first come this way and I will take you to your wonderful accommodation for your stay in the Algarve. All, of course, courtesy of the bride and groom.'

He paused for breath and then smiled again.

'The car is this way. I will take you the motorway route as you will want time to get ready for the ceremony. But there will be lovely scenery towards the end of the trip.'

Imogen glanced at Joe as they climbed into the four-wheel drive car. What was he thinking? It was impossible to tell from his expression but he must be feeling something. The one love of his life, the woman who had driven him to desperation—even if he was over her, even if he hadn't seen her for seven years—was getting married.

None of her business—she was sucked in enough; she couldn't risk getting further involved. That way led madness.

It was best if she concentrated solely on the scenery for the rest of the journey. So as the car glided down the motorway and then wound its way along bendy valley roads she inhaled the sweet breeze and soaked in the greens of the verdure outside until Luis said, 'Nearly there.'

Her vision didn't yield so much as a hut, let alone a villa, and Imogen frowned as Luis turned down a dirt track. 'Wow. So the villa is really secluded, then?'

'Villa?' Luis said. 'No, no—did no one email you?'

'No,' Joe growled. 'Should they have?'

'Yes. You see, all the singletons have been assigned the

villas. You have been given a yurt. You will *love* it. Full of luxury and romance. It is five-star.'

The scenery became so much irrelevant colour and the brilliant sunshine faded as Imogen struggled for breath. 'A *yurt*?' she coughed out.

'Do not worry. This is a state-of-the-art yurt. All mod-cons. Leila and Howard have had them specially put up for the occasion. You will be able to fall asleep together, gazing up at the stars.'

Tension ricocheted from Joe's body and no doubt collided with hers; in fact their mingled tension could probably power a rocket. All the way to the ruddy stars.

'Here we are,' Luis said cheerfully, apparently oblivious to the atmosphere as he parked the car and turned to look at them. 'Howard was very particular about your accommodation, so I hope I can report back to him that you are happy. Yes?'

Oh, hell and damnation. They were supposed to be a loved-up couple and Imogen had no doubt that Howard Kreel would much rather that was *exactly* what they were. It couldn't be much fun for the groom, having his bride's ex-boyfriend there for 'closure'.

This was clearly her cue to be adoring, when in actual fact the desire to strangle Joe with her bare hands was making her palms itch. 'Of course we're happy,' she said. 'How would it be possible *not* to be happy? Don't you agree, sweetheart?'

'Absolutely,' Joe said, with a credible attempt at enthusiasm and an overdose of heartiness. As if Joe had ever been *hearty* in his life. 'Imogen and I are sure to appreciate every second of our stay.'

'Excellent.' Luis sprang out of the car and opened Imogen's door. 'Then I'll take you on a guided tour of the site and leave you to it.'

Imogen tried to appreciate the fairytale beauty of the

site—she really did. It was a good few steps up even from a *glamp*site. Lord knew how much it must have cost to convert the area so spectacularly. Tipis and luxury tents dotted the area—all individually decorated and all, Luis assured them again, equipped with a variety of mod-cons. Two large wooden huts had also been constructed.

'There is the bar and the dining area. Meals and refreshments will be available all day.'

In addition to what money could buy was the wealth of nature's offerings—the colourful flowers, the vibrant vegetation, the lap of water from a small brook that wound its way down a rocky precipice and then meandered through the lush lime-green meadow.

And there in a secluded corner…

'Here we are,' Luis announced, gesturing at a pink canvas palace. 'You have guaranteed privacy. All the details about the wedding and the reception and the available activities are in a folder inside. The coach will arrive at four to take you to the beach ceremony.'

'Fabulous. Thank you *so* much, Luis,' Imogen trilled, forcing her lips upward, keeping the smile…aka rictus… in place as she watched his departing back.

Two more strides and Luis had climbed into the four-seater.

'Not! This is *not* fabulous, Joe. Look at it. It's got *turrets*! It's the yurt of love. What happened to the twin beds in a villa?'

'Yes, well, I obviously got upgraded from singleton to one of the loved-up people.' He thrust a hand through his hair. 'Let's not panic until we've actually looked inside.'

'Fine.' Imogen tugged the canvas door open. 'Um…'

Pink canvas walls were draped with beaded curtains and gauzy material. There were tasselled cushions, luxury pile rugs, an overstuffed sofa, a dressing table…and an enormous sleigh bed.

Below a porthole.

With a view of the stars.

For a fleeting second she wished that there could be a rerun of Paris—another rash decision to break the rules. But she knew that wasn't possible. Once was fine—could be chalked up to a magical experience. Twice… That was way too dangerous and she wouldn't go there. Couldn't go there for the sake of her own sanity.

She was *not* going to end up bedazzled, befuddled and controlled by lust.

Turning to Joe, she swept her hand towards the bed. '*Now* can I panic?'

Joe exhaled heavily and forced his features to neutral. What had he ever done to deserve this? A twin room in a populated villa would have been tough, but manageable. Worst-case scenario: he'd have stayed up in the lounge playing video games. All night.

There was nowhere to go in a yurt.

Chill. He needed to chill. He was a ruthless corporate businessman, for goodness' sake—not an adolescent.

Plus he had no one to blame but himself; this whole jaunt had been *his* damn fool idea. Now he would just have to suck it up.

'No need…' He stopped and cleared his throat, forced more words past the knot of panic in his throat. 'No need to freak out. I'll sleep on the sofa; you can have the bed.'

Rocking back on his heels, he swept a final glance around the tent and rubbed the back of his neck.

'I guess you need to change, so I'll leave you to it.'

Fresh air—that was what he needed. Fresh air and exercise. Perhaps if he walked a very, very long way he'd walk off the desire that urged him to turn round, rip open the door of the yurt and throw Imogen down onto the bed. Walk off the desire.

Master plan, McIntyre. But it was the only one he had…
It didn't work worth a damn.

An hour later, as he approached the yurt, anticipation unfurled in his chest. And when he stepped into the pink canvas bubble he stopped in his tracks. Because Imogen looked so beautiful she robbed his lungs of air. Her dark hair rode her shoulders in sleek glossy waves; a floaty floral dress gave her beauty an ethereal edge.

She rose from the dressing table and faced him, her lips tilted in an almost shy smile as she spread out her arms and gave a twirl, the orange and red flowers of the dress vibrant as they swirled around her.

'Do you think this is all right?' she asked. 'I chose it myself—no help from Mel, no ulterior motive. Just because I like it. But now I'm worried that it's not glam enough.'

'I don't think that's a problem,' he managed. Though his blood pressure might be approaching the turreted roof.

'You sure?'

'One hundred per cent. You look beautiful. I promise.'

Silence enveloped them; awareness hummed in the air. Time to distract himself.

Keeping his movements casual, he headed for the sofa and picked up a leatherbound folder.

'That must be the itinerary Luis mentioned,' Imogen said, her voice slightly high as she sat down.

'Yup.' He stared down at the words and forced his brain to make sense of them. 'So, as we know, after the ceremony there's a Bond-themed party on a yacht. We'll need to take a change of clothes with us. Then tomorrow there are various activities we can do. Leila and Howard will have left for their honeymoon, but they want all their guests to stay and have fun.'

'Activities?' Imogen looked up and there was genuine enthusiasm on her face as she no doubt worked out a way to avoid his company for the day. 'That sounds like a great idea. What sort of activities?'

Joe scanned the list. 'Sightseeing, beach yoga, surfing and…'

'And what?'

'There's an art class run by Michael Mallory, who is a lecturer at one of London's top art colleges. You should do that.'

Imogen narrowed her eyes. 'You don't give up, do you?'

'No. I've seen how talented you are—seems a shame for it to go to waste.'

'That is not your decision to make.'

'Agreed… But I just don't get why you are being so damn stubborn about this.'

For a second unease pricked his conscience. Why did it matter so much to him? Hell, it was way better to have this conversation right now than dwell on all the other things they could do in the Yurt of Love.

'Now is as good a time as any for you to tell me. No excuses—no need to nap.'

'I *did* need a nap.'

'Rubbish! No one sleeps with their body completely still and radiating tension. You were ducking out of a proper explanation of why you refused to go along with my report and help out on Richard's apartment. And please spare me the *I can't do any art because I need to move* crap.'

'It's the truth.' One defiant swivel and she presented her back to him, leaning forward to pick up a lipstick and peer into the heart-shaped gilded mirror. 'So I'll give the lesson a miss.'

'Shame.' Joe leant against the cushioned back rest and picked up the folder again. '"Michael Mallory: esteemed lecturer and mentor to Justin Kinley, Myra Olsten and Becca Farringham, all of whom exploded on to the art scene after graduation. Michael has planned an intense day in which you will learn how to express your artistic instincts and find your own definite artistic voice. This kind of near one-on-one tuition is an incredible chance to learn from a master and—"'

'Stop!' Imogen spun on the chair to face him, her chest rising and falling as she jabbed a mascara wand in the air. 'Just stop—OK?'

'Why? I'm just telling you what you're missing.'

'I get it. OK? I get what I'm missing and I'm good with it.'

Only she wasn't. Not by a long shot. He could see the sparkle of tears in her eyes even as she blinked fiercely. Sense her anger and frustration as she clenched her hands round the edge of her seat and inhaled deeply.

'Imo, sweetheart. You're *not* good with it.'

He stood, strode over the canvas floor and dropped to his haunches in front of her, covering her hands with his.

'Tell me. C'mon. I'm sorry I went on at you but I've seen your talent. That proposal—you made the sketches come alive. I could see the glitter of the mirror, feel the softness of the sheets, smell the freshly baked baguettes.'

'They were just a few pencil and charcoal sketches.'

'They were a lot more than that.' He shook his head. 'I don't get it, Imogen. Why don't you take the project further? I've seen how absorbed you've been, how much it matters to you.'

He had seen her frustration if it hadn't been perfect— the way she'd thrown crumpled bits of paper at the bin— seen the ink streaks on her forehead, the forgotten cups of tea and coffee, the food he'd forced her to eat.

'And that's exactly the problem!' she said.

'Meaning?'

For a moment she hesitated, and then a small reluctant smile tugged at her lips. 'I'm guessing you won't let up until I explain?'

'Nope.'

She leant back against the dresser and inhaled an audible breath. 'I told you my parents' marriage is less than stellar?'

Joe nodded.

'I didn't explain why. The main reason is my dad. He's an artist, and he's dedicated his life to his art even though he's barely sold anything. It's an obsession with him—more important than my mum, more important than me. Mum did *everything*. Worked at any job she could get to pay the bills and put food on the table. She wanted to study, to go to uni, but somehow it never happened. It couldn't because Dad wouldn't go and get a job, it was always, "When I get recognised, then it will all change."'

Her shoulders hitched in a shrug.

'Mum couldn't even leave me with him when she was at work, because he got so absorbed in his work he forgot me. It consumed him. I don't want that in my life.'

His throat tightened as he saw the pain in her eyes. So much made sense now: her desire for a job that didn't challenge her, her need for a partner who pulled his weight.

'Just because your father lost perspective it doesn't mean you would.'

'Not a risk I'm willing to take. And even if I were I couldn't do that to Mum. She had such high hopes for me. She wanted me to be a lawyer or an accountant. Make something of my life…do all the stuff she missed out on. When it turned out I couldn't achieve that she was devastated… I can't disappoint her even more.'

'But surely what your mum wants most for you is for you to be happy? You should talk to her about this. You can't live your life for your parents.'

Imogen shook her head. 'I'm not. Sure, Mum steered me away from art at every turn—but I don't blame her for that. I don't want to be bitten by the bug. Mum *does* want

me to be happy and so do I. I know what I want from my
life—I want to be secure, settled and comfortable. I want
a nice husband and two point four kids. Maybe a Labrador
and a white picket fence. The happy bonus is that I won't
make my mother miserable, watching her daughter follow
the same road as her husband.'

'The less than happy price is that you miss out on something you love.'

'Then it's a price I'm willing to pay.'

'Even to the point of not taking up art as a *hobby*?'

'I can't.' A small shake of her head as she looked at him
almost beseechingly. 'I've realised that these past weeks.
I did love doing Richard's proposal, I did enjoy working
on projects for Peter, but you saw what happened. I became obsessed.'

'That was one proposal—with a deadline. And you
don't have a family yet.'

'Doesn't matter. I have to draw a line under it now.'
As if suddenly realising his hands still covered hers, she
pulled them away. 'Do you understand?'

'Yes, I understand.'

Her words pulled a nerve taut. Years ago, after his parents' death, that had been his exact decision. With two
grief-stricken sisters to look after and a company to try
and sort out—responsibilities that had surpassed his own
dreams—he'd drawn a line under his surfing career. He'd
taken his board out one last time—and the memory of
the cool breeze, the tang of salt, the roll of the waves was
etched on his soul in its significance.

'But I don't agree.'

He rose to his feet and looked down at her. Lord knew
he did know how she felt—maybe that was why he was
reacting so strongly to Imogen's decision. But he'd had
no choice. His sisters were his priority—that was an absolute, and he had no regrets as to his decision. But this…

this was different, and he wished—*so* wished—there was some way to show Imogen that.

'Your talent—your art—is a fundamental part of you that you're shutting down.'

'Maybe. But by shutting it down I get to be the person I want to be.' Her lips curved into a small smile. 'It's truly lovely of you to care, and I appreciate it, Joe, but I made this decision long ago—it's the sensible option. And I'm all about the sensible.'

Turning, she picked up the abandoned mascara wand and leant forward to peer at her reflection.

Only she *wasn't* 'all about the sensible'. He'd seen Imogen Lorrimer at her least sensible and she'd been vibrant and alive and happy.

It's truly lovely of you to care.

Her words echoed round his brain and set off alarm bells. Caring was not on his agenda. Time to back off— Imogen's life was hers. He'd had his say and now it was time to join the Sensible Club.

'Have it your way,' he said.

CHAPTER ELEVEN

IMOGEN SWALLOWED PAST the gnarl of emotion in her throat; she didn't even *know* Leila or Howard, and yet the sight of them repeating their vows had tears prickling the backs of her eyelids.

In a gown that clung to her in diaphanous folds of ivory and lace Leila radiated bridal joy—her smile could probably illuminate the whole of the Algarve. But it wasn't that which touched Imogen most—it was the way Howard looked at his bride. Such love, such adoration, such pride that it was little wonder Imogen's chest ached.

Hollywood, eat your heart out. Imogen, get a grip.

Maybe she was overreacting like this because the setting was so damn movie-like: the golden sand, the lap of waves and the glow of the setting sun that streaked flames of orange across the dusky sky.

What she needed to remember was that this was a moment of time—not a happy-ever-after. Look at her parents: she had pored over their wedding photos as a child, in an attempt to work out how such rosy happiness could have evaporated into screaming and bitterness.

Her parents' dreams had crumbled to dust, their radiance no more than sex and foolish hope. Proof-positive that a marriage based on lust did not work—a marriage between two incompatible people did not work. But a marriage based on a tick-list would. Imogen was sure of it.

There was a collective gasp as Howard lifted his wife's veil and kissed her. As Leila slid one slender arm around his neck Imogen cast a surreptitious look at Joe. Did he mind? Was he revisiting the past, wondering what would have happened if Leila had agreed to marry him all those years ago?

Surely not. He didn't look like a man harbouring thoughts of the past—if anything he looked faintly bored. Unless, of course, it was all a façade—Joe was hardly a man to wear his heart on the sleeve of his grey suit, and that was even assuming he *had* one.

'You OK?' she asked under cover of the applause that had broken out as Howard and Leila continued their lip-lock.

'Why wouldn't I be?'

'You loved her once—whatever your reasons, you wanted to commit a lifetime to her.'

Broad shoulders hitched. 'I'm happy for her—happy that she is happy. That the damage I did has been mitigated. No more than that.' He glanced around. 'Come on. It's the receiving line. So don't forget to turn on the adoring look.'

'I think you've forgotten something.'

'What?'

'It's a two-way street. You have to look adoringly at me too.'

And she had to remember that this was fake. Needed to dismiss the wistfulness that wisped through her brain at the thought that Leila and Simone got the real McCoy version of the adoring look and she was stuck with the false one.

Joe raised his eyebrows, a small smile playing on his lips, and all thoughts of wistfulness blew away, to be re-placed by far more dangerous memories of the havoc those lips could cause.

'You think I can't do adoring?' he asked.

'I'm finding it hard to imagine.'

'Watch and learn, Imogen. Watch and learn.'

His cool broad fingers grasped hers and Imogen bit her lip to hold in her gasp. It was their first contact in days and her skin reacted like a parched plant in the depths of the Sahara to rain.

A little flicker of envy ignited in her as they approached Leila—even the stunning photos that graced the celebrity mags hadn't done her justice. Long blonde hair shimmered under her veil, exotic green eyes lit up as they rested on Joe, and her smile demonstrated the slant of perfect cheek-bones and the curve of glossy provocative lips.

'J!' she exclaimed in a melodious yet husky voice that fitted the setting perfectly.

Any second now birds would swoop from the sky and land on her and everyone would break into song.

Not that Imogen cared. Much. So who knew why a mixture of jealousy and mortification seared her insides as Leila threw her arms around Joe before stepping back and raising a hand to cup his jaw?

'It's so very good to see you, J. I do appreciate you coming.'

Imogen tried not to clench her nails into Joe's palm and made an attempt to access the voice of reason. Leila was the bride—no way was she hitting on Joe. Or should she say *J*? *All* ex-girlfriends didn't have an agenda to win back their boyfriends. This was closure. Yet…damn it… she wasn't imagining that proprietorial look on Leila's face.

Joe stepped back and put an arm around Imogen's waist, squeezed her against him. 'Good to see you too, Leila— and congratulations. This is Imogen.'

Imogen blinked—was that *Joe's* voice? Low and tender and…well…*adoring*? As if he were introducing someone special and precious?

The bride's perfect smile froze a touch—she was sure of it.

'Imogen. I am so happy to meet you. You and I must have a proper girl-to-girl chat at the reception.'

Well, wouldn't *that* be fun? 'Super,' Imogen said, managing a smile as they moved along to stand in front of Howard.

'Joe. My man.' The groom slapped Joe on the back with what looked like excessive force. 'Thanks for coming along, dude,' he said. 'It means a lot to Leila—which is why I told her of *course* I didn't mind. Oh, and from one surfing dude to another—make sure you take your board out while you're here.'

Joe's lean body tensed next to hers and Imogen glanced up at him. Surfing dude? Joe was a *surfing dude*? Could Howard be mixing him up with someone else? There was nothing in Joe's face to indicate his thoughts; his features could have been carved from granite.

'Imogen.' Howard grasped her hands. 'It is so very nice to meet you and to know that Joe is in good hands. Hope you like the yurt?'

'It's—' Before Imogen could reply she saw Leila's head turn.

'But I put Joe and Imogen in the villa, sweetie.'

'I changed the plan, sugar puff. Paid a bundle for that yurt—shame for it to go to waste.'

A small frown creased Leila's brow before she smiled her radiant smile. 'Wonderful idea.'

'It's incredible,' Imogen chipped in, before they moved along to where the bride's and groom's parents awaited.

'Phew...' She whistled as they walked away from the line. 'I don't think you're exactly Mr Popular—with Howard's family or Leila's.'

'No big surprise, given the way I treated Leila.'

Imogen frowned. 'I'm not sure that's the problem.'

'What do you mean?'

'I get the idea they're worried that Leila still has feelings for you. To be honest, if I was your real girlfriend so would I be.'

Come to that, even as his fake girlfriend she wasn't happy about the idea.

Joe shook his head. 'That doesn't make sense. This is Leila's wedding day—she hasn't seen me in seven years. And, believe me, she can't possibly have any good memories of how we parted.'

'I suppose.'

Joe had a point—maybe her imagination had gone into overdrive. So affected by Steve's defection to Simone that she found bugbears where there weren't any. But…

She shrugged. 'Well, bear it in mind as a possibility.'

Before Joe could answer Luis waved at them and headed over. 'It was a beautiful ceremony, yes?'

'Absolutely.'

'And now your change of clothes is in the beach huts. If you come this way, and once you have changed please head for the yacht. Women this way—men that way.'

Joe stepped onto the garlanded deck of the yacht and blinked at the dazzling array of glittering disco balls and spinning lights that strobed the deck with multicoloured lights. Men in tuxedos and women in various Bond girl costumes chattered, their voices mingling with the Bond-themed music. As he scanned the crowd for Imogen he realised that he had no idea what she would be wearing. Not that it mattered—he would know her by her stance, her glorious shape, the sweep of her dark hair.

'You must be Joe,' a breathy voice proclaimed.

Before he could sidestep her a curvy petite woman had launched herself at him on a wave of overpowering perfume.

'Oh, my! You're every bit as gorgeous as Leila said. I'm Katrina. Part of your line-up. I know you've come with some other woman, but I wanted you to see what you're missing, sugar.'

Was she for real? 'No need, thanks. I'm—'

'Oh, come on, darlin'…no man can resist me. Just one little kiss.'

As Katrina pressed her over-glossed lips to his Joe looked over the top of the petite blonde's head to see Imogen walking straight towards them, her gown a swirl of Bohemian tangerine-orange. Her smile dropped from her lips and she faltered for a heartbeat as she took in the scene. Then her lips tightened, and if she could have lasered him with her glare he'd be dead by now.

Taking Katrina firmly by the arms, he hoisted her away from him.

'I'm taken,' he finished.

Katrina turned on one stiletto heel and gave a little giggle. 'Dear me. Caught red-handed. Catch you later, Joe honey.'

'Why don't you chase after her, *Joe honey*?' Imogen asked.

The cool sarcasm caught him on the raw. Surely she didn't believe he'd instigated that interlude?

'Don't mind me.'

'I don't want to chase after her. That was Katrina. One of the line-up you're here to protect me from.'

'Didn't look to me as though you needed protection at all.' Imogen emitted a mirthless laugh as she gestured to his pants pocket. 'Apart from the type that comes in foil packets. And no doubt you've got plenty of those handy in your wallet.'

A flash of anger stabbed him as he leant back against the railings. Did she really think so little of him?

'You don't think you're overreacting a touch?'

'I'm the one who found you with a woman draped all

over you, her tongue practically stuck down your throat. And you think I'm overreacting?'

'Yes, I do. Nice imagery. Even better point: Katrina *was* draped over me—believe me, short of dodging her and letting her fall flat on her face there wasn't much I could do.'

'Oh, please. That is ridiculous—a big, strong man like you couldn't defend himself? I'm sure you have plenty of moves to avoid women of all shapes and sizes, and Katrina is hardly wrestler material. From where I was standing you looked pretty happy.'

Shaking her head so that the orange flowers woven into her hair vibrated, she hoisted her palms in a get-away-from-me gesture.

'I cannot *believe* I could have been so stupid as to come to this wedding with you. I actually bought that whole spiel you gave me.'

What the hell…?

'Spiel? It wasn't a spiel. I told you the truth.' Which hadn't exactly been a picnic for him.

'*Hah!* I just had the dubious pleasure of witnessing "the truth".'

Frustration mixed with bewilderment and he expelled a sigh. 'Imogen. If I wanted to get involved with Katrina why would I have brought you to the wedding at all?'

'Maybe you hadn't realised how attractive Katrina would be. Maybe you're regretting bringing me.' Imogen's blue-grey eyes narrowed and she clicked her fingers. 'Or maybe this is all a ploy to make Leila jealous. What are you hoping for, Joe? That she'll realise that she still loves you?'

For a second sheer disbelief froze him to the spot. Then… 'Enough!'

Propelled by sheer anger, Joe stepped forward and pulled her into his arms.

'Stop it!' Slamming her palms on his chest, she leant

back against his hold. 'No need to kiss *me*. Leila already believes we are an item.'

'Never mind that,' he growled. 'I'm going to show you what a real kiss is—and then you can understand that I was *not* kissing Katrina.'

The idea that she really believed he was such a bastard made his blood simmer in his veins and he sealed her mouth in one harsh swoop. He revelled in the lushness of her lips, the taste of mint and strawberry. Her body stilled and then she tangled her fingers in his hair. The angry stroke of her tongue against his sent a shudder through him and he pulled her tight against him, so she could feel his body's instant savage reaction.

OK. Stop now, Joe. Whilst you can. Point made.

Breaking the kiss, he stared down at her as their ragged breaths mingled in the evening breeze. '*That's* a real kiss,' he rasped. 'Do you really believe I'd bring you here as my guest and then go off with someone else? *Really?*'

Her slim shoulders lifted in a shrug. 'Why wouldn't you? If it was a tactic in your strategy to win Leila back, I'm sure you are more than ruthless enough to do just that.'

'What strategy? I do not want to win Leila back. Even if I did I'm not a complete bastard. I have too much respect for you to treat you as a pawn. I am at this wedding for all the reasons I told you. I have no interest in Katrina. I am *not* Steve. You are not second-best. It's your call whether you believe me or not.'

Before she could answer he saw Luis, wending his way through the tables towards them. 'Ah, here you are,' he said with a smile. 'Leila sent me to find you. She'd like a chat with Imogen.'

Joe bit back the urge to tell Luis to tell Leila to take a hike; he and Imogen were in the midst of an important conversation. It mattered to him that Imogen believed him.

Imogen, on the other hand, practically leapt towards

Luis, clearly relieved to be let off the conversational hook. 'Of course. I'll come straight away.' As Luis started to thread his way through the crowds she turned and murmured, 'Don't worry, Joe. I'll stick to my part of the bargain. *Whatever* your motivations for wanting me to.'

CHAPTER TWELVE

'ALONG HERE,' LUIS said, and led Imogen away from the thronged deck, where people shimmied and twisted to the beat of the music. Imogen followed on automatic, still processing what had just happened with Joe; trying to work out what to believe.

Instinct bade her to accept Joe's version of events, but her instincts were hardly the most reliable—she'd trusted Steve implicitly and that hadn't exactly ended well. Worse, it could be that her instincts had been skewed by that kiss, her brain deceived by a heady cloud of lust. Her lips—hell, her whole body—still buzzed from the aftershock.

The noise from the deck faded as she followed Luis down some stairs and into a private corridor. *Come on, Imogen—get prepared.* She'd told Joe she'd still play her allocated role—convince Leila that she was Joe's muchloved girlfriend.

Her brain whirled. Did Joe have a point? Why would he have kissed Katrina if he wanted this charade to play out? Because he wanted Leila to realise that he wasn't really in love with Imogen and that he was available? Her temples ached as she tried to work it out.

Luis pushed a door open. 'In here.'

For a mad moment Imogen expected him to announce her, but instead he simply flashed a smile and withdrew. Still, the feeling of being a subject granted an audience, or in this case summoned, persisted.

The spacious conference room was dominated by a

sleek oval cherrywood table, with Leila enthroned at one end on an ornate chair. She'd removed her veil, and also the train of her dress, so that now she was encased in a lace concoction that hit mid-thigh and moulded her model figure to perfection.

Suddenly the tangerine Bohemian look seemed a fashion disaster—maybe the black diamanté evening dress would have been better. She shook her head—why was she even thinking about this now? Maybe it was the slightly patronising I-am-more-beautiful-than-you-can-ever-be-and-we-both-know-it look in Leila's green eyes. Shades of Simone's cornflower-blue orbs, with their I-am-more-exciting-alluring-and-interesting-than-you-and-Steve-has-always-loved-me expression.

'Imogen. Thank you for seeing me in private.'

'No problem.' Choking back a sudden surge of hollow laughter, she tried to smile as she sat down.

'Howard and I are leaving tonight, and before I go I need to make sure Joe is in good hands.'

'Right. I see.' Or rather… 'Well, actually—no, I don't. Joe's happiness is not your responsibility.' Unless, of course, Joe's strategy was working and Leila was having second thoughts.

The blonde woman settled back on the chair and shook her head. 'You see, that's where you're wrong. I dashed Joe's hopes to the ground years ago—spurned his love—so I do feel that his happiness is very much my responsibility. He *loved* me so much. I was his world and then I rejected him.'

Hurt touched Imogen and she gritted her teeth, unable to help wondering what it must feel like to have Joe—correction, to have *any* man—think she was his world.

'I feel so awful that I broke his heart like that… And when he looked at me today I saw all that love as though it had never gone away…could be rekindled in a trice…'

The leaden realisation that she had been right plummeted in Imogen's tummy. Joe *did* still love Leila—she had been right on the money.

Wait. The word lit up her brain in neon and her gut screamed at her to listen to it as her brain replayed his words. *'I have too much respect for you to treat you as a pawn. I am at this wedding for all the reasons I told you.'*

She replayed their conversation over pizza in the Langley boardroom. His voice as he told her the truth about his past: the tragedy and its outcome. The guilt over Leila; his need to make amends.

Finding her voice, she met Leila's emerald-green eyes, tried to read her expression. 'Do you *want* to rekindle Joe's love? Do you still love him?'

'No. Not at all. Howie is the man for me. But now I know for sure Joe still has feelings for me I wanted to talk to you, so we can come up with a strategy to help him get over me.'

The hell with this. There was every possibility that she'd regret this, but somehow it wasn't possible for Imogen to believe that Joe had lied to her. Ruthlessness was one thing; dishonesty was another. Steve had lied to her. Joe hadn't. Not once.

'I think he *has* got over you.'

The words were liberating and oh, so right.

Green eyes blinked at her in sheer incomprehension. 'Darling, I know you want to believe that, but it's simply not true. I saw the look in his eyes when he saw me. I—'

'So did I. Joe told me he's over you and I believe him.'

'Then why hasn't he had a relationship since me?'

'Because he's spent the last seven years bringing up his sisters. You know that.'

'Don't I just? Those twins are devil children. I never understood how he could pick them over me. Without the twins maybe I could have stuck it out. Though I don't know… I remember the first time he dressed up in a suit to go and sort out his dad's company. He didn't look like my Joe any more. He'd changed so much. No more surfing— just dull, dull, dull business stuff. No more photo shoots, no more magazine articles, no more parties and travel… Joe could have been a surfing champion—famous, rich, having a life of freedom and fun. With me. He *knew* that was what I wanted, but he couldn't see sense.'

Surfing again. So it was true. Only Joe had been more than a 'surfing dude'—he'd been a champion, with a glittering career ahead of him. Her heart rended at the image of corporate, suited and booted Joe riding the waves, free and laid-back and happy, before tragedy struck.

'He chose the twins over me. And when I told him I couldn't marry him he heaped abuse on my head. I know it was because he was driven to distraction by my refusal and his love for me, but it *hurt*, Imogen. So much.'

For a few seconds Imogen could only open and close her mouth as sheer disbelief silenced her vocal cords. Joe had given up so much and then achieved so much, without complaint, regret or martyrdom. And this idiot couldn't see *any* of that. Could only see how the world revolved around *her*.

Drawing breath, Imogen tried to do as Joe had asked. 'Joe does feel terrible about how he treated you. He did actually write you a letter, apologising and…'

'*Hah!* I got that letter…'

Imogen stilled, a layer of anger laving the inside of her tummy. 'You *got* that letter? Why didn't you contact Joe?'

'What was the point?' Leila shook her head. 'His letter was full of the twins and how he'd won custody. It was too late for him to change his mind. Otherwise I'd have given him a second chance. If he'd seen reason it may not have been too late for us to recapture our love and—'

'Rubbish. You didn't love Joe. You wanted to hang onto

his board shorts and be carried to fame and fortune. And you didn't care what happened to the twins as long as you got what you wanted.'

'That's not true. If he'd loved me he would have put me first. That's what love is. I was trying to show him how to be happy.'

'Joe asked you to marry him. Spend your life with him. If you loved him wouldn't you have at least thought about it? Even if it was just to help him with the twins?'

Leila threw up her arms. 'Those damned twins.'

'They were people, Leila. Children—*grieving* children. How could Joe have lived with himself if he'd abandoned them?'

'Hooey.'

'Hooey?'

'Yes. Hooey.' Leila nodded in emphasis. 'Joe and I could have had a wonderful future together. He would have made a fortune—not just from surfing but from advertising and endorsements. We would have been as big as any of these football celebrity couples. We could have had it all—hell, by now we could have been on reality TV, with millions in the bank.'

'Is that what Joe wanted?'

'Of course. He loved surfing—and I'd have handled all the other stuff. But then he went and blew it.'

Anger was on a slow burn now, along with a feeling of wonder as to why Joe thought he owed Leila *anything*. 'It wasn't his fault his parents died.'

'No, but he didn't have to let it change everything.'

'But it *did* change everything!'

OK, so she'd yelled, but it had been either that or give in and shake some sense into Leila.

'Leila, you need to wake up and smell the coffee—or iced tea, or whatever. Just for a minute can you *please* try and look at this from a different perspective?'

For a second guilt prodded Imogen. Less than an hour ago she'd been just as bad as Leila, willing to condemn Joe because of her own fears and inadequacies. She had judged him unfairly. Now she could make amends. By standing up for him. And maybe she could achieve something more. Because whether he liked it or not Joe had been affected by his relationship with Leila. Maybe this was Imogen's chance to achieve closure for him. And if that meant bursting Leila's bubble then she'd enjoy every second.

'If Joe had done what you wanted and surfed off into the sunset with you what would have happened to his sisters?'

'Well...they...they would have been fine. He could have visited them, kept in touch. They could have come to stay with us every so often.'

'Visited them where, Leila?'

Red stained the blonde's cheeks. 'There must have been other relatives.'

'Nope.'

'The care system. Or...' Discomfort creased Leila's face.

'You didn't think, did you?' Imogen leant forward and slammed a palm down on the table, hearing the frustration sharpen her voice. 'Or rather you just thought about yourself. If it had been me all those years ago I'd have married him to help him through. I'd have stood by him. He's a good man. Who feels terrible about the way he behaved to you all those years ago. He believes he blighted your life. *Did* he?'

The green eyes skittered away. 'I would dream about his anguished face...his words of anger would echo in my eardrums.'

'Leila. This is real life. *Please*. There is a good man up there, beating himself up because he thinks he did you damage. A man who gave up his dream to look after his sisters. A man who built a new life for them and him.'

A man she had accused unfairly and owed an apology to herself. But that could come later—now her chest ached as she held her breath and hoped that her words had had some effect.

There was a long silence as Leila's glossy painted mouth opened and closed, and to Imogen's surprise she saw the green eyes swim with tears.

'Oh, hell,' Leila said. 'Double hell. Now my mascara is running.' A small sniff and suddenly she looked a whole lot more accessible. 'You're right.' She gusted out a sigh. 'I'm behaving appallingly. I've always felt terrible about the way I left Joe. I was young and shallow and, truth be told, I don't believe Joe and I really loved each other. I loved being a surfer chick and he loved having a hot blonde girlfriend.'

'That's OK.' Surprise and a sudden leap of elation at the knowledge that her instincts had been right after all fizzed in Imogen's tummy.

'But that doesn't mean I should have deserted him. And now—because I don't want to face what an outright bitch I was, and I certainly don't want Howard to know—I've rewritten history to suit myself. Without giving Joe a thought. I'm sorry.'

Imogen shook her head. 'It's not me you owe the apology to.'

'You think I should talk to Joe?'

'Yes, I do.' Imogen smiled—whatever her faults, it had taken guts for Leila to acknowledge the truth and want to make amends. 'That way you can both have closure.'

'And I can get on with doing what I'm best at. Being adored and fêted and looked after.'

'I think that's the bride's prerogative. Truly, Leila, I wish you and Howard very happy.'

'We will be, darling. And, Imogen?'

'Yes?'

'I'm sorry I tried to put you in the villa and gave you all those evil vibes. I know what it looks like, but I'm really not interested in Joe. I love my husband. It's just…'

'Just what?'

Leila sighed. 'I suppose I was so caught up in this story I'd concocted, about being the woman Joe would never be able to get over, that it was a bit of a shock to hear about you and then see that he is genuinely happy. But I'm glad he's found real love—truly.'

'Leila, I—'

'No, really. I know he doesn't love easily, but I can see how much he adores you. I'm glad he's found the happiness that I have. I *do* love Howie, so very much. And that's why I'll tell him the unvarnished truth. *After* the honeymoon!'

Leila winked and rose to her feet, and Imogen couldn't help but smile as she followed her out of the room.

Once back on deck, Imogen found a secluded spot and leant against the railings as Leila approached Howard, had a quiet word with him, and then kissed him with a long, lingering embrace before she headed over to Joe. Minutes later the two of them headed off the deck.

Imogen turned and faced out to sea, hoping that the long overdue conversation would help Joe to cut himself a little slack. The sound of the waves lapping against the yacht made her heart suddenly ache. Giving up surfing must have been tough for Joe, and it made his insistence that she try out that art lesson make way more sense.

For a while she lost herself in a daydream, trying to imagine a younger, more carefree Joe, master of the waves, travelling to different competitions, sponsored, fêted, and doing something he loved.

But he'd given that dream up—and done so without martyring himself or making his sisters feel bad. He'd done what Eva Lorrimer had been unable to do—how could she not admire him for that?

The hairs on the nape of her neck rose to attention: a sure sign that Joe was in the vicinity.

'Hey.'

The warmth of his body was right next to her as he leant back against the rails so he was looking directly at her.

'Hey.' She smiled at him tentatively 'How did it go?'

Joe opened his mouth and closed it again, poleaxed by the sheer beauty of her smile. The reddish-orange of her kaftan dress was vivid in the dusk, her eyes bright with a warm, questioning look.

'It was…great.' He felt as though he'd shed a weight he'd barely even known he carried. 'Thank you. Leila told me what you said in there. If you hadn't championed me we'd both have gone on looking back from a skewed angle. Now we've sorted out the good memories and got the bad ones into perspective—and that feels good. So I'll say it again. Thank you.' He paused. 'I take it I'm off the Katrina hook as well?'

'Yes.' She blew out air and brushed her fringe from her forehead. 'I'm sorry. It's just that's exactly what Simone did to get Steve back. Turned up at some party with another man on her arm. He made a beeline for her. Worst thing is, I trusted him—thought he was aiming for closure. Turned out the only place he was aiming for was the bedroom, and I didn't realise. He two-timed me for months and I didn't have a clue. When Steve finally told me the truth he told me I was monochrome, grey, whilst Simone lit up his world.' Slim shoulders hitched. 'But it doesn't mean I should have painted you the same colour!'

'Then he must have been blind. You aren't grey and you aren't monochrome. You're Imogen Lorrimer, smart and beautiful—hell, you practically light up the yacht. I promise.'

For a long moment she stared at him, and his heart

twisted as he saw doubt wrestle with her desire to believe him. His feet itched with the urge to get hold of Steve and kick him round the town for what he'd done to Imogen, undermining whatever self-belief her mother had left her with.

'Thank you.'

'You're very welcome.'

Awareness flickered into being. The strains of music and the raised voices faded and all there seemed to be in the world was Imogen—so beautiful, so damned kissable. *Snap out of it, Joe.*

He forced a smile to his lips. 'Hey, we could start a mutual admiration society.'

Imogen blinked as if to break the spell. 'I'll drink to that.'

'I can take a hint. Hold that thought.'

Joe glanced around and waved at a passing waiter, who came over with a champagne-laden heart-shaped tray, decorated with a photograph of Leila and Howard, arms around each other on a beach.

Seconds later they clinked crystal flutes. 'To mutual admiration,' Imogen said.

A silence fell. Not awkward; more thoughtful.

And then… 'Joe?'

'Yes.' His gaze skimmed over her pensive features, over the delicate curve of her neck, the glorious thick dark hair that waterfalled past her shoulders.

'Why didn't you ever mention that you were a surfing champion?'

He stilled. Even knowing that Leila must have mentioned it, he still didn't want to talk about it. 'It's never come up in conversation.'

'It must have been tough to give it up.'

'It was.'

'Like shutting down a fundamental part of yourself?' she asked, quoting his own words back at him.

Dammit. That was what happened when you started to care about other people. It came back to bite you on the bum.

'Yes.'

'Do you regret it?'

'No.'

Clearly the monosyllabic answers weren't doing the trick. Her expression showed a mix of compassion and admiration, and Joe didn't want either.

'I mean it. Holly and Tammy are way, *way* more important to me than being a surfing pro. It was never a question in my mind that there was any choice. And I've never regretted it. Not once. My sisters are two wonderful people, we've built up a cache of incredibly happy memories over the years and we'll continue to do so. I have a career that I love and that I believe has value. Maybe I lost something, but I gained more. Life is what you make it.'

He'd known that all those years before—been determined never to look back and have regrets.

Blue-grey eyes surveyed him and then she stepped forward. Standing on tiptoe, she brushed a feather-light kiss across his cheek before almost leaping backwards.

'I was right. You're a good man.'

Emotions mixed inside him—the desire to pull her into his arms and kiss her properly along with a residue of embarrassment.

'Hey, there were days when it was hard. Don't make me into a saint because I'm not.'

Days when, surrounded by the collapse of the family business, facing the fact that his parents had not been the people he'd believed them to be, trying to help the twins through their grief, all Joe had wanted was his old life back. He had craved the feel of the waves under him, the powerful exhilaration of meeting the challenge of the swell. He'd yearned for the freedom of the sea instead of the net of responsibilities that had sometimes threatened to drown him.

'When did you last surf?' she asked.

'Just after my parents died.'

Her hand rose and one slender finger twirled a tendril of hair. 'I'll do you a deal,' she said.

'What sort of deal?'

'I'll go to that art class tomorrow if you'll go surfing.'

Whoa. 'I'm not sure that's a good idea.'

'Why not?'

'I haven't been on a board in years. I drew a line under it long ago.'

'Then maybe it's time to rub it out. I understand why you gave it up years ago, and I understand how back then you were scared to surf because it would be too painful. But maybe now you could take it up again.'

'I'm too old and too unfit to go back to a professional surfing life, even if I wanted to. Which I don't.'

'Then what's the problem with just surfing because you enjoy it? For you?'

She laid a hand on his arm, her touch heating his skin even through the thick material of his tux.

'It's OK to feel sad that you had to give up something you loved, lived and breathed. It doesn't make your love for the twins any less, and it doesn't make you a bad person if sometimes you resented what fate did to you. Going surfing won't turn you to the dark side.'

How did she *do* that? Understand those deep, dark feelings of guilt and helplessness he'd experienced back then. Discomfort touched him. This was too much, too close, too…*something.* He needed to make a choice. Imogen had offered up a deal: art class in return for a surf session. So he needed to put his man pants on and get on with it.

'OK. Deal. I'll go surfing tomorrow and you'll go to the art class.'

'Deal,' she said.

Joe felt a little light-headed as silence blanketed them once more. This time it was a different silence. The kind that bound them together somehow. His muscles ached with the need to hold her in his arms.

As if on cue, behind them the strains of the music changed from an electro carnival beat to the pure sound of a haunting, melodic song of love and yearning.

The hell with it. He gazed down at her and the words fell from his lips: 'Let's dance.'

It was an awesomely bad idea, but for the life of him he couldn't bring himself to care. No more thinking—right now he wanted to dance with this woman and no other under the starlit sky. Stupid? Probably. But that was the way it was.

Without a word she pushed away from the railings, stood up straight and stepped towards him.

It felt ridiculously right to tug her into his arms, bringing her lush curves flush against him. Biting back a groan, he slid his hand round the slender span of her waist to rest on the flare of her hip.

A shiver ran through her body and she pressed against him, her breasts against his chest, her hair tickling his chin. As lyrics about desire and vows and promises were crooned onto the evening breeze they swayed together, their bodies a perfect fit.

Imogen looped her arms around his neck, her fingers brushing his nape, and this time he couldn't hold back the groan as his pulse-rate rocketed. His hands rested on the curve of her bottom and she looked up at him, lips parted, eyes wide and dark with desire.

How he craved her—with a longing that hollowed his

gut in an intense, deep burn of heat. There was only so
much flesh and blood could stand, and his had stood it.

'Let's go,' he said.

Rational thought tried to intervene.

'Unless you want to stay for the photographs? The paps
will be here soon.'

'I don't care. Let's go.'

There was no hesitation in her voice—just an acknowl-
edgement that her need was as great as his.

She swallowed. 'Though we should say goodbye to
Leila…'

'We'll write a thank-you note.'

Impossible to wait, to make the time to find the bride
and groom amongst the crowds. He clasped her hand, in-
terlaced his fingers in hers and pulled her towards the steps
leading off the yacht.

Imogen pushed the door of the yurt open, her heart ham-
mering against her ribcage and her whole body one great
big mass of need. Following behind her, Joe shoved the
door closed and she turned to face him, terrified he'd
change his mind even as she knew he wouldn't.

He was no more capable of stopping this—whatever
this was—than she was.

Every one of her senses felt heightened. Dizziness
swirled in her head, and her legs were like blancmange.
Staring at Joe, she thought he looked so defined, so focused, against the backdrop of pink canvas. The strength
of his jaw, the angle of his cheekbones, the sinful line of
his mouth…

Two steps and she was right up close as he leant back
against the door and pulled her into his arms. Reaching
up, she cupped his jaw, the roughness of his six o'clock
shadow tantalising her fingers.

His hand was thrust into her hair and he angled her

face for his kiss before his lips locked over hers in fierce demand. A demand she met without hesitation—met and matched—her entire being consumed by a need only this man, only Joe, could fulfil.

Her greedy fingers tugged at the buttons of his shirt and they pinged to the canvas floor. Not that it mattered. All that mattered was that she could now run her hands over the sculpted muscles of his chest.

He groaned as she stroked his skin, ran a thumb over his nipple. 'I want you, Imo. So bad.'

Joe broke their lip-lock to trail a sizzling stream of kisses along her neck, unerringly finding the sensitive spot that drove her frenzied. She arched her back to give him better access, and then gave a gasp as he scooped her up and resumed their kiss.

He tantalised and tormented her with his tongue as he strode over to the bed and lowered her down, stood above her. The sinful smile that tugged at his lips made her ache with a sudden poignant want as she etched this moment onto her memory. Joe looked younger, carefree, gorgeous, with his brown hair spiked and mussed from her fingers, his eyes dark and dilated with a heat that made her squirm.

As if her movement spurred him on, he shrugged himself out of his shirt, shucked off trousers and boxers.

Her gaze ran over his magnificent body.

'You like?' he asked.

'I want,' she replied and, sitting up, she reached to pull him down onto the bed.

CHAPTER THIRTEEN

IMOGEN ADJUSTED HER sketchpad on the easel, dug her flip-flop-clad toes into the warm crunch of sand and tried to concentrate.

The lecturer was fully living up to his promise—Michael Mallory was brilliant, and in any other circumstances she would be riveted.

Chill out, Imo. So what if Joe hadn't been there when she'd woken up that morning? It was no biggie that he hadn't even left a note. They'd had a deal—she would paint and he would surf. So maybe the waves only worked at a certain time of day…he'd had to rush. Maybe he hadn't been able to find a pen or paper. Maybe he'd written a note and a stray dog had crept into the yurt and eaten it. There were endless possibilities. There was no need for her tummy to be knotted with a sense of dread.

Instead she needed to enjoy the moment and anticipate later. After what they had shared last night—after falling asleep wrapped in each other's arms, her head on his chest, his strong arm encasing her—there was no need for doom and gloom. Later they'd swap stories, have a meal, maybe a glass or two of wine and then…to bed.

And what happens after that, Imo?

Nothing. Nothing happens. Get a grip.

This was lust—pure and simple.

Only…was it more than that? Hadn't they shared things on an emotional level? Could Joe tick the boxes on her list?

'OK,' Michael said. 'Listen up, if you haven't already.'

Imogen jumped and stared at the tall, lanky man who was suddenly standing right in front of her.

He stroked his beard and frowned down at her. 'Yes, that means you. Here is your assignment. You have two hours and then report back here.'

Imogen glanced down at the piece of paper and then around her, realising that the rest of the class had already dispersed.

'Sorry,' she muttered.

'Redeem yourself by producing a worthwhile exercise,' he returned.

Determination seethed inside her. Joe had gone surfing reluctantly, this she knew, and he'd done it so that she could reap the benefits of this class. It was time to do exactly that.

'I will.'

'Good. I've assigned you a place—go there and come back with a land or seascape with a difference. It doesn't have to be technically perfect—draw from your heart and dig deep into your soul.'

Picking up her sketchpad and pencils, she set off. Twenty minutes later she'd reached her destination. It was incredible—a tiny cove of rich golden sand at the foot of a cliff-face that swept the skyline.

As Imogen walked forward her mouth dropped open at the rock formations—arches and shapes that almost defied nature, rock pools galore. Other than herself, the place was completely deserted. It was if she'd gone through a portal and entered another world.

Ah!

That was how she would draw this scene—she would make it slightly alien, use the rock formations to indicate a time portal…subtly distort things… Her brain popped and fizzed with ideas.

Making her way to a handy clump of rocks, she opened her sketchpad and started to draw…

* * *

'Imogen?'

A shadow fell over the sketchbook and she whipped her head up so fast she heard her neck crack.

'Joe.'

'Sorry to interrupt.'

His voice was cool and formal—the tone one you'd use with someone you'd just met and were thoroughly indifferent about. Not someone you'd tangled the sheets with just hours previously.

'That's fine. It's probably good—I'd lost track of time.'

Feeling at a sudden disadvantage, she scrambled to her feet, clutched the sketchbook to her chest. The dreaded leaden feeling returned with a vengeance at the look in his brown eyes—cold with a hint of wariness. She took in his clothes—despite the blaze of the midday sun he wore a crisp white shirt and a lightweight jacket over chinos.

'Didn't pack your Hawaiian shorts?' she asked.

'No.'

'So when are you hitting the waves?'

'That's what I came to tell you.' His voice was even, his features unreadable except for the tension in his jaw. 'I'll have to take a rain check—I have to leave. Now. I've changed my flight but you should stay here—finish the class, soak up some rays.'

'Why do you have to leave?' *Please tell me there's an emergency. Nothing life-threatening but a genuine valid reason for you to go.* 'A work crisis? Do the twins need you?'

'Is that what you want me to say?'

Hell, yeah. Right now Imogen wanted to dig a hole in the sun-scorched sand and bury her head deep, deep down. But she wouldn't do that—that was what she'd done with Steve: refused to see the truth, painted an illusory fictitious relationship world.

'I want you to say the truth.'

'The truth is that after last night I think it's best to cut this interlude short.'

Anger imploded in her: a molten core of volcanic rage. 'Really? That's what you think? Jeez, Joe. What happened to respect? To what you said last night about respecting me? Is this how you show it? Slinking off after sleeping with me? Wham-bam, thank you, ma'am?'

Joe flinched, his mouth set in a grim line.

'That's not how it was. It's not how it is.'

'Then tell me how it is.'

'I don't *know*, goddammit.' He rammed his hands into his pockets and rocked back on his heels. 'I'm not sure what happens after a second one-night stand. It's a situation I've managed to avoid for the past seven years.'

Freaking fabulous. What was she? The flu?

'So this is your answer. Hell, Joe, I'm surprised you even bothered to come out here to tell me you were going. I'd have worked it out soon enough.'

'I didn't want to do that. I don't want us to end badly.'

'Then don't go. Don't run away.'

Joe's guts twisted. Anger at himself pounded his temples. Imogen was hurt; he could see it in the way she hugged that sketchbook to her like some sort of magical shield.

Of course she's hurting, dumb-arse. Your behaviour puts you up for the Schmuck of the Year award.

He should never have let this situation happen. Yet last night he hadn't given Rule Two a thought. Not one. Everything had been obliterated by his need for Imogen—his need to possess her, hold her and savour every centimetre of her. To gaze at the stars and dream.

Madness.

Even looking at her now—so graceful, standing so tall, her eyes challenging—his hands were desperate to break free from his pockets and hold her. The simple sundress she wore exposed her sun-kissed shoulders and the curve of her toned bare arms. So beautiful his heart ached. The sooner he got on that plane the better. And it would be Rule Three all the way. 'No Looking Back'.

'I'm not running away. It's more of a strategic retreat.'

Her lips didn't so much as quiver, and he knew himself the words weren't funny—even if there was an element of truth in them. He knew with a bone-deep certainty that he couldn't spend another night with Imogen.

'I'm leaving because it's best for both of us. Things are getting complicated, and the best way forward now is to draw a line before they complicate further.'

'I thought we were through with drawing lines?'

'Not this one. We got carried away by chemistry again last night; that wasn't meant to happen and I will not risk being driven by lust again.'

Her arms squeezed the sketchbook even tighter as her face leeched of colour and Joe knew she was thinking of her parents' disastrous lust-driven relationship. Which was good—that was what he wanted: for Imogen to be on the same page as he was, in agreement that this had to stop here.

'You want a relationship that isn't based on lust. You want a man who ticks all your boxes and I don't tick any. So it's way better to cut your losses right here and now and go and find him.' His hand fisted in his pockets; the thought of Imogen with another man made him want to hit something—preferably the man. 'It's best for *you*.'

Just like that her shell-shocked face changed, and he knew he'd said the wrong thing as her mouth smacked open in outrage. Eyes narrowed, she stepped forward.

'And what gives you the right to make that decision for me?' Imogen asked. '*I* know what's best for me—not you. All my life people have known what's best for me.

My mother, Steve, and now you. And you've known me all of a few weeks.'

The sarcastic cut of her voice slashed at him and flamed his own emotions to anger. 'You said it yourself, Imogen. That it should only be one night.'

'Then something changed,' she flashed back, before exhaling a sigh. 'Last night *did* happen and I refuse to regret it. Or at least I didn't regret it until now. You know what, Joe? You don't really respect me. Because if you did you would have asked me what I think, how I feel, what I want, what *I* think is best for me. I accept that you need to go, but it's because it's best for *you*. Don't kid yourself or try to kid me you're doing it for me.'

He opened his mouth and then closed it again. Imogen was right. Yet... 'Imogen, I do truly believe this is best for you, but if I'd asked you before I booked that flight what would you have said?'

For a second her gaze dipped away from him, and then she jutted her chin out and met his eyes. 'I'd have suggested we stay here until tomorrow, as planned. I draw, you surf, we have another night. Tomorrow we go home and go our separate ways.'

It sounded so reasonable, so tempting, so....terrifying.

'And what if that slid into one more night? One more week...?'

'Would that be so bad?'

Her voice was small and tight, and Joe hated himself even as he knew what his answer had to be. Everything was sliding out of control, complications abounded, and he needed to get both himself and Imogen out of the line of fire.

'Yes, it would. You're looking for a man who wants a relationship, a white picket fence, a family. I'm not that man. I do *not* tick the boxes.'

'How do you know you couldn't?'

The very thought made his head reel with images of his parents, presenting their perfect married image to the world, supposedly living out their happy-ever-after behind the picket fence. They'd had it all—love, a family, a successful business.

Yet the whole time it had been nothing but a façade.

Joe remembered piecing together the reality of his father's affairs—so many of them with employees and clients. Remembered finding the paperwork showing that his mother was filing for divorce. The family company had been a hotbed of scandal and corruption: funds embezzled, nothing as it was supposed to be, business relationships and personal relationships all a quagmire to be waded through.

The realisation had dawned that everything he'd grown up with had been an illusion. And then it had turned out everything he'd believed he and Leila had was nothing more than another mirage. His whole life had been askew and off-kilter, viewed through the wrong perspective.

He would never put himself in that position again. This thing—whatever it was with Imogen—was meant to fit his rules; Imogen had agreed, goddammit.

'There is no way I can ever tick your boxes. It is not going to happen. Not now, not ever. I do not want complications in my life. You do not want a relationship based on lust.'

'Is that all you think we have?'

'Yes.'

'You really believe that, Joe?'

'I—'

'And do you really believe that having a family and growing old together is just one big complication? Are you really such a coward that you'll always run away from any chance of getting close?'

'Yes, yes and yes again.' Better a coward, than a fool,

enmeshed in an emotional quagmire it would be nigh on impossible to break free from.

Imogen shook her head. 'Then you'd best go. Have a safe flight home.'

'Enjoy the art class.'

It was a monumentally stupid comment, but he was having difficulty unsticking his feet from the sand. Having difficulty doing the thing he needed to do.

'I hope this doesn't make you drop out of it.'

'Don't worry, Joe. Your conscience can rest. I keep my promises. See you around.'

The bitter taste of cowardice and confusion coated his tastebuds as she swivelled and started to walk away from him.

Without so much as a glance back.

He needed to do the same.

It was the only way forward.

CHAPTER FOURTEEN

Three days later

'HOW ARE YOU feeling, hun? Ready to go in there and freeze his balls?'

Imogen managed a smile at Mel's words, truly appreciating her best friend's attempts to cheer her up. Mel had been a rock—had plied her with tea and wine and chocolate and tissues as needed, listened to her rant and pretended not to notice when she cried.

Though who knew why she'd shed a single tear for a man who had made it more than plain that he wanted nothing more to do with her? Humiliation still burned inside her that she hadn't just let him go and feigned indifference. Honestly—she might as well stencil 'Doormat—Use Me' on her forehead.

Yet there had been a moment on that sun-kissed Algarve beach when the grim, haunted expression on Joe's face had twisted her heart—made her want to help with whatever inner demons tormented him.

Hah! More fool her. Inner demons, her foot—Joe had just been terrified that she would go emotional on him. Become a complication to his footloose and fancy-free existence.

Well, she'd show him. Joe had called a meeting at Langley with Peter and Harry, and Peter had asked her to minute it.

Pride straightened her spine. 'I am ready to go in and be arctically professional.'

Mel grinned at her. 'That's my girl. Well, you look the part.'

'Thanks to you! This dress is perfect.'

Imogen smoothed the skirt of the sculpted jersey dress with satisfaction. The demure yet tantalising rounded half-zip neckline, the way the Italian fabric clung to her body, dipped to just above the knee, made her feel professional from the sleek chignon atop her head to her perfectly pedicured pale pink toenails that peeped from a pair of killer heels.

'Show me "The Look".'

Hand on hip, Imogen focused on projecting icy disdain.

'Brilliant!' Mel clapped her hands together. 'Trust me, bits of him will shrivel! Go get 'em, Imo.'

Easier said than done. By the time she'd trekked the tube journey to work the thought of seeing Joe was filling her with a swirl of conflicted emotions. *Come on, Imo.* It was imperative that she crush any lingering stupid hopes, push down the insane lurch of anticipation.

As she approached the boardroom her heart pounded against her ribcage so loudly she'd probably deafen Joe rather than freeze him. Bracing herself, she pushed the boardroom door open and entered. Channelled every bit of her inner ice princess.

The Langley brothers sat on one side of the mahogany table facing Joe, who had his hands flat on the table edge, his gaze directed on Peter.

'You have got to be joking!' Peter Langley leapt to his feet, looking about to vault the table and throttle Joe.

'Peter. Sit down.' Harry half rose and grabbed Peter's arm.

Imogen cleared her throat. 'Sorry I'm late,' she said.

'You aren't.' Harry attempted a smile. 'We started early.

Peter and I just want to know which way the land lies. Come in, Imogen. We'd better minute this.'

'Sure.' Within seconds she'd seated herself at the table, notepad in hand, as foreboding prickled her neck. Something bad was clearly going down.

Yet even her apprehension couldn't prevent her brain from absorbing Joe's appearance. The immaculate charcoal-grey suit with a hint of pinstripe, the bright white shirt, dark blue tie. Professional from the spikes of his hair to the tips of his no doubt shined-up leather shoes. His face was neutral—no trace of any emotion whatsoever. It should be impossible to believe that this man had turned her life upside down, only—*dammit*—it wasn't. Her whole being was on alert, and it was taking every ounce of willpower to keep herself from staring.

'I'm ready,' she said.

Peter waved a hand. 'Go ahead, Joe. Explain your decision.'

'Langley is doing well, but progress has to be sustained and more. Ivan Moreton has come forward with a very lucrative buy-out offer.'

'*Ivan Moreton*?' Disbelief vied with horror.

'Yes.' The syllable gave nothing away. 'The deal he is offering is more than fair. In order to avoid the buy-out Langley needs to meet the criteria set out here over the next two months.' He pushed a bound report across the table. 'Again, I'll go through it for the record.'

As Imogen listened to the points, anger began to simmer. Glancing across at Peter and Harry, she could sense their worry and her tummy twisted in sympathy.

Head back down, she minuted the discussion until the three men had finished. Waited as Joe rose to his feet and shook hands first with Peter and then with Harry.

'You've got my number—any questions, just call. Otherwise I'll be back in two months to review the situation. I'll see you then.'

Hurt threaded through her building rage—Joe's glance had barely even skimmed over her, his brown eyes indifferent. Had he really managed to edit her out of his memory banks that easily—just another one-night stand to join the ranks? Just an anonymous employee in a company he was grinding in his corporate mill?

Well, hell, she was a lot more than that—and she would not just stand aside and let him do this. Forget freezing him—instead her palms itched with the desire to grab him by the lapels of that tailored suit and shake him until his teeth rattled. Her hands clenched into fists, all thoughts of professional cool forgotten

'Excuse me, Joe. Could I have a word before you go? In private.'

Just great. Exactly what he'd hoped to avoid. The meeting had been bad—for once knowing that his decision was financially sound and correct was not enough. Nowhere near enough. As for the effort of keeping his gaze averted from Imogen—his eyeballs positively ached.

Joe concentrated on maintaining his expression at strictly neutral. 'Of course.'

The Langley brothers exchanged glances. 'Stay in here,' Peter suggested. 'Harry and I need to go and come up with a plan of campaign for the next few months. Imogen, when you're done here could you please join us in my office?'

'Sure.'

She rose to her feet as they left the boardroom, and Joe braced himself to withstand the sheer force of her beauty and her anger.

'What can I do for you, Imogen?' he asked, sitting back at the table.

She slammed her palms down on the mahogany table-top. 'You can explain what the hell *that* was all about.'

'Meaning…?'

'Meaning I thought you said that you didn't like to close companies down.'

'I don't—and if you read the minutes you just took you'll see that I didn't.'

'Huh. Those criteria are nigh on impossible.'

'No, they aren't. They are difficult, I grant you, but they are doable.'

'Provided Harry doesn't have another heart attack and Peter doesn't relapse into another breakdown from the stress.'

Her voice caught and, heaven help him, guilt shoved him hard in the chest.

'How could you do this, Joe? It's wrong.'

'I have no choice—Ivan Moreton's offer is very generous.'

'Of course it is. That's because there is nothing Ivan wants more than to take this company down. He loathes Peter and Harry. You must realise that?'

Joe rubbed a hand over his face. 'Yes, I do. But that dislike gives Langley a profitable way out. He's even promised to keep the majority of staff.'

'So he can rub their noses in his triumph. Plus, he knows damn well neither Peter nor Harry would ever work for him.'

Something tugged in his chest; face flushed, eyes sparking, Imogen looked so beautiful he wanted to help. Wanted to give her whatever she wanted. Which was exactly why it was time to close this interview down. Before he did something stupid. *Again.*

Rising to his feet, he shook his head. 'This meeting is over, Imogen. I've given Langley a chance.'

For a second a doubt assailed him. *Had* his decision

been strictly business? Somewhere deep down had he reasoned that even if he'd refused to give Imogen a chance he could at least offer the company she loved one?

'I suggest you go out there and take it.'

A small frown creased her brow as her blue-grey eyes surveyed him.

He held out a hand. 'Goodbye, Imogen. And good luck.'

Her fingers lay in his for one brief final moment. 'Goodbye, Joe.'

Two months later

Imogen drew in a deep breath and looked around her tiny new studio apartment with approval. Spick and span, with nothing that even the most exacting parent could complain about. Fresh flowers on the small foldaway table, which was open and beautifully laid, complete with ice bucket for the champagne currently in the fridge. Hell, this would be a celebration even if it killed her. If it wasn't, and her parents went loopy, then she'd just drink the damn bottle herself.

Heaven knew she deserved it after the past months— but it had been worth every single lost moment of sleep as she and all of the Langley team had pulled together and managed to meet every criterion on Joe's list. Now Peter and Harry had met with Joe and Langley was safe—the knowledge was a constant warm glow inside her.

But that wasn't the reason for this lunch. Apprehension fizzed in her veins and as if on cue the doorbell rang. Her heart beating a nervous rhythm against her ribcage, she crossed the floor and pulled the door open.

'Hey, Mum. Hey, Dad.'

Panic roiled in her tummy at the sheer enormity of what she'd done and what she had to tell them. Even so, the certainty that she was right calmed her—Joe had been correct. She couldn't live her life for her parents, no matter how much she loved them. Any more than he would expect his sisters to follow a path of *his* choosing just because he had chosen to take responsibility for them.

Instead he'd encouraged them to live their dreams, and he spoke of them with love—never disappointment. Eva hadn't ever been able to do the same, and whilst that was perhaps wrong, what had also been wrong was Imogen's compliance in that. That was why Joe had urged her to embrace art.

Joe. Why did anything and everything always come back to Joe?

'Imogen? What's the matter? We haven't come all this way just to watch you daydream.'

Eva Lorrimer's querulous voice pulled her into the present.

'Sorry, Mum.' Imogen hauled in breath—no point dressing this up. 'Thank you for coming. I've got some fantastic news. I've been accepted into art college.'

Silence plummeted as Eva opened and closed her mouth, whilst Jonathan Lorrimer shifted from foot to foot.

'Is this some sort of joke?' Her mother had gone pale, her forehead pinched.

'No, Mum. It's for real. It's a top London college and I can start in January.' Imogen tried for a laugh…winced at the strangled gargle she achieved. 'So you know what to get me for Christmas.'

Eva shook her head. 'How could you be so stupid, Imogen? After everything I went through for you…'

Guilt surfaced, along with a hefty dose of self-doubt, but then she pushed her shoulders back and adhered her feet to the carpet. Joe might not be in her life, but he had taught her something life-changing. That life was for living and it was *her* life to live.

'Mum!'

To her surprise the interruption worked and Eva stopped talking.

'I know I've never managed to achieve what you wanted me to achieve, but that doesn't mean I'm stupid. Just because maths and science aren't my thing it doesn't make me useless.' She could feel a weight lift from her shoulders, was liberated by the words.

'I... I...' Eva rallied. 'I never thought that—I just wanted what was best for you. I wanted you to make something of yourself.'

'And I have done that. I'm proud of my work at Langley.'

'Being a PA is a good steady job...'

'It is—and I'm a good PA. But I've been more than that at Langley and now I want to pursue my dream, Mum. Not yours, but mine.'

'And end up penniless, knocking on my door for help?'

'No! I've thought all this through. Langley is safe now, and I've arranged with Peter to keep working there part-time. I've got a manageable student loan. I'll show you the figures, if you like. I can make this work *and* pay my own way. I'm so excited—please be excited for me.'

'I'm excited for you.'

Swivelling on her trainer-clad foot, Imogen surveyed her father with surprise.

'Truly I am, Imo. I may not have made it yet, but if you've been accepted into art college then maybe I can live vicariously through you. Well done, poppet.'

Poppet. He hadn't called her that for so many years. Not since those rare times when he'd sat with her as a child and shown her how to draw. Until either Eva had put a stop to it or he'd disappeared back to his studio, leaving her to fend for herself. But at least now he could find it in himself to be happy for her, rather than begrudge her a success he hadn't had, and she was grateful for that.

'Thanks, Dad.'

'*Tchah!* Well, *I'm* not excited for you, Imogen.' Eva sniffed. 'I can't stop you, and I won't try, but I still think you're making a grave mistake. You'll get caught up in this art malarkey and the rest of your life will pass you by. When will you have time to meet a nice man to settle down with?'

The question hurt, and she blinked hard as an image of Joe shot into her head. *Nice. Settle down.* Not words she associated with Joe—but it didn't matter. Like it or not, he'd insinuated himself into her heart and it was proving hard to prise him out. But she would—even if she had to get a chisel.

'You lost Steve, and now—'

'Steve loves Simone. And next week we can all dance at their wedding and wish them well.'

And she meant it—the thought of attending no longer had the sting it had held before. Steve and Simone were happy—that much was clear from the one conversation she'd had with Steve after he had voluntarily reimbursed her for the cost of the cruise. Further evidence had been provided by the stream of happy photos that Simone flooded social media with on a daily basis.

True, her stomach still dipped at the idea of being pointed out as the poor little ex, but she'd manage. At least she would be able to foil the sympathetic stares and prurient curiosity with her college news.

'So,' she said firmly. 'How about we open the champagne?'

One day later

Exhilaration shot through Joe's veins at the familiar feel of the surfboard under his feet. He felt weightless, suspended in time and nature, at one with the elements.

The power of the sea was both awe-inspiring and thrilling. Sheer adrenalin pumped in his blood as he caught the wave, and the screech of a seagull blended with the pounding in his ears, the tang of the sea spray on his skin causing sheer joy.

Just like the way he felt when he was with Imogen.

One week later

OK. She could do this. Imogen gazed out of the window as the train pulled in to the old-fashioned Devon station and she tried to block out her parents' bickering voices.

'Don't see why any of us are coming to this damned wedding at all,' Jonathan muttered. 'Though I suppose if you feel you need to go, Imo, the least we can do is come to give you some moral support.'

Eva sighed. 'I've explained time and again that we are going to this wedding because Steve was once part of our lives and he is the son of one of my oldest acquaintances.'

'The same acquaintance who looks at me as though I'm something she stepped in,' Jonathan grumbled as he lugged a suitcase onto the platform.

'Guys…'

Some things would never change—she would probably be playing peacemaker between her parents for ever. Yet it could be worse; she might have lost her parents in a tragedy like Joe had…

Not again. No thoughts of Joe, today of all days.

Raising her voice to drown out her thoughts, Imogen waved placating hands at her parents. 'For whatever reasons we are all here now, so let's just get on with it. At least the scenery is gorgeous, the church is beautiful, and maybe we can find time for a proper cream tea.'

A taxi ride later and Imogen scanned the churchyard, bracing herself for the sight of friends and acquaintances all waiting to pounce.

Instead…

She blinked and dropped her knuckles from her eyes in the nick of time. Rubbing her eyes was not an option— not with the amount of make-up she had on. It must be a hallucination, but however many times she blinked the man remained there.

Solid and real—he looked just like Joe.

Hallucinating—that was what she was doing.

The hallucination headed purposefully towards them, dressed to kill in the same dark grey suit he'd worn to Leila's wedding. Her nerves skittered, her tummy somersaulted—maybe it really was Joe.

'Hello, Imogen.'

'Joe. Um…what are you doing here?'

He raised his eyebrows. 'I'm here for the wedding, of course.'

Gathering her wits together, she managed an introduction, saw her mother's eyes scan from her face to Joe's and braced herself again. But to her surprise Eva tugged on her husband's arm.

'Come on, Jonathan. Let's get inside. Imo and her friend can follow us. I want a chance to talk to Clarissa.'

Her brain fried, scrambled and poached all at the same time—and if that wasn't bad enough all she wanted to do was launch herself at his chest and hold on for dear life.

Once her parents were out of earshot Imogen forced her vocal cords to obey her brain's command. 'So you're real?'

His eyebrows rose as his lips quirked upward. 'Last time I checked.'

Her whole being drank him in. She noticed that his hair was longer…even spikier. There was a touch of strain about his eyes, and as he rubbed his neck in that oh, so familiar gesture she would have sworn he was nervous.

'Is everything OK?'

'It is now. You're looking good.'

'Thank you. You too.' Hauling in breath, she asked the million-dollar question. 'Why are you here? Really?'

'I'm keeping my part of the bargain. You come to Leila's wedding, I come to Steve's—remember?'

Imogen hauled her senses into line. 'I kind of assumed all deals were off due to unexpected complications.'

'Nope.' His gaze latched on to hers with a seriousness that made her tingle all over. 'I've been surfing. All deals are back on.'

He'd gone surfing. Imogen's heart skipped in the sure knowledge that he'd done that out of honour. But that didn't change anything.

'I'm glad,' she said simply. 'And I appreciate this, but I'll be fine on my own.'

'OK.'

A curl of disappointment rippled inside her.

'I'll see you in there, then,' he continued.

'Huh?'

'I scored myself an invite of my own.'

'How?'

'I gate-crashed the wedding rehearsal and threw myself on Simone's mercy. I think she was quite pleased to see me.'

'You did what? What did you tell them?'

'I told them the truth. That I needed to see you. We need to talk. A bit more privately. There's a bench round the corner. We've got a bit of time before the ceremony.'

Imogen hesitated.

'Please.'

The word disarmed her. Joe was used to giving orders—plus he'd come all this way—plus… Plus she wanted to be with him, wanted to make the most of every minute, and wouldn't a proper closure be better than the way it had ended? No doubt that was why he was here.

'OK. But we can't be long.'

She followed him through the picturesque graveyard, tried to concentrate on the old gravestones, the feeling of history and peace, the autumnal smell in the air, the red-brown leaves on the trees.

'Here we go. It's secluded enough here and out of the wind. I checked.'

'How forward-thinking of you,' Imogen managed as she attempted to try and think through a haze of misplaced happiness. It was as though there had been a bit of her missing and now she was whole. She needed to get a grip.

'Isn't it?'

His eyes raked over her as she sat down and spread the swirl of her turquoise dress out so that he couldn't get too close. Close would be a bad idea. The man was uptight, rule-orientated, cold. A man who thought three nights was a commitment he couldn't deal with. But despite herself she craved the warmth of his body.

Her memory was flooded with the way he'd held her, the way he'd shown her so much about herself, the way he'd made love to her.

'Joe, it's OK. I'm OK. You don't have to explain anything. Everything has worked out fine. As you know, better than anyone, Langley is safe. I'm not going to melt down or be permanently affected by the time we had together or the way you behaved. Though, for the record, it sucked.'

'You're right. It did. And I'm sorry.'

The flare of hope she hadn't even realised she'd harboured died. He was here to apologise—nothing more.

'Apology accepted. Now, please don't feel you have to stay. Steve and I are good. We've worked out our differences. I can more than manage on my own.'

The words were true but oh, how she wished it wasn't like this. Her heart ached; her chest was banded with pain.

'So I guess this is goodbye. Again.'

* * *

This was *so* not the way it was supposed to play out—hard to understand how he who could grasp control of any boardroom meeting—anywhere, any time—couldn't manage this situation.

Panic sheened the nape of his neck with moisture. Imogen was saying goodbye—he'd obviously blown any available bridge sky-high.

'No.'

Was that croak his voice? Time to step up—because no way was he losing this woman without at least a fight.

'No,' he repeated firmly. 'It's not.'

'There is nothing more to say.'

'That's where you are so very wrong. There is a load more to say. But first I need to say the most important thing.'

'What's that?'

'I love you.'

Joe wasn't sure what he'd expected, but the sceptical rise of her eyebrows wasn't it—nor the determined shake of her head as she slipped her hands under her thighs.

'Don't, Joe…'

'Don't what?'

'Lie.'

'Lie?' She thought he was *lying*?

'It doesn't make sense. I haven't seen hide nor hair of you for two months. Last time I saw you, you couldn't even contemplate more than two nights with me—this is taking "absence makes the heart grow fonder" too far.'

He was making an incredible mess of this. Had he really thought she'd fall into his arms in a swoon of delight? He needed to make her believe him. This was his last chance.

'Imogen, I love you. I loved you back then and I love you now. That's a fact. Love isn't logical, and you can't put it in a tick-box. I panicked on that beach on the Algarve because for seven years I'd lived by my self-imposed rules and then you came into my life and changed everything. Broke down all the barriers I'd built to keep my life from complications.'

Imogen swept her fringe to one side as she contemplated his words. 'I'm not sure I want to feature in your life as an unwanted complication.'

'You won't.' He shoved a hand through his hair and tried to summon up coherence. 'I…I've done a lot of thinking over these past two months. And I've realised what I did after my parents died. I closed down.'

'That's understandable. It's part of the grieving process.'

'It was more than that. They left a mess behind them. Turned out their marriage was on the rocks and the family business was so far up the proverbial creek a hundred paddles wouldn't have been enough.'

He shrugged.

'I had no idea. I thought they had an idyllic marriage and the business was thriving. It was all an illusion. Tax evasion, fraud, infidelity, wrongdoing… My father was higher than a kite, funded by clients' money. Women… clients, colleagues, secretaries…he slept with them all. My mother turned a blind eye for the money, but the money was running out so she was filing for divorce. It was all very…complicated.'

'Oh, Joe.'

Her face was scrunched up in compassion as she twisted her body to face him, placed her hand on his thigh, her touch so warm, so right.

'I can't begin to imagine how confusing, how incredibly emotional it must have been for you. To have all your memories twisted—and you couldn't even ask them why. No wonder you decided the best way forward was no complications.'

He shifted his body to face her, amazed at how easy, how right it felt to share.

'All I wanted was to sort it all out, look after the twins and make sure I never let complication into my life again. So that's what I did. Then I met you and you changed everything; you've shown me how to feel again, to care, to love, and I don't care how complicated it is. I'll become the man you want me to be, Imogen, if I have to try all my life long. Give me that tick-list and I'll do my best.'

'No!'

The word hurt, slammed into him like a cannonball. But then she shifted along the bench, her warmth right next to him.

'There is no tick-list,' she said. 'I've shredded it and burnt the scraps.'

'Why?'

'Because you made me see what a stupid idea it was. How can someone conform to a tick-list? I tried to do that. For Steve. I tried to make myself fit his list and the result was a nightmare.' She laid her small hand on his thigh. 'I can *so* see why you closed down after your parents died. I didn't close down, but I built myself a comfort zone and I was too scared to leave it—too scared I'd repeat my parents' mistakes, too scared I'd be like my father and fail. Meeting you changed that, made me see how exhilarating it is to push the boundaries and go for what you want.'

She smiled at him—a smile that lit up his world.

'I've been accepted at art school.'

Happiness for Imogen and the world opening out to her warmed his chest. 'That's amazing news, sweetheart.'

'It all started from that art class. Mike, the lecturer, made me promise to keep in touch and he really encouraged me. He's been so supportive and...'

Jealousy and pain tackled him at the same time, twisted

his gut with a hurt he knew he had to conceal. 'So…you and this Mike guy…?'

'No! Don't be daft.'

Blue-grey eyes widened as she stared at him.

'Oh, Joe. Don't you get it? I love you.'

'You do?'

'Yes, I do. Every bit of you—from the spikes in your hair to the tips of your toes. I love how you've made me strive to live the dream, the way you make me feel protected and like I can do anything. I love how you talk about your sisters and I love how you give one hundred per cent of yourself to what you do. I just *love* you. Full-stop.'

He grinned at her, his heart full with the sheer joy of hearing the words. 'One thing you should know, though…'

'What's that?'

'I'm expecting plenty of lustful goings-on in our marriage, whatever you think.'

In one fluid movement she landed on his lap and cupped his face in her hands. 'Well, Mr McIntyre, that's lucky—because I wouldn't have it any other way.' Then she froze. 'Did you say marriage? You mean…?'

'If you'll have me. Imogen, I can't imagine anything better than being your husband and waking up every morning with you in my arms. I want it all—white picket fence, kids, the lot.' He pulled her closer, his arms round the slender span of her waist. 'Because what we have, Imogen, is way more than lust. We have liking and respect and love.'

She nodded. 'I know. That's why these past two months I've missed you so damn much. Talking to you…laughing with you. I've missed the way you need that first cup of coffee, the way your hair spikes up. I've missed your scowl and your smile. Your touch, your taste, your smell.'

'I know exactly what you mean, sweetheart. I've spent weeks trying to stick to Rule Three and not look back. But you—you've haunted my days and my nights. I'd wake up in the night and swear I could feel your hair tickling my chin. So many memories… I couldn't stop looking back, though God knows I tried. Filling my days with work and…'

'Your nights?'

'My nights were filled with fantasies of you. I love you, Imogen Lorrimer. You've made me see love can be real. Not an illusion. So, Imogen, if you want me in your life I oh, so definitely want you in mine. For ever. Will you marry me?'

'Absolutely, Joe. I am all yours. For ever.'

He smiled a smile that lit her world—a smile that made her feel like the most beautiful, wonderful, desirable woman in the world. A smile that spoke volumes, spoke of everlasting love and all-encompassing joy.

'Then let's live the dream, Imogen. Starting now.'

EPILOGUE

Dear Diary

In case you've forgotten me, as I've neglected you shamefully over the past few months, my name is Imogen Lorrimer—until tomorrow, when I will become Imogen McIntyre. Because tomorrow I am marrying Joe McIntyre, who I no longer have to dream is in my bed because he has taken to making a regular appearance there. Naked.

I love him.

Think sexy rumpled hair. That I love to run my fingers through. Think chocolate—the expensive kind—brown eyes that gaze at me with love in their depths. Oh, and a body that I plan to worship for the rest of my life.

Joe is kind and loving and altogether perfect. He has taken up surfing again and, believe me, watching Joe on a surfboard is a privilege. He's thinking of setting up some sort of surf school for teenagers in the future. Our long-term plan is to move out of London and settle in Cornwall—though first I want to finish college.

Which is utterly amazing—and Langley has been fantastic at being flexible so I can work and attend college. Mum is way happier about the whole art college scenario now I am marrying Joe. In fact I don't know how he's done it but he's even charmed her into admitting one of my pictures was 'not bad'. Which from Mum is a compliment of the highest order.

Dad has found work in an art supply shop, and whilst he still spends all his spare time in his studio, I have the feeling Mum and Dad are getting on a little bit better.

Holly and Tammy are fantastic—it's like having the siblings I always dreamed of. They are going to be bridesmaids, with Mel as chief bridesmaid. So, you see, life could not be better.

Tomorrow, dear diary, I will be walking down the aisle towards Joe, and I know with all my heart and soul that this is the man I will love for the rest of my life. And that he will love me right back.

For ever

Night-night

Imogen xxx

* * * * *

MILLS & BOON®

Why not subscribe?
Never miss a title and save money too!

Here's what's available to you if you join the exclusive **Mills & Boon Book Club** today:

✦ *Titles up to a month ahead of the shops*
✦ *Amazing discounts*
✦ *Free P&P*
✦ *Earn Bonus Book points that can be redeemed against other titles and gifts*
✦ *Choose from monthly or pre-paid plans*

Still want more?
Well, if you join today we'll even give you
50% OFF your first parcel!

So visit **www.millsandboon.co.uk/subs**
or call Customer Relations on **020 8288 2888**
to be a part of this exclusive Book Club!

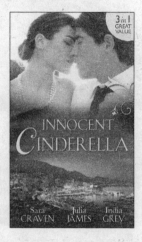